It began as an experiment . . .

In his chilling new novel of scientific adventure, the bestselling author of *Neanderthal* probes the very essence of creation—of what makes us who we are.

New York, at century's end: A mutilated body has been found, its face and fingerprints removed, a coin-sized circle carved into its upper thigh. On a remote island off the Southeast coast, a young man is running from a place he cannot survive, toward a world he cannot comprehend. And in the echoing canyons of Manhattan, another young man—a journalist—is moving closer to the truth about his own past, and to an encounter that will alter everything he has ever believed about himself.

For thirty years a colony with its own laws, values, and complex living systems has been growing. Covertly supplied with the latest technology and DNA materials, its leaders carefully monitor their human trials and conceal the inhabitants from the outside world. Now someone has escaped. When Jude finds him cowering in the shadows of his apartment hallway, he will understand why this ragged stranger who calls himself Skyler is so frightened.

They share the same face.

Now Jude and Skyler are running together—bound by a new, secret science—hunted by unknown pursuers as they search for the mystery of their birth. Aided by a doctor with her own dangerous secret, they flee across the country, drawing nearer to a conspiracy at the very heart of America's power structure . . . survivors of an experiment that has gone tragically, irreversibly wrong.

From the microscopic mysteries of the genetic code to a horrifying truth beyond all imagining, *The Experiment* blends cutting-edge science with adrenaline-pumped suspense to provide a cautionary tale for our time.

# THE EXPERIMENT

**Also by John Darnton**

*Neanderthal*

# THE EXPERIMENT

John Darnton

A DUTTON BOOK

DUTTON
Published by the Penguin Group
Penguin Putnam Inc., 375 Hudson Street, New York, New York 10014, U.S.A.
Penguin Books Ltd, 27 Wrights Lane, London W8 5TZ, England
Penguin Books Australia Ltd, Ringwood, Victoria, Australia
Penguin Books Canada Ltd, 10 Alcorn Avenue, Toronto, Ontario, Canada M4V 3B2
Penguin Books (N.Z.) Ltd, 182–190 Wairau Road, Auckland 10, New Zealand

Penguin Books Ltd, Registered Offices: Harmondsworth, Middlesex, England

First published by Dutton, a member of Penguin Putnam Inc.

First Printing, September 1999
10 9 8 7 6 5 4 3 2 1

REGISTERED TRADEMARK—MARCA REGISTRADA

LIBRARY OF CONGRESS CATALOGING-IN-PUBLICATION DATA
Darnton, John.
The Experiment/John Darnton.
p. cm.
ISBN 0-525-94517-2
I. Title.
PS3554.A727E97 1999
813'.54—dc21 99-28860
CIP

Printed in the United States of America
Set in Bembo
Designed by Julian Hamer

PUBLISHER'S NOTE
This is a work of fiction. Names, characters, places, and incidents either are the products of the author's imagination or are used fictitiously, and any resemblance to actual persons, living or dead, events, or locales is entirely coincidental.



This book is printed on acid-free paper. ∞

For Kyra, Liza and James, made the old-fashioned way,
with memories of Jingo and the House of 1,000 Rooms

And for Nina, with unstoppable love

Surely some revelation is at hand;
Surely the Second Coming is at hand.
The Second Coming! Hardly are those words out
When a vast image out of *Spiritus Mundi*
Troubles my sight: somewhere in the sands of the desert
A shape with lion body and the head of a man,
A gaze blank and pitiless as the sun,
Is moving its slow thighs, while all about it
Reel shadows of the indignant desert birds.
The darkness drops again; but now I know
That twenty centuries of stony sleep
Were vexed to nightmare by a rocking cradle,
And what rough beast, its hour come round at last,
Slouches towards Bethlehem to be born?

—W. B. YEATS

# THE EXPERIMENT

# Chapter 1

Skyler and Julia crept to the basement door of the Big House and looked around to make sure they weren't being watched. A breeze stirred the humid air, rustling the Spanish moss that hung from the old oaks that arched over what used to be the approach road. It made a dry, whispering sound.

It was dusk, at least, which meant they would be hard to spot in the shadows of the old manor—but not that hard if someone walked around back.

Skyler felt the fear as a tingling in his groin; from there it spread upward to his belly and reached his arms and legs.

*This is crazy,* he thought.

If they were caught—he couldn't even imagine the punishment. Nothing like this had ever happened at the Lab.

They weren't sure what they were going to do. They had no plan, really, other than to break into the Records Room and search for clues to explain what had happened to Patrick. They had to do something, try to find something, or else the reason for his disappearance would never be known. It would remain forever mysterious, like those of the others on the island, who had been taken away and never returned.

That morning Patrick had appeared fine. He had eaten breakfast with the others in the Age Group and then gone off to calisthenics and chores. But by the early afternoon they had heard the rumors: he had been summoned for a physical—not the routine weekly examination but a *special* physical. That was a signal that something was wrong, that perhaps a dreadful illness had been discovered, and sure enough, the Elder Physicians had convened a meeting before dinner to inform them that Patrick had been "called away." The phrase had been uttered ambivalently, as it always was:

in sadness certainly, for the Physicians had loved him as they loved them all, but also with a hint of reverence—as if he had made some sort of noble sacrifice.

At the doorway Skyler moved closer to Julia. He smelled the familiar scent of her hair, and it plucked up his courage. He grasped the doorknob and turned it slowly, and pushed. Nothing happened. He held the knob firmly, lifting it while he rocked the door gently with his other hand, and it suddenly gave way. So, it was not locked. That made sense: the leaders of the Lab would not have worried about security.

*Who, after all, would be foolish enough to open it?*

He slipped inside and heard her light tread behind him. She was breathing in long spurts. When he closed the door, darkness engulfed them. Above their heads, they could hear footsteps creaking along the old floorboards and the indistinct murmur of voices. Skyler listened; he couldn't identify them. One was high-pitched and sounded a bit like Baptiste when he was excited or angry. Skyler felt a rush of complicated emotions and a strange sense of longing. What would happen if they just marched upstairs and demanded to know everything? He darted a quick glance outside. The wind was up and the moss was waving on the branches of the old oaks. Twilight was upon the island.

*What are we looking for?*

Julia had already moved across the room. He hurried to a bank of filing cabinets and began tugging at a drawer, but it would not open. He saw that it was locked in place by an iron bar that ran across the front, secured by a padlock on one side. He looked at her quizzically. She knew this place, the Records Room, from her afternoon career chore. She would come in to dust and straighten up, although of course she was not permitted to touch the machines or files or even any of the thick textbooks that lined the shelves. But while refilling printers and stacking paper and washing the floors, she had observed a lot. She had made a game of carefully watching the computer operators, and once, left alone, she had even tried to work the machine.

Before Skyler knew it, she was seated at the computer. She clicked it on, and instantly a greenish glow filled the room. Damn! They hadn't anticipated that! Julia took off her shirt—*what is she doing?*—and then Skyler understood as she draped it over the screen and poked her head under it. The glow shrank within her little tent, and it shivered with her movements.

Skyler moved away and stood guard, his back to a wall. His eyes were now accustomed to the dark, and he scanned the room. The interior walls were hewn from rock and whitewashed, the exterior ones constructed with cinder blocks. The floor was linoleum, and the ceiling was covered in acoustical tiles marked in one corner with a widening pool of brown water stains. There was not much furniture: the computer Julia was sitting at and one other on a plain wooden desk, metal file cabinets, a bookshelf, a standing lamp and a green Naugahyde chair with a rip down one arm.

He looked at Julia, who seemed oddly at ease now that she had something to do, and he admired her coolness. He had never before set foot in the Records Room, and he felt he was trespassing upon forbidden ground.

He watched the windows for movement outside, but he knew that the real danger was closer at hand—the staircase. If they were discovered, it would most likely happen because one of those voices above decided to come downstairs. What if an Orderly needed to fetch something? He tried to push the thought away. Julia's head was still hidden; he could almost hear her thinking as she pecked at the keys, trying different combinations. Then she removed the blouse from the screen and looked at him, a ghostly radiation upon her cheeks.

"Sky, come," she whispered.

He raced over and peered across her bared shoulder at a blank screen.

"I can't get anything," she said, distraught. "I don't know how to work this thing. It's hopeless."

She turned the machine off, and the green glow shrank to a dot and disappeared. She stood and put on her shirt. Skyler glanced outside one last time and approached the only other door in the room. From the moment he had seen it, he knew he would have to open it. He suspected that it led to a place about which he had heard rumors for as long as he could remember. As children, it had loomed large in the dark corners of their fearful fantasies.

He turned the brass doorknob and pulled.

There was a white metal table in the center, and domed lights above, shining brightly. The floor was graded slightly and led to a drain. Cabinets lined the walls, stocked with medical equipment. Tanks of gas with rubber tubing and a mask stood next to a bed in one corner. The room was scrubbed more painstakingly than any he had ever seen.

Slowly, he stepped inside, and Julia came behind. The room was warm and stuffy. There was yet another door, thick and heavy like the vault of a meat locker. He crossed the floor and pushed the door lever, and it moved swiftly inward, opening onto a black void. He found a switch and flipped it, and a blaze of light blinded him momentarily—mercifully—until finally he focused upon the terrible sight before him. For there, stretched out upon a slab, was a body.

At first it looked like a small statue, pale and strangely shrunken. It was lying upon its back. The feet lay pointing outward, as in repose. There was a yellowish-green hue under the neck and spreading in half circles around the armpits. Male genitals slumped to one side, swollen with fluid. Skyler tried to avoid looking at the chest, but found his eyes drawn inexorably to it. The chest was gone. In its place was a cavity, sliced open, neat as a gutted fish. Flaps of squared-off skin hung down on either side like shutters on a window, and the rib cage had collapsed inward around a dark hole that was ringed in dark red—dried blood.

It was Patrick.

Skyler jumped as Julia slipped up behind him and touched him lightly on the arm. He felt her stiffen as she saw the body, and he heard her next to his ear, a quick intake of breath.

"Look," he exclaimed in a voice gone small. "His heart's gone."

He heard her resume breathing. They stared for some seconds.

"But why?" she said.

He had no answer.

They backed out and turned off the light and closed the vault. In the Records Room, Skyler stood watch while Julia examined the desk and computer with trembling hands, making sure there were no traces of their presence. When they got outside and shut the door behind them, they looked around quickly to make sure the coast was clear.

They ran as fast as they could and didn't stop until they were deep inside the now darkening woods. Even there, the only sanctuary on the island left to them, Skyler and Julia no longer felt safe.

They stopped, gasping for breath. She sat on the ground, and he leaned against a tree. When she spoke, her voice was so low that he could also hear the stirrings of small animals in the underbrush, and he tried to listen to both. He kept watch.

"I don't understand," she said. "Why did they have to take everything out of him? What did he have?"

"I don't know, but it must have been deadly. Fast-acting and deadly."

"How do we know?"

"Why else would they cut him up like that?"

"Do you think it was some horrible disease?"

"Maybe that's what they're trying to find out."

"Do you think it's contagious? Maybe we got it."

"We were only there a couple of seconds."

"His heart was missing—you saw that. Where was it? Why would they take it out?"

"I don't know—unless, maybe, they're analyzing it or something."

His tone didn't sound convincing, he realized, when he heard himself.

"I don't know," she said, standing up and walking around. "I hate this—it's frightening. There's so much we don't know. *Something* is going on."

Skyler knew what that meant, where she was headed. For months her doubts and suspicions had been growing, faster even than his. And when they got together for their secret meetings, which seemed to both of them more and more risky, sooner or later she broached the subject. She was becoming obsessive.

"Patrick's not the first to die"—Skyler noted that she did not mention Raisin by name, and he was at least grateful for that—"and he's not the first to be called in for a special physical. Why don't they ever discover something during the *regular* physical?"

"I don't know. Sometimes they do."

"But not always. And that makes it seem like they know something's wrong *beforehand*—don't you see?"

He did. And as so often happened, he knew without knowing; on some level he had had the same thought, but he hadn't cared to examine it until she held it right in front of him. She was always like that; her mind was swift, unrelenting. She could brave things that he preferred to look away from.

He nodded and glanced at her in the fading quarter-light, her long dark hair hanging in strands against her cheek, the paleness of her underarms as she reached out.

"It's horrible," she said. "Just horrible."

She put her arms around his back, and they held each other tightly. They had done that hundreds of times, but still, at the first touch, there was always that flash—the forbidden. The Lab did not allow boys and girls to mingle, and now that they were older, the prohibition was backed by a punishment so severe that no one even knew what it would be. No one had ever violated the rule. Until them.

He realized, as he began to calm a little, that he had been trembling since he had seen the body.

"We have to go back," she said, pulling back at arm's length and looking into his eyes. "They'll miss us in the dorms. *What if somebody comes?*"

Skyler knew she was right—what they were doing was dangerous—but he did not want to let her go. He was reluctant to be alone with his thoughts.

They held hands as long as they dared, until they reached the outskirts of the Campus. Then they separated and moved toward their separate barracks, passing the Big House in the distance. A full moon was on the rise, and Skyler could see the mansion through the shadows of the oak trees that surrounded it. The moss hanging from the branches obscured part of the facade, but the moonlight reflected off the upper windows like a glow from within.

At one point, Skyler looked back and saw Julia slipping from behind a tree to the pedestal of a statue of a Greek goddess, and as the moonlight caught her, it froze her in his mind forever, so graceful and vulnerable.

In bed, lying upon the thin mattress that covered his wooden bunk, Skyler listened to the sounds of the others breathing in their sleep, sounds that he had heard his entire life, and tried not to think about Patrick. He almost thought the sounds were a little altered, that he could detect one missing.

There would be, he knew, a funeral service, and Baptiste would speak, as he had at the other services. Skyler didn't want to think about those either.

Instead he tried thinking about the past, when he'd been young and everything had been different. The island had been his universe to explore. How he had loved the scientific excursions into the forest, the mad search for bugs and plants. How happy he had been on those occasions—like Baptiste's birthday—when the doors of the Big House were thrown open to them. How he used to relish those nights sleeping out of doors to learn about the stars, scanning the skies with telescopes; in the mornings he would awaken early and lie still, identifying the birds by their calls and watching the first thin rays of the sun shimmer over the water.

Jimminies, the children were called, though where the word came from or what it signified, they were never told. They were all about the same age, a year or two different, no more. So they were especially close.

Growing up in the Lab, they had felt secure and content. Neither Skyler nor any of the others had ever really questioned not having parents, even though they knew that children on the mainland—"the other side," it was called—possessed them, In reality, all the Elder Physicians were their parents, they were told, and they were lucky to have "not two, but twenty" figures of respect who raised the children according to scientific principles and treated them all with an equal hand.

And, anyway, Skyler and the other Jimminies were special. They were "pioneers of science," participants in a noble experiment. On their island paradise, they would live long and fruitful lives through a regime of mental purity and bodily health. If they were lucky, they would never experience "the other side," that cesspool of pollution and violence. They would never get any closer to it than the movies and TV programs they were allowed to watch on special occasions.

But it didn't always feel like paradise: the endless medical examinations, the pills and vaccinations, the blood and urine samples, the calisthenics and rules against running games that might be harmful. And then, too, there were the Orderlies, three of them, so much alike and each with that peculiar slash of white in his hair, who ruled over them like stern older brothers. It was hard not to dislike them.

Skyler had a distinct recollection of the time long ago—more than ten years now—when he'd first become restless. He'd been fourteen years old at the time. Like so many of his memories, this one was bound up with his best friend, Johnny Ray, or Raisin, as Skyler himself had named him.

It had begun to happen on a summer day after the science lesson in the lecture hall, a one-room wooden structure set high on cinder blocks. Even with windows on two sides propped open, the hot, thick air barely moved. Above the blackboard was a customized couplet, printed in handsome script:

> Nature and Nature's laws lay hid in night:
> Bacon said, *"Let Newton be!"* and all was light.

In unison they had recited Rincon's First Law, named after the Lab's founder, Dr. Rincon, who did not live on the island and was known to them only through his teachings and his research: "Human life alone is sacred; its preservation and extension is our mission." Scientific facts were drummed into them, learned by incantations and memorization. They learned the periodic table of elements, the name of every part of the body, the biological kingdoms and phyla, all the known planets of all the known solar systems, even the four-letter coded DNA sequences surrounding a hundred and twenty disease genes. On this particular day they received back papers they had written, most with high marks. Outside the lecture hall, Raisin pulled Skyler aside.

"It's phony, you know—this whole thing."

"What is?"

"Writing papers, getting grades. They don't even read them."

"How do you know?"

"I tested them. After the first two paragraphs I made it up. I wrote complete gibberish."

He showed his paper and the grade he had gotten, scrawled at the end: VERY GOOD.

"I don't think they care whether we learn or not—you ever get that feeling?"

In fact, Skyler realized, he did have that feeling sometimes, but he had never put it into words.

"But then why would they teach us?"

Raisin shrugged. "I don't know. Maybe to keep us busy."

For days afterward, Raisin kept up a tirade. He harped on the restrictions that circumscribed their lives: the books in the library that they could not read because they were "not fit," TV shows that they saw advertised but were not permitted to watch, games of roughhouse they could not play, questions the Physician Teachers never answered.

One hot afternoon, through the open windows, they heard, as they sometimes did, distant cries carried by the wind—the sounds of younger children at play at the Nursery. The Nursery was a small adjacent island—it could be reached across a narrow sandbar at low tide—but the Jimminies were not allowed to go there. Nor were the toddlers ever brought onto the mainland.

"Did you ever wonder," Raisin asked later, "why we never see them? What would be the harm in it?"

There was another group with whom the Jimminies were permitted no contact—the Gullah, a tiny community of black people. Skyler and Raisin had heard—from where they did not remember—that these were descendants of slaves, and that many years ago scores of them had inhabited the southern half of the island. Now there were only a dozen or so, mostly fishermen living in shacks on the western shore. A few brought fish to the Big House, and they were objects of fascination to the Jimminies, mysterious silent beings who walked on the paths, carrying glistening trout and yellowtail on long fronds ripped from the fan-shaped palmettos.

"They have boats," said Raisin. "Why don't we have any boats? Why is the only boat in the Lab locked up inside the boathouse?"

Skyler finally turned on Raisin, demanding that he stop posing his stupid, troublesome questions. "Why are you doing this?" he shouted.

Raisin smiled. "Asking questions is supposed to be part of science," he replied. "It's called the scientific method. Remember?"

And then gradually a strange thing happened: Skyler began asking questions, too—to himself—little ones first and then bigger ones.

One Sunday morning, he gazed up at Baptiste during Dogma and had a remarkable sensation. Not so very long ago he had been enthralled by Dogma. The services had given structure to his week, in the same way that science gave meaning to his life. Even before he understood the full meanings of the words, he loved to hear Baptiste roll them out, starting softly and then raising his voice gradually until, gripping the lectern with both hands, he was practically yelling. Skyler would sit there spellbound.

But this day he felt nothing. He looked at the symbol upon the wall, the twin-headed snake coiled around a staff. He looked at the blown-up photograph of Dr. Rincon in his white coat, gazing off confidently as if he were surveying a future in which Reason and Science had triumphed. And he looked at Baptiste, whose coal black hair was pulled tightly around his head, accentuating a skull that seemed as narrow as an ax blade. And he felt nothing.

The Chief Elder Physician spoke.

He spoke about the "beauty of reason and organization over the chaos of superstition and religion." What did he mean? He spoke about "the pendulum of the historical-cultural cycle swinging to our side." The words sounded hollow. It used to make Skyler feel privileged, all this talk of how they were so special, raised by the Lab as acolytes of science. *A chosen tribe*—stronger, healthier, purer, longer-living. How they were kept away from "the other side" to avoid contamination from the "modern-day Babylon" of the United States. But now he didn't know what to feel—he didn't feel much of anything.

How strange it was. Baptiste kept speaking, but Skyler blocked out the words. He stared at this man who had been the magnetic force at the center of his life for as long as he could remember. And it was then that the remarkable sensation happened: slowly, as he looked, Baptiste began to appear smaller, frail, aging with specks of gray in his hair and crow's feet around his eyes. He even seemed—was it possible?—slightly ludicrous.

Skyler leaned forward and turned slightly to catch a glimpse of Raisin. He could tell by his posture, hunched in on himself as if in concealment, that he was undergoing the same epiphany. They locked eyes, and Skyler saw an ember of defiance burning there. At that moment the two exchanged an unspoken, unspeakable secret—apostasy.

* * *

The next year the restlessness got worse. The questions wouldn't go away. Odd things kept happening. A girl named Jenny disappeared into the surgical ward for six days, and when she returned, they were told her left eye had been diseased; in its place she wore one made of glass. A boy was taken away in the middle of the day, held in the ward for two days, and then just as mysteriously released—the attending physician said his illness had been successfully treated.

Raisin, tall and gangly with his hair sticking out in all directions like animal fur, was turning strange. He had always been different. For one thing, he was an epileptic, subject to sudden fainting spells. Though it was never stated outright, both he and Skyler knew that the illness was troubling to the Elder Physicians—anything less than perfect health was deemed a failure.

For another, Raisin had stopped taking the daily pill handed out to all the Jimminies at evening meal. He insisted the pill robbed him of energy. Proudly, he showed Skyler how he concealed it under his tongue when the Orderly passed, saving it for a collection stashed in a tin can under his bed. Wherever he went, he secretly carried a child's toy, a wooden soldier four inches tall, so bruised and knocked about that its blue and red paint was largely gone; even when they went on forced marches around the Campus, he kept it in his pocket, and sometimes at night when the others were sleeping, he would take it out and play with it and show it only to Skyler.

Increasingly, Raisin was on the verge of open rebellion. He had become a target of attack at the Lab's Self-Criticism sessions. He was denounced by the Orderlies for various offenses and spent hours with the Psychologist Physician. Three times he was punished for disobedience, forced to spend the night hungry and alone locked inside "the Box," an old chicken shed at the edge of forty-foot pines; the sounds of the animals foraging in the darkness around him frightened him, and in the morning he was welcomed warmly back into the group and given a large breakfast. For days afterward he behaved himself, but it didn't last.

The only saving grace was that Skyler and Raisin and many of the other Jimminies had turned fifteen, and so their schooling stopped and instead they took on chores. Skyler was a goatherd. Every morning he rounded up a band of the scrawny animals from the barnyard, shepherded them to distant pastures and brought them back in the late afternoon when the sun was low in the sky. This brought him a taste of freedom.

Raisin was given the worst chores, but one of them had a hidden blessing. Once a week he was sent to collect honey from beehives in the woods—a job few others were brave enough to do—and these turned into occasions for celebration. He would abandon his honey jars and meet up with Skyler. Away from the Lab together, they could do whatever they wanted.

Sometimes when the two of them were alone in the woods, Raisin would have a seizure, and Skyler learned to care for him. As he lay thrashing about on the ground, Skyler would hold a stick in his mouth so that he wouldn't swallow his tongue. Afterward, Skyler would cradle his head and murmur gentle phrases to him as he came back to consciousness, surfacing from some dark depths, blank-minded and confused. They, of course, kept the fits a secret.

Way up in the northern forest, Skyler discovered a hidden meadow reached through a narrow passage in a ravine. It was hemmed in with boulders and trees, and, ringing it around with branches and underbrush, he turned it into a makeshift corral for the goats. By confining them inside, he was able to roam free. From then on, when he met with Raisin, their horizons expanded. For a few watchful hours at a time, they had the run of the wild area to the north. They explored the swamps and dense woods, running along the paths made by wild boar and deer. They gamboled in the fields and climbed trees so tall that they could see the whitecaps of the ocean. That such dangerous activities were proscribed made them that much more delicious.

On one particular spring day, when the outlying blanket of cordgrass waved in the ocean breeze and the loblolly pine smelled fresh of sap, something extraordinary happened to them.

With the goats securely tucked away in their enclosure and the honey jars already full, they were lying upon their backs in a field, when Raisin, a piece of straw sticking from his mouth like a cigarette, turned to Skyler and suddenly announced that he wanted to explore the western shore.

"But that's where the Gullah are," protested Skyler.

"That's the whole damn point," he replied, using the one profane word he had picked up from TV.

And before Skyler could think of an objection, Raisin was on his feet, off and running. Skyler kept up and followed, but he was at pains to keep up, running as fast as he could. They tore along a path toward the shore and then through a patch of swampland, sending the water splashing around them. Raisin lengthened his lead. Skyler saw his back receding ahead of him, zigzagging between the trees until he disappeared altogether. Then suddenly Skyler heard a sharp cry, followed by a long moan. He recognized it instantly—the onset of a seizure. By the time he caught up, Raisin was writhing on his back, his limbs jerking in spasms and his eyes turned up in the sockets.

Quickly, Skyler covered him with his own body and placed a stick between his teeth. He thrust his head to one side and held on with all his might, trying to deaden his weight to keep Raisin close to the ground, riding out the seizure like a wrestler pinning an opponent. Gradually, he felt the spasms subside and the body beneath him turn limp. But as he rolled off, something lashed his arm, thin and strong as a whip. For an instant, he imagined Raisin had sprouted a tail. Then he saw what it was, and as he leapt up and turned the body to one side, the snake was hanging there, its fangs embedded in the back of Raisin's leg. He got a branch and beat it until finally it released its hold and curled up. He smashed the head until it stopped moving and then ran back to Raisin.

"Don't move him, child!"

The command came over his left shoulder. He obeyed it instantly without even thinking about it. He was pushed aside, and a pair of coal black hands ripped Raisin's pants open, exposing a red welt and two tiny black-blue holes in the milky flesh. A knife came out, moving quickly to make four slits in a crosshatch. The elderly man with gray hair bent down, pursing his lips and sucking the wound with a slurping sound. He turned and spat out venom and sucked some more, and soon he was extracting mouthfuls of blood and expelling them upon the leaves of a berry bush. Raisin began to stir.

"Hold him still," the man directed, and Skyler did as he was told. The old man made deeper cuts and turned Raisin on his side so that he bled into the ground.

"Don't pay to take no chances," he said. "That'd be no ordinary snake. That's a water moccasin."

Soon, Raisin was awake, and Skyler was ordered to carry him. He did, and followed the large elderly man, who was dressed in a bulky blue sweatshirt and wide-bottomed blue pants. They went down the path until finally they came to a clearing and he could smell the mudflats. Ahead was a grove of cypress, and on the other side, a shack no bigger than a garage, made of shingles painted blue. As he carried Raisin inside, he looked to his left and saw an expanse of water coming right up to the grassy bank. There was an old wooden dock, and tied to it—Skyler's heart skipped a beat when he saw it—was a boat with an outboard motor.

"Put him down," the man said, gesturing to a sagging iron-frame bed covered with a quilt. Skyler was dying to ask all kinds of questions—he had never been inside such a place, with so many new and intriguing objects—but he kept silent as the old man bound up Skyler's wound and even sewed together his pants leg.

"No reason to go around talkin' about this," he said. "Those people you live with, they don't take to your talkin' to strangers. You go tellin' anyone, and you're going to have to deal with me—and I got my ways."

The man cast a hard glance at Skyler, who was sitting quietly in an overstuffed easy chair, and at that point the boy suddenly recognized him—one of the fishermen who brought their catch to the kitchen window of the Big House.

"We won't, I promise," he said.

"Damned right—we won't."

Raisin suddenly sat up in the bed, surprising both of them.

The old man took Skyler over to a window and pointed at the backyard, a jumble of long weeds and engine parts. To the rear was a tupelo maple, and from its branches hung more than a dozen round, shiny objects—hubcaps, Skyler later realized. They turned, glistening in the sunlight.

"I have my ways," said the old man. "You ever heard of juju?"

Skyler shook his head.

"Magic. You talk about this and it'll be the last talkin' you do. You'll just open your mouth and nothin' will come out."

Raisin, intrigued, asked his name.

"I don't go tellin' my name till I know the other 'ns."

They introduced themselves, awkwardly. They had never done that before.

"I'm Kuta."

"How come you're called that?" asked Raisin.

"How come you're called Raisin?"

"I don't know. It's just a nickname."

"Mine's more than a nickname. It's a story."

And the old man settled into the easy chair. Skyler sat next to Raisin on the bed.

"Kuta's Gullah, what some folks here speak, though you wouldn't know nothing about that. It means *turtle*. I'm called that, 'cause when I was born, I was such a little thing, the midwife held me up in the palm of her hand, lying on my back, and I was so small they didn't expect me to live. She says:

'Why, this little babe's no bigger than a turtle.' And so I was. But I kicked my legs and I kept on kicking and I just willed myself to keep on living. Even when I was growed, the name stuck."

"And what's that?" asked Raisin, pointing at a trumpet hanging from the wall by a peg.

Skyler knew Raisin knew the answer; they had seen bands playing on television.

*"That,"* said Kuta proudly. "That's my *instrument.*" He fixed Raisin with a stare. "You usually ask so many questions—or is that the snake talking?"

But he didn't wait for an answer. He told a long tale about his younger days playing the trumpet in jazz bands on the mainland. He talked about juke joints in New Orleans and life on the road, playing for ten bucks a night and gambling it away and waking up next to beautiful women whose names he could not recall.

"Nothing like the travelin' life," he declared, rubbing a gray beard that stood out against his black leathery chin. "Broadening to the spirit. Good for the soul. A man needs travelin' the way a fish needs the ocean."

And as he talked, Skyler looked at Raisin and could see that he, too, was entranced.

They stayed, that first day, more than an hour. Kuta saw them off, standing on his doorstep, leaning his bulk against the frame, while Raisin asked one final question—could they come again to visit? Kuta pawed his cheek, thinking.

"You know you ain't supposed to be 'round here."

Silence again. Finally, the old man looked them over, sizing them up.

"Shoot. I guess it's no harm, so long as you don't go tellin' nobody. Specially those Orderlies. I don't want no trouble, now."

When they returned to the Lab, Raisin limping on one leg and Skyler trying to shoulder his weight, they talked excitedly. Skyler hadn't seen Raisin like this in years. It seemed a whole new world had opened up, and their minds were suddenly reeling with new possibilities.

"We got to be careful," Skyler said as they approached the Campus. "Can you walk without a limp?"

"Damn right I can."

And he did.

The boys returned six days later. Kuta was sitting under a palm tree, repairing a fishing net, which was spread out on the sand before him. Raisin walked up and sat on a rock five feet away, silently watching as the bony black hands moved a three-inch needle back and forth through the wire mesh. Skyler sat next to Raisin and they stayed like that, awkward and silent for quite a while, until finally Kuta broke the silence.

"What you lookin' at, child?"

Raisin shrugged, gave a hint of a smile and replied simply: "You."

"What's a matter? Never seen a body work before?"

"Not sitting down."

And so was born an unusual friendship.

Skyler and Raisin visited Kuta about once every two weeks, whenever they could get together and whenever they dared to risk it, moving cautiously along the path to make sure they were unobserved and looking in his window to see if he was alone. He always was. He had been married twice, but both women lived on the mainland and he hadn't seen either for years. He seemed equally fond of both wives, and he loved talking about them—especially how good they were in bed.

Talk like this intrigued Skyler and Raisin because they had been separated from girls for the past year and any mention of sex was forbidden at the lab. They asked so many questions about it, that one day Kuta slapped his knee laughing and vowed to take them to a house he knew in Charleston—a prospect that almost literally took their breath away.

Raisin jumped at the idea, then sulked when Kuta said he was joking. He was always trying to get Kuta to take them out in his boat—"just to go fishing," he pleaded, though Skyler suspected there was more to it than that—and Kuta kept coming up with excuses: the boat needed repair, the engine had thrown a valve, the tide was wrong. Finally one day he looked Raisin straight in the eye and said: "You know those people in that Big House would have my hide. They *own* just about the whole island. What you tryin' to do to me, child?"

Still, the old man seemed to luxuriate in his role as life guide. He filled their heads with Gullah history—recounting such stories as the ancestors who had stepped off a slave ship onto this very island and turned to march directly back into the ocean toward Africa, a mass drowning. At times, talking about the Lab, he would turn serious, shaking his head and pronouncing "something wrong-headed" about its strict doctrines. He thought it peculiar to get all those inoculations—"they turning you into pincushions, for what?" he demanded. And he derived a pleasure in dispensing subversive notions.

"Don't see no harm in running," he would say. "A boy's gotta stretch his legs if he's to become a man. And what's wrong in leaving the island? It don't make no sense to stay cooped up here your whole life."

For their part, the old man was a window to the outside world, the only person they had ever met who was not in the Lab. They loved the forbidden hours in his shack, sitting on the bed with broken springs, hanging on his every word. The trumpet was always hanging from its peg upon the wall, and on special occasions—meaning when the spirit moved him—Kuta would take it down and play a riff or two, his cheeks bulging like a blowfish.

He had a television, but they preferred listening to the radio. It was turned during the afternoons to a DJ called Bozman, who spilled out the words in singsong Gullah.

"Disya one fa all ob de oomen. Dey a good-good one fa dancin."

And Kuta would translate: "This one's for all the women out there. It's good dance music."

The broadcast—from the mainland—almost made them shiver, it was so illicit and enthralling.

It did not escape Skyler that all this talk of freedom and sex was feeding Raisin's discontent. Increasingly, he began talking of his dream of going to "the other side." As the months passed, he became more and more rebellious, always in trouble of one kind or another. He began standing up to the Orderlies, talking back, openly obstreperous. And punishments lost their effect. His head was shaved bald, which was meant to humiliate him; he seemed to wear it as a badge of honor. Food was withheld; he grew uncomplainingly thin.

One morning, Raisin was called in to see the Psychologist Physician. There was a report that he had been seen masturbating, which he did not deny. Nor did he deny hiding the dinnertime pills; he seemed to enjoy leading a search party of three Orderlies that marched straight to the barracks and found the cache of tablets under his bed.

The Elders confined him to the Campus—he had long since lost his right to gather honey—which meant he could no longer slip away to see Kuta. Skyler realized that the prohibition would be hard to bear. One afternoon, Raisin was discovered in the woods; Skyler alone knew where he had been. He was removed from the barracks and consigned for three nights to solitary confinement in "the Box." Skyler tried to visit him there. The first night, he got close enough to hear Raisin talking to himself, playing with his toy soldier, but he had to leave when someone approached.

The next night, he found that the Orderlies had placed the guard dogs around it, and their fierce barking kept him away.

Soon, Skyler saw Raisin only at a distance in odd moments, his bald head bobbing as he carried out garbage from the Meal House or cleaned the toilets or submitted to some other discipline. He was confined for days on end in the basement of the Big House—locked inside a room at night, according to the rumors. It was Patrick who told Skyler this, and he broke the news gently, out of deference to their friendship.

One hot morning, Skyler was crossing an upper field on the Campus when he walked by the vegetable garden and heard his name being whispered. He looked around, but saw no one. Again, he heard it, coming from behind a row of waist-high corn.

He ducked behind it and there was Raisin. He had been sent to do weeding, and his head and cheek were smudged with dirt. His hair was growing back in ungainly clumps, his eyes looked pink and watery, and he was disturbingly gaunt. He had a wild look about the eyes.

"I have to get away," he said, grabbing Skyler's arm and squeezing it so tightly it almost hurt. "You have to come, too. The things I've learned—down there, in the basement. You have *no idea* what's going on. Horrible things. We all have to get away."

Skyler didn't want this. He was scared. Raisin was acting so strangely—there were little bubbles of spittle at the corner of his lips, and he seemed to be babbling with the urgency of what he wanted to say. The others would be coming right behind him and—Skyler felt a stab of guilt—he knew he would get into trouble for being with him.

Still, Raisin was his friend, his oldest friend. He needed him. Skyler would hear him out and do whatever he wanted.

"I want you to come with me," Raisin said. "I can break out. Tomorrow night. We'll meet at the boathouse and take the boat. We'll go on to the other side. We'll be out of here—for good. We'll be safe."

Skyler agreed. He felt dread in his stomach. The others were approaching.

"Eight o'clock," whispered Raisin. "Eight o'clock at the boathouse. Don't be late!"

The next night Skyler felt his heart pounding as the hour approached. He listened carefully for the chiming of the grandfather clock in the Big House and heard it strike seven. He made a small bundle—two shirts, an extra pair of socks, a small pocketknife, a paperback book on Charles Darwin—to carry with him.

*The mainland! What would it be like?*

His hands and feet felt cold with fear. I'm a good friend, he told himself—a loyal friend.

Then something unforeseen happened. There was a noise way off in the distance, a thin crash that sounded a bit like glass breaking. It could have come from the Big House, though he wasn't sure. He listened intently, but everything was quiet.

Five or ten minutes later, he heard footsteps, a heavy tread on the pathway leading to the boys' barracks. The door swung open and in stepped an Orderly. He surveyed the room, pulled a chair up against the door and sat in it, his arms folded. The other Jimminies were stunned; nothing like this had ever happened before.

Gradually, they settled down. One by one Skyler heard them drop off to sleep, the sounds of their steady breathing. He stole looks over his blanket at the Orderly, sitting there, implacable.

Skyler waited. He watched. Then he, too, fell asleep.

He awoke sometime in the early morning hours. The chair was beside the door, empty. Otherwise, nothing had changed. He leapt out of bed, dressed and went to the door, leaving the bundle behind under his bed. When he stepped outside, he could see dawn was already coming up in the east.

He ran to the boathouse. And then his heart soared. The lock was broken—the door was swinging open a half foot or so. He crept up to it, softly placed a hand upon the latch and pulled it wider, peering inside. The light was dim. There was the slip inside between two narrow docks that hugged the walls, the sound of water lapping the base of the piers. And on the other side the bay doors were open—he could see straight through to the bay. The boat was gone!

Outside, four feet from the door, he saw a small object. He bent to examine it and then picked it up and held it in his hand. Raisin's toy soldier.

That afternoon, he learned that Raisin had never made it to the mainland. He had lost his way in the marshes, they were told, and at high tide the boat had been caught in the treacherous currents. It had capsized and he had drowned. The boat had been discovered floating upside down a half mile from shore, and when it had been turned upright, Raisin had been found, his lungs filled with water, his face a ghostly blue and one leg caught under the wooden seat.

At the funeral service, Baptiste theorized that the escape had brought on a seizure. He managed to say some good things about Raisin. Julia, Patrick and many of the other Jimminies wept openly; something in Raisin's whole saga touched a chord of tragedy in their world, and they sensed it would never be the same. As for Skyler, he was too devastated even to cry. He felt he had lost his only brother.

He put some of the blame on Kuta. For a while, he stopped coming to the shack, but then, when he found he missed the old man a great deal, he resumed his occasional visits. He still basked in the warmth of his company, but it wasn't the same. When there had been three of them, the old man talking and the two boys drinking it in like wine, it had felt like a family.

Lying in bed, Skyler marveled at the human mind. Here he had tried to avoid thinking about Raisin and his death a decade ago. He had tried to construct roadblocks to prevent thinking about it, and his mind had led him on a back route to that self-same destination.

He felt his hands and feet go cold again, just as they had that fateful night.

He reached under the bed and searched with one hand for the object. When he didn't find it at once, he feared that it was missing, but then he struck it with his finger. He lifted the wooden soldier up and placed it under the thin blanket.

Raisin dead. Now Patrick. Who would be next? How many more would there be? Had Raisin been right: were none of them safe?

# Chapter 2

Jude Harley had been on the West Side anyway to conduct an interview, and so he'd decided to walk to his office at the newspaper on Fifth Avenue. He passed a traffic snarl on West Forty-sixth and watched a taxi driver lean on his horn, sending a blast echoing up and down the street. Blocking the road ahead was a flatbed truck piled with steel girders; on top of them stood three construction workers in yellow hard hats, looking up. Jude followed their gaze. Thirty floors above, a girder being hoisted by a crane rocked at the end of a cable like a balancing pencil. The taxi honked again.

Jude was a bit put off by the new, sparkling Midtown. Not that he would have willed it back to the old days of the pushers and the prostitutes—it was simply that so many of the new stores were slick and shallow. Crass commercialism had triumphed again. He passed a shop and peered into the window at statuettes of the Empire State Building and Miss Liberty, plates emblazoned with the skyline, foot-tall dummies of Charlie Chaplin and Madonna and Elvis. Not long ago, it had been one of his favorite bars, a darkened den with wooden booths, a jukebox of Sinatra songs and a painting so blackened by grit that only old-timers knew it was of Joe Louis delivering the knock-out punch to Max Schmeling.

That was another problem with change—it made you feel old. And at the ripe age of thirty, with young adulthood finally behind him, reasonably secure in his career, unattached or free—depending upon your point of view—and standing in the middle of the tumult of the greatest city in the world, one thing he did not want to be feeling was old.

He walked east past the towering office blocks of Sixth Avenue until he came to Fifth Avenue, then turned uptown. The crowd was light for a Saturday morning, but it thickened when he came to Rockefeller Center. He was in no hurry to get to work, so he ducked down the walkway lined with airlines, bookstores and chocolate shops. His reflection popped up in the plate-glass windows, dogging him.

Jude Harley had a thin, angular face with long dark hair that fell into his eyes when he leaned over the keyboard to type a story. His looks were protean, a woman had once told him: one minute he might be almost ordinary, but the next—seen on a street corner with his collar up, reading intently by a fire, telling an outrageous joke at dinner—he could catch the eye and dazzle. He had been flattered by the description. So how come he had been alone for three months now?

He came to the sunken plaza. With the warm weather, the skating rink was gone, and in its place was a forest of umbrellas. Too bad. He enjoyed watching the skaters cutting figure eights with their long-legged strides, their sheer exhibitionism. But something about the place also unnerved him; even as a newcomer to the city years ago, he had felt its oppressive anonymity. Out of nowhere, he thought of Holden Caulfield, the eternal alienated adolescent, coming to skate with his "phoney" date with the cute ass, and he felt a stab of loneliness.

He resumed his walk up Fifth Avenue. Otherwise—meaning professionally—things were breaking for him. He was getting good assignments at the *New York Mirror* and had hit his stride with three or four bylines a week. At this rate, he might get a column, someday, a perch that would allow him to trumpet his talent. He liked the rough-and-tumble world of the tabloid, and he knew he was good at it. He had sharp elbows and natural instincts. Once he had gone for a job interview at *The New York Times*; he'd been put off by the self-satisfied smugness of the editor who'd met him in the reception room, and by a newsroom as deadly as an insurance office. He'd skipped the second interview.

There was something else: a novel that he had written years ago and peddled fruitlessly around town had finally been published. Much to his surprise, it was even doing well, thanks in part to the publisher's vigorous advertising and publicity campaign. He had to admit, he got a kick when he strolled into a bookstore and saw the display built around that familiar cover, a dark blue jacket with a grotesque face in white plaster of paris. The title, *Death Mask,* was printed in raised silver letters.

Jude stopped at a coffee wagon on Fifty-fourth Street, an aluminum-plated trailer run by Bashir, an Afghan. Bashir loved to talk, especially about the Taliban, the religious fundamentalists who had overrun his country.

Jude had been to Afghanistan for a series on refugee camps—two years ago, when the *Mirror* had been printing foreign news in a bid for respectability—and Bashir had been delighted to discover someone who at least knew the names of the provincial cities. He treated Jude as a special friend.

But today Jude wanted to preserve his solitary mood, and so he plunked down his two quarters for coffee—regular with milk and extra sugar—with a wordless nod.

In his lilting New Yorkese, Bashir asked him if he had heard that a northern village—the name was hard to make out—had fallen.

Jude said he had not.

"They control ninety percent of the country now," said Bashir sadly. "The situation is very bad."

Jude nodded sympathetically.

"I don't know what will happen. My poor country. The way they treat people is horrible."

"I know," said Jude, accepting his coffee in a brown paper bag with the neck twisted into a handle.

They shared a moment of silence.

"You have a good day," exclaimed Bashir, suddenly smiling and showing a gold tooth.

Jude responded: "You, too."

Ducking into the building, he thought about Bashir, and people like him who had real problems, struggling to make ends meet. His coffee wagon seemed so compact and homey. Photographs of beautiful, dark-haired children were taped onto a side window; change piled up on a kitchen towel spread on the counter as he bustled about amid the thick fumes of Colombian coffee. He was moving up in the world, making something of himself. With a twinge of middle-class guilt, Jude found that he envied the man—his certitude, his striving, even the political convictions that gave an organizing principle to his life. Most of all, he admired his passion.

The *Mirror* occupied three floors at 666 Fifth Avenue, a nondescript skyscraper that nonetheless rose high enough to cast its red neon number into the haze sometimes overhanging mid-Manhattan. The sight of 666 up in the sky had caused one wag with Biblical knowledge to call the newspaper "the Beast." For the literate, the nickname also carried an allusion to the newspaper in Evelyn Waugh's *Scoop*, and so it had stuck.

It also had the ring of descriptive truth. The owner was R. P. Tibbett, a

New York real estate mogul who was assembling a media empire and had moved his headquarters to Washington, D.C., to be closer to the politicians he financed. He used the tabloid shamelessly for vendettas and payoffs. The *Mirror* was not so much the flagship of the Tibbett fleet as its garbage scow. When he wanted to campaign for more TV licenses, he did it with a steady drumbeat in its pages, and when he wanted to skewer an enemy, which happened more and more frequently these days, he did it with the stiletto-sharp prose of its best writers. To cloak their shame, the reporters espoused the mystique that their paper was street-wise and "in touch with the people"—whatever that meant.

Jude passed an honor box in the lobby—Tibbett was too cheap to give the paper away even to the people who produced it—and recoiled at the hype of the page-one headline: KILLER FLU STALKS CITY. Apparently, two people were in the hospital.

The elevator stopped on the third floor, and as the doors were closing, a hand intruded to send them skittering back. Jude saw long, curving fingers bearing an opal ring, and his heart sank—he knew that ring. Betsy entered, and her eyes widened in surprise, which she quickly tried to damp down.

"Oh, it's you," she said icily.

Jude was nonplussed. He didn't know how to answer that statement—"Yes, it's me"? So he simply said: "Hello."

His voice echoed without a response, as she stared straight ahead at the doors. In the silence he could hear the elevator cables grinding. Betsy was a fellow reporter; they had lived together for nearly a year before she'd thrown him out three months ago—or more precisely, when he had decided to leave but let her salvage a bit of pride by showing him the door. He recalled how furious she had gotten during their tag-end fights, and how she had slapped him once, tearing a bit of skin on his cheek with her ring. She had screamed that he was incapable of feeling, "emotionally retarded." What did she expect? she said, given his abysmal childhood. Then she had cried, which he hated.

Still, they had had some fantastic lovemaking. Working nights, they used to sneak into the library and make out among the boxes of microfilmed newspapers. He looked at her out of the corner of his eye, and he could tell she was doing the same. The elevator came to her floor, and she gave him a pinched smile and a flat but reasonably warm "Good-bye," as if to say: I now care so little, I can treat you like anyone else. When she was gone, he was relieved.

The elevator door opened, and he stepped out on his floor.

"Morning, Barry," he said to the receptionist, a fellow with a heavily waxed blond handlebar mustache that gave him the lugubrious look of a water buffalo.

"Well, if it isn't the big novelist."

Jude groaned inwardly. He was in no mood to deal with sarcasm.

The newsroom had that familiar Saturday feel—people casually dressed, hoping for catastrophe to strike somewhere but not right on deadline. Only a dozen or so reporters were in; they were keeping their heads down, out of the line of sight of the editors.

Jude was up for a good breaking story. The interview he had just done had been a bust. He had recently finished a takeout on gun control, complete with wrenching stories of children who had found loaded revolvers and shot their siblings, and he wanted something neat and fast—"quick and dirty" was the newsroom expression—to wipe his synapses clean.

Jude looked up at the Metro desk. Leventhal, the editor in charge on weekends, was holding a huddle with the sub-editors. That was not a good sign. When Jude had first joined the paper, he had heard an old-timer remark that no good story ever came from a meeting of editors, and he had found nothing in his experience to contradict the axiom. Still, Leventhal liked him, or at least appeared to respect his work. If there was something good around, he might throw it his way.

Jude sat down at his desk and clicked on his computer. The screen leapt to life; he signed on, and promptly swore out loud. The message light was glowing, and he knew what that meant: questions about his piece. He was right, and as he scrolled through the story, his heart sank. He saw long dark patches of comment mode placed there by an unseen editor. He spent the next three hours piling through his notes, checking facts and calling up sources, who didn't exactly feature the idea of wasting a Saturday on the phone with him. For revenge, he took a long lunch.

When he returned, his phone rang. It was Clive, the young news clerk on the Metro desk, speaking in hushed, conspiratorial tones. Clive owed him—more than once, Jude had helped him shape a story—and as their eyes met across the newsroom, Jude picked up the signal: payback time.

"A murder, sounds good," said Clive. "Don't know much about it, but the wires are saying it's strange. Mutilation. Maybe a ritual killing, maybe a Mob hit."

"Who's the victim?"

"No ID yet."

"Where?"

"Not far. Tylerville. Near New Paltz."

Jude did a quick calculation; he could get there in an hour and a half, maybe two; have an hour to report it out and half an hour to write it. He could make the deadline. Monday's paper was a good one, read by people starting the week and looking for something to gossip about around the proverbial watercooler. He felt a familiar rush—a quickening of the pulse, not much more—and he knew that he was hooked.

He sauntered up to the Metro desk and stood next to Leventhal, who ignored him until he cleared his throat.

"Hey," said Leventhal nonchalantly.

"I finished the revision on gun control," Jude said noncommittally.

"Weren't you out on some story this morning—what was it?"

"The psychic who got rich on the stock market. It didn't pan out. She lives in a railroad tenement in Hell's Kitchen. I'd like to leave if you have nothing for me. I've got to go upstate tonight."

"Upstate—where?"

"New Paltz."

"New Paltz." Leventhal raised one eyebrow slightly. "What're you doing up there?"

"Nothing much. Dinner with friends."

Leventhal paused, as if he were deep in thought.

"Well, as long as you're in the area . . ."

He made a point of fishing through papers on his desk, even though the printed piece of wire copy was right on top. He finally seized it and handed it wordlessly to Jude, with a sideways cock of the wrist that said: this is no big deal, but it could amount to something.

On his way to his desk, Jude congratulated himself on the stratagem. He had known it would succeed because it tickled two primitive spots in the editorial cortex: fobbing off an assignment and disrupting a reporter's private life. As he grabbed his coat and a fresh notebook and hurried out the door, he looked at Clive and flashed him a V sign.

# Chapter 3

Skyler lay in bed, listening to the birds and identifying them. There was the bubbling chatter of the yellow-throated warbler, and he imagined it hopping from branch to branch. Nearby came the fluted cries of the chachalaca; he knew how it looked when it rippled its feathers to shake off the morning dew. And far in the distance, he heard the jingle of the white-eyed vireo, "the drunkard" as Kuta called him, crying out *quick with the beer check.*

The moment he had awakened, he'd thought about Patrick. He had done the same every morning for the past week, since he and Julia had discovered the body. The image of it, shrunken and gutted on the cold table, rose up unsummoned. Part of him—the part that was so assiduously listening to the birds—tried to block it out. But that was impossible.

Maybe today something would happen—something that would bring to a head the confusing and frightening chain of events. Patrick's death had rekindled all the doubts that he had tried to lay to rest over the years. There had been a service for him, of course. A simple wooden coffin had been placed under the photograph of Dr. Rincon, and Baptiste had delivered a eulogy. But Skyler had not listened. Instead, he was envisioning the wounds in the corpse, his mind reeling with questions.

Thank God for Julia. Thinking about her was a balm to his fevered imagination. He needed her more than ever, now that his world was turned upside down and people that he had once loved and trusted had become objects of suspicion and fear.

He conjured her up in his mind's eye—her flowing dark hair, her bright laugh quick as a sandpiper, the fullness of her thighs and hips that never ceased to excite him, her body that schooled him in wisdom, and her mind that seemed to range always to the next horizon and welcomed him when he arrived there.

How long had he loved her? It was impossible to say. Forever, it seemed.

He remembered her as a young girl, and almost blushed in recalling how she used to trail after him and Raisin, and how the two would run off into the woods without her. Once they'd pretended to ignore her, and lured her deep into the forest and then abandoned her. It had been a great lark. They'd laughed and returned to Campus. But as the afternoon shadows lengthened and she still had not returned, Skyler had felt dread in his stomach. He'd scanned the treeline, unable to confess his mounting alarm, until finally close to dusk, he'd spied a tiny white spot—her shirt!—and felt such a rush of joy and relief that he actually gave a little leap of happiness.

Not long after that had come a second, even more frightening scare.

He came to dinner at the Meal House one evening—this was back when boys and girls were still allowed to mix—and noticed that she was not there. The next morning, he drew aside a girl from the Age Group and asked where she was. The girl lowered her voice to a whisper.

"Didn't you hear? She went for a physical and then right into surgery. Nobody knows what it is, but it sounds serious."

For five days he didn't sleep at night, and barely ate. During Science, he thought of nothing but her. On the evening of the fifth day he could no longer stand it. During dinner, he feigned a stomach ache and was consigned to barracks. He slipped out while the others were eating, crossed the yard to the Big House and located the window to the sick bay on the first floor. He opened it and climbed inside, and there she was, sitting up in bed, throwing him a big smile. Before he knew it, he was at her side.

"I was lucky," she explained. "They found something wrong, but they operated on it and now I'm all better."

She turned over in bed and raised her pajama top to expose her back, where an eight-inch-wide bandage was wrapped around her waist.

"I'm going to have a great scar."

She sat up again, and he reached over and touched her hand. It was a shock to be holding it—already the Elders had been laying the groundwork for the precepts against contact between the sexes—and he felt a thrill when she squeezed his hand in return.

From that time on, things were different.

He did not try to put a name to his feelings for her, because that was too complicated and upsetting, but he knew that she had come to occupy a central place in his scheme of things. He laid down the law: he and Raisin would no longer exclude her; they were offically a threesome. Raisin accepted the change, but not as easily, and once in a while, talking late at night in the barracks, his friend would reminisce about the good old days.

Then the Lab itself did something to solidify the relationship among the three of them. They were chosen, along with several others, to participate in storytelling sessions. Every few days, they would be taken out of class and placed in a room in the Big House itself. They lay down on cots and a nurse gave them injections from a big needle, which hurt. But then they got to stay there and listen to stories played on a tape. They hated the injections, but it was fun to lie around while others were studying. And they felt pride in being special, in being "an experiment within an experiment," as Baptiste had put it.

In retrospect, those were the halcyon days, the carefree years when the three of them were together, before all the questions and doubts.

And then Raisin had died.

Julia had been just as profoundly affected by the death as he'd been, and so they felt a need to comfort each other. It was natural for them to seek each other out and to begin meeting secretly, going to great lengths to plan ways to be alone together even when it became clear that doing so was against the rules.

"How can this be wrong?" Julia asked one time, as they strolled through a meadow near the hidden pasture. "It doesn't feel wrong. It's the rules that have changed, not us. We're not doing anything different."

But, of course, they were. They had begun touching and holding hands. And one morning when Skyler was lying on his back, she asked him why he'd come to visit her in the sick bay that time, and as he tried to explain, searching for the words, she leaned over and kissed him on the lips. He was shocked and scared and thrilled all at once. And he wanted more.

They began meeting regularly. Her job gave her some leeway two days a week—when she delivered mail to the small airstrip on the island's eastern bulge—and Skyler met her nearby. They began touching and kissing as soon as they were in the woods. The Lab said sex was wrong, but Kuta preached a different doctrine, and what he said seemed to make sense. Skyler followed Raisin's example: he didn't take the little pill that was proffered every evening, and Julia stopped, too. Soon their bodies felt different, more sensitive, alive and subject to sudden exciting urges.

One hot, silent afternoon, they explored the southern end of the island, where they had never been. They followed the remnants of an old road scarred with ruts from wagon wheels. It skirted a line of scrub brush and loblolly pine and led them to a sand dune. They walked around it and saw an astonishing sight—a forty-foot tower rising up from a rocky peninsula. It was made of brick. Painted bands of red and white ran up the side, now faded to pastel hues, and on top was a round glass cabin encircled by a walkway and topped by a round metal roof. It was an abandoned lighthouse.

They ran to it. Skyler pushed the wooden door, which gave way with a bang, and they stepped inside. Suddenly, the air was alive with the beating of wings—scores of birds flapping and circling and rising to disappear out open windows. It was gloomy and there was an acrid smell from bird droppings that coated everything. A spiral staircase clung to the sides and mounted toward a shaft of light above. They went up it, and halfway to the top, there was a two-foot wide breach. They crossed it, clinging to iron rivets in the brick wall, Skyler first and then Julia. They continued up and finally reached a circular glass room flooded by light. In the center was a huge lantern with a four-sided lens set upon a rusted rotating track. They stepped outside onto the round balcony. A strong wind blew against their clothes. They could see for miles over the green-gold marshes and curving brown creeks and distant mudflats—all the way to the mainland.

They stepped back inside the glass room. They hugged and lay down on the warm concrete floor. As the birds resumed their roosting on the metal railing outside, they kissed. Then slowly, trembling, they removed each other's clothes and came together naked. Skyler caressed her body and she caressed his. They knew instinctively how to touch each other and where. Skyler felt Julia's breath hot in his ear, and he clenched her tightly and told her he loved her. She squeezed him back, so hard that at first he thought he was hurting her, and she told him that she loved him, too—more than anything in the world, more than life.

They made love. Afterward, they examined one another's body thoroughly, taking it all in, all the turns and curves, including the blue marks on the thighs. Then lying in each other's arms, listening to the sound of the birds outside, and in the distance the waves slapping upon the shore, they said again that they loved and would always love each other. Skyler was amazed that he felt no regret, no feeling that he had done anything wrong. On the contrary, he knew he had done something right. And he also knew deep inside that now there was no turning back.

The lighthouse became their refuge and escape. They came whenever they could get away, and after making love they would sit in the glass room at the top, holding onto each other and looking over to the mainland like two castaways in a crow's nest.

On Campus, they studiously ignored each other, which made their trysts in the lighthouse all the more passionate. To arrange them, they evolved a code using a smooth gray rock the size of a fist at the base of an old oak tree; if either of them moved it from the right side of the trunk to the left, that was a signal to meet in the lighthouse that afternoon. How Skyler's heart would soar when he saw the rock had been moved!

It was not long before the meetings turned subversive. After making love, they would talk about everything, sharing their doubts and fears. In addition to lovers, they became confederates.

Once she startled him when she looked out at the distant banks and said: "You know, I've been thinking more and more lately that we should go to the other side."

Since Patrick's death, Julia had been on a campaign to get to the truth. She had stepped up her spying in the Records Room. She had stolen a glimpse at two folders in the filing cabinet, which looked like the results of their physical examinations, she said. And by close observation, she had learned some computer commands. Twice, when left alone, she had used them and even gotten the computer to respond. But she needed to find the right passwords, she said—two of them. Without those two words, she would get nowhere.

The danger she was running made Skyler wild with fear. He tried to drive home the risks of discovery: she could be caught at the computer at any moment; for all they knew, it made a record of its use. But she would have none of it. She was so caught up in the chase that she was throwing caution overboard. She insisted he was letting his imagination get the best of him.

But as he tossed around in bed, he thought again about Patrick's body laid out in the morgue and recoiled at the image. *That* was not imaginary.

Skyler rose and pulled on his jeans as the morning light began to stream in through the windows. The other Jimminies were beginning to stir in their beds, shifting around, clearing their throats and making other waking noises. Benny, a small boy who had slept above Skyler for as long as he could remember, let one arm dangle over the side rail of the upper bunk, as he did most mornings. Skyler looked at it; the meat of flesh on his under-arm was filthy. He was often in trouble for lack of cleanliness.

From outside came the clanging of the ranch bell, the signal to get started, which roused more movement in the bunks. They had heard it so many mornings now, it was almost subliminal.

Skyler combed his hair in the mirror. He looked at his face looking back at him—his dark eyes and thick dark hair and broad forehead. He had never thought one way or the other about his looks, until Julia, but he did now. He liked it, lying in her arms when she told him how handsome he was, but he was not sure he believed her.

He glanced at the corner where Patrick's bed used to be; it was gone. The same thing had happened with Raisin years ago—as soon as he had died, the bed had been taken away, as if somehow that would help them forget the loss. He wondered who made decisions like that, how they could be so obtuse.

The young man in the next bed, Tyrone, cleared his throat, ran a hand through his flaming red hair, and rose up on one elbow.

"Up early—as usual," he said.

It was a pointless observation, meant to be social, but Skyler let it go with a nod. He didn't like Tyrone and he didn't trust him. From time to time he wondered how the Elder Physicians knew so much about what the Jimminies were up to, and whether or not there was a spy in their midst. One time, when they were watching a TV show about the Second World War, a spy entered the plot and the Orderlies turned the program off without explanation. If there was a spy, Tyrone, with his need to be loved and appreciated by the Elders, was Skyler's candidate.

But perhaps he was being unfair. Ever since he had begun his lonely quest to try to unravel the mystery of their existence on the island, he had been struck by how much he had changed—how often suspicion dominated his thinking and how apart he felt from the others in the Age Group. They were strangers to him—as he was to them.

He stepped outside onto the cinder block that was the front stoop and onto the packed brown earth. The screen door closed behind him with a loud thwack. He looked up at the morning sky—overcast, with some bite to the wind. They were at the beginning of the hurricane season. He remembered how the great storms used to excite him—how the wind would bend the branches and the moss would come alive, large hunks detaching themselves and flying through the air twisting like a nest of snakes.

But this storm would blow over quickly. He had spotted a small window of blue high in the sky over to the west.

The screen door banged, and the other Jimminies traipsed out of the barracks and joined him. They all washed their faces in the fresh, clear water in the battered white metal basin sunk in the concrete. It was so cold they gasped. From time to time, one of them would stand up to give the pump handle three or four plunges and the water would poke reluctantly out of the rusted spout and slosh into the basin. It was a routine performed without thought every morning.

But today might be different, Skyler thought—he felt it in his bones.

As they walked to the Meal House, Benny fell in beside him. "You all right?" he asked in his slow drawl.

"I've been better," replied Skyler.

Benny was the only other member of the age group whom Skyler trusted enough to share some of his secrets. He had told him about the expedition to the Records Room and how Julia and he had discovered Patrick's body. Benny's face had turned ashen; he clearly hadn't known what to make of it.

"He must have been very sick," he had said. "Otherwise, it just doesn't make sense."

By way of reply, Skyler had shrugged.

Benny said he was worried that Skyler was going to get into trouble—"big trouble, serious trouble."

"You remember how Raisin was getting—before he died. You're getting like that now, a little bit," he had said haltingly, looking at the ground.

Now he was silent as they walked past the Big House.

Skyler looked at the decaying mansion. The sight of the place filled him with dread. Cracks ran through the faded pink walls, which were darkened by stains. The four tall columns at the rear entrance were peeling, the paint hanging off in flower petal strips. The bottom of the swimming pool, which had not been filled once in their lifetimes, had buckled. It was rent by foot-high weeds sprouting out of miniature cones of dirt. The ancient marble statues around the pool were blemished and green-black with mold in the crevices of their elbows and joined thighs.

His eye was drawn to the basement door, which was closed—inscrutable.

Farther on they came to the Meal House, raised two feet off the ground on wooden stilts set in concrete. It was screened on three sides and attached to a jerry-built kitchen that contained a wood-burning stove, a refrigerator and a bookcase used as a pantry. As always, the young men fixed their own breakfast, scooping out granular cereal from wooden barrels and searching through the bins for fruit that was not bruised or overripe. The milk, straight from the cows, was warm.

They ate mostly in silence, which was unusual. Everyone's still upset because of Patrick, thought Skyler.

They barely had time to swallow their food before an Orderly banged on the door with the side of his fist—it was time for calisthenics. The sun was behind his darkened silhouette, so it was impossible at first to know which one it was, since they could best be distinguished one from the other by the location of the white streaks in their hair. It turned out to be Timothy, their least favorite.

Timothy marched them to the familiar worn ground of the Parade Field, and they fell into formation. He unfolded a wooden chair, sat upon it and barked out the commands. Their grunts filled the morning air. Skyler held back, performing the exercises at half strength and going full out only when the Orderly was looking. But he rapidly worked up a sweat in the humidity.

At last came the moment Skyler was waiting for.

"Push-ups!" yelled the Orderly. The group swiveled to the left and fell to the ground, a position that allowed Skyler to keep one eye on the women's barracks. He watched and waited, and eventually they came out, all in a group, walking toward the Meal House. They were chatting, moving in and out of his view as they passed behind trees and bushes.

He felt panic rising in the back of this throat, but then at last he spotted Julia. A wave of relief swept through him at the sight of her familiar figure, the long dark hair trailing down her back as she moved gracefully along the path.

In an instant Timothy stood up, clapped his hands, and calisthenics was over. Skyler and the others walked across the Campus, and by a miracle of timing, they arrived at an intersection of paths just as the women did. For several seconds the two groups mingled. Skyler walked behind Julia, so close that he could have leaned over and kissed her. Then, as he was about to step away, she turned around, leaned toward him and whispered. "I think I know it. I think I know the password."

He was so surprised, he was speechless. He watched the women walk off down the path. Then he looked out over the marshes, now touched by sun, and watched the last of the morning mist rising. The wind was picking up and the leaves were showing their pale green undersides. It looked like a storm was brewing after all.

# Chapter 4

Cruising down Main Street, Jude had no trouble finding the Tylerville police station, a squat red-brick building at the center of town, like dozens of others he had seen in decaying towns around New York. He parked in the grease-stained vanilla-colored macadam lot in the rear, under a narrow window that he took to belong to a jail cell, and walked around the building to enter by the front door. Cops got funny if they saw you taking shortcuts on their turf.

The desk officer showed him typical respect, as he read a *People* magazine without lifting his eyes from the page. Jude knew the article, and the author of the article, and he toyed briefly with the idea of informing the officer that about forty percent of it was true. Instead he placed one hand on the desk, within the range of the man's peripheral vision. The cop acknowledged his presence with a grunt and finally looked up. Jude pulled out his wallet to identify himself, flashed the laminated bright pink New York City press card with a practiced flip of the wrist, and stated his business.

"You'll have to talk to Sergeant Kiley."

Not a good sign. Public relations officers were usually sergeants.

"Who?"

"Kiley. He's in charge of public relations."

The deskman resumed his reading.

"Who's heading the investigation?"

"You'll have to talk to Sergeant Kiley."

Jude was about to enter a grim-looking waiting room, when he saw a reporter he knew from the *Daily News* seated with his back to him. He ducked outside and walked to the corner. He fished in his pocket for a quarter, dialed the local paper and asked for the night editor. This was a calculated gamble: some local papers liked having a big city reporter in town and felt flattered by the sudden collegiality; others viewed him as competition and froze him out. Jude struck it lucky. He dropped a name or two and was connected to the reporter working the story, a woman called Gloria, who told him she was about to visit the medical examiner, and invited him along.

Ten minutes later, he was standing next to Gloria, a young woman about his age with a pleasing, open face, on a porch outside the office of Norman McNichol, M.D., medical examiner for Ulster Country. The office was in a white clapboard house on Broad Street, an elm-lined avenue where the overgrown lawns sloped down to a sidewalk whose slabs tilted wildly because of the irrepressible roots underground.

Idyllic small-town America, thought Jude, looking up and down the street. Gloria raised a finger with pale green nail polish and pressed a round white pearl button. They heard the muffled singsong of a bell within. Below the button was a discreet brass sign: MCNICHOL FUNERAL PARLOR.

"So the M.E. moonlights as a funeral director," said Jude. "He can funnel business to himself—there's more than a whiff of conflict of interest in that."

"Oh, he's okay. He's a character. Buried everyone around here. Parents, children—you name it. He just keeps going on."

McNichol, a tall, slender man of indeterminate age, with a trimmed gray beard, opened the door and gave Gloria a peck on both cheeks, European-style. He pumped Jude's hand vigorously. Jude felt she was right: he was okay.

"We've got to go to Poughkeepsie," he said. "That's where our boy is waiting for us."

He disappeared inside and reemerged, carrying an old-fashioned black leather doctor's satchel.

"Hop in your car," he said, bounding down the steps. "You can follow me."

McNichol drove like a maniac—typical, thought Jude, of someone who treats death like a work buddy. In no time they pulled up to an imposing brick building with a circular drive, in the center of which stood a thick metal sign with embossed letters: POUGHKEEPSIE PRESBYTERIAN HOSPITAL.

They followed in McNichol's wake, past the reception desk, where he breezed by and sent papers fluttering, to a staircase at the rear. It led to the autopsy suite in the basement of the maternity wing. A large red sign in block letters—RESTRICTED—was plastered on the main door. They entered through a side office, walked past a rabbit warren of cubicles with gray metal desks for the residents, and entered the scrub room. The walls were lined with lockers, hampers and two deep sinks. In a cupboard were stacks of faded green gowns, thick white aprons, masks and white slip-over shoe covers. On a table were two dispensers of cream-colored latex gloves.

"Suit up," ordered McNichol.

Jude hung up his jacket, switched his wallet to his back pants pocket and put his arms through the sleeves of a backward-facing gown, trying to suppress a look of amazement. He had never attended an autopsy before. He approached the sink basin and looked up questioningly.

"Go ahead." McNichol was chuckling. "This scrubbing's for *him*. To protect him from you and all the little microscopic critters you're carrying. You'll want to scrub thoroughly on your way out—that one's for *you*. To protect you from him. I'd say it's more important."

He disappeared through swinging double doors.

Jude turned to Gloria, who had tied her smock tightly around her waist with a neat bow.

"I don't get it," he said. "He's going to allow us in?"

"Oh, he does it all the time. Like I said, he's a character. And we don't get that many homicides, so he likes to show off."

They pushed through the swinging doors and found themselves in an anteroom. McNichol was waiting for them. It was cool and damp, like a walk-in meat locker. There were two doors ahead. On one was a printed sign that read: *Please indicate* No Head *if the brain is restricted. Thank you.*

"That's the isolation room," said McNichol. "Quarantine. It's for bodies with communicable conditions. By that I mean *seriously* communicable. Self-evidently, virtually any disease can be passed from one individual to another. In there we put tuberculosis, certain fevers, Creutzfeldt-Jakob . . . that's mad cow disease. We've never had one of those, knock wood"—he reached over to knuckle-rap the arm of a chair.

He saw Jude look at the *No Head* sign. "That's to prevent disposal—in these kinds of cases—without safeguards."

They took the other door, which led to the autopsy room.

The first thing that hit Jude was the smell, a combination of antiseptic and something else that gripped his stomach and made him want to retch. That would be formalin, a fixative, explained McNichol. They were in a room with chipped yellow paint, green tiles that rose three-quarters of the way up the walls, and large fluorescent ceiling lights. Glass cases lined two walls, filled with bottles and sterilized implements and various floating objects that Jude did not care to inspect too closely. Along a third wall were large sinks giving way to stainless steel counters, upon which stood five huge plastic containers of chemicals.

McNichol handed Jude a blue jar of Vaseline and told him to dab some in his nose. "Trick of the trade," he explained. "Overwhelms the olfactory sense. I don't require it. I lost my smell of death many years ago." He somehow made it sound like a deprivation.

Gloria passed up the blue jar. Jude was impressed; how many dead bodies had she seen?

In the center of the room were two L-shaped stainless steel tables, their long sides running parallel to one another. The long portions of the tables had a perforated surface, which, Jude theorized, would allow liquids to flow to tiny sinks at the angles of the L. The short sides were lined with various tools, small Tupperware containers that McNichol said were to hold tissue samples. Nearby were metal boxes, called "coffins," for eviscerated organs. Both were filled with formalin.

McNichol moved to the rear of the room, where large white drawers were set in the wall. He pushed a metal gurney alongside one, opened it full length, dropped a railing and moved to the other side so that he could hold the gurney in place with his hip.

"We don't have a single diener on duty today," he said. "They're the ones who are supposed to transport the body to and from the morgue. Technically, I shouldn't be doing this."

He leaned across and reached for a black body bag.

"The dieners are charged with 'running the gut.' It's a particularly heinous piece of work—you slit the gastrointestinal tract along its length and check the walls of the gut, as well as its contents. But the dieners like to do it—would you believe they actually choose for the honor?"

He grunted, and with a single smooth motion, pulled the top of the bundle onto the gurney. Then two more movements—one to hoist the hips, the other to center the feet—and the body was centered on board. It was all done quickly, as if he had done it hundreds of time, which Jude figured he probably had.

"Now, if you wouldn't mind lending a hand—"

McNichol gestured with his head toward the glove dispenser. Jude was surprised—surely asking a bystander to assist in an autopsy was a breach of medical protocol. But Gloria was already at the counter, dusting her hands with talcum powder and rolling the thin gloves up the fingers like an expert, and so Jude joined her, trying to act casual.

They helped McNichol place the bag upon the L-shaped table. He unzipped it and removed white sheets that were inside. Then they helped to shed the corpse of its plastic cocoon and laid it gently to rest upon the cold metal surface. Jude was horrified and thought he might be sick. The body was white-bluish in color. The man's face had been shredded, so that it was a mass of caked blood and bone and reddish muscle. The eyes were missing, as if they had been stabbed or poked out; even the ears were ripped off. Only the dark cavity of the mouth was recognizable. Inside it, the tongue was swollen and seemed to be floating on a sea of reddish fluid.

"My God!" exclaimed Gloria.

McNichol was silent, busying himself with the micro-details of the routine of the external examination. He made frequent notes with a ballpoint pen on the autopsy sheet and kept a running commentary: "Caucasian male, approx. twenty-two to twenty-six years. Weight one hundred seventy-five pounds. Height five-ten." He inspected every inch of the body, turning it this way and that, looking for marks, scars and wounds. Then he measured the circumference of the head and chest, and the length and circumference of the arm and leg.

He took skin samples. He scraped under the fingernails, swabbed the wounds, weighed specimens and put them into tiny bottles. Finally, he stepped back and took a broader view.

"Well," he said contemplatively, "I certainly can't inspect the eyeballs."

For the first time, he seemed to take in the entire corpse, and the grotesque nature of its wounds.

"I've seen this kind of thing once or twice before," he said in a portentous tone. "But this one's a bit different."

"How do you mean?" asked Jude, thankful that his voice sounded normal.

"Well, customarily disfigurement is a sign of rage. The victim is hated by the murderer—passionately hated. So much so that the murderer attacks him and mutilates him and sometimes carries on mutilating him even after he's dead. It's almost as if he's trying to eradicate him, to wipe him off the face of the earth. Then there's another scenario, closely linked to that. In this case, the murderer is suddenly struck by remorse and attacks the dead body—almost as if he is trying to erase his crime, as it were—to blot out all traces of what he has done. Either way, there's passion involved, a lot of emotion. Which usually points to an intimate relationship between victim and perpetrator. And that makes the police's job a lot easier. A husband, a lover, a stalker. The odds are overwhelming that it'll be solved within forty-eight hours, and the perpetrator will be led into the station house in handcuffs, break down and confess to the horrible deed in tears."

He fell quiet.

"And this one?" prompted Jude.

"This was clearly done to thwart identification."

"How do you know?"

"For one thing, it was done methodically."

McNichol touched the skull at the dome of the forehead, where there was only bone. "Incisions were made here and the skin was pulled away like bacon strips. Look how neatly it was done. Painstakingly, patiently. The killer—assuming for the moment that it was the killer who also did this—took his sweet time. And then there are the hands."

McNichol raised the dead man's arms and twisted them roughly so that they fell back palms up. Jude leaned over, losing his squeamishness now that he was engrossed. The tips of the fingers and thumbs were blistery and black.

"Burned off," McNichol continued. "No chance of any prints here, except maybe a partial print of this one." He grasped the ring finger of the left hand and held it up. "Looks like our fellow had a whole bag of tricks. Not to mention the strangest of all."

McNichol waited. He wanted to be asked, and Jude accommodated him.

"And what's that?"

"Take a look at this." McNichol moved to the bottom of the gurney, lifted the corpse's right foot and twisted it slightly, so that the cadaver's swollen genitals were thrust up and the pink inside of his right thigh was clearly visible. In the center was a deep cut, almost perfectly circular, the size of a silver dollar.

"God knows what that's all about. But again, it was done methodically and precisely." The examiner replaced the foot, moved to the thigh and traced the rim of the wound with his forefinger. "He stuck a knife in at an angle and spun it in a circle, like extracting an oyster."

Jude wished he would dispense with the culinary metaphors.

"Maybe there was a birthmark there, or a scar, or some identifying feature," Gloria ventured.

"Maybe. But it's not a visible place. And it's hard to imagine anyone keeping a record of it. So why go to all the trouble of removing it?"

Jude felt the deadline nipping at his heels.

"What's the cause of death?" he asked.

"Ah," said McNichol, as if the bright kid in the class had finally asked the pertinent question. "Shot to the back of the skull. Professionally done. Probably a .32-caliber, but we don't know that yet for sure. His wrists have bruises, I'd say he was tied up and on his knees when the bullet was fired from above. He was killed first and disfigured afterward."

Maybe it was a Mafia killing after all, thought Jude. But then he recalled from the wire copy that the body had been found in the woods, dumped in a thicket. When the Mob wanted to keep a killing secret, the body didn't end up where it could be found, and certainly not on an M.E.'s examining table.

Over in the corner was a clear plastic bag with what looked to be clothes inside. Jude thought he saw a red shirt, all bundled up. McNichol followed his glance.

"His clothes," he explained. "We'll examine them in detail later."

Jude looked at his watch. "Anything else worth seeing?"

"One other thing, but you'll have to wait."

For a half hour McNichol worked on the body with a long-handled scalpel and a #22 Becton Dickerson blade, keeping up a running commentary as if he were describing a motoring vacation through an exotic piece of countryside.

"The primary incision goes from the front of the armpit along the anterior axillary line just under the nipples, to the sternum. That is the xiphoid process. Then we move south with a slight detour around the umbilicus to the top of the pubic symphysis, which is right here."

The M.E. glanced up at Gloria.

"Incidentally, I should add that this procedure is not recommended for an open casket."

He went back to work.

"Now, as you see, we have allowed exposure to both the thoracic and abdominal cavities."

Jude held his breath and looked. It was not so bad. McNichol cut back the skin flaps and abdominal musculature. Then he picked up an oscillating saw and cut the clavicles and ribs along an angle, creating a wedge-shaped piece. He lifted the chest plate off intact, like a headwaiter raising the domed cover of a main course.

Jude looked again. This time the sight was revolting. The heart, which looked like a strapped-down slab of red meat, the pathetically deflated lungs, the thymus gland—all so compact and neatly packaged, swimming in a bouillabaisse of mucus and fluid. He inconspicuously rested one hand on the side of the table to steady himself.

McNichol, meanwhile, was working quickly. He used a syringe to suck up the serous fluid between the thoracic organs and the chest wall and squirted it into a plastic container to save it. He took photographs of the heart and lungs and measured and recorded the ratio of the width of the heart compared to the width of the chest. Then he tied off the carotid arteries, clamped the trachea and esophagus, cut through the diaphragm and the pleural sac, and removed the heart and the lungs together.

He peered deep into the abdomen and took more pictures. He took out the intestines, clamping the gut and cutting proximally between the first and second segments of the small intestine and distally just before the rectum, and put it aside for later analysis. He reached in with a wide embrace and lifted out a cornucopia of digestive organs—the liver, gall bladder, pancreas, esophagus, stomach and duodenum.

Jude could see all the way to the back of the abdominal wall. He was able to identify the urinary system—the kidneys, ureters and bladder—but barely; just at that moment they were lifted out in a single block.

"Check the sheet," McNichol told Jude. "How old did I say this guy was?"

"Twenty-two to twenty-six years."

The examiner looked momentarily confused—the first time his self-assurance had slipped a notch.

"Too young. I can tell by looking at these organs—that's way too young. How could I have been so wrong?"

Laboriously, McNichol examined each organ closely, like a jeweler holding a gem up to the light. Each was cleaned of blood and fat, weighed, photographed, and cut into sections, or "breadloafed," as he called it. Each was probed and secreted fluid that was sucked up by the ever present syringe and yielded silver-dollar–sized sections that were placed in the plastic bucket, or "the coffin." From here, McNichol said, they would be sliced thin as a hair, mounted on slides, and put under the microscope for histological examination.

Finally came the pièce de résistance—the brain. McNichol cut a perfect line across the top of the scalp from ear to ear, and retracted the skin flap. He used the vibrating saw to cut through the bone, creating both a shrill sound and an acrid smell, then removed the skull cap and placed it to one side with a preoccupied gesture, like a chess player discarding a captured pawn. He was looking, Jude surmised, at the fatal wound.

McNichol picked up a serrated knife and cut through the dura, the tough outer covering of the brain, then reached down hard and sliced the blood vessels at the base. He lifted the brain out, held it high in one hand and said, "Here we are." With a gloved finger, he reached into a hole and flicked out a snub-nosed bullet, which he placed in a small bottle. He put the brain in a large jar of formalin.

More than ever Jude felt the deadline rushing at him, and again he looked at his watch. McNichol seemed to be cleaning up, replacing the skull cap and chest plate, and wiping the body with blue cloth.

"I don't mean to rush you," said Jude. "But what was that thing you said would be worth waiting for?"

"I haven't forgotten," replied McNichol.

He stood at the top of the gurney, behind the head of the body that was now cut and lined and red with blood. He leaned over and pried open the mouth, which was now drained, and directed Gloria and Jude to look inside. They did and were flummoxed.

"I don't get it," she said. "I don't see anything."

"Precisely," retorted McNichol, puffing up with pride. "You don't see anything. Not a single cavity. Every tooth strong and perfect. On a grown man. When was the last time you saw a mouth like that?"

Jude and Gloria looked at each other.

"Of course," continued the M.E., "it just compounds the problem."

"The problem?"

"Of identification. It looks like he's never been to a dentist. No prints and now no dental records. That makes him practically untraceable."

Jude asked for an office with a telephone line and found one on the second floor with a desk looking out onto the back parking lot. A secretary brought him a cup of coffee, which he drank heartily.

He plugged in the computer and typed in the slug for his story—*slay*—the time-honored slug for the day's most sensational killing. In a half hour he was done. He wrote seven hundred words, going heavy on the forensic material—the burned fingertips, the perfect teeth—details that made it clear he had personally witnessed the autopsy. He also took care to portray McNichol as something of a hero, recalling as he did so the advice of a long-departed editor who used to tell him: "It pays to be generous to people who can return the favor." He attached his modem to the phone line, dialed up the special number, heard the whining hiccup of a connection, and sent the story to 666 Fifth Avenue.

* * *

On the drive back to the city in the evening, Jude thought about Gloria. After he had filed, he had driven her back to her paper.

"You want to go out later, when I'm through?" she'd asked, a touch less than matter-of-factly. "I know a good health food restaurant, if you're up for that kind of thing."

He wasn't. He suspected the offer entailed more than dinner, and somehow when he thought of the long drive back and the gory scene in the autopsy room and even, for some reason, Betsy and the hurtful names she had hurled at him months ago—mixing it all up into one complicated, exhausting package—he felt drained of desire.

He'd held out his hand to shake good-bye.

She'd held hers out and smirked.

"In a hurry, huh? Big-time reporters like you come up here for one day. Then we help you, and the amazing thing is, you still manage to get something wrong."

That had hurt.

Still, he thought, the story he'd filed was not a bad one. And he hadn't gotten anything wrong, he was sure of that.

He flipped on the radio, caught the headlines on 1010, and was pleased to note that there was not much competing news. He began conjuring up front-page headlines for his story, a favorite pastime: "Mutilating Mangler on the Loose" or "Body Tells No Tales" or "Faceless Horror Upstate." He lowered both windows to let the wind whip through the car, found a rock station and turned the volume up.

That didn't feel bad. Not bad at all.

The next morning, however, when Jude went out in his shorts and T-shirt to fetch the paper from a newsstand, he had a shock. Not only was the story not on page one, he couldn't even find the damned thing! He rested the paper on a mailbox, started on page two and began flipping the pages—his anger growing with each flip. Finally, he spotted it—way back on page 42, crammed in with the bra ads. And it had been reduced to four paragraphs. Barely enough for a byline.

*Jesus Christ!*

All that work. Driving all the way up there, talking his way into the autopsy, beating out the *Daily News.*

*All that—and they cut it to shreds and bury it.*

He raced back upstairs, changed and went to the office. Spotting Leventhal across the newsroom, he bellowed out his name.

Leventhal motioned him into his fishbowl of an office, equipped with a full-size picture window so that he could see out into the newsroom. The trouble was, the newsroom could see in. Jude didn't care. He had righteousness on his side.

"I don't get it," he yelled. "That was a great story. Why the hell did you short it?"

Leventhal looked at him blankly, pretending confusion. Finally, comprehension dawned.

"Oh. You mean the New Paltz thing. That's what's got you raving like a maniac?"

"Damn right. That should have been front page."

"Front page!"

Leventhal searched around for a prop, and found it: today's paper, which he threw dramatically down on his desk.

"Now, that's front page."

Jude read the headline: DOUBLE TROUBLE. A subhead explained: *Identical Twins Held in Murder Rap. Which One Did It?*

He read the first paragraph. The story was about twin lawyers, one of whom was suspected of strangling a blonde woman on the Upper East Side. The other one was going to represent him as soon as their identities were untangled.

Jude hated to admit it, but Leventhal had a point.

"Still, you didn't have to bury my story like that."

"Bury it? It got all the space it deserved, Harley. Yeah, it's got some gory details, but right now it's just an anonymous body. You get me a name to go with the corpse, then we'll see if it goes anywhere. OK?"

Jude tried to revive his anger, but it had been defused by Leventhal's one-two punch. He looked up and tried to count the colleagues staring in at his discomfiture. Half a dozen, at least. Leventhal noticed them, too, and his face turned red.

"Goddamn it," he said. "I'm the weekend editor, and I decide what goes in the Monday paper. I'm sick and tired of people second-guessing me. Now, get out of here!"

Jude left. But when he thought about it later, it seemed odd. Leventhal usually didn't yell like that. It seemed like he had gotten *too* upset. Jude mentioned this to Clive to see what he thought, but the news clerk simply shrugged.

# Chapter 5

Skyler knocked on Kuta's door. He knew the old man was in because he had seen his weather-beaten boat tied to the dock, its grimy engine mounted on a stump nearby, undergoing the perpetual repairs. The waves on the small bay were turning rough in the wind.

He was feeling scared. He had been feeling that way all morning and then all afternoon, taking the goats to pasture, ever since he had encountered Julia and she had whispered her message about the password. He had waited for her near the air strip as long as he could. When she hadn't appeared, he'd left a message for her in the mailbox, telling her to meet him at Kuta's this afternoon—the first time he had dared do such a thing and a mark of how desperate he was. Now he was going to wait for her and see with his own eyes that she was safe. But he had a bad feeling about the whole thing.

The door opened, and Kuta fixed a bloodshot eye on him.

"Child, you look a mess. What you been up to?"

Without waiting for a reply, he turned and led the way. It felt cool inside.

"Take a seat," he said, motioning toward the easy chair. He put on a pot of water for tea.

Skyler sat quietly for a while and then slowly unburdened himself. He told about Patrick's death and how he and Julia had discovered the body in the basement morgue; he talked about the funeral service and Julia's detective work. He spoke in a general way about his fears for her, but this was hard to do—the words seemed to get tangled in his throat. Finally, he dropped off into silence.

Kuta shook his head slowly from side to side.

"A lotta strange goings-on," he said finally. "I've been saying that for years. A lotta strange goings-on. And don't this beat all. It ain't natural for a boy that young to die. I believe those people in that Lab are some kind of Satan worshippers. Some kind of anti-Christ."

In recent years, Kuta had been turning religious, and he'd even tried teaching Skyler the Scriptures, to counter what he called "all that false instruction."

He rose, took two battered mugs out of a cupboard, put a tea bag in one, and poured hot water into them. After a minute, he switched the tea bag.

"That explains the airplane," he continued. "Seems like every time there's one of them deaths, that little airplane goes off. I heard it come back no more than two hours ago." He was referring to a small propeller plane that was stored in a tin hangar next to the strip runway. Skyler had heard it at various times, but never paid it much attention.

"What do you mean, *explains* it? What do you think the plane's doing—aside from carrying mail?"

"That I can't say. What I can say is I notice it flying off whenever there's some kind of trouble—you know, a medical emergency."

"What do you mean? What are you saying?"

Skyler was getting upset. He was sorry he had come.

"I'm not saying anything. I'm not meaning anything. Hush up and have your tea."

A minute later, Kuta asked a question.

"You think they was operating on him?"

"On Patrick?"

"Yes."

Skyler nodded. He didn't want to speculate with Kuta. He felt close to him, closer than to anyone else except Julia. But he didn't feel like trying to put words to the suspicions and fears that so preoccupied him—all that belonged to a different part of his life, which he wanted to share only with her. And he especially didn't feel like talking about it now, with her maybe missing out there somewhere.

He got up and turned on the radio that was set on the old refrigerator. Out came the strains of a fiddle and guitar and the slides of an accordion—Zydeco, Kuta called it. Skyler sat back down in the easy chair and waited for Julia.

By the end of the third song, he became convinced that something had gone wrong. He glanced over, for the hundredth time, at the old kitchen clock mounted on the wooden wall with its slow-moving, thick black hands. Her chores in the Records Room should have ended more than an hour ago.

He stood up abruptly and turned off the radio. At least he could go and look for her. As he brushed by Kuta, he detected a look of worry in the old man's face and his wrinkled brow, but again he did not feel like explaining—this time because he didn't want to linger another moment. For, suddenly, his anxiety had burgeoned into a gnawing, uncontrollable fear. He imagined he heard a small voice inside his head—*her voice*—calling to him for help.

He bolted through the door, and by the time his foot hit the ground, he was running. And now the voice inside him was screaming.

Halfway up the path, he thought he saw someone in the bushes, a startled face watching him—it was Tyrone. Maybe he had followed him, was spying upon him. He didn't care. It barely registered. As long as the face was not Julia's, he would not stop. He dashed through the woods, dodging trees and leaping over fallen branches. The storm was gathering force. The wind was picking up and the Spanish moss was waving in the air above, and as he heard his footsteps strike the earth, he felt his heart pounding in his rib cage. *Something has gone terribly wrong.* The fear was growing into a certainty and it propelled him along the path, running with all his might.

By the time he reached the main grounds of the Campus, large raindrops were mixing with the wind. As he ran, his lungs burning now, he could feel them slap his face and arms. He looked around quickly as he raced on, crossing a small brook and the Parade Field. No one was around. Just as well—surely, they would have seen his desperation and called out the Orderlies. He leapt over a bench, ran to the men's barracks, yanked open the screen door and tumbled inside. He came to a halt, sweating and shivering, in the middle of the semi-darkened room. A dozen faces looked up in astonishment. The Jimminies were scattered about, most lying on their bunks, except for a cluster in a corner listening to music. They stared at Skyler, slack-jawed, as he gulped for breath.

"Julia," he blurted. "Where is she? Have you seen her?"

He read the answer in the dumbfounded looks and didn't wait for anyone to speak, but instead turned and bolted out the door. He crossed the Parade Field again, with the rain coming down harder. Now he had to break into a fast walk, holding a stitch in his left side. Already, puddles were accumulating in the hollows and potholes of the barren ground. Behind him, staring out through the screen door of the men's barracks, he could almost feel the eyes of the others upon his back.

What he was doing—heading toward the identical wooden structure across the field—was unheard of. No man in the Age Group had ever entered the women's barracks.

He heard the voice inside himself again. *Help! Help me!*

When he burst in upon the women, they leapt back in fright, and a group huddled against a wall with more than a touch of melodrama. But he knew, he could tell right away, that they had surmised why he had come, and something about their reaction and the looks on their faces told him that his fears were well founded. Something *was* wrong. And one quick glance told him that Julia was not among them.

"Where is she?" he demanded.

The reaction was instantaneous. Some looked down at the floor uncertainly, others turned away. But one woman, Sarah, a friend of Julia's, found her voice and approached him sympathetically as she spoke.

"She is not here," she said softly. "They came for her about noon. They said they had found something wrong in her tests."

The words cut into Skyler. It was what he had feared all along on some level that he'd never articulated. *"Something wrong"!* That's what they always said. He felt his heart skip a beat and freeze up. The image of Patrick upon the slab rose before his eyes. Why did he let her do it? Why, why, why?

He turned and ran out the door into the storm. He no longer felt the rain or the ache in his side. He was surrounded by a numbness that seemed to extend into the air around him. He thought of only one thing: Julia. He had to find her. He had to see her. He had to save her.

Skyler entered the basement of the Big House through the same door that he and Julia had used only days before. This time he didn't worry about being seen or leaving signs of forced entry. He turned the knob and knocked the door open with his shoulder.

It was dark inside and he flicked on a light switch. The Records Room looked just as it had before. There was a pile of papers on top of one of the desks, held in place by a rock. He moved slowly now—not out of fear but out of dread. He walked across the room, tracing the same path he'd taken before when Julia had been seated at the computer. The vision of her sitting there came to him in a flash—her long dark hair, her bare shoulder when she'd taken off her shirt.

He came to the door of the operating room, felt the clammy, cold weight of the brass doorknob in his hand, steeled himself, and gave the door a shove.

Instantly, he saw the body.

A pale cone of light shone down from above, bathing it in a yellowish hue. She was naked, lying on her back, her hands at her sides. Her perfectly rounded neck was turned slightly. Her hair rippled out around her head, cascading onto the white metal table as if she were floating on a lake. Her features were serene and cold like porcelain: her brow unfurrowed, her eyes closed, her perfect nose tilting up slightly. She looked as if she were about to speak.

Skyler couldn't think, couldn't feel. He was past thinking and feeling. He walked in a daze slowly around the table and the cone of light that shone upon it, looking at the body, the one person he had loved with his life. And now he seemed strangely detached, unfeeling—as if it were too much, as if his mind refused to take in the information offered by his eyes. He reached out and touched her on the shoulder. The body was not cold.

It was then that he saw the incision, a dark red, angry cut beginning low down on one side. It curved around the belly, and he suddenly realized that part of her viscera was missing. That was why, come to think of it, the body seemed so small and shrunken. And now that his brain was functioning again on some primary level, his eyes began to function, too. They began to take in things, like the small pool of blood that had coagulated under the curve of her spine. And to see where it had dripped down onto the concrete floor, a little rivulet of red leading to the drain to one side of the table.

Skyler couldn't hear. He couldn't breathe. The shell of numbness was too thick—but it was about to break. He felt a spasm overtake him. It started at the base of his back and fishtailed upward through his spine, like a corkscrew drilling upward, exploding in a whiteness in his brain. *Help!* He heard the little voice again. *Help, help!* But it was no longer calling for her. Now it was calling for him.

He tried to think, to calm down. She had been operated upon—that much he could discern. Suddenly, the wave of incomprehension struck him again: the person that he loved, that precious body—cut into, hands moving inside of her, organs fondled and removed. *The barbarians.*

*Gone. She's gone.*

And as he thought it, he was conscious that it was the first thought he'd been able to have. He felt he was rushing to the surface from some numbing depths underwater. He had other thoughts. He knew that they would come to kill him next. But strangely, he did not feel afraid, because he was too much in shock and horror for that. The shell of numbness around him was still there—it was his friend.

Skyler steadied himself by leaning against a counter behind him. His eyes swiveled and held, now taking in everything. The counter was cluttered with medical implements, jars of liquids, cotton balls, syringes, a small saw whose teeth were covered in blood. He picked up a knife and held it, the blade, too, covered in blood. He began to breathe deeply again, taking in oxygen in gulps, like a runner after a race, and looked around again. In a corner was a metal pole on wheels, and hanging down from it, a bag and a tube. Nearby was another counter, and above it, rectangular basement windows hinged at the top, leading to the outside.

He saw the body again, and her death, the reality of her non-being, dealt him another body blow. It kept coming and coming, like being struck by the blades of a windmill. He grasped the counter and held on. He had an impulse. Should he pick her up? Should he wrap her up in something and carry her away? But to where?

Suddenly, he heard a sound, footsteps on stairs. He raced across the room to the door and turned a key and heard the lock click. He heard the footsteps approach the door on the other side. The doorknob turned, once at first, then twice in surprise, then insistently it began to rattle. Skyler bounded across the room, leapt onto the counter and pushed the bottom of the window. It opened out and he heard the raindrops smacking against the glass. He threw the knife outside, jumped headfirst into the window, held himself in place by his elbows, and wriggled upward. His feet swung wildly and struck the IV stanchion and sent it smashing to the floor. He squeezed harder, and suddenly he was outside in the pouring rain. On his knees, he looked back through the open window and saw the body lying in the cone of light. He pulled away just as the door cracked open with a tearing sound, an instant too soon to see who was there. He picked up the knife and ran, holding it upright, through the rain.

He decided to head north toward the forest, but he had to make one stop first. He burst into the lecture hall, empty and darkened in shadows, and ran up the central aisle to the podium. He stood before the portrait of Dr. Rincon, staring for a moment at the distant, familiar, unknowable face. Then he raised the knife and plunged it through the glass, smashing it and sending shards raining upon the floor. The blade went in deep, up to the hilt, and he pulled it out. Before he turned to run back outside, he noticed that a trickle of red blood—*her blood*—had spread on the black and white photograph. It looked as if the good doctor had taken a fatal blow right in the center of his chest.

If only it were true!

# Chapter 6

*Jesus Christ!* Jude muttered to himself as he walked down York Avenue on his way to the interview.

An hour earlier, the city editor himself, no less, had used the loudspeaker to summon him to the city desk. This was a particularly denigrating way of handing out an assignment, perfected by the *Mirror* over generations of abusing employees. It compelled the reporter to walk past rows of competitors who wished him failure or ridicule—or, in many cases, both.

"Dead man walking," muttered a forty-year-old rewrite man out of the side of his mouth as Jude passed.

The spleen behind the remark held out a slender reed of hope—maybe the rewrite man knew the assignment and was simply envious—but it was dashed by one look at the city editor, Ted Bolevil. His brow was creased, a sign that he had succumbed to shallow guilt. Bolevil was a short, ruddy-faced Australian who was regarded as little more than an errand boy for Tibbett and was consequently detested throughout the news room. His nickname—not always out of earshot—was, naturally, "boll weevil." In preferred short form, it was "the weevil"—preferred because it was close to weasel.

"Harley. I want you to do a sidebar. Identical twins. What makes them and why."

*"What?"* Jude knew it was a hack assignment. The paper was trying to string out the story of the mix-up of the homicidal twin and his upstanding brother; today's headline, over the revelation that one of them raised race-horses on the side, was: WHICH TWIN HAS THE PONY? The story was running out of gas, and they wanted to pump it up with a bunch of sidebars. Jude

didn't care to waste time on a sidebar. He wanted to follow the New Paltz murder.

"You heard me. People want to know. Identical twins. Maybe *separated at birth*. You ever see that feature? Two photos of people who look alike. You know—like Tony Blair and the mule boy from *Pinocchio*."

Jude just looked at the man. Bolevil got flustered.

"But this should be serious. Scientific. What happens to them? Why do they both end up doing the same dead-end job? Or marrying blondes—that kind of thing. You know—get the point?"

Jude was afraid he did.

"Throw in new research," Bolevil added. "Scientific types up in arms. New breakthroughs. Why is one good and one evil? How to tell which one's the bad seed? You know, that kind of thing."

His tendency to speak in sentence fragments was only one of his annoying habits, and by no means the most.

"Make for good pictures," he said. "We get only one twin, we can shoot him twice—ha ha."

Bolevil turned his back to Jude and dug into his in-basket, with a small sigh intended to suggest the burdens of newspaper leadership. End of discussion.

*Mule boy in Pinocchio!*

Jude found the address he was looking for, 1230 York, the gated entrance to Rockefeller University. He walked up a hill, past men mowing a patch of lawn on tractors, and entered ivy-covered Founders Hall. A bust of John D. greeted him. He leaned upon the reception desk, fished out a piece of paper and read the name he had found in the *Mirror*'s electronic morgue.

"Dr. Tierney, Research," he told a uniformed guard. He anticipated his question and cut him off open-mouthed: "She's expecting me."

He was told to take a seat. After the appropriate New York waiting time of ten minutes—not enough to be impolite but sufficient to establish that the visit was an intrusion—he was escorted to the fourth floor. He sat in another chair, across from a secretary who was pecking at a keyboard. She eyed him up and down and lifted a phone receiver languidly.

"The gentleman from the *Mirror*," she said, lacing ironic spaces between the words.

The door opened, and through it walked a young woman in a blue skirt with a white lab coat, a pair of glasses tucked into the vest pocket. She had long dark hair that fell upon her shoulders and interesting-looking hollows under her eyes.

"I'm Dr. Tierney," she said, looking at him closely as she extended her hand, which felt strong and warm. "Elizabeth Tierney," she amended.

"Jude Harley."

"I'm sorry to have kept you waiting. I wasn't told you were here."

The secretary lifted one eyebrow.

Jude liked the apology—she was clearly from out of town, and in fact her speech hinted at the broad vowels of the Midwest. She was about thirty, he thought, his age.

They stood in silence for a moment, until she turned slightly and said: "Won't you come in?"

Her office was a mix of the official and the friendly, bound medical volumes next to books of poetry. Jude spotted Yeats, Blake and Baudelaire, for openers. There were stacks of computer printouts and personal clutter—mail, a model sports car made from wire hangers, a bulging Filofax and photographs on a windowsill. On the wall were a dartboard with Freud's face, a Kandinsky print, a large poster of a single human cell, framed degrees and a bulletin board pinned with postcards, many of tropical settings. Above her desk were two African carvings.

"Would you like some coffee?" she asked, motioning him to a couch.

He nodded yes, told her he took milk and sugar, and was pleased to note that she fetched it herself, from some sort of adjoining pantry. Two points.

He was also pleased, when she returned, that she did not take up a position behind her desk, but sat on a chair beside the couch, angled toward him, her knees pointing up. Proximity always helps an interview, he thought as he pulled out a tiny tape recorder from his pocket and propped the half-inch mike onto a metal clip facing her.

"Just for insurance," he said. "I thought you might get scientific and technical. But I won't use it if it bothers you."

"Not at all," she said, and her tone suggested she meant it. She was nothing if not confident. She crossed her legs, and with her knees at an incline, he could see several inches under her skirt, a disturbing patch of white thigh disappearing into darkness.

"I suppose you're here because of that murder case—the two lawyers," she said. "Horrible business."

"That's right. For our paper, the more horrible, the better."

She nodded knowingly. "For all of them, I'm afraid. Still, I like your sports section."

Now he was really impressed. Three points.

He looked at the pair of African carvings mounted on thick white blocks on the wall, resplendent in beams of light from the ceiling lights. The statuettes were about eight inches tall, worn smooth and dark as ebony. At first they looked identical: disproportionately large heads with wide-open oval eyes, bulging cheeks marked by slanting scars, and elaborately carved little caps painted blue. Each was adorned with a beaded waistband, a brass ringlet around the left wrist and a small shoulder cape of cowry shells. But from the exaggerated genitalia it could be seen that one was a man and the other a woman.

Dr. Tierney followed his gaze.

*"Ibeji,"* she said. "They come from Nigeria, Yorubaland in the south. The Yoruba carve them whenever they have twins."

He was taken by the carvings, and it occurred to him that he might somehow work them into his story. She read his curiosity and continued.

"The parents commission them from master carvers, and they pay a great deal, the more ornate the better. Each statue represents one of the twins. They are kept carefully stowed away, and if the twins achieve adulthood, well and good, the *ibeji* are meaningless objects to be tossed out—or these days more likely sold for a pittance to a trader who gets a hefty markup when he sells them to foreigners.

"But if one of the twins should die—which happens more often than not—the statue representing that twin takes on enormous spiritual value. It is dressed like the child, it is given food and put to sleep at night and takes its rightful place at all birthdays and ceremonies. The idea is that this is the only way to appease the missing twin. Otherwise, it will become jealous and angry and come up to claim the living twin and drag him down into the netherworld."

She smiled. "That's because the two twins have only one soul between them. At least, that's the theory."

Jude looked at them more closely—at the gently curving bellies, the serene smiles, the slitted oval eyes. They were eerie and majestic-looking, existing in another, timeless world. They reminded him, strangely, of fetuses.

"They're beautiful," he said.

"I'm glad you like them," she said, genuinely pleased. "I do, too."

After a moment's silence, Jude switched on the tape recorder, pulled out his notebook, and said: "Well, time to get started."

He began with some warm-up questions. Her age: thirty (so it *was* the same as his). Her hometown: White Fish Bay, Wisconsin. Her parents: her father was a doctor, her mother a housewife. Her background: Berkeley, and then Minnesota for postgraduate work and three years of medical school at Duke.

She was not, she explained, a practicing doctor, but a medical researcher in biology. Research on twins studies was a recent sideline.

He jotted down her replies. The notebook was largely a prop, since the tape was recording every word. He had learned to use note taking to adjust the flow of information—he could open the spigot by scribbling enthusiastically and shut it down by tapping his ballpoint in boredom. But he quickly realized that this woman needed little encouragement to talk about her research, which aroused an enthusiasm that burned in her dark eyes.

"Do you know why scientists are so passionate about identical twins? Every year we trek to their gathering in Twinsburg, Ohio, and set up booths and hound them unmercifully to get them to participate in all kinds of studies. Do you know why?"

Jude nodded ambiguously; it could have signified yes or go on. She went on.

"Twins studies are a powerful research tool."

Jude wrote that down.

"Monozygotic twins—twins that come from a single fertilized egg that splits—are an accident of Nature. It's like a little slippage of the gears, a crack in the mirror that allows us to see through it to the other side. It provides us with two separate individuals that have the exact same genetic makeup. Their genes are, for all intents and purposes, the same."

"I see." Jude stopped taking notes.

"So here you have two identical people, the same from the point of view of what they inherit from their ancestors, different in circumstances. It's a miniature experiment, aimed at solving that age-old conundrum: what counts more, hereditary or environment? Nature or nurture?"

"I remember," said Jude. "Biology 201."

"More likely 101. The introductory course. You probably know the salient features of the studies. All those coincidences that seem to defy belief—they're part of common lore: how two identical boys or girls, raised in separate cities and with no contact or even knowledge of one another, end up leading lives that have all these spooky similarities. Scientists love to study them, newspapers love to write about them, and we all love to read about them."

She walked to her desk and rummaged through a drawer. "Here, look at this," she said, handing him a yellowed clipping. "An old article from one of your competitors."

It was a story from the *New York Post*, dated May 9, 1979, about identical twin boys born in Piqua, Ohio, to an unwed mother in 1939. They had been adopted by different families, raised forty-five miles apart and had met up again nearly forty years later. The article enumerated astounding similarities. It quoted one of the twins, and Jude copied it down: "When I went to meet my brother the first time, it was like looking in a mirror."

"Watch out," said Dr. Tierney. "This stuff can become habit forming. A Danish shrink, Juel-Nielsen, came up with a name for it—'monozygotic monomania.'"

She smiled, sat back down, and noticed that he was still copying.

"I don't mean to say anything," she said, "but is that allowed?"

Jude looked up. He saw that she was looking at his moving pen.

"Oh, you mean writing all this down from the *Post*. You know what they say: 'Good writers borrow, great writers steal.'

She did not seem to be amused, and so he added, "No, it's perfectly all right, as long as you attribute it."

Nodding, she continued.

"A lot of the twins-reared-apart studies were done at the University of Minnesota—the Twin Cities, naturally. There's a man there I had the honor to work with, though only briefly, Professor Thomas J. Bouchard, Jr. He founded something called the Center for Twin and Adoptive Research. He got hooked in 1979 and—you'll be happy to know—it was a newspaper story on that same set of twins you just read about that did it.

"Jim Lewis and Jim Springer. By coincidence, they had both been given the same first name. They looked almost exactly alike in every way—lanky, six feet tall, about a hunded and eighty pounds, dark hair, brown eyes. Not all monozygotic twins retain the physical resemblance to such a high degree. But the real surprise came when they started comparing the narratives of their lives: each had married a woman named Linda, then gotten a divorce, then remarried a woman named Betty. Jim Lewis had named his firstborn child James Alan, spelled A-l-a-n. Jim Springer named his first James Allen, which he spelled A-l-l-e-n. What's really intriguing is the similarity in all the little details, the fabric of their daily lives. When they were kids, they both had dogs named Toy. Their families went to the same beach in Florida for vacations. Each of them worked in law enforcement. They liked the same hobbies—blueprinting, drafting, carpentry. They even liked the same beer, Miller Lite, and smoked the same brand of cigarettes, Salem. Their results on various tests were carbon copies—so much alike that it looked as if the same person had taken them twice."

Jude was writing it all down. This was good stuff. It had been printed before—some of it going back two decades—but still, maybe he could recycle it into the body of the story.

"You don't have to take notes," she said. "I don't mean to discourage you, but most of it appeared in a magazine article just a few years ago."

Jude's heart sank. She rose, thumbed through a stack of papers on her bookshelf, and sat down with a copy of *The New Yorker*. He glanced over at the date and jotted it down: August 7, 1995.

"Let me find a passage about Bouchard's early work." She flipped to a page marked by a paper clip, skimmed the article, and summarized it:

"Among the first pairs he studied were two women, Daphne Goodship and Barbara Herbert. They had both been adopted and lived apart near London for thirty-nine years. They met at a railroad station in May 1979. Each of them was wearing a beige dress and brown velvet jacket. They had dozens of little similarities—both had identical crooked little fingers, for example, which had kept them both from typing or learning to play the piano. Both had weak ankles from tumbling down stairs at the same age, fifteen. At sixteen each of them had gone to a local dance, where she met the man she later married. Each had suffered miscarriages during her first pregnancies; each then had two boys followed by a girl. They had little tics and gestures in common, giggling and this habit of pushing up their noses when they laughed—which they called 'squidging.' And so on. It goes on and on, twin after twin."

Jude jumped in with a question:

"But given all the possible variables in a lifetime, all the people out there and all the twins, wouldn't you expect some crazy coincidences? I mean, if you and I compared our lives in minute detail, wouldn't we come up with some details that seemed eerie because they were the same?: we went to the same rock show in 1976, we use the same toothpaste, we have uncles with the same first names. Especially if we were *looking* for the similarities. And we'd naturally discard all the dissimilarities that didn't fit in."

She smiled and nodded. "I applaud your skepticism—I imagine when you're a reporter, it comes with the territory. And to be truthful, I share it to a large extent—or I did."

She crossed her legs, and Jude saw that disturbing band of white thigh again. It was hard not to look at it.

"But the universe of people we're talking about here is small. The number of monozygotic twins is growing, thanks to fertility pills, but it's still not all that large. A little under four births out of every thousand. And of those, the number who end up being raised apart for various reasons is minuscule. Back when Bouchard began, there were only nineteen recorded cases of twins who separated and reunited. Now there's more. The literature contains references to a hundred and twenty-one, and there have been more than thirty books and articles written about them. Still, that's not a lot, and the remarkable feature is the high coincidence of similarities among such a small sample.

"Yes, any two people of roughly the same age—you and me, say—we could sit down to compare notes and pore over our lives and our habits and our tastes until we came up with a whole array of things in common."

She smiled at him here, and he smiled back. He wondered: Was she saying *especially you and me?*

"In fact, I've done that—I mean, I've set up control groups using two strangers chosen at random to see what they'd come up with. You lock them in a room together, and they're usually able to establish some pretty amazing congruities. But not as many as separated twins, and not in so many different aspects of life. What's interesting about these studies is how the congruities keep occurring over and over in the same areas, as if there were certain categories in which they are allowed to operate. It's almost as if the similarities were preordained. A predispositon to alcoholism or smoking or suicide or insomnia—if you find it in one twin, chances are you'll find it in the other. Why should they end up having the same number of marriages and divorces? Or the same careers and hobbies? Even a lot of their social and political *attitudes* are alike. Why should twins end up with the same feeling about the death penalty or working mothers or apartheid? Why should their tastes run the same in coffee? But not—and try and figure this one out—in tea?"

She glanced at his empty cup.

"Speaking of which . . . would you like some more?"

He shook his head no. He didn't want her to stop.

"What will really blow your mind is the parallel tracks of physical development. Twins often get the same diseases at exactly the same ages—okay, you might expect that. But the parallels are so finely tuned. There are cases in which they each grow a blackhead in the exact same spot on the nose at the exact same time. How do you explain that? Is there some vicious little gene lying around whose whole goal is to inject a little spot of misery into the life of an adolescent? Is our whole makeup nothing more than a giant time-release capsule?"

Her eyes were blazing now.

"What's the causative factor—how does this happen? What's the explanation? There are similarities between any two of us, granted. But in monozygotic twins they go beyond the law of averages, and they keep happening in the same spheres. Coffee and not tea—what is that all about?"

The secretary knocked; Dr. Tierney was needed down the hall.

"I'll only be a few minutes," she told Jude. She tossed him *The New Yorker.*

The article by Lawrence Wright was titled "Double Mystery." It began with a description of identical twin girls, Amy and Beth, born in New York City in the 1960s and placed for adoption in separate homes. They sounded cute: "fair-skinned blondes with small oval faces, blue-gray eyes, and slightly snub noses." By chance, the two families were outwardly similar—Jewish, with stay-at-home mothers and an older son as a sibling. But Beth seemed to have drawn the lucky card. Her family was more prosperous and more solid. More important, Beth's mother was loving and accepting; she doted on her new daughter, drew her into the bosom of the family, and provided her with everything she could possibly want. The father was attentive and supportive.

Amy's mother, on the other hand, was overweight and insecure and began to feel competitive with her daughter and regard her as a threat. The family—mother, father and son—closed ranks against the adopted child and excluded her as an outsider. As might be expected, Amy developed problems. She bit her nails, cried when left alone, wet her bed, and had nightmares. By ten she showed the signs of a rejected child—she was shy and insecure, made up illnesses, had an artificial quality that came out in role playing, was confused over her sexual identity and suffered from a serious learning disorder. What would you expect, given her home life?

But how about Beth, with all her advantages?

That was the part of the story that astonished Jude. For she, too, displayed the same signs of inner turmoil as an infant—thumb sucking, nail biting, blanket clenching and bed wetting. She, too, became a hypochondriac and fearful, and as she grew older she, too, fell into an artificial dimension of role playing and had problems with friends and in school. There were some differences, of course. But fundamentally, the secure and loving family, all the advantages, the step up in life—they didn't count for very much when it came to conquering the inner demons.

Jude was fascinated. Why should Beth turn out to be as troubled as Amy? That contradicted common sense and reason. Was there such a thing as total biological destiny? Did it override everything else in determining character—family life, education, inculcated values, chance? And where was free will in all of this? The conviction that comes from the marrow of our bones that we are actually making choices and that we can change ourselves if we try hard enough? All his life, Jude had thought—when he thought about it at all—that he would have been a different person if he had been raised by his parents instead of foster parents—less lonely somehow, more secure, more *giving*, as Betsy would have put it. Was that wrong?

Dr. Tierney returned, and he closed the magazine. She had changed her doctor's coat for a tweed jacket, worn over a white silk blouse, and he could see one side of a strand of pearls hanging close to her neck and disappearing past the unbuttoned collar. She was clearly getting ready to leave. He was disappointed—he had assumed that they would have more time for the interview, and he was reluctant to break it off.

"I'm afraid—if it's not an imposition—I need a bit more of your time."

"Of course." She smiled faintly. "I'm sorry I have to go now—something's come up. But we can meet again."

"Would tomorrow be okay? I've got to finish this story by the next day at the latest."

"That'll be fine."

"I can meet you somewhere else if it's more convenient. I'll give you a call."

She nodded.

"Thank you, Dr. Tierney. This is a great help."

"Please—Tizzie. That's what most people call me."

"Tizzie, then."

They shook hands.

He took a final look around her office. He saw with a new eye that the framed photographs were mostly of an elderly couple, presumably her parents. There was another one of a beautiful Irish setter and still others of groups—what looked to be friends on a rafting trip and posing by a convertible. He did not, however, see a photo of her alone with a man.

On the street outside later, he wondered why it seemed to matter.

# Chapter 7

Skyler ran through the rain, drunk with grief, his clothes soaked through and sticking to his chest and the front of his thighs like weights. He did not know where he was going—he had no plan, other than to get away, to leave them all behind, to find a refuge where he could stop and take his time and formulate a life plan centered on this new thing growing inside his gut like a beast—the need for vengeance. They would pay for her death, he would see to that. Nothing else mattered.

He was aware that his feet were carrying him northward toward the forest, and he dimly thought that the escape route made sense. He knew the paths and the rivers, the ways of snakes and deer and boar. He knew how to live there and he felt at home there; he would hide out and dedicate himself to cultivating and appeasing the beast. He remembered the Shell Ring where he and Raisin had played, a vast circular mound of ancient clam shells and mussel shells and other mollusks built hundreds of years ago, it was said, by the Indians for defense; no one could sneak up on you there. That was the place to be.

Then he heard the dogs.

At first, it was an indistinct sound, rising and falling like the wind. Then came a clap of thunder, and it was as if it cleared the air and made way for the baying, the excited, bloodcurdling cry of animals on the spoor. Suddenly, the sound seemed much closer. Skyler could visualize them, the Orderlies holding thick leather leashes, and the hounds straining and sniffing the ground ahead. If the Orderlies found him, he would be done for. They might kill him on the spot, without a moment's thought. Or maybe they would tie him up and carry him back to the Big House and cut him open the same way they had cut open Julia, for whatever it was she had discovered. He ran faster, but he knew he could not keep it up much longer.

He left the path and found himself knee-deep in swamp water. He plunged ahead, with water now on all sides, above and below, and promptly lost his footing and fell into the murky water up to his chest. He struggled up and moved on slowly, taking the drag weight in his thighs. He felt something cold in his right hand and looked down and was surprised to see that he was still clasping the knife.

The swamp slowed him to a crawl. He tripped over a submerged log and fell again, face forward. When he raised his head, he saw the surface bouncing around him with rain pelts as if it were boiling. He came to a tiny island of a single tree and pulled himself up, leaning his shoulder against the trunk, his chest heaving. A rope of Spanish moss hung across his shoulder, and he flung it to the ground. The rain was coming down in a thick blanket now. Turning and staring into it, he could see only ten feet or so into the grayness, but he could still hear the hounds. They sounded higher-pitched, frustrated and whining, as if they were being held from pursuit of their prey. A good sign perhaps. Maybe they'd reached the swamp's edge and the Orderlies wouldn't let them go on. Maybe they would lose the scent and be unable to follow him through the water. The thought gave him hope and pushed him onward. He jumped into the water and moved through it by swiveling his upper body and taking long strides. He kept at it and soon he fell into a rhythm, which made the going easier. Despite the rain and the cold, he was sweltering with heat; sweat was pouring down his temples and the back of his neck.

From time to time, the image of Julia's body, immobile and shrunken and ripped open, flashed through his brain, and it filled him with anger, and deepened his resolve to fight the storm and elude his pursuers. Minutes went by, long minutes, then tens of minutes, then a half hour. He had stopped thinking, had slipped into a fevered daydream as he slogged ahead.

Abruptly, he came to. He noticed that the rain seemed to be lightening, and as he walked, he had the sensation that the water was receding—it was down to his knees now and the bottom felt more secure. He kept walking until he looked down and saw that he was on solid ground. He had passed through the swamp. Then he collapsed and lay there for a long time, not thinking at all.

He sat bolt upright. His head had cleared. How long had he been there? He had no idea. His muscles were aching. He listened—he could no longer hear the baying of the hounds. Looking up through the canopy of branches, he saw that the storm clouds had dissipated. Dusk was coming on. He would need a safe place to spend the night.

He took stock of his situation, which was not good. They would not stop looking for him—that he knew. They would never stop. They would hunt him down, no matter how far into the northern forest he ventured. And sooner or later they would find him. There would be a slip-up—a bit of telltale smoke from a fire or he would run into them as he went tearing down a path after some animal. Or perhaps the dogs would comb the woods and pick up his scent. He couldn't hold out forever. His only chance was to leave the island. But how? Raisin had tried it and he had died, pulled down by the treacherous backwater currents of the marshes. How could he succeed where Raisin had failed?

The answer came to him instantly, so clear he felt he must have been close to it all along. Kuta's boat. It was not running, because the engine was out of commission, but Kuta could fix it, and he could negotiate the shoals to reach the mainland. He was the only one Skyler could turn to—surely, he would not refuse him, not when it was a matter of life and death. Once on the mainland, Skyler could bide his time and plot revenge. Somehow, he would survive to do that. But the prospect of going "to the other side" filled him with fear. He had no idea of what he would encounter there or what it would be like.

And first he had to get to Kuta's shack. That would be tricky. He would have to wait until dark and then double back and walk around the swamp to the meadow. From there, he would slip behind the Campus and reach the thin strip of shore peopled by the Gullah.

Evening came quickly and was eerily quiet. Skyler moved stealthily through the woods, using the knife from time to time to cut his way through the undergrowth. Finally, he found a path that went roughly in the direction he wanted. All around he heard the deep croaking of bullfrogs. Every so often a bush or clump of marsh grass on either side of the path would twitch suddenly, the flight of a panicked creature, and each time he startled at the sound. The sky above was clear, but darkening, and through the branches he could already see stars coming out.

The path was crossed by another one, slightly wider, that veered off at an angle. He took it and followed it for a half hour or so, until he came to the meadow. He stood at the edge and stared—it looked unearthly and serene. The moon was out and it hung low in the sky, casting a ghostly glow upon the long yellow grass that waved in the breeze. Skyler stepped into the meadow and heard it rustling around him. As he walked, the straw brushed against his legs and he felt like a ship pushing through a golden sea. Except that his passage was hardly smooth—he stepped upon clumps of knotted earth and grass that made his ankles wobble and slowed his stride. Above his head, there was movement—angular forms zigzagging through the night air. Bats, swooping and dive bombing. He suddenly felt vulnerable, walking in the open in the moonlight, but gradually the fear melted away and he felt strangely disconnected, out of time. The feeling was opposite to the panic that had gripped him in the swamp. And he realized that some primal core where fear is born had been eviscerated, and that he no longer cared what happened to him.

On the far end of the meadow, he stepped into the woods and melted back into the shadows. He saw off in the distance the gleaming lights of the barracks. The windows appeared bright yellow in the darkness and, looking so warm and cozy, they beckoned him. He turned and moved in the other direction, stopping behind a tree to pick his route carefully, ten steps at a time, to the next tree, and listening intently. There was a cascade of noises, of buzzings and chirpings and croakings, but nothing more than that.

Soon he was on the path he knew well and that he could negotiate with his eyes closed—the path to Kuta's. Ahead was the darkened outline of the shack, and the window was lighted. He slipped around it and approached the water, shining in the moonlight. He saw something glimmer, a flash of metal. It was the outboard engine, still resting on the stump. But when Skyler walked over to the dock, he saw something that stopped him in his tracks. The boat was submerged a half foot under water, its rope emerging and still tied to the rail. He could see to the bottom of the boat, where there was a gaping hole near the stern, and near it a large rock.

He turned quietly and stared behind him. Now he saw that the front door of the shack was smashed inward, hanging by the upper hinge. Cautiously, he crept over, bent under the window and straightened up to look inside.

An Orderly was there! He was sitting on the bed, his back to Skyler. Even from behind, his thick neck and hunched back gave him a thuggish appearance. He sat there motionless, apparently waiting for someone—*for me,* Skyler realized.

He looked quickly around. Kuta was not there or at least not in sight. And everything seemed in place, except for the door and a rug that was crumpled in a corner.

He backed away quietly, then turned and ran. When he reached the woods, he kept running. *So they've come. Someone did see me here earlier—Tyrone. But what did they do with Kuta? Did they hurt him?* He feared the answer to the question. These people, whom he had known his whole life, whom he had trusted and even loved—they were monsters. They were capable of anything. *But why? What are they after? And why would they kill Julia—what was it that she had discovered in the computer?*

Self-preservation told him one thing—to flee. He heeded it, racing steadily along the path, like a hunted animal. He retraced his steps and came again to the lights of the barracks and then to the meadow, stopping on the edge to spy for signs of movement. His eyes crisscrossed the waving field, studying all the dark spots in the grass until he was satisfied it was empty. Then he examined the night shadows in the border of the woods on the other side, peering with his head slightly cocked to improve his vision. It looked safe and he took a stride forward.

Again, he felt a sudden rush of vulnerability once he was in the open, only this time it combined with a palpable fear and the sense that danger was close. He stopped for a moment to stare around and saw nothing and continued, rebuking himself for not skirting the meadow through the woods. His heart quickened and the alarm within sounded more urgently, so much so that he dropped to the ground and then slowly raised his head and looked in all directions. Still nothing—only the soft whispering of the long grass. The straw dug into his arms and stomach. The bats were gone, and the stars winked against black velvet.

He stood up and resumed his trek, now staring straight ahead and relying upon his ears to cover the rear. The fear rose again instantly and it turned to panic, and he found himself quickening his pace and then running flat out, though it was difficult to find footing through the clumps of earth. The more he ran, the more frightened he felt and the more he tried to shut out everything around him and concentrate upon a narrow tunnel straight ahead.

Then suddenly something rose on his right side, a shadow coming out of the grass. A flash of movement and then a sound, a low growling. He turned as he was running, just in time to see a furry body thrusting at him, teeth bared and glistening in the moonlight. It was a dog, swiveling in fury as it twisted in the air, coming at his throat. Instinctively, he turned his shoulder to it, hearing the growl turn deep and feeling a rip across his upper arm. He raised his hand, without thinking. From a distance, he watched as the hand moved up, bearing the knife, and the blade sank deeply into the fur. It went in right at the neck. The power of the animal's lunge carried it onward as the blade sliced the jugular, so that the dog continued to fly through the air and to bleed and lose life as it flew. When it landed in a heap in the grass, it was a dead weight. Its back legs twitched, its lungs heaved, and it gave out a thin groan. Blood gushed upon the grass.

Skyler stood back and stared in shock. He felt his shoulder—his shirt was ripped and his upper arm bleeding, but it looked like a scratch. He had been unbelievably lucky. He looked around, then turned again and ran as fast as he could, out of the meadow and into the woods.

He ran and ran until his lungs ached. He had recognized the dog, having seen the pack of them behind a chain-link fence in a kennel near the Orderlies' compound. It had been so quiet in its approach, it must have been stalking him. He wondered if there were others out there looking for him. If so, he had made their job easy; he had left his scent in a clear trail. He found a path and headed north, toward the forest, and slowed to a walk.

After fifteen minutes he came to another open field, this one long and narrow with the grass cut short. There was a large metal shed at the far end. He recognized it instantly—the air strip. But how had he come here? He must have been going the wrong way. Now he was totally confused, and he was too exhausted to figure out the right direction and make good his mistake by putting distance between him and his pursuers. He approached the shed. There was a small door in one side. He turned the handle, and was surprised when it opened.

Inside it was dark, but he felt a light switch and flicked it on. The long, sleek machine, the airplane, looked powerful and ready for flight, even at rest, its wheels lodged against wooden blocks and its nose pointing upward. The propellers were strapped to one side. He opened the metal door in the side of the craft, went back to turn off the light, and in the darkness felt his way. He climbed inside, closed the door behind him and felt a metal enclosure at the rear that had two small bags in it. He crawled inside and found a tarpaulin, which he pulled over himself like a blanket.

There, he collapsed, listening to his heavy breathing in the darkness. From time to time he felt sleepy, but he couldn't drift off—he would stiffen and raise his head with a snap because he thought he heard the sound of hounds baying. But he couldn't be sure. Was the baying real and, if so, was it getting closer or farther away? Or perhaps his fatigue was playing tricks on him and his mind was echoing the sound that had pursued him earlier in the day.

# Chapter 8

"So where were we?" asked Tizzie, balancing the glass of chardonnay by the stem and peering into Jude's eyes.

"Well, let's see," said Jude, sipping a scotch and trying to sound business-like. "You were telling me about the Minnesota studies. After our meeting yesterday, I went to the library and read up on some of them."

"And?"

"And I see what you mean. They're addictive. I see why you scientists are attracted to them."

"Not just scientists—writers and poets, too. Shakespeare and Dostoevsky, for openers."

"I understand why. The stories are gripping—they're like tales from the Arabian nights. The one about the two separated Japanese brothers who both got tuberculosis and developed a stammer—"

"Kazuo and Takua."

"That's it. And one becomes a Christian minister and the other becomes a thief and goes to prison."

"And yet despite that, underneath they're both the same. Both were vacillating, weak-willed men who needed to submit to something that could impose discipline. They both gave themselves over to institutions that took over their lives."

"And Tony and Roger, the two who found each other after twenty-four years and moved in together and began dressing the same and acting the same, so that they practically merged into a single person."

"Talk about being weak. Neither felt complete without the other, and each of them tried to become the other."

This time, Jude was not using the tape recorder, only the notebook. He had wanted a more informal atmosphere—better for this kind of interview—and had suggested a drink after work. She had agreed. And so they found themselves sitting at an outdoor table at Lumi, a café restaurant on Lexington Avenue, on a balmy June evening. A breeze rustled the leaves of a maidenhair tree, which grew from a sidewalk plot of earth covered in posies and protected by iron wickets. A dachshund, tethered to a man wearing a blue suit and a red bow tie, sniffed it.

Tizzie was wearing a dark blue, double-breasted pinstripe suit. She did not have on a blouse as far as Jude could tell, which afforded him a perfect view of her collarbones and the pearl necklace. He had to admit, she looked good.

But he was here for work, he reminded himself.

"How do you explain the findings when it comes to personality?" he asked. "The fact that twins who are reared apart can turn out to be so similar."

"It's complicated. The literature's confusing. There was a seminal article by Bouchard in 1988, which set the groundwork. Basically, it compared identical twins raised separately and identical twins raised together, and concluded there were no substantial differences—they share more or less the same cluster of personality traits."

"There you go again—defying common sense."

"It gets worse. There are some studies that suggest that twins raised apart are actually *more* alike than twins raised together."

"More? How's that possible?"

She chuckled, took a deep sip and put her glass down.

"The best guess is that twins raised together sometimes go to great lengths to be distinctive, to *appear* more different than they are. They want to carve out their own identities, which is only natural. The emotional dynamic between twins growing up together is more complicated than we can ever imagine."

"But it's paradoxical. How can twins who haven't even laid eyes on each other until middle age be more alike than ones growing up in the same household? That contradicts what common sense tells us—that character is forged by experience, by family and upbringing."

"I admit it's a lot to swallow. Can it be that all that stuff—families, home life, schooling—doesn't really carry much weight in the final analysis? Doesn't it matter whether we have parents who love us uncritically or freeze us out, siblings who support us or undermine us, grandparents who pass on traditions and values or who are in the grave? Doesn't any of that shape us irrevocably?"

"It has to. I have to think two people in the same environment have a better chance of turning out similar. Think of all the influences—going to the same kindergarten, hearing the same Sunday sermons, being subjected to the same mother hugs and the same whacks of the belt from dad. Doesn't all that count?"

"So you'd think," she said. "The alternative is that all that is minimal in terms of forming our character. In a determinative sense, who we are depends upon other variables."

"Such as?"

She sipped her wine. "There are two possibilities. One is that personality is much more genetically determined than we give it credit for, that it unfolds more or less on its own, like film pouring off a spool. That's a kind of frightening hypothesis, because it doesn't allow much room for change or variation—what we like to think of as free will."

"And the other?"

"Simply that we haven't identified the formative variables. Maybe they are experiences so profound and basic to early childhood that they supercede the influences we usually point to. Maybe different ways of delineating the self. Or coping with loss or coming to terms with death. Or maybe something in the mind and the way it interacts with the outside world, something in how we process experience. Outwardly, things could appear very much the same for any two people. But inwardly, internally, the two might be living in two completely separate and disengaged universes. For them, life could never be remotely comparable."

Tizzie raised a finger and poked an ice cube.

"I don't know if you've known identical twins. Most people have. And the remarkable thing is that, though they do look the same, once you know them you can always tell them apart. They are truly very different as people. And of course there's one bit of good evidence to back that up."

"Which is . . . ?"

"Which is that while it's clearly possible to fall in love with one twin, I don't know of anyone who's fallen in love with both. Spouses of identical twins make for a good talk show—how do you fight down your attraction to the other one, that sort of thing. But it doesn't happen much in real life. The more interesting question—from the point of view of what we can learn from research—is to look at it from the twins' point of view. Are identical twins, those raised apart, attracted to the same type of person?

"When it comes to their love lives, there are a lot of coincidences. They'll start dating about the same time, have the same sexual hang-ups and dysfunctions, get divorced a comparable number of times, even—if they're women—start their periods at the same time. But the choice of a mate is still elusive. The jury's out on that one. One study done at Minnesota seems to suggest that the spouses end up being wildly different. On the other hand, you hear some interesting stories of mental swapping—maybe it just means that love is still a mystery after all."

Jude looked at her glass, which was empty. She followed his gaze, gave him a quizzical nod, then caught the eye of the waiter and ordered another wine and another scotch.

"There's so much that's unexplained in this field," she continued. "I suppose that's why I like it. We're still at the stage of asking basic questions. Fraternal twins, for example—we all know that they happen when two separate eggs get fertilized at the same time. But did you know that even they share a number of physical traits, more than ordinary siblings—that their teeth are more symmetrical, for one thing. Why in God's name should that be true?

"In some cases, maybe they come from a single egg that splits before fertilization. We don't know. We don't even really know why twins occur to begin with—what is it that causes two eggs to drop or one egg to break apart. But we do know—now, at least—that it occurs much more often than anyone suspects."

"What do you mean?"

"Now that we have ultrasound to record early pregnancies, we've learned that double pregnancies happen many, many more times than the results suggest. About one in ninety live births produces twins. But, believe it or not, about one in eight of all pregnancies start out with twins."

"That's amazing."

"It is. You talk to gynecologists these days, and you hear some interesting tales. One day a woman comes in, he examines her with ultrasound, and she's bearing two tiny embryos. A month later, she's back and there's only one."

"The other one died."

"Right."

"So a few of us had brothers or sisters in the womb we never even knew about."

"More than just a few. Estimates are that between ten to fifteen percent of us so-called singletons began life in utero with a sibling snuggling up to us or fighting with us or kissing us—all of which goes on there, by the way."

"We're just the ones who won out."

"Yes. The great Darwinian struggle. It begins with the sperm swimming up to the ovum, but it doesn't end there. It goes on during pregnancy."

"Incredible."

"But true. It's been happening since time in memoriam, but of course no one ever realized. One week the mother-to-be has a little extra blood, doesn't think much of it, and that's it—it's over before it's even had a chance to start, so to speak. There's a word for the phenomenon."

"What?"

"Vanishing twins."

Jude wrote it down.

"Vanishing twins. I like that. Talk about drama."

She looked at him intently and continued. "An awful lot of people have a vague notion that they might have had a twin somewhere along the line. Nothing they can pin down—just this sense that somewhere out there is—or was—someone they were incredibly close to. In a few cases, they turn out to be right—unbeknownst to them, a twin was separated out and reared somewhere else. In the other cases . . . who knows? Maybe a prenatal memory. There's no reason your brain can't register something inside the womb as well as outside.

"Incidentally," she went on, "I can't help noticing, you take notes with your left hand. You are, obviously, left-handed."

"Yes, so what?"

"Interesting."

"What's interesting about it?"

"Not to put too fine a point on it," she replied, "but I was just thinking—there is, you know, a higher incidence of left-handedness among twins. In fact, it may be only a matter of time until someone comes along and claims that every left-handed person is the mirror image of a vanished twin."

Jude stopped writing. He looked at her square in the eye and couldn't tell whether she was joking, but her mouth had a mischievous laugh wrinkle on one side.

Their drinks came. He took a deep sip of scotch and felt it hit him. She ran her fingers through her hair, which made it billow outward and fall gently on her shoulder.

There was a brief, uncomfortable moment of silence, and Jude decided to break it.

"You know, at the library I even read a few of your studies."

"Oh, you did," she said, pleased. "And what did you think?"

He struck a judgmental air. "Not bad."

"That's all? Not bad?"

"Shows promise. I like your style."

"I see," she said, lifting her glass and looking over the rim. "My writing style, I presume."

"Absolutely. Your use of metaphor, the color, the drama, all those linguistic flourishes. I had no idea *The Journal of Personality and Social Psychology* could be so gripping."

"How about my character development?"

"I think your character is developing just fine."

She ignored that. "Well, modesty compels me to point out that a good editor can do wonders."

"You don't say." He paused. "Personally, I've never met one."

"What—a good editor?"

"In fact, I've never heard those two particular words uttered in the same sentence."

"Ah-ha," she exclaimed. "What have we here—a little professional animosity?"

"Not really animosity. Hatred, maybe."

"I understand. That's always the way with unequal relationships. On the one side, there is the power, and on the other, there is only . . ."

". . . charm."

She smiled.

"There's this joke . . ." he began, then said, "Christ, I can't believe I'm telling you a dumb joke."

He stopped.

"No, please, go ahead," she pleaded. She sounded as if she meant it. "Well, you see, an editor and a reporter are crawling across the desert, dying of thirst. Suddenly, they come to an oasis. The reporter rushes ahead, he's drinking the water, swimming in it, having a grand old time. He looks back and what does he see? There's the editor, standing at the edge, pissing into it. 'Hey, what the hell are you doing?' he shouts. The editor draws himself up and replies: 'Improving it.' "

She laughed while he drained his glass.

"Would you like another drink?" she asked. "Maybe in honor of your vanishing twin, you should make it a double."

# Chapter 9

It was the clanging of the large metal door that startled Skyler awake—that and a blast of light that came from the front of the shed. It took him only a second to remember where he was, and when he did, the events of the previous twenty-four hours came flooding back, like pieces of a nightmare assembling themselves into a horrific whole. Along with it came the by now familiar hollow in his stomach.

He pulled the tarpaulin over his head and tried to read the noises that reverberated inside the metal shed. Another door clanged, and he knew the hangar was now wide open and he envisioned the plane facing the end of the grass strip runway. He heard footsteps treading upon the ground, approaching the plane and moving away and again approaching. He heard a metallic pounding, then the sound of liquid being poured into a tank and he smelled gasoline fumes. Finally, he made out a dull *thunk*, followed by a skittering sound—the block under the tire being kicked away, he thought—and he knew he was right a moment later when the *thunk* came again, and the plane rocked almost imperceptibly. Suddenly, the tail lifted, he heard a stream of curse words surprisingly loud through the thin metal skin of the plane.

"Jesus Christ! Son of a bitch!"

The words came only a few inches away from his ear. He could not recognize the voice. It felt like he was being gently carried. He heard fingers slap against the metal for a better grip, and then a series of grunts. A final heave-ho and the plane's tires cleared the threshold of the shed, and as the craft moved onto the grass and into a slightly declining slope, it gained momentum and rolled by itself—so much so that the fingers grabbed it again, and with more cursing it was brought to a shuddering standstill.

Then Skyler heard the door open and a foot step onto the ladder. He held his breath and froze under the tarpaulin, tensing every muscle. He had to prepare himself—if the cover was lifted and he was discovered, he would jump up and attack whoever was there. Surprise was his only ally. His heart seemed to somersault: *Where was the knife?* Then he remembered: he'd lost it in killing the dog.

The door snapped shut, and he heard footsteps on the wing and another door open and close. More grunts, more curses, the snap of a seat belt. A long silence, one minute, maybe two—and then the sounds of toggle switches being flipped, a window sliding open, and finally the roar of the engine. The plane was vibrating crazily, and he smelled fumes of burning fuel.

In no time, the plane was bumping awkwardly down the runway and shaking from side to side. And then, just as the engine whined as if it was about to explode and the whole plane seemed about to give up the ghost, magically it lifted off and soared upward. Skyler felt his stomach swoon.

For a long time, he listened to the sound of the engine, echoing off the ground and then sounding suddenly quieter as the plane lifted. They droned on alone in space. Slowly, cautiously, he moved the tarpaulin from his head and, looking up, he saw a metal siding, painted cream color and chipped, revealing a green undercoat; it divided his tiny compartment from the interior of the plane. He blinked his eyes in the light, and looked down at two small leather bags. He was at the bottom of a baggage compartment, separated by the siding from the interior of the plane. He raised his head to peer over the edge into the cabin. Ahead were four empty red seats, lined up on either side of a narrow aisle. Above the seats were tiny knit hammocks, apparently for storing things, and little nearby nozzles pointed downward. In the front were the backs of two black seats; one was empty, one occupied. A red fire extinguisher lay underneath.

He could see the back of the pilot's head, a baseball cap held in place by thick black earphones. Before him was a panel of instruments with fluctuating needles and dials and knobs and blinking yellow numbers. The pilot held a U-shaped stick with both hands, and a similar stick extended above the empty seat, turning in synchronicity as if by a ghostly hand. Above was a long window, through which Skyler could see the sky and huge white-gray clouds billowing upward like frozen smoke.

A wing dipped, and suddenly the view shifted and Skyler saw a vista of deep blues and bright blues extending as far as he could see, with slashes of whitecaps—the ocean, he realized with astonishment, seen from above. Fear seized him, but it was ameliorated by a sense of wonder. Off to one side, he caught a glimpse of a green mass, and it took him more than a second to identify it as land—yes, there were the tops of trees rising and falling like the folds of a blanket, and rocks and marshes ringing the whole. It was an island—maybe even his own little island—and then the knowledge struck him almost with the force of a physical blow, that he had already left it behind, his world, the only place he had known. He was on his way to "the other side," to the land he knew only through the radio and through Kuta's stories, to Babylon, as Baptiste called it when he railed against America's obsession with religion and superstition.

The idea intoxicated his mind for a while and kept him on edge with the lure of danger and possibility, but gradually fatigue ambushed him. He lowered his head and curled up under the tarpaulin in the confined space. Soon, the drone of the engine and the rocking motion of the plane lulled him, and so the passage that was to have been the most momentous in his life was lost to sleep.

# Chapter 10

Jude was pleased when she called the next day to say that she liked his sidebar. Like many journalists, he disparaged his profession outwardly—it wasn't cool to be idealistic about anything, especially at the *Mirror*, where journalists called themselves "hacks"—but inside was a different story. He believed newspapers tried to do good, and once in a while actually succeeded.

"First of all, you got the facts right, which is a virtue not to be overlooked," she said. "Then there's the matter of your style—I like it. Straightforward, matter-of-fact, no bullshit."

"Well—you like my style and I like your style. We're getting somewhere."

And so they were. Before she could hang up, Jude, summoning up his courage, had blurted out an invitation to dinner. Much to his surprise, after a small hesitation, she had accepted. And it had gone on from there. Now they were strolling along on the boardwalk at Brighton Beach, on one side the waves lapping the long expanse of deserted brown sand, on the other a jumble of knish shops, Tastee-Freez, food emporiums and scores of people, mostly elderly, sunning themselves and gossiping in half a dozen different languages. They had just finished a leisurely meal at the Primorsky, a Russian establishment tucked away in the shadow of the elevated train that was one of Jude's favorites; the moment you walked in, everything said you could be back in Moscow, from the open vodka bottles and sad little beet salads to the bouffant hairdos and color-clashing beaded dresses of the heavyset women. It had not disappointed.

This wasn't a date, exactly, more like a casual Sunday afternoon spent in each other's company. They had met only a week ago. Tizzie had never been to Brighton Beach, and Jude, who knew the neighborhood somewhat from a series the *Mirror* had done on the Russian Mafia, had offered to show her around.

Tizzie sat on a bench and looked out over the ocean, and Jude sat next to her.

"This puts it all in perspective, doesn't it?" she said, turning her face to the ocean.

"What?"

"Oh, the whole thing. Work, love life, parents, friends, the ozone."

Jude was struck, as he had been several times, by the feeling that she was hard to read.

"Something's bothering you," he ventured.

"No," she said, then, "Yes."

"Tell me about it."

"Not much to tell, really. It's my parents. They're old and failing—my father especially. It's difficult when you grow up thinking they'll last forever."

Jude nodded and followed her gaze out to the water. Seagulls circled above, and there was a strong smell of salt in the air.

"That's why I had to leave the other day—when you were interviewing me. I'm trying to arrange medical care. It's hard to do long distance."

"Where are they?"

"Wisconsin. White Fish Bay—that's outside of Milwaukee. Beautiful place, green lawns, white clapboard houses, the works. I loved it growing up there—a daughter of the suburbs. An idyllic American childhood."

"You sound sarcastic."

She laughed. "But this is no fair. You've already interviewed me. You know all about me, but I don't know anything about you."

"There's not much to know."

"I'll be the judge of that," she said firmly, resting her hand on his. Her tone was encouraging.

"Tell me about your name. It's unusual. Where did your parents get it?"

He paused a moment, tried to come up with a joke, but couldn't.

"The strange thing is, I don't know." He paused. "And I can't ask them."

She looked at him questioningly.

"They're dead."

She put her hand on his arm. "I'm sorry. How did it happen? How old were you?"

And so he took a deep breath and he told her, and he found as he went along that it was surprisingly easy to talk to her about it. He told it straight out—at first in a flat, neutral voice that was self-consciously drained of all affect, lest he be accused of self-pity but then, gradually with color and feeling. He recounted the story of his life, just the way it had happened and the way he had felt at the time. He told her about his idiosyncratic early childhood, his first years in Arizona, where his parents—and this he knew from the vaguest of memories—had belonged to some kind of cult in the desert mountains. It was the 1960s, he said, and people did that sort of thing then.

Tizzie nodded.

He told her how his mother and father had met there. "I was told—although I don't know who told me, and maybe I just imagined it, but I think it's true—that they got married at the direction of the cult leader. He was one of those guys who wanted to build a perfect society away from the world and then ended up running it like a demented dictator, I guess. Anyhow, I came along. Then my mother died, of natural causes, I don't really know what it was."

"How old were you?"

"I must have been about five or so. I can't remember her. I can't even picture her face, and I didn't have a photograph or anything to help me."

Jude looked at her and then out to the ocean. It was easier to talk that way.

"The strange thing is, I used to try to conjure her up, with all my might. I used to lie there and try to think as hard as I could about what she looked like. And when I did this—I haven't done it in years—I couldn't come up with an image, nothing visual. But sometimes I came up with a fragrance. Not a fragrance, really, more of a smell. And I know this sounds weird, but it wasn't a good smell. It was strong, pungent. It was almost antiseptic."

At that, he felt Tizzie's hand touching the inside of his elbow, and he continued.

"Anyway, my father drifted away from the cult. I don't really know what happened, but he was probably devastated by the loss of her—at least, that's what I've always believed. It stands to reason, if he loved her at all. And I guess that happens, even with arranged marriages. We moved to Phoenix. And then he died, too, in a car crash. It was some kind of horrible accident on a crossroads at night. The driver of the other car was drunk."

"And you were how old?" Tizzie sounded deeply moved.

"Six, or maybe seven. I'm not really sure."

"Then what happened?"

"I was taken in by neighbors, people who lived down the block. The Armstrongs. She was some kind of lawyer, and he—I don't know what he did, I think he sold insurance. I hated them. I know it's not fair, they were probably good people—I mean, who else would take in a little kid like that? But still, I hated it in their house. They slept in separate rooms, not just in separate beds. I remember these long dinners with one of them at one end of the table, and the other at the other, and me in the middle, these long silences where all you would hear was his false teeth clicking as he chewed his food. It was an unhappy house—you pick up all kinds of things as a child. I never heard them argue outright, but I knew that they were always at each other, little things. And so when they split up, or I heard they were splitting up, I was actually relieved, I think. I went to a foster home then."

Jude looked at her and anticipated her question. "I was fifteen. Then I won a scholarship to a prep school back East, Phillips Academy, Andover. In Massachusetts. I don't know how I got it. But anyway, I went there, and that place kind of saved me, I guess. I can't say I liked it a lot, though I didn't mind it too much at first. A lot of rich kids, well educated, sons and daughters of Republicans, that kind of thing. Vacations, I'd stay at the school and eat in the cafeteria with the help. Or I'd be invited to some kid's home and I'd sit there around the Thanksgiving table, trying to remember my manners and turning red with embarrassment when the parents would ask these soppy questions about my past. I can't say I fit in, but I got a helluva education."

Jude felt his recital winding down. It hadn't been painful—quite the opposite: it almost felt good to talk about it.

Tizzie wasn't quite ready to stop. "So your early life in Arizona—you really don't remember anything about it?"

"No, not really. Just little things here and there. Stupid little meaningless things."

"Like what?"

"The heat when we'd go down to the desert. We were up in the mountains, so the days were bearable, but down below, it was miserably hot and the nights were freezing cold. There were some kind of mines there."

"Mines?"

"Yeah, tunnels and shafts, I remember playing in them—exploring them, hiding in the dark, dropping rocks down hundreds of feet. I used to play a lot with this girl."

"Who was she?"

"A tomboy. That's what I nicknamed her—Tommy. Her parents were in the cult, too. We spent a lot of time together." He stopped.

"What is it?"

"It's funny, but I was just remembering. When my mother died, I didn't cry. When my father died, I didn't cry. But when we left there, when my father took me away, I cried my eyes out. It was all because of this girl. She raced along the side of the road as we drove away, and both of us were bawling our heads off. I just looked and looked out the back window as she got smaller and smaller in the distance. We went to some kind of motel. I remember crying for nights afterward. I thought my life had come to an end."

Jude looked at Tizzie, who sighed and squeezed his arm.

Then they stood up and walked back down the boardwalk toward the elevated train rattling in the distance.

# Chapter 11

The Valdosta Baptist Church was a low-slung wooden structure whose sole adornment was a square, chimney-shaped belfry, but no bell. The window panes were covered with decals of garish reds, blues and greens, separated by black squiggly lines, meant to evoke the stained-glass grandeur of the medieval cathedrals of Europe.

In the basement, sweltering despite an air-conditioning unit that groaned and dripped a steady stream of water on the garbage cans outside, Skyler lay upon a cot. It was uncomfortable, made of canvas tightly stretched upon crisscrossing wooden legs, which rendered it easy to dismantle with all the other cots when the screaming children came in for morning day care and the homeless were given a quick bowl of cereal and put back out on the streets.

He was depressed. He had every reason to be depressed. He had been there for—how long?—days and days, it seemed, more than a week surely. Lost, hungry, desperate, he had wandered the streets of the city in a crash course to come to grips with the insane new world he had dropped in upon so unthinkingly. He felt like a voyager from another planet. The frenzy, the noise, the filth—it all crowded around him and pressed in upon him in an overload. Never mind understanding it, just try to survive it. The cars careering around corners, the crowded sidewalks, the menace lurking in every shadow. It was like the worst of the TV programs shown back on the island.

On his first day, after walking away from the airfield and pushing through a hedge, he'd approached a young girl to ask where he was, and she'd turned and fled. Children made fun of his old clothes, dogs barked at him. It began badly and got worse.

That first morning was forever imprinted upon his memory. The plane was still droning on when he awoke with a start; panic rose up as palpable as the bile in the back of his throat. His nap had left him disoriented and frightened, and he felt claustrophobic in the baggage compartment. His arm was sore where the dog had lunged at him. He had an irresistible urge to take his bearings, to scout out the situation, and so, cautiously and slowly, he raised his head to peer into the cabin.

There was the back of the pilot's head, baseball cap in place just as before. But outside through the windows, everything had changed. Gone was the blue expanse of water. Instead, there was only land—and so much of it! It extended in all directions as far as he could see, patches of dark green for trees and long strips of brown soil that looked deep and rich, the way fields back home looked at planting time. There were chocolate brown rivers snaking through the landscape and rounded humps for hills—all of it wreathed in a fog that made parts of it disappear and reappear.

There were long black ribbons—roads—and upon them were cars that moved slower than the plane and turned this way and that like little animals that had minds of their own. And as the plane flew on, they came to a more populated area, roofs and roads, and a bright green field with brown paths that puzzled him until he realized it was a baseball diamond. They were flying lower now: more houses, more roads and cars, and a large round wooden tower with writing on it. What was that for? The plane banked, and Skyler saw something large and dark on the ground that was moving below them, and he was alarmed until it dawned on him that it was the plane's own shadow.

Suddenly, the pilot spoke. Skyler dropped down in terror and didn't move. The pilot spoke again, but in a casual, disengaged way, so that Skyler surmised that it had nothing to do with him. Once more, he dared to look over the partition, and he saw the pilot in profile, with a little tuft of gray hair poking through the forward hole of the backward baseball cap. He recognized him—Bryant, the handyman in the Big House. Knowing who it was made everything seem more real and even more frightening. Bryant was holding a receiver in his hand, and Skyler presumed that he was communicating with someone on the ground.

Not long after that, the plane banked again and came in for a landing, setting down on the runway with a bump. The engine abruptly squealed louder, and at that moment the aircraft began to slow; then it turned sharply to the left, and moved ahead until the engine tapered off and stopped with a sputter. There were more noises close by—clicks and snaps and footsteps coming down the aisle toward Skyler. He realized that Bryant was standing right above him; he could almost feel him looking down upon him. He stopped breathing and held every muscle rigid, the pulse pounding in his temples. Then, suddenly, the tarpaulin moved. Skyler was ready to spring up, and was gathering his strength to do so, when he heard the door swing open. He moved his hand; the suitcase that had been at his side was gone. Bryant was already outside.

The footsteps disappeared, and Skyler waited until he could hear nothing. He got out of the plane and stepped onto the tarmac in the shade of an open hangar under a corrugated metal roof. He looked in all directions: no one in sight. Nearby was a two-story tower topped with large, square windows and a rotating metal object. Beyond that was a brick building with windows that reflected like mirrors, and a parking lot half filled with cars. To Skyler's left was a metal fence, and farther on, a hedge, and through that he could see a road. It was already hot as blazes.

He ran—just ran straight out as fast as he could, and when he came to the fence, he vaulted it, cutting his arm on the uppermost metal spike, and then he struggled through the hedge. Then he ran some more up the road, turned and looked behind him. No one was following him. He slowed to a quick walk and looked around. There were large signs on stilts. One said AQUALAND and showed children with their mouths open plummeting down a slide filled with water. Another was for a gas station. At a crossroads, he came upon a sign with red letters against a yellow background, mounted on rubber wheels, which read: COME JOIN US FOR DINNER. But no one was around. Then he approached the young girl walking down the sidewalk and asked her for help, and she turned and ran away.

For two days, Skyler had wandered the streets, eating out of garbage cans outside restaurants and begging for loose change, which he had never seen before and had to learn to use. His beard grew to a stubble, his stomach ached constantly, and his skin became pasty and he got as thin as a saint. One morning, when he awoke in a park, he saw that the sky was filled with dark, billowing clouds and the wind was whipping up; he knew a storm was coming. The streets emptied out, and just as the rain started to hammer down, a police car came along and picked him up and took him to the homeless shelter in the church basement.

It turned out it was not just a storm, but a hurricane, and it was a terrifying experience. While the wind howled and the rain pounded outside, the men fought inside. There was a lot of drinking and stealing, which scared him. Once, a man who had been talking to himself wounded another man with a knife and was expelled; he left, shouting vile words. At night, the man on the cot next to him, who grunted that his name was "Smokey," taught him to roll his clothes up in a bundle and sleep on them so that they wouldn't be stolen. Skyler began to wonder if Baptiste hadn't been right—maybe the mainland was one great big cesspool.

The religious people who ran the place gave him an extra shirt and a pair of pants and insisted that he attend services. He was amazed to see a statue of the crucifixion on the altar; he kept quiet, his eyes wide with amazement at the reverence with which they read from the Bible. He liked the singing, though.

His bunkmates taught him how to earn a few bucks by bagging groceries, weeding gardens and washing windows, and collecting bottles to refund at the Winn-Dixie market. He saved a pathetic fistful of coins, and lived on the shelter's cereal and sandwiches, and on bread and french fries that he snuck from the cans behind Karla's Fish & Crab.

For the next couple of days, he and Smokey joined a small gang of Mexicans and Salvadorans that picked peaches. The first morning, everyone made fun of him, because he was too terrified to mount the open back of the truck that was to carry them.

"Boy, where you from?" shouted the owner, pushing up the wide brim of his straw hat. "I seen backwoods boys before, but I never seen one like you."

Just as he was about to drive off and leave him, Smokey whispered something to two other men, and they jumped down and hoisted Skyler onto the truck bed, where he rode sitting down, bouncing among the crates and burlap bags. The orchard was miles away. Smokey taught him how to carry a long white ladder on his shoulder, and a young Mexican girl with a stunted thumb taught him to pick the peaches by stretching up with one hand and pinching them off. They were given cards with numbers on them, and when they picked a bushel basket full, they carried it to the foremen, who inspected the peaches and poked a hole in a grimy card with a handheld punch. Skyler was embarrassed that even the small children filled more baskets than he. It was exhausting work that hurt his back; peach fuzz stuck in his skin, so that when he rubbed his arms across his forehead to wipe off the sweat, it felt like hundreds of microscopic splinters.

They were not paid the first day, and so had to return to the orchard the next morning. That day, finally, the foreman looked at their cards and doled out dollar bills grudgingly; they were small denominations but fresh bills that still smelled of ink, and no one objected. Smokey took Skyler's pay as well as his own, but then they got separated and he disappeared for two days. When he returned, stinking of gin, he handed over only twelve dollars.

The next morning, Skyler changed his clothes and walked four blocks to Hill Street, passing the Southern Salvage Company, an army and navy store, and Currie's Body Shop, until he came to a lot where there were two large, rusted storage tanks fitted with a tall white flagpole, from which drooped an American flag. Next to it was a blue and orange sign that said: HARDEE'S—VALDOSTA'S PLACE TO EAT—and underneath, in smaller letters: *All you can get, gravy Sunday.* But they were only serving breakfast. And when he came back later, the waitress insisted upon seeing his money before he could be seated, and he had to spread out everything, including the coins, on the counter. They sat him alone near the kitchen door. He ate ravenously, and after he returned to the shelter he felt sick.

Smokey had been around, and he liked to tell stories starring himself that suggested he knew the ways of the world.

"You know," he confided one evening as Skyler lay on his cot, staring at the acoustical tiles above, "this town will give you money just to leave it. That's a fact. You go down to the police station and they'll take you right over to the bus station and buy you a bus ticket to anywhere you want to go. Only thing is, you have to stay gone."

Skyler took to escape by daydreams. In the evenings, his stomach half full from the baloney and peanut butter and jelly sandwiches served by the shelter, he would retire to his cot and cover his eyes with one bent arm and spend hours in drifting memories of the island. He did not even know its name or how far away it was, and he did not want to tell Smokey or anyone else about it.

Mostly, he thought of his early years there, when life had seemed simple, straightforward and joyful. He thought a lot about Raisin, but he was not ready to think about Julia—that was still too painful.

One evening, Skyler's daydreams were summarily interrupted. Big Al, the supervisor of the shelter, a man who stripped to his waist and so showed a mountainous belly and thick shoulders covered in a carpet of hair, walked over and kicked a leg of Skyler's cot.

"Follow me," he commanded.

Skyler did as he was told, and trailed behind the big man into his closet of an office. Unbeckoned, he sat across from the desk, which was cluttered with phone books, rags and papers, an ink stand and a teddy bear. The wall was festooned with mechanics' calendars of women bending over to show their bosoms and thrusting out their pelvises.

"I just don't get it," said Al, shaking his head as if genuinely confused.

Skyler was the one who was confused. And Al's tone of voice did not augur well.

"You guys coming down here, taking advantage of Southern hospitality."

Skyler looked him in the eyes, but all he could read there was anger.

"I suppose you think it's cool. Big-time writer, grow a beard, come down here, pretend to be what you're not."

Al sat back in his chair, slightly more reflective, ready to strike a pedagogic note.

"I tell you, I don't mind a man being poor, no crime in that at all. But I can't stand a man pretending to be what he's not. Especially if that something is lower than he is. 'Cause that makes him just as low as he's trying to be. You get what I'm saying?"

All Skyler could do was shake his head in dumb incomprehension.

Al sat forward, hunching his elbows on the desk. The air conditioning set the hair on his shoulders moving in waves.

"Let me ask you—you collecting stuff for a new book? You getting lots of—what do you call it?—*material?*"

Skyler knew it was incumbent upon him to say something.

"I don't know what you're saying. I have no idea what you're talking about."

"Oh, you don't, doncha?"

With that, Al picked up a newspaper and threw it. It struck Skyler in the chest and fell onto his lap. He picked it up and looked at the page that it was opened to. He still didn't understand.

"Look at the picture," commanded Al. Skyler did. It was a photograph of a man, and it looked a lot like him.

"I have to admit—you almost had me fooled. All that nonsense about being slow and so confused. You should get an award for best actor. I have to hand it to you."

He looked at Skyler hostilely and shook his head. "I'll give you five minutes to collect your stuff and get out."

In no time, Skyler found himself out in the back alley, a small bundle under one arm.

"Here," shouted Big Al after him. "Take this as a souvenir of your sojourney down South." He threw the newspaper at Skyler's feet and closed the door with a slam.

Skyler picked up the newspaper. It was called *USA Today*. He looked at the photograph and saw that it didn't look exactly like him, but close enough to make someone think it was. It appeared to be an ad for a book of some sort. *Death Mask.* It mentioned New York. He read the name of the author and tore the page out, folded it up and put it in his pocket. Then he shuffled off toward the police station.

# Chapter 12

Jude was late for work, and so he approached Bashir wary of a long conversation. He was tempted to duck into the neighboring deli for his morning container of coffee, but the Afghan would have probably spotted him, since his coffee stand was positioned to keep the competition in sight. That would have constituted betrayal and opened a breach in their relationship.

"Morning, Bashir," he said.

He got a gold-toothed smile.

"Morning, boss."

Bashir often called him that.

The Afghan wiped his hands on his apron, plucked a container from the top of the upside-down stack, flipped it under the spout and pulled the tiny black bar toward him, leaning back slightly.

"So," he asked, "everything okay?"

"Things are fine. How about you?"

"Hunky-daisy."

"Hunky-dory."

"Okay."

The handsome olive face clouded over. Bashir moved closer and leaned down to the window.

"Boss, let me ask you"—the voice dropped to a conspiratorial level—"you okay? You in any kind of trouble?"

Jude was nonplussed. "What?"

"Are you in trouble?"

"No, of course not." He was confused. "Why do you ask?"

"Nothing, nothing."

Bashir hesitated, as if he were loath to cross some invisible boundary. He decided to.

"It's just that I see things."

"Like what?"

Bashir was practically whispering now, and moved his eyes around, in almost a parody of looking vigilant.

"I think you're being followed."

"Come on!"

"I mean it. I've seen the guy. Big, muscles, mean-looking. He's got a streak in his hair, like white paint or something. You can't miss it."

"Why do you think he's following me?"

"Because I've seen him. More than once."

Jude laughed it off.

"It's true. He stays back and watches you and then he comes."

"C'mon, get out."

But one look at Bashir's face told him that he was not joking. The man really believed what he was saying.

As Jude walked away, clutching the coffee, he shook his head at the absurdity of the idea. Still, the Afghan *was* serious. He wasn't making it up. Before Jude entered the *Mirror* building, he turned to look up and down the sidewalk. No one was there—or rather, a lot of people were there, but no large, muscular man with a distinguishing streak in his hair.

He had to admit, sitting there at his desk, that he was feeling a bit spooked. *Who wouldn't be? Being told you're being followed.* His mind ran through the possibilities. *Someone angered by a story? Someone's boyfriend? Some ancient enemy?* Nothing clicked, and he decided it was futile. *Nothing to it, I'm sure. Just Bashir being . . . Bashir.*

It would help if he got a decent assignment. He hadn't had one in almost two weeks—not since the mutilated body up in New Paltz. That had been a good story—quickly reported and written like a dream, even if it had been cut to shreds. *What the hell*—the story that muscled it off the front page hadn't been a total loss: it had led him to Tizzie. She was the best thing that had happened to him in a long time.

After their stroll on the boardwalk Sunday, he'd taken her home to her apartment on the West Side, and she had invited him up for the famous cup of coffee. She hadn't even got around to opening the beans before they were on the couch. His disclosures had evidently touched her deeply. She was passionate and responsive, but still, he felt, somewhat restrained, as if holding herself back. As for him, he was as sweaty and excited as an adolescent. But he didn't want to press things—it was all too important for that. He wanted everything to go just right.

They'd said a warm good night and had seen each other the night after, club hopping in the Village. They were going to meet again tonight. Three dates in the space of one week—for him that constituted clutter on his social calendar.

He watched the editors conferring and thought he'd check the New Paltz story out again, see if anything had happened worth a follow.

He decided to call Raymond La Barrett, an FBI agent and one of his best law enforcement sources—truth to tell, one of his *only* law enforcement sources. Jude was not the kind of guy to hit it off with cops or Feds. He had met Raymond three years ago while working on an article about the ten biggest drug dealers in New York, guys who plied their trade more or less openly. The cooperation had been intense and had entailed trust on both sides to skirt the libel laws and get enough about the thugs in the paper to put heat on the police. The article had worked, resulting in six indictments and four convictions. Jude and Raymond had met for a celebration at McSorley's, downed a few drinks and exchanged a few jokes, and struck up a mutually advantageous working relationship.

Raymond was eight years older, an advantage that prompted him to call Jude "kid." Until the FBI man had moved to Washington a year ago, placed in charge of a division with the ominous-sounding title of "Special Operations," they had seen each other every other month or so, and twice gone fishing upstate. They'd worked several stories together and even evolved a loose code on the phone to arrange meetings: if one suggested it was "time for a beer," that was the signal; they alternated—one time at a bar near Jude's apartment, the next near Raymond's place. "Just dumb enough to work," observed Raymond, when he set it up.

Jude knew his number by heart.

"Special Ops."

The call was answered by a secretary, who put him through.

"Yeah."

"Raymond, this is Jude."

"How're you doing, hot shot?"

"Okay. How about you?"

"Good. Still working for the same old rag?"

"More or less. And you, I see, are still wasting taxpayers' dollars."

"Flushing them down the toilet as fast as I can. So what's up?"

"No much. I wonder if you can help me with a homicide up here. A strange case, happened a couple of weeks ago."

"You know we don't get involved in that. Strictly local. Unless there's an angle."

"I'm hoping there is. To tell the truth, I'm at a dead end. I was thinking you might have something."

"Go ahead. Hit me." Raymond's tone sounded dubious.

"Up in a small town called Tylerville, near New Paltz. The body turned up and hasn't been ID'ed yet. The face was ripped off and the fingerprints were missing—at least all but one."

"What's so strange about that?"

"Well, I haven't seen it before."

"You *saw* it?"

"Yeah, the M.E. let me in during the autopsy. I practically embalmed the guy."

"Jesus Christ. That's not kosher."

Raymond's stint in New York had broadened his vocabulary.

"No, and neither was what they did to the body."

"Aside from removing the face and burning off the prints, what else?"

"There was this gouge mark on the inside of the right thigh. About as big as a half dollar."

"C'mon, you have to do better than that. You haven't seen a half dollar in twenty years."

"You want the exact measurements?"

Jude flipped through his notebook.

"What's that?—that sound?" asked Raymond.

"Nothing. Just my notebook."

"He let you watch. He let you take notes—who is this guy?"

"His name's McNichol. Something McNichol."

"*Norman* McNichol."

"Yeah. How did you know? Do you know him?"

"Know him, shit. Everybody knows him. He's a kook. The ghoul of Ulster County."

Raymond dropped his voice half a notch and added: "Between you and me, let me tell you something—don't trust the guy. He's a number one weirdo, and he can put you on the wrong path in no time."

"Here it is. The hole measured exactly 3.6 centimeters in diameter. It was almost perfectly round."

"So what's that prove? They opened him up like a bottle of wine?"

"McNichol thought it had something to do with a distinguishing mark."

"He would. Listen, kid, it could be anything. Some kind of wound he got before, an accident transporting the body. I wouldn't pay it too much attention."

"Could it be a Mob hit?"

"Could be. Who the hell knows? If they cut off his dick and stuffed it in his mouth, I'd say you got something. But a little jab to the thigh? It doesn't tell you a helluva lot."

"Will you check it out on your end? See if you've got anything at all?"

"Will do, but don't get your hopes up. And anything involving McNichol's bound to be fucked up."

"Thanks. That's what I needed to hear right now."

"Hey, kid, let me ask you—you recording this conversation?"

"You know I am. Standard operating procedure on all my stories."

"Well, it's not standard fucking operating procedure on my end. So cut it out."

"Okay, next time it'll just be you and me and whoever else is listening in on your end."

"Very funny, kiddo. I'll get back to you."

"See you."

"Right."

The line went dead.

Jude's curiosity had been pricked, and he wondered: could he have misheard? He removed the wire from the receiver, reached into the drawer for the recorder and rewound the type, listening through earplugs. It took him four or five stabs to find the place he wanted. But soon enough, there it was, in Raymond's twangy accent: *"Aside from removing the face and burning off the prints, what else?"*

That's strange, he thought to himself, and he played the tape from the beginning to make sure. *I never told him that the prints were burned off. I just said they were missing.*

He shrugged. It could have been just a lucky guess. But it didn't make Jude feel very comfortable about all these mysteries that seemed to be cropping up around him. In fact, he felt the opposite. Definitely spooked.

---

Jude wrapped himself in a paisley print bathrobe from El Corte Ingles in Madrid, slipped on rope-bottom sandals from an Eritrean shop in the Village, and padded off to the refrigerator in search of more wine. He was feeling pretty good.

Their lovemaking had been even better this time. She had been anything but restrained, even wild at times, tossing her long hair with such abandon that twice it had whipped him across the face. For his part, he had let himself go and plunged into a state of surrender that combined a dreamy vagueness with sharp-eyed focus; it shut out everything but their two bodies, turning and moving together perfectly. He shook his head in amazement, as he collared a half-filled bottle of chablis with one hand and pinched together two glasses with the other.

*Damn.* He had not lost himself like that for some time.

When he returned, Tizzie was propped up against the headboard, looking sphinxlike. Standing beside her, he poured them each a half glass, and as she reached for hers, the blanket slid down to reveal her breasts, small but perfectly rounded with the nipples erect. He gave an appreciative nod and raised his glass in a toast.

"Here's looking at you, kid."

She reached over to pull the tie on his bathrobe, which fell open, revealing his nakedness, and returned the toast.

"And you, Louie," she said. "This could be the start of a beautiful friendship."

He smiled and walked around the bed and sat down beside her, shoulder by shoulder. She asked about the objects in the room, and so he explained the artifacts of his life—where he had gotten them and why he liked them. There were paintings and odd pieces of sculpture and knickknacks from flea markets. She was inquisitive and seemed interested, and he found he enjoyed talking about the objects and noted again that he felt at ease with her. But he couldn't help thinking that this was not the intimate postcoital conversation he had expected.

"And how about that?" she asked, gesturing toward the half-opened closet, where a black negligee hung. It was Betsy's.

"That's the remnant of something that probably never should have happened and in any case is over."

"Don't think I'm jealous," she said. "Because I'm not."

"Not that type or just not now?"

"Neither." She sipped the wine, looking thoughtful. "She must have been pissed off if she didn't come back to get it."

"You're right about that."

"A critical mistake—leaving clothes behind. You never know who might end up wearing them. It might fit me, for example."

"Be my guest," he said.

"Actually, it's not yours to give away, is it?"

It sounded like a rebuke, and he was quiet, choosing instead to put his arm around her. With his free hand he traced the outline of her body, following the curves and dips until he encountered something; it felt like a seam. He lowered the blanket and looked at her side, where there was a long scar, raised and white.

"What's that from?" he asked.

"An operation."

"I figured that much. What for?"

"Years ago, many years ago, I was sick and I lost a kidney."

"A kidney—how?"

"I was given an antibiotic that didn't agree with me. Gentamycin, it's called—it's fairly common. You get it for a urinary infection, which is what I had. Anyway, in some very few cases, it causes nephrotoxicity. It wipes out the kidneys. So I got a new one."

"Christ."

"It's no big deal. It happened long ago. I don't even think about it anymore. I even like the scar."

"I like it," he said. And he leaned over to kiss it.

After another glass and some small talk, he was surprised to find that he was aroused, more aroused than he had been for a long time. He reached over to caress her back, and she immediately turned and moved on top of him. They made love again.

Afterward, he was daydreaming. His mind flitted over the day's events. He thought of telling Tizzie about Bashir's strange warning and the phone call to Raymond, but it all seemed silly and inconsequential now. Something much more significant was happening to him.

He wanted to hold her in his arms, but she pulled away after a short while. She couldn't sleep that way, she explained.

The next morning, Friday, Jude had a set-to with Jenks Simons.

Simons was one of those insufferable, cocky types—every paper has one—who make it a point of pride to know everything that is going on, not in Bosnia or City Hall or some other hot spot, but in the newsroom. He lived not for news, but for gossip. He was rumored sometimes to omit the most compelling morsel from his stories—such as the police knew the murderer to be a man because a bloody fingerprint was found on the underside of the toilet seat—because he enjoyed serving it up at a dinner table. He liked being the center of attention. To make things worse, and to add a firm foundation to the general disregard in which he was held, he was talented.

Jude bumped into him between the two doors of the men's room—Jude going out, Simons going in.

"So," said Simons with a smirk, which looked slightly grotesque at such close quarters, "now we know why you got that twins assignment."

"What? What are you talking about?"

But Simons had already disappeared inside, so that Jude had to wait for him outside in a busy aisle of the newsroom. He waited a long time—so long that he actually began pacing, which was usually all it took to set off rumors that a reporter was having trouble with a story.

Finally, Simons emerged, a flicker of satisfaction on his face that Jude was still there. Jude could care less—he needed to find out what Simons knew.

"So what do you mean?"

Simons feigned incomprehension. "Mean?"

"The twins thing. What in hell are you talking about?"

"Simply that it's obvious why you got it. Because you have a *twin* yourself."

Jude was too stunned to speak. He felt light-headed.

"If you don't have a twin, then I guess it must have been you in Central Park yesterday, rummaging through garbage cans. At least, that's what Helen said—Helen, in real estate news. She said he looked a lot like you. Except of course the way he was dressed—not up to your standard, apparently. She also said that he . . . I think I'm right in saying *he* instead of *you* . . . I mean, giving you the benefit of the doubt and all that—"

"Simons, so help me, I'm going to wipe that smile off—"

"All right, all right. Calm down. What she said was that he looked pathetic. *Like a whipped dog* was the expression she used."

Jude looked as if he was about to belt him.

"Look, take it easy. So it's not a twin. But you ought to know there's somebody going around who looks a lot like you."

Jude turned and walked away, but Simons made him look back with one last jibe.

"There, now, wasn't that worth waiting for?"

* * *

At noon, Jude ran into Betsy in the cafeteria. He had just finished consuming a mound of spaghetti, when he saw her pay the cashier and venture into what was euphemistically called the dining area, carrying her tray high before her as if it were an offering. He looked deeply into his peaches, but she spotted him and sat down directly across from him. He smiled, but not for long: what he read in her face was disconcerting—solicitous concern.

"Jude, tell me, are you all right? I mean, you would tell me if you weren't—true?"

She was thrilled. Only his total self-immolation could make her shine more brightly.

"Yes. I mean, I'm fine."

He did not ask why she was concerned—in fact, he had conspicuously not asked why—but he had a feeling that she was going to tell him.

"I've heard these strange things about you—Simons said you were roaming the streets like a bum. Foraging for food in garbage cans. If it wasn't you, it was somebody who looks like you. What's going on?"

It struck him that she fancied that *she* might be the cause of his misery—that he was a casualty of love. That would account for the sprightly tilt of her head.

"Helen," he said.

"I beg your pardon."

"Helen in real estate news. Apparently, she saw someone who looks like me, and she's been spreading these stories. I'm sorry to disappoint you, Betsy, but I really don't know anything about it."

"I see," she said, looking down her nose at him, almost as if he were rifling through a garbage bin right now.

In ordinary times Jude could have sloughed these encounters off. But they were getting to him. He was feeling a vague floating anxiety. It had started with that unsettling exchange with Bashir. Too bizarre. *A man with a streak of white in his hair.* The little Afghan had seemed so damn sure. And now all this talk of a doppelganger. *What the hell was that about?*

Jude did not use *paranoid* loosely. Being a purist when it came to language, he believed the word was bandied about too often in these conspiracy-minded days. But right now if someone had asked him how he felt—assuming, of course, that he would answer truthfully—he would have replied: "Paranoid."

* * *

Over the weekend—on Sunday—Tizzie and he had their first fight.

Saturday night, she had seemed distant and distracted while they were dining at a restaurant on Third Avenue. At one point, he saw her peer over his shoulder, her eyes widening before she glanced away. Jude turned and, looking through the window, he thought he saw someone, a man perhaps, or a shadow, sliding off into the darkness. Tizzie made light of it and said it had been nothing, really, just a horrible-looking man leering inside. She had not finished the main course, and they left soon after.

The next day, he was feeling ill and decided to stay in bed. Tizzie came over, letting herself in with the brand-new key that he had given her—to him a symbol of a turning point in their relationship, but to her little more than a convenience. She had not, he noticed without remarking on it, given him a duplicate of her key.

He was running a fever. She busied herself in the kitchen, making him soup and tea. When she brought it to him, he didn't want any. She tried to take his temperature; he resisted. She added an extra blanket, and he took it off. All her fussing bothered him—this female need to nurture—it seemed almost as if she were nagging. He snapped at her.

"What I really need is to be left alone."

She flinched. He saw a hurt pass across her face that quickly turned to anger.

With that, she spun on her heel and walked out, slamming the door.

He kicked himself: why the hell had he acted like that?

He called her later and apologized and she seemed to accept it, but her voice had taken on a cold tone, which was disturbing. He was bothered by how much it bothered him. They had known each other for scarcely two weeks and he felt—for the first time with a woman—that he cared for her more than she did for him. He wasn't accustomed to the seesaw turning that way up. Maybe he liked her too much, he thought—maybe that was why he couldn't accept her ministrations.

From the first, he had felt comfortable in her presence, able to speak his mind honestly and drop the poses that he had adopted with others. He discovered, with a bit of surprise at first, that she seemed to actually like *him*, and not some image of him, and he relished the candor this brought out in him. Maybe she could finally open him up, the way other women had said they wanted to.

But did *she* want to? That was the question. He had thought they were going great guns. If it was up to him, they would move in together, but he was loath to bring the idea up—new honesty be damned—because he sensed that she would not go for it. Something about her remained out of reach, inscrutable, and it fed a fear in him that her interest in him might soon flag.

Face it, he told himself, you are more involved with her than she is with you. He wanted to know everything about her—what she'd been like as a child, where she spent her vacations, how her day had been, what she was thinking. She was reticent to fill in the blanks. Some role reversal—*he* had always been the one accused of being unreachable.

And now it was the beginning of a new week and Tizzie was away on a trip—she had not even told him where she was going. He kicked himself again for acting like a jerk. When she came back, he'd have to do something especially nice for her.

On Monday, feeling better, Jude did some book publicity.

He was still a little mystified by *Death Mask*'s success, thanks in part to the gobs of promotion dished out like scoops of mashed potatoes and gravy. The publisher, coincidentally Tibbett's own company, had gone so far as to mail tiny white death masks to the major reviewers. Jude had to admit he was impressed.

During the day, he gave interviews about the book. He found it trying—he was accustomed to asking questions, not answering them, and it bothered him that with each interviewer he fell into a set piece of patter. The whole thing was more than a little unreal. He would hear a tape of himself speaking; the words were recognizable, he remembered saying them, but his voice sounded like a stranger's. It was like seeing his picture turning up in the newspaper ads; when he came upon it out of the blue, the sensation was strange, almost as if he were looking at a photograph of someone he vaguely knew.

Christ, he thought. Get a grip on yourself.

The book signing that afternoon at Words Ink down in SoHo had all the earmarks of a disaster. Jude got there late, trapped in sweltering heat for twenty minutes while the number six train sat in semidarkness between stations and a voice on the p.a. system told them what they already knew—that the train was delayed. He got out at Astor Place, and at that precise moment, the sky opened and let loose one of those torrential summer downpours.

He ran to the store and burst through the door out of breath, his hair plastered down and water streaming from his brown corduroy jacket onto the thickly polished wooden floor. The manager, a woman in her fifties who wore her hair in a tight bun, greeted him with a bony handshake and a pinched smile. He looked around: a small writing desk with a leather top had been set up near the window with a stack of his books to one side; a poster was draped across the front showing his picture and the ubiquitous white death mask. Across the way was a sideboard with crackers laid out in a circle and cubes of bright yellow cheese, cracked like parched earth. Next to them was a cluster of green wine bottles and a battalion of plastic glasses—many more, he could see in an instant, than there were people to drink from them.

The manager followed his eyes and read his thoughts.

"We don't usually have signings for . . ."—she was searching for the right word—"your kind of book."

It sounded like an accusation, and any doubts that he had on that score were swept away by her next statement:

"The pressure from our uptown office was intense."

Jude was still working on a clever retort when she cupped her hand under his elbow, guiding him to the desk. "Why don't we just position you here?" she said, in the officious tone of a teacher taking a new boy into the classroom.

"I need a glass of wine. To steady my nerves."

Since she thinks I'm Jeffrey Archer, Jude thought, I might as well play at being Dylan Thomas.

"Certainly. We'll bring it to you."

He wondered who the "we" was. Aside from the two of them, there was one clerk and a few scattered customers, skulking around the Travel and Biography sections. The scene was every author's nightmare: a stack of unsold books and no one to sign them to. He downed the wine in one gulp and held out the plastic cup for a refill. She carried the glass to the sideboard, her face drawn in disapproval.

Jude draped his wet jacket on the back of his chair and settled in behind the desk. It was made of fine mahogany and so comfortable it almost inspired him to want to write something, maybe in longhand with a quill pen. He wished a customer would come by so that he could compose a florid inscription. The rain outside was still pounding down. He picked up a book off the top of the stack, opened the page at random and started to read. The prose struck him as overwritten and amateurish, so he closed the cover loudly and downed another cup of wine. This time he got up and replenished it himself. He picked up a book on the way back, a copy of *Catch-22*.

A young woman in a green trenchcoat with the belt tied at a jaunty angle came in, wandered over to the desk, and looked at the poster, then at Jude, then back at the poster.

"Yes, it's me," he said, in what he took to be a droll voice.

"It's *I*."

"Beg your pardon?"

"If you're a writer, you should know the correct way to say it is: *It's I*."

"I'm not that kind of a writer," he said.

"What kind are you?"

He hadn't expected that question, and said the first thing that popped into his head.

"A people's writer. Ungrammatical. Idiomatic."

"I see."

She picked up a book and leafed through it, her brow furrowing. Jude tried to read her forehead: was it concentration or disdain? Then to his amazement, she carried it to the cashier, paid for it and held it out to him to sign it, her slender fingers cradling the spine as if it were a delicate animal.

"Jude Harley," he wrote in expansive slanted letters. "Power to the People. Seize the Day."

"Unusual first name," she ventured, quizzically.

"It's short for Judas. From Judas Priest. The heavy metal band. My mother was a groupie."

She smiled uncertainly, closed the book and left, closing the door gently behind her. Jude took another cup of wine and realized that he felt terrific. Judas Priest: he was going to have to use that one again.

Over the next forty-five minutes, a dozen or so people came in, and three of them bought his book. Between sales, Jude read *Catch-22* and practiced a disinterested, *poet maudit* slouch, and now that he was on his eighth cup of wine, he was feeling no pain.

Then a remarkable thing happened. A tour bus parked down the street, and the store was invaded by a throng of sightseers, glad to be in out of the rain and laughing and joking in broad Midwestern accents. They seemed bigger than the shop itself. And when they saw Jude behind the desk, they were fascinated, approaching him with a mixture of curiosity and caution, as if he were an exotic dog chained to a stake.

"Well, look at this," said one gentleman, wearing glasses with no-nonsense clear plastic rims.

Jude grinned uncertainly.

A gray-haired woman posed two friends next to him and took a snapshot, the flash of the camera temporarily blinding him.

"Emma, I know you'll have a story to go with this one," piped up one of them cheerily. They all laughed.

"You bet," Emma shot back.

She walked over to the desk and picked up a book, weighing it with one hand as if it were a cucumber.

"What's this about, young man?" she demanded.

Jude did some cold calculating. "New York in the nineties. The night creatures, the bars, the netherworld. Life in the belly of the Beast."

"Is there sex and violence?"

He calculated some more. "A little."

"Of which?"

"Both."

"Sold," she proclaimed, loud as an auctioneer, and the others laughed, crowded around and grabbed at the stack. He was signing away like a man possessed, engaging in chitchat, tossing off clever ripostes, asking first names, writing "to Vickie" and "to Herman" and "for Babe" and "with best wishes" and "fondly" and "with memories of New York" and even throwing in the odd quote from *Catch-22*, when he chanced to look out the window.

The rain had turned into a downpour, a solid curtain of water pounding onto the pavement. Looking at it from inside was like looking out through a waterfall—everything was blurred and smudgy, an Impressionist painting. Suddenly, in the middle of it, a face appeared. Jude froze and stared. He felt from some instinct, as surely as if chords of music had sounded, that this bleary vision would prove meaningful. He stared harder. It was a man, drenched and hunched over. The figure moved closer to the window through the curtain of rain, so that gradually its features became more distinct. And as Jude stared, his mouth dropped open. He thought it looked exactly like him, his own visage staring back at him. The face was perhaps a little younger, but that was hard to tell—it was unshaven, grisly, deranged-looking. Their eyes met for only a second, and Jude thought he detected a current of recognition. Then the figure backed away, became blurred again and was gone as quickly as it had appeared.

Jude pushed his chair back and jumped up and ran to the door. He couldn't get it open immediately, and he saw the manager approaching out of the corner of his eye, but he gave a final tug and then pushed and it flung open into the rain. He ran outside and was instantly drenched and looked in all directions, but could see nothing. He ran up the street, then doubled back and ran the other way, then back again. But he found no one. The apparition had vanished. He stood there, in a doorway, for a long time, wondering what to do.

When he got back to the shop, the tourists were leaving, eyeing him suspiciously. He stood in the rain until they had all departed and then went inside. The manager was toying with a button on her blouse. Jude walked over to the desk, picked up his jacket, and stood before her in a puddle of water. He mumbled an apology, but he was too distraught to make it eloquent, and he saw that she was looking at him with genuine sympathy.

Jude made his way through the stygian gloom of the Times Square subway station, half in a daze. Above him was "the crossroads of the world"—the place to meet anyone. But he had never heard of an encounter such as the one he had just had, running into himself.

In SoHo, he had grabbed a bite and drunk three cups of coffee to sober up. Sitting alone in the diner, he couldn't get the image out of his mind. It was an image he had seen his whole life—*his own face.* At moments, he recalled it as clear as a bell—as if his own visage had lunged out of a mirror to grab him by the throat. In particular, it was *the eyes.* When he'd stared into them for that millisecond, he'd felt he was peering into the recesses of his own soul.

But at other moments he could convince himself that he was mistaken, that he was ranting on because of some tramp that had been attracted by the lights and warmth of the bookstore window. Nothing more than that. And then of course there was the wine, the excitement, the heady feeling that came with signing all those books in that strange Dickensian shop. Could that matron have spiked the wine? Possibly, he told himself. But unlikely, he admitted. He knew what hallucinogenic experiences were like, and they were not like that. He had been slightly drunk, but otherwise in possession of his faculties. And then, of course, there was that other sighting—who was it? Helen. She had undoubtedly seen the same man.

He'd left the diner and boarded a subway home. Now, in the Times Square station, he turned a corner. On the left were three young men in track pants and high tops lurking near a bank of wall telephones. To the right, across a pavement studded with black globules of old chewing gum, was a newsstand manned by a bored-looking Pakistani. Unsold stacks of the *Mirror* towered above its rivals.

He negotiated a path through the crisscrossing crowd toward the shuttle to go to the East Side. He waited with two dozen others under a crackling sign that eventually flashed the track number, and then they all moved on together, purposeful as a lynch mob. They crossed over a makeshift bridge of iron slabs laid across the tracks, past open darkness and screeching trains, and ran into a flood of exiting passengers. It took a full half minute to move ten paces.

The car was already full when he stepped across an eight-inch gap to board. The line of seats were taken by exhausted faces of all colors and hues, eyes deadened. He reached for a strap and held on as the train left with a lurch, pressing him into sweaty bodies on both sides.

"Excuse me," muttered a woman who spiked his left foot, sounding not at all sorry.

He looked across the ragged white-scalp part in her jet black hair to study the ads above for hemorrhoids and blurred vision and facial skin peels. The sound of punk rock, distant and tinny, came at him from a pair of earphones to his right. His eyes drifted across the sea of heads and hair and gear toward the rear of the car, and through the back window into the car behind.

It was then that he saw him. A large, muscular man, with a white slash through his hair. The man was looking at him, and Jude caught him in mid-expression; it was an ugly look—he seemed to be almost leering, brazenly—and Jude thought it was directed at him. *But why?* He had never seen him before in his life. For a moment, their eyes locked, then the man dropped his glare and made a half turn so that his back was to Jude. Jude looked around the car hurriedly, then again through the rear window into the car behind. The man's back was turned in a slouch. He was swaying with the rhythm of the train and rocking his shoulders slightly, like a boxer. People around him were giving him a wide berth.

Jude tightened his fist around the handgrip. He felt his pulse quicken and his stomach tighten. He scrutinized his fellow passengers. No one was noticing, no one was paying any attention. The eyes were deadened. He tried to think; the white streak, the very thing Bashir had mentioned. Could it be a coincidence? Surely, in a city this large . . . And anyway, what could happen to him in the middle of a crowded subway?

He held his breath, turned slightly, and looked again through the rear window. *He's staring at me.* Again, the man turned his head away. The white spot, a streak above the left eye, looked like a dab of paint.

Instinct took over. Jude fled. He let fly the strap, turned and plunged through the throng toward the car ahead. He spotted openings, little spaces between people, and he made his way to them, squeezing through like a wedge, not caring who he pushed.

"Hey, motherfucker, watchid."

People swore, frowned, stared daggers.

He reached the door to the forward car. An elderly woman was leaning against it, and he practically picked her up and trundled her to one side, grabbing the metal door handle and thrusting it to the right. It resisted, then abruptly gave way. He stepped out. There was a sudden rush of hot wind and the screaming sound of metal wheels rounding on steel track. The door behind him slammed shut. He was between the two bouncing cars, one foot on each, dancing madly. Groping in the semidarkness, he finally found the other door handle. He grasped it with both hands, swung it wildly back and forth until it clicked and the door retracted.

Jude turned to look behind him. He saw faces staring at him in puzzlement and annoyance, but he did not see the man. Ahead was a wall of people, but he did not hesitate. He bent his head and dove through the wall, twisting and turning through the sweaty bodies. People backed away from him in alarm, and just as he reached the exit doors, he felt the train grinding to a stop. The doors opened and he bounded out and sprinted without a backward glance.

He ran, dodging the oncoming passengers. He raced down the platform, under the stairway to Grand Central and into the tunnel that would take him to the Lexington Avenue line. It was surprisingly deserted, and the newsstand at the entrance was locked behind a metal gate. His own footsteps echoed back at him, and he could hear his heavy breathing. He slowed and looked back. No one was following him—in fact, there were only a few scattered souls, walking slowly. Ahead, there was no one at all, and the tunnel darkened and narrowed. It looked frightening, and so he resumed the pace, feeling a stinging on his soles as his feet slapped down on the concrete. In the foul air, his lungs began to ache.

At the end, the tunnel opened into a subterranean labyrinth of columns, passageways and descending stairways. Jude knew the route, and without skipping a beat, he cut straight across the oppressive concrete concourse, half as wide as a football field. Ahead was a staircase with a black and white enamel sign reading UPTOWN, and as he reached it, he paused for a moment, held onto the handrail and peered back the way he had come. No one. He felt relief, and still catching his breath, he made every effort to collect himself and amble down the steps as if nothing had happened.

The platform was deserted—almost. Ahead of him, pacing slowly in the opposite direction, was a figure, a man in a leather coat. Jude stopped dead in his tracks. He squinted in the half-light and looked hard. Something about the figure was already familiar, an arrogance to the rolling stride. Instantly, a wave of fear passed through Jude. He did a double-take. *It couldn't be. But it was. It was the same man!*

He was unmistakable—there it was, the patch of white, gleaming like a wound. Jude slipped behind a column and hid there, his heart pounding, holding his breath and standing stiff, so that not a stitch of clothing would show. He could hear the man walking up and down the platform; once he cleared his throat, an unpleasant bark of a sound. It was dumbfounding, beyond belief, there was simply no physical way for the man to have arrived ahead of him. *How did he do it?* For the moment, Jude banished the question and concentrated upon escape.

He chose his time carefully, waiting for a convergence of distractions. Soon enough, a subway pulled in two tracks over, emitting an ear-splitting racket that drowned out everything else. He watched until the man resumed his pacing and turned his back, and then he bolted and took the stairs two at a time, stopping at the top to look back. He could see the legs, still pacing. He raced across the concourse and through the turnstiles to the exit, then up more stairs and into the twilight air cleansed by rain.

Once outside on the sidewalk, Jude did not stop running. He ran to Third Avenue, then north for four blocks until he spotted a cab with a rear door swung open, one leg and high-heeled shoe dangling outside. Inside, a woman in an evening dress was laboriously counting her change. Jude held onto the door handle. She smiled at him as she stepped out, and he weakly smiled back, then jumped inside and gave his address. He fell against the backseat, spent and frightened.

The traffic was heavy and the cab moved slowly. It was not air-conditioned, and Jude lowered both windows as far as they would go. He could smell the perfume of the previous occupant, a powerful, exotic scent. A matchbook and a half-smoked cigarette lay on the floor. The driver switched on the radio, and a talk-show host was attacking a caller in an aggressive, nasal voice; something about welfare. Jude scanned the pavements on both sides. People were walking home from work, carrying briefcases and groceries. A young couple strolled down the sidewalk, arms around each other, easy as royalty.

The cab took a sharp turn, cutting off a pedestrian whose face, two feet away from Jude's, registered anger. It pulled up to Jude's building, a five-floor rent-controlled walk-up on East Seventy-fifth. Jude paid, tipping heavily, and looked both ways as he stepped out. Nothing untoward. The sun was hanging westward over the city, bleeding red upon the street.

Opening the front door, he entered the vestibule and passed his mailbox, filled with letters. He unlocked the second door and stepped into the dingy central stairwell with tiny, cracked black-and-white-tile floors and a rough staircase whose heavy banister was encrusted with layers of mud brown paint. It was a depressing space, and he usually hurried through it.

But this time he paused. He was breathing normally, but his senses were still alert from his flight from the subway; his vision was strong and hearing sharp, and he felt ready to spring at a moment's notice. And he thought he heard something—not much, nothing loud, a whisper of a sound from the shadows under the staircase. It was an indistinct rustling, the vague sound of someone drawing breath.

Jude took his foot off the first step and walked halfway down the hall, close enough to see a shivering, pathetic-looking figure in the shadows. Too small to be the man with the white hair.

"Come out of there," he commanded in a voice whose authority surprised even himself. "I can hear you. I know you're there. Come out."

Jude stepped closer.

There was a hint of movement in the darkness, more rustling, and then suddenly and all at once, a person materialized and stepped forward into the glare of the light from a dangling cord.

Jude was transfixed, struck dumb.

Before him stood a quivering tramp in rags, his long hair matted and falling to his shoulders. But there was no question—take away all that and it looked like Jude himself, almost exactly like him. It was his double, though oddly youthful despite the grime upon the face.

Then it spoke.

"Don't hurt me. Please don't hurt me."

The voice was shaking, scared. It carried an odd accent, slow and Southern-sounding, but unlike any Jude had heard before. And what really struck Jude was the timbre of the voice—it sounded just like the tapes he had heard of his own interviews. It sounded just like himself.

# Chapter 13

"What's your name?"

It was such a basic question that Jude felt stupid for not asking it earlier. Certainly he was not thinking clearly. He was still reeling from the first sight of Skyler, this apparition that seemed like a nightmarish version of himself, all bony and straggly-haired like some Old Testament prophet come to preach Armageddon.

Nothing had fully prepared him for the shock of standing face to face with someone who looked so much like him—not the rumors and talk, not even the brief sighting outside the bookstore. Yes, he had been perplexed and intrigued by all that, but he hadn't seriously contemplated the reality that he had a double and that the double would one day step out of the shadows of the stairwell and sit down in his living room.

He kept staring at the mouth, the chin, the nose, the eyes. They looked just like his own. *How can this be?*

It was impossible. Yet it was real.

"Your name. What's your name?"

Jude repeated the question to the pathetic-looking figure perched on the edge of his couch, as he had had to repeat various other questions over the past twenty minutes. So far the double had done little to shed light on the enigma of his appearance.

"Skyler."

"Skyler? Is that your first or your last name?"

A look of bewilderment.

"Do you have parents? Brothers or sisters? Do they have the same name?"

Jude was feeling exasperated, and his interrogation was taking on a hard tone—probably not a good idea, he thought.

"No."

"Then let's assume it's your first name. How about a second name? Do you have any other name?"

Skyler hesitated, but only a moment. He was thinking.

"I guess you could say Jimminy. We were all called Jimminies."

"Who is *we*?"

"All of us in the Age Group. On the island."

"What island? Is that where you come from? What's the name of the island?"

Again came that look of bewilderment, descending like a curtain.

"We didn't call it anything. We just lived there."

"What state was it in? What country? Is it America? Are you American?"

Skyler shrugged.

"I think so."

"*Think so! Jesus Christ.* How is it possible to grow up and not even know what the hell country you're in?"

The truth was, Skyler was wondering the same thing himself. He was also feeling wary. With good reason, for all he knew. He was not as shocked as Jude was to see a double of himself—the thought of finding Jude had been the sole purpose for coming to New York, and he had been searching for him for almost two weeks. Still, he recalled the jolt when he'd first set eyes on him in person as he was hiding behind a stoop across the street. Jude had stepped out of the door and there he was—someone who looked virtually identical and even had the same way of walking.

Skyler had every reason to proceed cautiously. He knew as little about Jude as Jude seemed to about him. Who was to say what role Jude had played in the terrible events on the island? Did Jude have any connection to the Lab or to Dr. Rincon? And what if he was in some way responsible for the death of Julia—the memory of which cut into Skyler afresh every time he thought of it, like the knife cutting into Rincon's portrait.

Skyler had contemplated the unknown Jude during the bus trip north, as he'd stared out the window at the converging roads and railroad tracks. It had been a harrowing trip. The names of the cities and towns had come and gone in a mindless profusion. He'd sat glued to the window; there'd been a flow of frigid air from the vents around it, which made him shiver nonstop. Next to him had sat a succession of outsiders and rejects, some garrulous and others frighteningly taciturn, lost souls all. Late one night, when the overhead lights were extinguished, a man with tobacco on his breath had reached over and touched his leg, and Skyler had pushed him away and had to change seats.

He had had no idea what he would discover in Jude, provided he succeeded in finding him—whether he would be a friend or an enemy. Then had come more than a week of hellish days and nights in the city, scrounging for food and sleeping in Central Park. He'd tracked Jude down when a bum on a park bench had told him he could look him up in the phone book. Other than that, no one had spoken to him; he was an alien. It would not have surprised him if people had begun to stone him. He became desperate. He saw an ad for the book signing, but had gotten frightened when he saw Jude close up. He'd waited outside the building on East Seventy-fifth Street and slipped inside behind another resident and hid in the stairwell. Throwing himself on Jude's mercy had been a branch grasped by a drowning man.

There was, too, something else. Skyler had seen Jude being followed by the Orderlies. He was thunderstruck with fear when he saw them—and he rapidly deduced that they must be looking for him—but it was at least somewhat reassuring to see them on the trail of his double. They would hardly be doing that if they were all in league together. The enemy of my enemy is my friend, Skyler reasoned, and so he decided for the moment to trust Jude—but only up to a point.

Jude tried to pry out more information. "How did you find me?"

"I tracked you down."

"But I mean: how did you *know* about me?"

"I saw an ad in the newspaper. For your book."

"Where did you see the newspaper?"

"In a place called Valdosta."

"Hallelujah. At last, a name."

Jude fixed his uninvited guest a meal of leftovers from the refrigerator, some chicken wrapped in tin foil, rice in a plastic bowl and salad. Skyler ate ravenously, chewing with his mouth open and hunched over the plate with his elbows on either side, as if protecting it. Jude recoiled from the sight at first and then became fascinated, watching wordlessly and examining him closely from top to bottom. He took in the dirt tracing the wrinkle lines, the leather skin, the foul-smelling oversized pants, the hair on the back of his head encrusted with mud.

He had to admit, he was fascinated. His guest *did* look an awful lot like him—except younger perhaps, definitely younger. It was hard to tell under all that dirt. And there were a number of little gesticulations and mannerisms that they had in common, tics almost, which he had already noticed. When Skyler had looked at him searchingly a few moments back, he had tilted his head ever so slightly to one side, the way Jude was wont to do. And standing in front of the kitchen table, before sitting down to eat, Skyler had rested with his weight on one leg, the left leg, which was a stance that Jude often adopted—he had even had that pointed out to him once by a woman who had found it sexy.

But did Skyler look *enough* like him—to what? . . . be a relative, a brother perhaps or even something closer? Jude knew that in the back of his mind, he was toying with one outlandish possibility—that this person stuffing his face at the kitchen table was nothing other than a long-lost twin. That was, he had to concede, one conceivable explanation, and it had the virtue of providing a rational explanation for what he saw with his own eyes. Occam's razor, they called it in science, the principle that the simplest hypothesis is the best to account for an unexplained phenomenon. And this was certainly an unexplained phenomenon.

*But was it really possible?* On the one hand, Jude thought, such things happened. In fact, coincidentally—almost *too* coincidentally—he had just written an entire article on the subject. And, after all, Jude knew almost nothing about his own childhood or his parents; they had been members in that cult. It was not altogether inconceivable to imagine that his mother had given birth to twins and that the infants had been torn apart by happenstance—perhaps even by the command of the cult leader. If ever there was a candidate for this kind of stupefying twist of fate, it was Jude. *Vanishing twins*—that was the catchphrase Tizzie had used. How strange it was that he had just learned it.

On the other hand, maybe the whole thing was just an amazing accident, some bizarre confluence of chance that defied the laws of probability. Maybe they weren't related. Maybe they just happened to look an awful lot like one another. Was that out of the realm of possibility? What were the odds that two people born of different parents in different parts of the world could end up looking the same? Jude was not ready to dismiss that hypothesis, but he had to admit that the more he examined Skyler, the more he inclined to the proposition that they were, in fact, twins. Strangely enough, he seemed to feel the truth of that inside him, a subliminal knowledge that had always been there, the same way he'd felt a shock of recognition when Tizzie had suggested his left-handedness could mean that he had shared the womb with someone else.

The dawning possibility made Jude feel guilty for thinking bad thoughts about Skyler. He *did* look repulsive, the way he ate. And he appeared hopelessly clueless, way out of his depth. Even accepting that somehow they were separated twins, Jude couldn't help wondering where Skyler had been raised, that he had grown into such an ignorant creature. That mystery, Jude told himself, was well worth solving, and he suspected that if he could just find the key, it would also open the door to his own lost childhood.

Jude went to a cupboard, pulled out a bottle of scotch and poured himself a full glass. He took a gulp, then sipped it reflectively while waiting for Skyler to finish.

"Let's take it from the top," he said finally, handing Skyler a napkin to wipe his face. "How old are you?"

Skyler looked him directly in the eye—for the first time. He seemed calmer and better disposed after eating.

"Twenty-five or so."

"Or so?"

"It's a difficult question, because we didn't have birthdays. We tried to keep track on our own, us Jimminies. But I can't be exact. I know I'm about twenty-five."

"But you could be older?"

"I could be, but I don't think so."

"You didn't count the years?"

"We counted the years, but not from the beginning. And as I said, we didn't mark birthdays. We were told that aging was not a natural process to be celebrated—on the contrary, it was something to struggle against, to overcome with the help of science."

"Who told you that? Your parents?"

"No. None of us knew our parents. We were told that we belonged to the Lab, and in particular to Dr. Rincon and to his servant, Baptiste."

"Can you tell me everything you know about these people?"

And so, with a scarcely audible sigh that amounted to a figurative toss of the dice, Skyler began the lengthy narrative of his life. He told of his earliest memories on the island, of growing up with only a dim, half-formed idea of life on "the other side," of taking the goats to pasture and running through the woods with Raisin, and going to the lecture hall on campus for science lessons. He told of Baptiste's lectures and Dr. Rincon's law, and how the Lab detested religion and believed in extended life and a new age, the dawning of rational, scientific living. He also told about the Orderlies and about Kuta and his own special education in his shack and his growing doubts and fears. And finally, he told of his escape.

He mentioned Raisin's death and Patrick's death, but he did not go into detail, and he spoke not a word about Julia. She was his and his alone; the love that had defined his life for so long was private, and that loss was not for the sharing.

Jude was far from satisfied. Too many questions were bouncing around in his brain, and he had been at pains to hold himself quiet until Skyler finished his story, loath to break the spell now that he was finally learning some basic facts. Then he forgot some of the questions. He had refilled his glass three times and found that his initial shock at seeing Skyler was now padded with numbness. He was not thinking altogether cogently.

"This Rincon—what was he like?"

"He was a demi-god." He had heard that expression on television once. It seemed to fit.

"Did you ever see him?"

"No. He came to the island once, but we were kept away."

Jude took another gulp of scotch, a big one.

"So you've never been to Arizona?"

"Arizona?"

Skyler's blank look supplied the answer.

"How about some early memories—anything about going underground, playing in mines?"

"No. Nothing."

"Anything about a desert, a place where it's hot by day and cold at night?"

"No. Nothing except the island. My first memories are all of the island. I'm sure that's where I grew up."

"Did anyone ever tell you had a brother?"

"No." Skyler paused. "Is that what you think we are?"

Jude ignored the question and came back with one of his own.

"How could you not know your parents? Didn't you know anything about them? Didn't you hear anything? Didn't you miss anything?"

"You don't miss what you never know. The way we were raised, all of us—it's hard to explain—we felt all the older people on the island were like our parents. They all looked out for us."

"But why did they have all those strange titles—physicians and things like that?"

"That's just what they were called."

"It sounds like some big hospital. Was it some kind of medical place?"

"I don't know what you mean. It was just the way we were raised. We were looked after carefully, and anytime anything was wrong, it was fixed right up."

"But they didn't love you."

"I used to think so—or else, why would they have done it? I don't think so anymore."

Jude was stumped. He drained his glass and set it down.

"Tell me again about these Orderlies, the guys who did the enforcing."

"You've already met them," replied Skyler, and Jude knew instantly who he was talking about. He felt a certain relief, but not all that much, in realizing that his paranoia had a foundation in reality.

"The guy with the streak of white in his hair?"

Skyler nodded.

"You said *them*. There's more than one?"

"There's three."

"Three?"

"Yes, and they all look a lot alike, except you learn to tell the difference. The white patch isn't quite identical."

So that explained it, thought Jude—how the thug had managed to outflank him in the subway. There had been two of them. But three? He looked at Skyler. "Three guys who all look the same? Identical triplets—I've never heard of such a thing."

"I don't know if they're identical. They look a lot alike, but like I said, you can learn to tell them apart." Skyler shrugged, a gesture to end the discussion.

"Jesus Christ."

Skyler looked at him. "Why do you keep saying 'Jesus Christ' like that?" he asked.

"What do you mean? What kind of question is that?"

"I was just wondering. You say it all the time."

"I say it whenever I need to say it. Which right now happens to be a lot."

"I see."

Jude got up, walked into the living room and poked around his bookcase. He returned a few minutes later carrying under his left arm a large blue book, which he laid upon the kitchen table. It was an atlas.

"Okay, you say you were raised on an island. Let's locate the sucker. You say you ended up in Valdosta. That's in Georgia."

He flipped through the index, found "southern United States" and turned to pages 178–179. His finger traced the outline of the coast. He was distressed to see how many islands there were. Scores and scores of them. And lots of little ones that weren't even named, at least not in this book.

"Let's see . . . Valdosta, Valdosta. There it is."

He was surprised that it was so far inland.

"What kind of plane were you in?"

Skyler conjured up the memory—the cabin with its four seats, the baseball cap on the pilot's head, the dials with needles fluctuating and lighted numbers.

"A small one. Red and white."

Jude's face showed his exasperation. "Propeller or jet?"

Skyler looked blank. "I know what you're going to say now," he said.

"What?"

"Jesus Christ."

"Very funny. You've been here an hour, and you think you already got me down pat."

Fifteen minutes later, Jude was prepared to concede defeat, at least for the time being. He figured that the island had to be off the coast of Florida, Georgia, South Carolina or, stretching it, maybe North Carolina. The number of islands along that expanse of shoreline was staggering. Furthermore, he knew that his atlas was incomplete and omitted hundreds of small islands. He had once been to Pawley's Island off South Carolina, and a local had taken him out crabbing in a rickety rowboat; he remembered being amazed at how many uninhabited bits of land there were tucked away in the marshes.

For his part, Skyler was hopeless in providing clues. All he could say was that the aircraft had put down in that one town in Georgia. He couldn't even estimate how long the plane ride was that had brought him there, since he had slept through some and perhaps most of it—a statement so patently ridiculous that Jude was inclined to believe it. Maybe later Jude could get some data on the fuel tank capacities of various planes and estimated flying times in order to try to plot a radius of likely distance traveled. This would at least narrow the search for likely candidates to an area of . . . what?—maybe five hundred miles. But he would need some more information to do that. In the meantime, he had to figure out what to do with Skyler, who seemed to fear for his life.

"These guys—what did you call them? 'Orderlies.' That's a peculiar name—I wonder what that signifies. A moment ago, you said they're brutal. What did you mean?"

"Just that. They were in charge of us. They were friendly when we were growing up. We looked up to them like brothers. But I began to feel that they kept us on the island by force, that if we tried to leave, they would hunt us down."

"And what would they do? I mean, would they actually kill you?"

Skyler said he didn't know.

"So that's why you think they're after you now—to kill you?"

He shrugged, then nodded yes again.

"But that doesn't make any sense. Why would they want to kill you? Just for leaving the island?"

"Maybe there's another reason."

"What?"

"To prevent this, what just happened."

"And what's that?"

"My meeting you."

The answer stopped Jude cold, and he spent some time in thinking it through. It didn't make sense. So what if he did have an identical twin brother, and so what if they were separated at birth, either intentionally or through some sort of accident? Why in God's name would anyone take such drastic steps just to keep them apart? On the other hand, why were those guys on the subway following him?

He looked across the table at Skyler, who appeared exhausted. He slid the bottle of scotch to him.

"Here. Try some of this. Maybe it'll buck you up."

Skyler raised the bottle to his lips, took a swig and felt the fiery liquid grab the back of his throat. He sputtered, leapt to his feet, grabbed his neck and ran to the sink, ran the tap and took a long draught of water. He turned, water dripping down his shirt, his eyes wide.

"Jesus Christ," he exclaimed.

Jude could not help himself—he laughed, so hard that he rocked back and forth in the chair, and at that sight Skyler smiled himself and even let loose a chuckle. It sounded for all the world like a chuckle that Jude might make.

"Here, sit down," said Jude, pulling a chair out from the table. "Before we go any further, there's something I've got to do."

Skyler sat in the straight-back wooden chair. Jude rummaged around in a drawer and came up with a large pair of kitchen scissors. He clicked them twice in the air, pulled out a dish towel, and stood behind Skyler, placing the towel around his neck and tucking it into his collar. As he placed one hand upon his shoulder, feeling the thinness of the bone underneath, Jude realized that it was the first time that he had touched him.

The hair came off in great swaths, falling onto the towel and Skyler's shoulders and onto the linoleum in little piles.

"Nothing fancy," Jude said, turning to look at Skyler's face head-on and measuring the sides with a critical appraisal. "We'll get you a real haircut tomorrow. This is just to get you through the night. You can't stay here looking like that. Shit, any neighbors see you, you'd give me a bad name."

With his locks sheared, Skyler looked halfway presentable. He also looked more like Jude—though thinner and more raw-boned. Also, thought Jude, he looks younger than before.

Maybe it was the liquor, but Jude was beginning to feel bound to Skyler. He felt a strange ambivalence. Some moments, he felt protective of him, as if he were a feral boy who needed a kindly human hand. At others, he felt repelled and even angry, as if Skyler was an interloper who had no right to thrust himself into Jude's world—to claim a piece of him, as it were. And he noticed that as his feelings kept flipping back and forth, so too did his perceptions. One moment he would acknowledge the uncanny similarity between the two of them and think they were virtually identical; the next he would reject it and wonder what he was doing feeding and tending a total stranger. He felt as if he were looking at a double-illusion painting, but he could not find a reference point to hold one image steady and he had not the slightest idea which was real and which was fake.

In any case, he had already made a decision that he would help Skyler out of his difficulty, whatever it was. His mind was running ahead to tomorrow. He wondered if he was placing himself in danger and—if it came to that—how big a risk he was prepared to run. He didn't know. How extraordinary. He thought: I've known him for all of an hour, and already on some level I know that he is going to change my life in some significant way—perhaps irrevocably.

"You better get some sleep," he said. "You can take my room. I'll sleep on the couch. I'm not ready for bed right now anyway."

He put a hand on Skyler's shoulder to guide him. They walked through the living room into the bedroom. Jude went to the dresser and pulled out a pair of blue-striped pajamas, and tossed them on the bed. He looked at Skyler's face, already familiar, and read his mind.

"They're called pajamas," he said. "We wear them at night when we sleep. Welcome to the twentieth century."

Jude showed Skyler the bathroom, especially the taps, and thought he would be impressed by hot and cold running water. He did not know that Skyler had stopped listening, that Skyler was no longer paying attention to anything he said.

Skyler's mind was roiling. His pulse was racing, and he was exerting a huge effort simply to try to appear normal, to control his emotions, as if nothing had happened. It was almost impossible for him to do.

For he had just seen something that had turned his world upside down. When he had stepped into the bedroom behind Jude, his gaze had taken in the bureau drawers, the pine shelves crammed with books, the large bed. And then it had fallen upon a bedside table and something that was on top of the table.

"Good night," said Jude.

And Skyler mumbled a few words in return.

As soon as Jude left the room, Skyler rushed over to the table and clutched the photograph of Tizzie. He held it up and studied it minutely, then sat on the bed and stared at it some more. His pulse raced even harder.

The hair was different, more luxuriant, falling in waves. The cheeks were not as full and the cast of the eyes looked a bit older. But other than that, there were no major differences. There was no doubt about it—the face under the glass, looking back at him with a smile, was Julia's.

When Jude awoke on the couch, his head ached and his mouth felt as if a vacuum cleaner had sucked it dry. The hangover preoccupied him for a moment or two, blotting out everything else. Like an inchoate but cumbrous shadow, the improbable happenings of the night before loomed in some back corner of his mind. But not for long. The memories sprang to life, and the shadow vaulted onto center stage. In the morning light that streamed in through the blinds, amazement mixed with incredulity.

Was it possible? he asked himself, half hoping that he had dreamed the whole episode.

But then he heard Skyler, already up and stirring.

He found him in the kitchen, sitting at the table, doing nothing. He appeared drained and exhausted, with yellow circles under his eyes. The haircut Jude had given him was showing its imperfections, with tufts of longish hair sticking out here and there, and his unkempt beard brushed the top of his chest. He was still in the blue-striped pajamas, so that sitting there, and looking up somewhat wide-eyed as Jude entered, he had the appearance of a lost and bewildered man-child. Which was pretty much the case, Jude reflected.

"Coffee?" asked Jude, already running the water and pouring out the coagulated pancake of yesterday's grinds from the filter cup.

"No."

Jude set the coffee going, cupped his hands under the cold water and splashed some onto his face. He looked for the dish towel to dry off and then saw it over on the counter, crumpled up with a pile of Skyler's hair sticking out. He used a paper towel instead. Then he took four aspirin.

"Well, I see you're not a morning person," Jude said. "Funny thing, neither am I."

Skyler looked at him, but remained silent.

"Okay, have it your way," said Jude.

He cooked them a large breakfast of orange juice, toast, bacon and sunnyside-up eggs. Again, Skyler ate hungrily, though not quite as slovenly as the night before, and when he finished, he carried his plate streaked with egg yolk over to the sink and sat back down at the table.

"I want you to know . . ." he began haltingly. "I mean, I'm grateful for all this, for the food, for the bed. I just don't know . . ."

He trailed off and looked away.

"I just don't know what to do. Where to go. I don't have any idea . . . how I am going to live."

Jude looked at him. Skyler's voice had a slight trembling to it. Jude thought that his own voice caught in the same way when he was upset.

"Now, c'mon," said Jude. His hangover had abated, and in its place he felt a light-headedness. "You don't have to worry. No one's going to hurt you. I'll see to that. We're in this together."

He wasn't convinced all that was true, but he thought it would make Skyler feel better. He could see that he was getting more and more upset.

Skyler gripped him on the arm and squeezed, so tightly that his fingers dug into the muscle of his forearm. When Jude looked up, he saw that Skyler's chest was heaving up and down, though no sound was coming from him.

"C'mon. What's the matter?"

As soon as he said it, he thought it sounded fatuous, but it seemed to strike a chord in Skyler.

"I just don't understand what's going on."

"Well, I can't blame you. I don't understand, either. And I have to say, it's one major shock to come home and find a twin in your hallway."

"Who is that woman in the picture?"

"Picture?"

"The one by your bed. Who is the woman?"

Skyler was still gripping Jude's arm, holding on as if for dear life.

"She's my girlfriend. Her name's Tizzie."

Now Jude was confused.

"Why?"

Skyler didn't answer; he just looked away and let go of Jude's arm.

"Listen, you don't even have to meet her. But don't worry, you can trust her. She comes here sometimes."

A new thought occurred.

"Jesus Christ. I don't know what the hell I'm going to tell her."

Skyler stood up and started pacing around the kitchen. Neither of them spoke for a while. Eventually, Jude, as host and man of the world, felt it was incumbent upon himself to come up with a plan of action. He moved into the living room and motioned to Skyler to follow him.

"First thing we do," he said. "is we've got to find you a place. It's not safe for you to be out wandering the streets, and it's probably not a good idea for you to stay here."

He walked over to stand beside the blinds with his back to the wall and lifted them with two fingers to peer out. There seemed to be nothing unusual on the street.

"Pretty soon we'll have more Orderlies around here than a god-damned hospital."

He sat Skyler on the couch and talked to him in a tone that was slightly patronizing.

"Soon I'm going to go out and find a place, nothing fancy. You stay here and don't move. Whatever you do, don't answer the phone. If somebody comes to the door and knocks, don't answer it. Understand?"

Skyler nodded.

"You look horrible. I'll bet you didn't sleep all night. I'm going to give you some pills—they're sleeping pills—and I want you to take one. No more than one. It won't hurt you, it'll just put you to sleep. But first, you've gotta get cleaned up. Take a bath. You know how to shave?"

Again, Skyler nodded.

Minutes later, Skyler was standing in the bathroom. As Jude had instructed, he had deposited his old clothes in a plastic bag to be thrown out. Some new clothes, Jude's, were piled on a chair. Hot water was running in the tub, and the mirror before him was steamed over. He tugged at his beard with the razor; it was tough going and he cut himself two or three times, but eventually he got it off, watching as the bits of black hair and shaving cream swirled down the drain. He wiped the mirror with the palm of his hand and looked at his reflection.

Jude had been right about one thing—he had been up all night. How could he possibly have slept after his discovery?

He was hopelessly, totally confused. Once he had begun to talk to Jude, after the frightening encounter in the stairwell, he had gradually begun to trust him. For one thing, Jude had seemed so completely stunned when he first laid eyes on him. And then the more Skyler told him, the more he had seemed perplexed; he'd ended up sounding as much at sea as Skyler was. And as Jude was puzzling it out with him, sharing his theories and his amazement at the story of the island and the lives of the Jimminies there, Skyler had begun to feel something he hadn't anticipated—a comradeship, a sense of alliance. Maybe it was because he was so lonely and desperate. He needed Jude to be on his side if he had any chance of discovering the truth about the Lab. But Jude himself inspired some of the feeling: he did not *seem* to be playacting. He *appeared* trustworthy.

But now Skyler did not know what to think. The photograph had changed everything. Or had it? It was impossible for there to be another Julia in the world. And yet the person—Tizzie, he had called her—was a dead ringer. She looked as much like Julia as Jude looked like Skyler. But how could that be? Was the whole world peopled with doubles? Could it be that Jude was playacting after all, that he was part of some conspiracy that had killed Julia because she had learned too much and now would do away with him? He would have to be on his guard.

Skyler took off the pajamas and flung them into a corner.

He stepped into the tub and lay down. There was something else that he did not admit to in thinking about the photograph. It had shocked and saddened him, arousing memories of *her*. But it had also awakened something—a quickening in his pulse, a dream, a wisp of hope. There was, it seemed, someone who looked like Julia. Maybe in certain ways, impossible as it was to contemplate, she would act like her—maybe she could almost *be* like her.

From somewhere Skyler heard a sound, the splashing of water on a tiled floor.

Jude lay on his bed, arms behind his head, staring at the ceiling. He had put on a little charade for Skyler to give him a gift of hope. He had pretended that he had a plan of action, so that they could at least believe that they were doing *something*. But truth be told, he didn't have the vaguest idea of what to do or where to turn. This was the damnedest thing he had ever heard of.

He would have to take it step by step, figure things out one at a time. He would have to play this chess game by instinct, to move the pawns at the start and worry later about the endgame. First, it was important to get Skyler out of harm's way. He would probably need a disguise of some sort. Jude wondered: would Skyler be more in danger or less in danger if he looked like him?

Maybe he should reach out for help. Sooner or later, Tizzie would have to know. On impulse he dialed her number, but there was no answer. Still out of town, wherever she was. Her message voice sounded coldly formal, and he left just his name on the machine.

It was when he was hanging up the phone that he heard something—the sound of water splashing.

*Jesus Christ.* The guy's a real hick—he can't take a bath without overflowing the tub.

Jude ran over and flung open the door. The tub was overflowing, and Skyler was turning off the faucets. When he finished, he lay back and stretched out in the tub.

Then it was Jude's turn to be puzzled. For he noticed something on Skyler's body, a little blue mark on the inside of his right thigh. He pointed toward it.

"What the hell is that?" he asked.

"That's our mark. We all have them."

*"We?"*

"The Jimminies."

Jude looked at the mark more closely. It was a little larger than a quarter, and it was a curious design; it looked like two babies facing each other, joined at the hands.

"Holy shit," exclaimed Jude, actually raising one hand in a gesture of astonishment. "It's a tattoo. Someone gave you a tattoo."

He stared at Skyler.

"And you don't mean *Jimminy*. You mean *Gemini*."

---

Jude was speeding across the Tappan Zee Bridge. The car was moving so fast that the steel supports of the span flickered in the light like an old black-and-white movie. The Hudson below winded off to the north as far as the eye could see, and sails dotted the blue water, white commas.

His mind was racing. None of it made sense. The mark on Skyler's thigh was clearly significant, and the fact that he and the other members of his "Age Group"—whatever that was—called themselves "Gemini" was also significant. What that significance was, Jude couldn't say. But the mark had triggered an association. Was it a coincidence? Or could the victim in Tylerville have been carrying a similar mark on his thigh? A mark that someone—the killer—felt compelled to obliterate? It seemed that the mystery was widening and deepening at the same time.

At least the clue gave him something to do, a starting point. As a reporter, as someone whose job was based on digging out truths that others didn't want exposed, that's what he needed—a starting point. Now that he was on the trail, he would follow it like a tracker, taking care to pick up more clues and avoid the wrong ones. He would stay the course until it led him to a dead end or to paydirt.

For the moment, he was flying. His destination was New Paltz. The room for Skyler could wait. This was more important.

His first move, after Skyler was cleaned up and wearing a presentable pair of blue jeans and a T-shirt, had been to place a phone call. He'd done it from his kitchen, so that Skyler wouldn't hear. It wasn't that Jude distrusted him. He simply felt that at this point, until things became a little clearer, the less Skyler knew, the better.

"Special Ops," the secretary answered.

Jude gave his name. This time, almost a minute passed before Raymond picked up.

"Hey, kid, how you doing?"

"Good. You?"

"Fine. Just fine."

Jude was making an effort to flatten his voice, to drain it of any sense of urgency, and he had the feeling that Raymond was doing the same thing.

"So I'm just checking in. Still following up that murder in New Paltz. I wondered if you got anywhere—if you were able to get an ID on the victim."

"Shit, yeah. It just came in. I should of called you. I meant to, but you know how it is—I've been busy."

Jude opened up his notebook. "So who is it?"

"Well, that guy McNichol did some job. The one print was no good. But it turned out the guy was in the DNA database—not ours but one of theirs. He sent it through and he got a hit. What sealed it was that the guy was right from there. A judge, I think."

"Do you have the name?"

"Hold on, I'll get the file."

Raymond put the receiver down. Jude heard a rustling of papers, then Raymond's voice again.

"You know, I'm not supposed to do this. It's not our jurisdiction, so this call never happened."

"Okay, understood."

"Where you calling from, anyway?"

Raymond didn't usually ask a question like that. Where did it matter where he was calling from?

"The office."

"Kind of early to be at work."

"I'm trying to clear up a lot of stuff," Jude replied. Then he added: "I'm thinking of going away for a while."

"Oh yeah, where?"

Jude was sorry he'd opened up that avenue. In fact, he wasn't really planning a trip.

"I don't know yet."

Raymond gave a grunt—it seemed a sound of disbelief. "Well, here's the name. Got a pen?"

"Yeah."

"He's a judge, like I said. Joseph P. Reilly. 197 West Elm Drive. Tylerville."

"Got a phone?"

"Unlisted."

"Yeah, but you have ways."

"Like I said, it's not our case."

"Anything more on the judge? What kind of judge is he—was he?"

"Not sure. Some kind of state court, I think."

"Okay, thanks. Oh, one more thing."

"Yeah."

"How come the judge was in the database to begin with? I thought that was for convicted felons."

"Ours is. So's New York's. But some of these agencies freelance. As an officer of the court, he had to set an example. As I understand it, at least according to McNichol, the guy didn't want to at first. It raised a ruckus in the local papers."

"Interesting. Anything else worth knowing?"

"Nope. Strictly routine. Except, of course, the murderer's still on the loose."

"Yeah. Okay, thanks again."

"Don't mention it. You can write a flattering article about me someday—the way you did with McNichol."

A small alarm bell went off in Jude's head. "But that didn't get in. The story was cut to shreds."

"Enough got in. It was a blow job. You should be ashamed."

After the call, Jude had made Skyler promise to stay put in his apartment. He was getting a little tired of playing nursemaid. After the bathtub incident, he'd felt he had to show him everything if he wanted to keep the apartment in one piece: where the light switches were, how to work the stove, and how to lock the door. Again, he'd cautioned him about the telephone—only answer it, he said, if it rings three times and then stops and then rings again. That was their code. He'd told him again to take the sleeping pill and said he'd be back by evening.

Then Jude had grabbed his jeans jacket and tape recorder. As he was closing the door, something in his conversation with Raymond registered. He went back into the kitchen and left a few minutes later, with two filled Ziploc plastic bags stuffed into the left jacket pocket.

McNichol wasn't at his funeral home in Tylerville, so Jude drove over to the hospital in Poughkeepsie. He walked hurriedly by the front desk, ignoring the receptionist who waved to get his attention, and dashed down the staircase. Below was an office he hadn't seen, and the door was slightly ajar. He leaned around it and saw McNichol sitting at a desk, his glasses propped up on his forehead and a pile of papers spread before him.

McNichol did not seem especially pleased to see him, and the bonhomie of the other day appeared to have vanished. As Jude made an apology for bursting in upon him, the M.E. kept looking distractedly—even longingly, Jude thought—at the paperwork on his desk. Jude concluded he must have been miffed because the story had gotten such measly play.

Jude felt he was working on borrowed time, so he went right to the point—flattery.

"I heard you got a successful DNA match. That's good work."

"Well, yes, as far as it goes."

"And the victim turned out to be a judge?"

"Listen, ah . . . what's your name again?"

"Jude Harley."

"Mr. Harley. As far as anything about that is concerned, you'll have to go to the police. It's all in their hands now." He paused. "I don't understand what happened. It's been nothing but trouble."

Jude understood. The death of a judge could be big news. The M.E. had undoubtedly gotten into a heap of trouble for letting them observe the autopsy. That reporter from the local paper, Gloria, had probably blown him out of the water. Publishing so many details about the cause of death could definitely put a crimp in the police investigation.

"I'm sorry if the story made your life difficult."

"Difficult—that's an understatement. Would you believe somebody broke into my lab? They stole the autopsy specimens. That's never happened to me before."

"Why would anyone do that?"

McNichol shrugged and turned away.

It was time to switch the subject.

"Actually, I'm not here about that," he said. "I'm here because of a mystery, and I wondered if I could ask your help."

At the word "mystery" McNichol seemed to perk up. His eyes forgot his papers, took on a sheen of curiosity, and bored into Jude's quizzically. Jude reached into his jacket pocket and pulled out the two plastic bags filled with dark swirls. He held them up, swinging them ever so slightly, like a present. One contained Skyler's hair and the other had a matching swatch; only someone examining the back of Jude's head with a magnifying glass could have said where it had come from.

Jude left the hospital and found himself in a cluster of municipal buildings. He walked two blocks to the courthouse, a magnificent red-brick structure with a bas relief of blinded justice above the entrance. He stepped inside a phone booth, pulled out his notebook to find Gloria's number at the paper, and dialed it. As soon as she heard his voice, she said she was on deadline on a story about electrical rates and gave him the brush-off. He shrugged. Too bad—she could have filled him in on the judge's death.

He stepped inside. On one wall was the listing of courtrooms and offices, a glass casement of white letters stuck into bands of black velvet. He scanned it. COUNTY COURT JUDGE JOSEPH P. REILY. Room 201. The name leapt out at him—it hadn't yet been removed. A fine example of small town delicacy, he mused.

He thought he might at least drop by the office to see if he could get some information about the deceased. Conceivably, the judge's secretary would have a bio of him or perhaps even a copy of his obit. He walked up to the second floor and knocked on a wooden door with a large frosted glass that had 201 stenciled in black. A female voice told him to enter. He did, and saw that it belonged to a black woman in a red blouse. She looked as if she did not brook fools lightly.

Jude introduced himself and expressed his commiseration, which succeeded only in drawing a dumbfounded look.

"Just what exactly do you want?" she demanded.

"The judge . . . Judge Reilly . . ." Jude began.

"He's in chambers, three doors down on the right."

She turned away.

Through his fog of astonishment, Jude found the judicial chambers. He stepped inside, into a crowded room done entirely in oak veneer. The benches were crowded. It was a warm afternoon and three windows were wide open, but they let in little breeze. Up front, on a raised dais, with an American flag on one side and a blue New York flag on the other, sat the judge, a remarkably young man. His nameplate was in front of him. He looked vigorous and, more to the point, he looked very much alive.

And more than that: Jude noticed that the judge did seem to bear a resemblance to the corpse he had seen—more or less the same height, the same build. Other than that, given the condition of the body, he could not say.

His mind reeled. So the judge was not dead. But then whose body was it? And why was there a resemblance?

Jude sat down on an aisle seat. He had the impression the judge had been watching him as he'd entered the room.

Now he was certain of it—the judge was staring at him.

Abruptly, the judge frowned, looked away and looked back at him again. He seemed to turn pale. He rose and turned as if to leave, collected himself and came back to strike the gavel once, and then he did leave. A bailiff followed the judge out of the chambers, looking uncertain. He soon returned and banged the gavel himself. Peering out over the crowd, now milling about, unsure of what to do, he declared: "Court is in recess."

# Chapter 14

When Tizzie arrived at Jude's apartment, she let herself in with her own key, juggling her purse in one hand and a gift-wrapped parcel in the other hand. She knew no one was home. Up and down the street, lights were blazing in the windows in the gathering dusk, but those on this floor remained dark.

She had picked up his message on the answering machine—no message, actually, just his name. She'd decided to see him, even though she was tired from her trip, so she'd jumped onto a cross-town bus. She would have preferred to go right to bed, but there was that nagging sense of guilt. She had been distant toward him lately, cold, and she hadn't wanted to be. She had received mixed messages from him; he seemed to want intimacy, but every time she took a step toward him, she felt him pull back. And she was holding something back, too. In an odd way, as much as she cared about Jude, she was uncomfortable with him and she didn't know why. That was what made her feel guilty. It was partly to appease that guilt that she had bought him a handsome cable-knit sweater in a tiny shop in White Fish Bay.

She put the box down on a hall table, stepped into the kitchen and switched on the lights. Her eye deconstructed the mess: an empty scotch bottle stood on top of the counter, and the sink was filled with dishes, including two plates with egg stains. There had been company, that much was clear—a night of drinking and then breakfast, no less. But what in God's name was that kitchen towel doing over there with that dark stuff in it? She examined it—bits of hair. What the hell was that doing there?

The living room told her the couch had been slept in, and she had to admit she felt passing relief. At least Jude had not been unfaithful—either that or the woman was a loud snorer, she joked to herself. She nicked her knee on the coffee table and cursed softly.

As soon as she entered the bedroom, she could tell from the faint sound of his breathing, spaced and steady, that he was there, asleep. That was strange—why would he be asleep at dusk? She approached the left side of the bed and looked down at him in the half-light—the smooth cheek, the long eyelashes, the familiar tousle of brown hair on the pillow. He looked defenseless and wholesome lying there, almost like a young boy, and the sight filled her with a complicated rush of emotion, an amalgam of maternal affection and womanly longing.

She thought that perhaps she should try to take a nap, too; the trip home had exhausted her. She walked around the bed, sat in a chair and unstrapped her shoes and took them off, placing them to one side. She stood up and unzipped her dress, letting it fall to the floor in a heap and bent down to pick it up and drape it over the back of the chair. She slipped her thumbs into the waist of her panties and slid them down her legs, placing them over the dress. Then she unfastened her bra and placed it on top. From the bed, she heard his breathing shift as he moved to a different level of sleep.

She walked to the right side of the bed, lifted the sheet and slipped underneath, pulling it up to her chin. The cotton felt cool to her skin. She wiggled her feet, then glanced over at the man sleeping next to her in the semidarkness. He was turned away so that all she could see was his back, rising and falling so minutely the motion was barely perceptible. She contemplated it for a moment. Even in repose, his back muscles looked strong. Then she scooted over and snuggled up behind him, putting one arm around him and pressing her breasts into his back. She slid her legs behind his. They were like two spoons in a drawer.

He stirred a little, still deeply asleep. She snuggled up against him even tighter, lifting a leg up and placing it gently upon his thigh, which was surprisingly warm. She felt again that unsettling ebb and flow of mother and lover. Again, with her encircling him, he stirred ever so slightly. Then his breathing steadied and she pulled back, retreating to her side of the bed.

She thought he was probably dreaming. She wondered idly what it would be like to make love to someone who was dreaming of making love. Then she turned over, lying on her side and bunching the top of the sheet into a small bundle under her chin, she began to quickly drift off.

Some time later—it was impossible to say how much later, in sleep time—a din broke out. It was the phone ringing, insistent, on the little table on her side. Why wasn't Jude answering it? Grumpily, resentful at being dragged back to the land of the waking, she reached over and lifted the receiver. Who in God's name could be calling at this hour? She cocked herself up on one elbow and brought it to her ear. She was vaguely aware of the body behind her, now moving, also gradually struggling to come to the surface. He was sitting up.

"Hello," she said.

The familiar voice over the phone snapped her to attention immediately.

"Tizzie?" said Jude. "What are *you* doing there?"

She did not respond immediately, so he repeated: "It's me. *Jude.* Is that you, Tizzie?"

"Yes," she said hesitantly, staring over at the man next to her, who was staring back at her with wide-open brown eyes. It was so bizarre beyond all reckoning—to see Jude's likeness before her and hear his voice on the phone—that she was stunned into silence.

"Tizzie," came the voice over the phone. "You must have met him by now. I know it's a shock. You won't believe what's been happening."

She found her voice, finally.

"I'll say," she said.

Jude couldn't say when he first became aware of the headlights trailing him. In retrospect, he thought it was somewhere in the South Bronx when he turned off the Major Deegan for the Willis Avenue Bridge, a shortcut that saved the $3.50 toll but that also meant driving through a stretch of back streets.

He wasn't really paying attention because he was deep in thought, turning the puzzle over and over in his mind. He looked at it from every conceivable angle—and it didn't make any sense from any of them. Hours earlier, he had driven up to New Paltz with the name of a dead man, suspecting only that the murder victim was somehow connected to the group Skyler was involved with. He hadn't known what he would find, but he had hoped that a little digging into the victim's past might turn up something, anything, one more clue to carry the tracker further down the trail. And what happened? He was driving back to New York even more confused than when he had left. It turned out that the victim was not a victim at all, but a living, breathing person, and a prominent local judge to boot. If that was so—and it clearly was—then who had been killed and mutilated? And why did his

DNA perfectly match the judge's? And then, of course, there was the biggest question of all: Why was the judge—whom Jude had never laid eyes on in his life—so upset at seeing him walk into his courtroom? The last riddle was especially disconcerting; it was one more indication that Jude was being dragged by the scruff of his neck into some nefarious plot about which he knew nothing. It was like coming into a movie halfway through—and finding your own face up there on the screen.

Jude had spent the rest of the day trying to unravel the mystery. He checked back in with McNichol, who was doubly annoyed by the second intrusion. Jude didn't want to alienate the temperamental medical examiner for fear he wouldn't perform the little chore he had left with him, but he questioned him enough to ascertain that McNichol stood one hundred percent behind his DNA analysis of the victim.

"Look," the M.E. had finally exclaimed, "I don't see how I could have made a mistake. Some of these hits aren't as clear as others. Some are doubles, some are triples. This one was a home run and it was out of the park."

Then Jude had run a check on the judge. He went into the local library, parked his computer in the "electronic work station area" and called up Nexis to retrieve the computerized file of newspaper clippings. He was surprised at how voluminous it was for someone so young—his own age, thirty. There were numerous articles about the various decisions he had handed down; he seemed to have a knack for drawing the big cases upstate. There were sex-abuse charges, school board zoning disputes, income tax violations, even one on silicone-breast implants. There were a few more profiles in the local press—Jude saw a byline by Gloria, and regretted more than ever that their relationship had soured before it had started. She might have proved useful.

He pulled out his notebook and jotted down the details: names of clubs and associations such as the Lions, Rotarians, and the Century Association in New York; judicial organizations like the American Bar Association and the Ulster County Bar Association; and various do-gooder groups like the Hudson Valley Conservancy, the Poughkeepsie Council for Better Hospitals, and Friends of the New York Neurological Research Organization. There were feature articles and brief mentions and photos taken at galas and society affairs. Jude found the clearest picture, which showed a smiling *Judge and Mrs. Joseph P. Reilly at the Sacred Heart Benefit for the Physically Disabled*, and downloaded it into his computer and then printed it out. There was even a short *New York Times* article dated June 2, 1998, when the judge had been appointed to a group called the Committee of Young Leaders for

Science and Technology in the New Millennium, which was described as an association of "eminent people under thirty-five years of age in business, law, science and politics" whose purpose was to "open the doors to scientific innovations and set priorities for technology in the next century."

*It seems like our small-town judge cuts a big-time figure,* he had thought.

Jude looked in the rearview mirror. Headlights that had been behind him for some time on the Deegan—they were identifiable because one was tilted up a bit and gave off an annoying glare—took the same turnoff that he did. When Jude stopped at a light, the car stopped, too, but it hung back thirty feet or so. No other car was nearby.

Jude registered this somewhere in the periphery of his consciousness, but paid it little attention. He was still absorbed in thinking about that afternoon.

From the lobby of the library, Jude had called Richie Osner, the computer whiz at the paper who could hack his way into any system if he was sufficiently motivated. Jude had given him the judge's name, gone out for a cup of coffee and a stroll, and come back to check his e-mail. Osner had been motivated, all right.

Jude had scrolled through the records he'd dug up. There were three months of the judge's credit card bills, which showed him to be a high spender with a penchant for hang-gliding and racecar driving; his selections in books and CDs, which revealed a taste for trashy novels and cabaret songs; and his driving record—no violations whatsoever, which was not surprising, considering that cops are occupationally reluctant to ticket a car with a judge's license plate. There was even a listing of the judge's prescriptions: various antibiotics, a monthly supply of Pravachol, for high cholesterol, and something called Depakote. Jude made a note to check that one out.

Frightening, he thought, how much you can find out about a person these days by just sitting down at a keyboard.

And, of course, most important of all, Osner had provided the judge's home address.

Jude drove out and found it on a dead-end street in the suburbs of Tylerville. The judge's house was the last one on the street, following a parade of ostentatious mansions that used a variety of stone walls and hedgerows to block the view of passing commoners. Exactly how ostentatious the judge's mansion was, Jude couldn't see, because it was hidden by a ten-foot-high Spanish-style wall of whitewashed rocks topped off by red tiles. How the guy had managed to buy such an estate on a judge's salary was beyond him. He had to be privately wealthy.

Securi-Corps signs were posted at strategic intervals on the strip of bright green grass in front of the wall; they featured a German shepherd guard dog, snarling and preparing to pounce. There was a large metal gate, and next to it a doorbell in its own foot-tall casita sunk into the wall.

For a moment, he contemplated ringing it. What the hell—he could pretend to be looking for someone or to be lost. Or he could just throw caution to the winds and ask for the judge and demand to know why his presence had discombobulated him so. Somehow, looking over at the decals of the guard dogs, these did not seem to be viable options.

Down the street, in the direction from which he had come, was a crew of three men standing beside a pile of dirt and rocks and looking down into a hole that was apparently of their own making. The markings on a truck nearby suggested they were workers for the town water-supply company. They were on a break, smoking, and from time to time they looked up at Jude—not in an unfriendly way, he thought, just curious.

He walked over to them and engaged them in conversation with his practiced reporter's banter, until one of them who had been staring most trenchantly asked him if he was a detective. Interesting question, that. Why would anyone possibly suppose that?

"No, not at all. I'm a reporter for the *Mirror*. Why did you think I was a detective?"

The answer threw Jude for a loop, and it also constituted the only genuine break that he had had all day. When the worker delivered the information, his face assumed that self-satisfied, anticipatory look people get when they are about to impart shocking news.

"Well, this place had been crawling with cops for days. Ever since that body was found, you know, the one that turned up in the landfill. They said he was wearing a red shirt. We seen a guy wearing a red shirt hanging around here days before. He looked like he was trying to get into the judge's house, just like you were."

Crossing the Willis Avenue Bridge, Jude moved over to the right lane to reach the approach to the FDR, and the car behind with the glaring light did the same. Other cars were converging in the lanes to either side, but the company did not make Jude feel less nervous. The car followed him down the FDR.

*Get a grip on yourself. What makes you so sure he's following you?*

Jude calmed himself with the thought that he was, after all, on a major approach to the city. The shortcut he had taken was hardly a secret. *You think you've got a monopoly on it?*

Earlier, he had stopped at a rest area on the Thruway and called his own number to check on Skyler. He had been about to hang up after the third ring when Tizzie had answered. He hadn't foreseen that—what the hell was she doing there?

She'd sounded upset, confused, unable to take it all in. But what did he expect? How would he feel if he suddenly dropped by her apartment one day and found another woman there who was *her* exact double? It sounded like a scenario from *The Twilight Zone*. He hadn't been able to be much of a comfort to Tizzie—his mind had been all over the lot, on the day he had spent and the judge's reaction to him and the worker's bombshell. He'd tried to explain as best he could that Skyler had turned up out of the blue, that he needed help, that they were going to try to "get to the bottom of this." He'd mumbled something about trying to clarify everything, insofar as he could clarify *anything*, when he got home in a few minutes. He had hung up feeling he had botched it.

He came to the sign for the Seventy-first Street exit with the car still on his rear end and flicked on his turn signal and looked reflexively into the rearview mirror. His heart skipped a beat—the car was signaling, too. He slowed down. His palm on the steering wheel suddenly felt sweaty, and he checked the mirror again. The car was hanging back about twenty feet, and its front turn signal was flashing yellow in the darkness. The exit was approaching—Jude had only a few seconds to make his decision. Abruptly, at the last moment, he swerved the wheel to the left, and the right front tire rode over the exit lane divider, so that his car shuddered back onto the highway. In the mirror, the car behind swerved gracefully back on track, directly behind. Its turn signal went out. *Still on my tail.*

Now Jude was truly spooked. There was no question that he was being followed. He floored the accelerator, felt the sudden speed thrust him back against the seat and drove so fast that he didn't dare take his eyes off the road to check his pursuer. Ahead were two cars, one in each lane; he passed one, slipped in next to the other and gunned it, leaving them both in the dust. He checked the mirror briefly, but couldn't make out the cockeyed headlight in the blur of lights and movement behind.

In no time, he came to the next exit, Sixty-third Street, and he swung the car violently to the right, fishtailing around the turn, and hit the gas again. At the end of the block, he turned on a red light to go up First. The lights were running with him, so he kept his speed at forty-five until he came to Seventy-fifth Street, where he hung a left and went two blocks until he found a space across the street from his building. He pulled in and doused the lights and waited. Nothing. He waited some more. There were no cars moving on the side street, only the lights of vehicles moving at right angles, up Third and down Second. On the sidewalk a man and a young boy passed, talking earnestly.

Jude locked the car and crossed the street with one hand in his pocket, holding ready the key to the front door. When he reached it, he opened it quickly, looked up and down the street, and darted inside. With the door behind him, he felt a wave of relief, the illusion that home provided sanctuary.

Standing in the entryway, he took stock. Again, he had precious few hard facts at his disposal. He didn't know who was following him or even how many people were following him, not to mention why. And he didn't know if he had really shaken them off or if they had merely dropped away, already knowing where he lived. His name was still in the book—regrettably. If they knew his name, they knew where he was. Even Skyler, *for Christ's sake*, had been able to track him down. Funny how he was beginning to date the start of his misfortunes to Skyler's appearance on the scene.

He opened his mailbox and pulled out a small penknife, extracting the blade and using it to pry out a thin piece of plastic with his name embossed upon it. He closed the mailbox.

It's not paranoia, he thought as he began the long climb up the stairs. *It's not paranoia to think someone's after you if you're actually being followed.* Under the circumstances, removing his name from the mailbox was a sensible precaution—but not, he realized, a very effective one.

Jude found Tizzie and Skyler sitting far apart in the living room. Tizzie was a mess. Her hair was uncombed, her dress looked as if it had just been tossed on, and she leaned upon a table, cradling her chin in both hands. Skyler was dressed in a pair of blue jeans and a black T-shirt—both belonging to Jude, naturally—and he sat grimly on the couch. The atmosphere seemed charged with emotional tension, as if a storm had passed through Jude's tiny apartment. The two looked up at Jude as if he could rescue them.

Jude tried to start off on a positive note.

"I'm glad at least to see you two are all right."

Tizzie stared at him. "What do you mean?" she asked. "Why shouldn't we be?"

"I don't know, exactly. But a lot of crazy stuff has been going on."

Jude looked at Skyler, who sat motionless in some sort of shock, and then walked over to sit down next to Tizzie. He took her hand, but she seemed barely to notice that he was holding it.

"Look," he said. "I wanted to reach you to tell you about all this, but I didn't know where you were. I know it seems crazy—and maybe it is. I can't make any sense of it myself. I've been trying to figure it out all day, and all I come up with is dead ends."

She looked at him quizzically, and he continued.

"All I know is that this guy"—he made a vague motion toward Skyler with his free hand—"turned up on my doorstep. Literally on my doorstep. I couldn't get much out of him at first. His name's Skyler, and he says he was raised on some kind of weird place that sounds like something from *The Island of Dr. Moreau*."

"What's that?" asked Skyler.

"Nothing. It's a book. It doesn't matter," Jude replied irritably.

At the sound of Skyler's voice, Tizzie stirred. She turned and looked at him, and he looked back, his eyes blazing.

"You know, he sounds exactly like you," she said to Jude. "This is really amazing. There are two of you."

"You don't know the half of it. Anyway, on this island—and he doesn't know where it is, by the way—there's a group of people like himself—"

"The Age Group," put in Skyler.

"Whatever, the age group. And they're raised to uphold science instead of religion, and they undergo strict physical regimens to make them strong and healthy, but basically, they're prisoners. They're not allowed to leave. If they do, they're tracked down by guys who are called Orderlies, who use bloodhounds. And every so often people on the island die."

At this, Tizzie looked again at Skyler, her eyes wide in disbelief.

"But Skyler did manage to escape. And after a couple of weeks in Georgia, he made his way up here, and he tracked me down through a picture in the newspaper, because—as you can see only too well—he looks just like me. And we can't figure out the explanation for that."

Now Tizzie looked at Jude.

"There's one possibility—that he's a relative, or maybe . . ." Jude hesitated for a second. "Maybe he's even my twin brother."

"But . . . but," Tizzie was so confused she was stammering. "You didn't have a twin brother when you were young."

"How do you know?"

"You never . . . talked about it."

"Maybe I had one and just didn't know it. You know—separated at birth."

"Of course, I know. That's my whole field. But it's just too remarkable, too much of a coincidence."

Now, marshaling his argument, Jude talked faster. "Think about it. What do I know about my parents? Practically nothing—except that they were die-hard scientists who belonged to some kind of scientific cult. Maybe they were engaged in some kind of elaborate experiments. When twins were born into the group, they would separate them—ship one out and raise him under totally different conditions, a controlled environment."

"To what end?" asked Tizzie.

"To tease out all the variables—you know, nature versus nurture. All the things we were talking about before."

"But where's the comparison?" She was looking from one to the other. "Where's the test?"

"It hasn't happened yet."

"That's a lot of trouble to go to for one experiment," she said. "Not to mention the immorality of it. Separating brothers, not telling them about each other. Raising one of them with all the advantages—at least I assume you would have had the advantages, if your parents had lived—and raising the other . . ." She looked over at Skyler with a hint of sympathy. ". . . in a so-called controlled environment."

Jude noticed that Skyler was stealing stares at Tizzie every so often. Yet when she looked directly at him, he glanced away as if it was hard to bear.

She continued: "People do separate twins, of course—I know that more than anyone. Usually it's an unwed mother who has to give them up for adoption and some stupid, unthinking agency that doesn't realize it's healthier for them to be raised together."

Now she was sizing up Skyler. She spoke about him in the third person, as if he wasn't there. "He looks younger than you," she said.

"Maybe not younger, just thinner," replied Jude. "He's been through a lot."

Suddenly, Skyler talked. "Let me ask . . ." he began hesitatingly. "How often does this happen?"

"What?"

"That identical twins are born."

"Not very often," said Jude.

"About four births out of every thousand," said Tizzie.

"So any group of scientists could not have a reasonable expectation that its members would produce twins."

"That's a point," Jude conceded.

"And if it happened twice in a small group, that would really defy the odds," Skyler continued.

"So what are you saying?" Jude asked.

Skyler shrugged. "Maybe they found a way to create twins," he said.

Skyler had not expected his remark to carry such weight, but it did. Jude sat there, at first a bit stunned, and then shot him an appraising look, as if to say: I might have overlooked something here. Tizzie appeared to be a little upset, as she had been throughout the discussion—in fact, as she had been since Jude's phone call, which had caused her to leap out of the bed, grab her dress, and regard Skyler as if he was some kind of freak.

Jude told Tizzie about the man who had been following him on the subway, and he filled them in on the murder in New Paltz and the mystery of the DNA match. But he did not tell them that the victim had a hole gouged in his thigh or that he himself had been followed—at least *thought* he had been followed—on the trip back. They were already nervous enough, he figured, and both of them looked as if they still had some recovering to do from the shocks they'd already received.

"It's just too . . . strange, too unbelievably strange. It's unthinkable," she said.

"What? Which part?" asked Jude.

"All of it. But to think that people might set up some vast scientific experiment . . . playing with human lives, I just can't believe it. And yet, damn it, you two do look alike.

"And, look," she said, "you're both frowning in exactly the same way, one hand to the head. Do you notice how you're positioning yourselves unconsciously? Sitting across from each other, almost like you're mirror images. This is amazing—if you guys really are twins. I've sat in on a lot of interviews with separated twins, but never at the moment when they were reunited."

"We don't know that that's what happened," said Jude. He noticed the split in her: the scientist in her was excited by the possibility of identical twins, but the woman who cared for him appeared distraught. He would say anything to console her.

Skyler seemed upset that Tizzie was upset.

The time had come, Jude thought, to take the situation in hand.

"Listen," he said, looking at Skyler. "The first thing we've got to do is make sure you're safe. You're not safe here, because chances are, they know you're here—whoever *they* are. Tomorrow we've got to find you a place of your own. I think we should disguise you, too. I don't know if it's better for you to look like me, for people to think you're me, or if it's worse. Given all that's happened lately, I suspect it's not a good idea.

"Tizzie, I think you should stay here tonight and not go out. That way we can all get started together tomorrow."

He wanted her to stay for her own safety, and he was also feeling moved that she was so upset by the fact that he had a twin. It could only mean that she felt deeply for him. Maybe he had been wrong about her drawing away.

But she insisted on leaving. She was anxious to spend the night at home, she said, since she had not been there for days.

"Where were you, anyway?" he asked as he walked with her down the stairs.

"Milwaukee," she said. "At my parents'."

"How are they?"

"Not at all well. Just old age, but it's happening so fast. It's like night falling."

He hailed a cab for her, and when she got in, he leaned over to kiss her on the cheek. She smiled at him, but it was a brave, false smile.

A few moments later, as he was undressing for bed—this time with Skyler on the living room couch—Jude was again struck by the sheer implausibility of the events of the past two days. More and more he was coming to the belief that Skyler was his brother and perhaps his twin. No one would have believed that this was happening, and yet it had happened—and on top of that, everything was turning out to be such a remarkable coincidence. Here he had met Tizzie while researching an article on identical twins, and he turned out to have one of his own. He went out on a murder story, and the victim had something to do with Skyler. What were the odds of things like that happening?

He had had the strangest sensation some minutes back, when the three of them were in the living room together. So much was going on around them that was unfathomable, and so much was going on among them that was unspoken. He felt that the three of them were locked inside some phantasmal shifting labryinth, that they were a trio picked out by fate.

Jude got up early, fixed himself a cup of strong coffee and checked the want ads for a cheap room. He found three or four and circled the ads, including one around Astor Place that sounded right. It read: 1 bdroom, partly furnished, short-term, no pets/smokers, $800/mo.

He left a note for Skyler, grabbed his jacket and went outside, inspecting the street carefully before getting into his car. Nothing suspicious anywhere. It was one of those beautiful New York June days, a blue sky with wisps of clouds and sunlight shining through the leaves on the side streets, dappling everything on the sidewalks below.

He got to Astor Place in no time, beating the rush hour. A barrel-chested man in a white strap-sleeve undershirt sat in front of the dilapidated brownstone, his chair tilted back to rest against the stucco façade. The wall behind him was covered with graffiti, which seemed to blend with the tattoos on his shoulder muscles. With a dispassionate wariness he watched Jude park the car, waiting for him to walk over.

"Are you the super?" Jude asked.

The man remained tilted back in his chair, grunted noncommittally, and looked at Jude up and down. Finally, he leaned forward, stood up and turned to go inside, motioning with his head for Jude to follow.

The apartment was on the third floor to the rear. The door had so many coats of battleship gray paint it could only be opened with a kick, and the floors, covered in linoleum, slanted and creaked. The first room was the kitchen, with a chipped enamel stove and a refrigerator with a round cooling unit on top. Off to one side was a narrow bathroom with a half tub under a shower and a pink flowered shower curtain. The back room was the bedroom with a square table, an upended steamer trunk that had drawers, and a couch of two large pieces that could be reconfigured into a bed. It looked out over a fire escape leading down to a back alley.

The place was clean, so Jude decided to take it.

"I imagine you'll want references," he said, eyeing the cracks in the plaster ceiling. "I can provide them."

The super looked back with narrowed eyes. "No," was all he said.

"Do you mind if I take it in someone else's name?"

The super grunted again. "As long as she don't smoke," he said.

"No danger of that."

Jude wrote a check for the first month's rent, then another for the same amount as security.

"The name's Smith," he said. "Jim Smith."

"Why not just say John Doe and be done with it?"

"Too obvious."

Two hours later, Jude was at his desk at the *Mirror*, trying to dodge Judy Gottman, the assignment editor, who paced the aisles holding a piece of paper as if she were stalking game. When he saw her approaching his cubicle, he grabbed the phone and launched into a highly arresting and also highly fictitious conversation. He made it sound as if he were squeezing gruesome details out of a reluctant assistant district attorney. She stood by his desk, chewing gum impatiently.

"I want this to be exclusive—*you hear me,*" Jude barked into the receiver, an undertone of threat in his voice. He looked over and raised his eyebrows, as if seeing Judy for the first time, then covered the mouthpiece with one hand and whispered: "Sorry—can't talk. This could be big."

Judy walked away, and he saw her corral another reporter.

He was putting off the call he knew he had to make. Finally, he inhaled deeply and picked up the receiver.

"Special Ops."

"Raymond La Barrett, please."

"And this is?"

"Jude Harley."

"One moment, please."

Jude used the few seconds to go over what he wanted: he needed to know if the FBI had taken over the New Paltz case and what they made of it.

"Hey, kid, how are you doing?"

Raymond's voice sounded natural. They kicked around some small talk for a while. Jude noticed that this time Raymond did not ask where he was calling from; perhaps he already knew.

"Raymond," he said finally. "I need more help on the New Paltz thing. It doesn't make any sense."

"How so?"

Raymond's voice still sounded nonchalant.

"Once I got the ID on the victim"—he was careful not to say, "Once *you* gave me the ID"—"I went up there to check it out."

"And?"

"And it's the damnedest thing. The victim's not the victim."

"What do you mean?"

"It was a judge, you remember? Well, he's alive. So someone else is dead who's got the same DNA."

"That's impossible. McNichol must have screwed up, that's all."

"That's what I thought. But he's dead sure he got it right."

"You talked to him?"

"Yeah, and that's not all."

"What else?"

Raymond's voice sounded suddenly guarded. Jude hesitated, then thought: what the hell; in for a dime, in for a dollar.

"Some workmen in front of the judge's house saw a guy they thought was the victim hanging around there some days before."

"Did they describe him?"

"Not very well. Only what he was wearing—a red shirt. That kind of thing."

Raymond paused for half a heartbeat. "What do you make of that?" he asked.

"I don't know," Jude replied. "Maybe he was trying to reach the judge, to contact him for some reason."

"What kind of reason?"

"I don't know. But a lot of strange things have been going on."

"Really? Like what."

"I can't say exactly, but take my word for it."

"*Can't* say or *won't* say."

"Maybe a little of both."

"Listen, kid. I don't know what you're smoking, but my advice is to keep away from this whole thing. It's a wild goose chase. You've got an unsolved murder and a nutty M.E. who made a bad call—that's all."

"Are you guys on the case?"

"Let's just say we've been informed about it. A homicide like this—the body all beat to shit and cut up—chances are, it's a Mob job. So we get brought up to date. That's not to say we're running anything, understand?"

"Yes. So you've got nothing to add?"

"Nothing that amounts to anything."

"Okay. Well, thanks anyway. If you get anything, will you call?"

"Sure thing. And, kid . . ."

"Yeah?"

"Keep your nose clean. It's about time for a beer."

Jude's mouth went dry. "Sure thing. Your place or mine?"

Raymond laughed. "Mine."

"Right. See you."

"Okay. Take care."

When Jude heard the click, he put the receiver down slowly. So Raymond had asked for a meeting. Something was up—something that his casual tone was at pains to conceal. And when had he ever ended a conversation with the admonition to "take care"? That didn't sound like him. Was it just one of those things people said—or was it a warning?

On impulse, Jude called his apartment. He let the phone ring three times, then hung up and dialed again. Skyler's voice came on the line, sounding nervous. He said the phone had been ringing all morning. Jude told him to stay put, that he'd be there soon.

When Skyler hung up, Jude spotted Judy, still on the prowl with assignments, and so he sat there for a moment, the receiver still at his ear. Then he heard it, a distinct sound—a second click. He knew from stories he'd done that that sound could only mean one thing: someone else on the line had just hung up. His home phone was being tapped.

# Chapter 15

Jude was anxious to get home and make sure that Skyler was all right, but he had one more thing to do. He called up Nexis from his desktop computer and used a password borrowed from the research department to get into "Deep Nexis," a compilation of clips from all the major newspapers, magazines and scholarly journals. As an information-retrieval system, it reached into every publication of importance; Jude needed to cast a wide net. He didn't know much about the creature he was fishing for.

He ran through the names of the major coastal islands, then Valdosta, Georgia. There were literally hundreds of articles—too many to read thoroughly—but even when he narrowed the search, he came up with nothing helpful. He then tried the names Skyler had mentioned. "Baptiste" yielded nothing; there were dozens and dozens of listings, but without a first name, it was impossible to pinpoint the search. He scanned them; none appeared to suggest an affiliation with a scientific organization. He tried "Rincon, Dr." There was a single listing—for a Dr. Jacob Rincon of Santa Monica, California, arrested for embezzlement and fraud during a federal investigation into misuse of Medicare funds three years ago. That didn't sound right. A search for the word *Lab* ended with a small box on the screen, inside of which was written: "Your search has resulted in 0 articles. Please try another category."

Jude signed off. He left his computer screen on, opened an old notebook and put it on his desk, and scattered around some books and papers and a ballpoint. Then he took his jacket from a locker, draped it across the back of his chair, and snuck down the back corridor. He took the freight elevator down to the first floor, cut through the lobby and took a staircase down to the basement, where the old morgue had been relocated. The morgue was the memory bank of the newspaper; it contained stories that had appeared in the *Mirror* since 1907, laboriously cut out by hand and filed away under scores of topics, by minions long since retired or dead. In times past, the morgue had held pride of place in the main floor of the newsroom, but ever since it had been discontinued in 1980, when Nexis had taken over, it had been consigned to purgatory. Rarely these days did anyone visit the subterranean vault. Its corridors were poorly lighted by dangling green lamps and banked by filing cabinets extending off into the funereal gloom. The files were packed with yellow clippings so brittle that they broke to the touch like ancient butterfly wings.

The morgue had its own Phantom of the Opera. It was presided over by J. T. Dunleavy, a dyspeptic attendant of indeterminate age. His famed attribute was his photographic memory, which, while it did not pretend to reproduce perfectly the contents of hundreds of thousands of files, had penetrated to the inner logic of the system so that he, and he alone, could comprehend it—he could say which oyster was likely to contain the pearl.

The only problem with Dunleavy was that to get good service, you had to get on his good side. Luckily, for some reason he had always liked Jude—maybe because Jude was one of the few reporters his age who had respect for the past. Dunleavy himself went beyond respect, into reverence—he was a Boswell who was compelled to record even the most trivial of human transactions.

He was sorting through a bin of odd clippings, placing them in piles. His bony fingers moved as fast as a Vegas dealer.

"What is it this time?" he demanded, but not in an unfriendly way, scarcely looking up from the counter.

"I need everything you've got on cults—in the 1960s."

"That's an armful. It was, you know, an interesting time."

Jude reflected. "What would you suggest?"

Dunleavy asked a few questions, nothing that probed deeply but enough to get an idea of what Jude was after. He padded off down the central corridor, the cone of light from a green lamp reflecting off the dome of his bald pate. Four minutes later, he returned with a folder marked CULTS SCIENTIFIC, and underneath that a further subdivision—WESTERN STATES. He poured the folder onto the counter; out fell three bundles, each tied with a thin cord that was lashed to a circular fastening stuck on a cardboard backing.

Immediately, Dunleavy frowned. "Something wrong here," he said portentously.

One of the bundles was labeled ARIZONA, and it was skimpy. It held only four articles, which Jude quickly ascertained were of no interest.

"But see here where the cord is bent," said Dunleavy. "That's what I mean when I say something's wrong. The file used to be much thicker. Here, look over the names of those who checked it out—maybe that will tell you something."

He handed Jude a sheet of paper from inside the folder that had names and dates scribbled upon it. Most were from the early 1970s; only one was recent. The handwriting was hard to make out, and Jude tried to read it out loud.

"Looks like Jay Montgomery, Jay Mortimery, something like that."

Dunleavy grabbed the list, looked at it, and cackled low.

"Aha. I knew something was funny. The name doesn't matter. But see that little mark beside the name, the black dot? I made that. I always added a telltale sign when the person requesting the file was a non-*Mirror* representative."

"You mean, somebody outside the paper using the morgue?"

"Precisely."

"So who was this?"

"We don't know who he was, but we know where he came from."

"Where?"

"Blue for the police. Red for the CIA. Green for NSA. And black for—"

"—the FBI."

"Precisely. And so we deduce that someone from the FBI took this file out—let's see—four months ago, and kept it. A most unorthodox behavior, I might add, and given the fact that there is a Xerox machine not more than twenty paces away, something that was most decidedly not done merely to keep a record of it."

"It was done to deny the file to someone else."

"Or perhaps to deny it to *anyone else*."

Jude felt he was at another dead end.

"Isn't there any way to track the clips down?"

Dunleavy began unwrapping the other two bundles. The only hope, he said, was that an article or two had been replaced erroneously in the wrong pile—which happened more often that you would think, he added.

He was soon proved right and held up a small piece of yellow paper, four paragraphs from an article that had been accidentally ripped in two.

The story had appeared on November 8, 1967, and it concerned a group called "the Institute for Research into Human Longevity," which had fielded a list of candidates to run for local offices, all of whom had been soundly defeated. A spokesman for the group, who the article said refused to provide his name, issued an ungracious statement, saying that the organization was "turning away from politics forever and would pursue its goals through research alone." He said the group had "changed its name to W."

*"W."* What the hell does that mean? wondered Jude.

The bottom of the story was missing, but that was not essential. Now that the date was known, Jude could retrieve it from the microfilm files. And, besides, the top of the story carried what was the single most important piece of information, the dateline. It was *Jerome, Arizona,* and as soon as Jude read it, he knew it was right, for it had struck a long-buried chord in his memory.

"Hello. Doctors' office."

The voice on the telephone sounded efficient, with more than a touch of that nasal New York brusqueness that tells the caller to get down to business right away.

"Is Dr. Givens in?" Jude asked. *Not that there's a chance in hell that he would come to the phone.*

"No, I'm sorry."

Funny, she didn't sound sorry.

"He's out all week."

Jude was glad—he was calling on the off chance that Dr. Givens, his assigned doctor in the HMO United Comprehensive Care, was *not* there. He wanted any doctor *but* him. Finally, he thought, something is breaking right for me.

"This is one of his patients, Jude Harley. I need a physical exam right away."

The words "right away"—and the presumption they conveyed—did not sit well with the receptionist, who told him to "hold on." He heard his name being punched into a computer, and then a silence while she read his records. Thankfully, they were short and dull—*but they're about to get more interesting.*

"What seems to be the trouble, Mr. Harley?"

With a torrent of lies and inventive explanations involving heart palpitations and sudden blackouts, a family history of dreaded diseases and the anxious pleadings of a friend who happened to be a doctor, Jude managed to convey some urgency.

"I'm sorry, but your medical plan does not authorize coverage of a physical exam unless it is performed by your own physician and for a verifiable symptom or complaint likely to lead to a diagnosis."

That figured—the company health plan that Tibbett had negotiated into the last contract was notoriously skinflintish. But when Jude said he would pay for all of it himself, no questions asked, and wanted "the works," her tone changed to something approaching helpful. She said she could fit him in that afternoon if he didn't mind being seen by a young doctor who had just joined the group.

Jude hung up the pay phone with a feeling of satisfaction and gave a thumbs-up signal to Skyler, whose puzzled expression indicated that he had not the remotest idea what it meant.

Tizzie joined them at the unisex hair salon on Lexington Avenue. Jude had called her shortly after he had smuggled Skyler out of his building through the basement and out the rear exit. Skyler had been outfitted with a golfer's cap and dark glasses, which lay beside the basin in which his hair was being dyed blond.

"You're going to make him look ridiculous," she said.

"No, I'm not. Anyway, the less he looks like me, the better."

"I see. And the way to make him look not like you is to make him look like a fool?"

Jude couldn't think of a retort.

The hair stylist came over, a young woman chewing gum.

"So what is it? You guys are twins and you're tired of looking alike?"

"Something like that," said Jude.

"I can give him a Leo. Or maybe something younger, you want punk? Only thing is, he already looks younger—I mean, you guys still want to be the same generation, right?"

Jude nodded.

The stylist looked over at Skyler, waiting in the barber chair with a white-and-black-striped cloth tied around his neck; he was looking at his new head of blond hair in the mirror and then at Tizzie's reflection.

"He says to ask you," she insisted.

"Give him a buzz cut," replied Jude.

"Not you," she said, then turning to Tizzie. "You."

Tizzie smiled.

"Give him a handsome haircut, like that," she said, pointing to a larger-than-life photograph of George Clooney on the wall.

"You got it."

The stylist walked away.

"I see you're already casting your spell," remarked Jude.

The visit to the doctor was an ordeal. Skyler needed a great deal of persuading even to enter the office, which lay behind a small side door next to an imposing entrance under a green awning on East Eighty-sixth Street.

Jude remained outside. Over and over, he had explained to Skyler why it was important to him to undergo a medical exam that would establish once and for all just how much alike the two of them really were. Skyler had had too much experience with doctors in his short life, Jude figured. His reluctance to submit to a physical was understandable, but it had to be overcome if they were to get any answers. Finally, Jude had prevailed upon Tizzie to accompany him, and it was only then that Skyler had agreed.

Skyler jumped when Tizzie rang a bell and the door was buzzed open by the receptionist. The lock, she explained, was intended to keep people out, not in.

The patient was so obviously nervous that the receptionist, the same one who had talked to Jude on the phone, was touched. She smiled sympathetically as she handed the file to Tizzie—*Jude's* file—and told them she would try to push his name ahead on the list. The waiting room was crowded, and they took the last two empty seats.

Tizzie asked him about the medical care on the island. He told her about the weekly examinations, the urine and blood tests, the obsession with vitamins and health food.

"Tell me," she asked. "Were you all in good health?"

"Yes, perfect health."

"But sometimes people got sick?"

"Sure, we got sick."

"And sometimes they didn't recover. That's what you told us."

"Most of the time they did. But not always."

"And when they didn't recover, what happened?"

"They died."

"Just like that? They died?"

"Yes. We never saw them again. We went to their funerals."

"Did you know why they died? Did they tell you?"

"Not really. They just said they died."

"But when they recovered . . . they were all right?"

"Yeah. But sometimes they were missing things—like an eye."

Tizzie was visibly upset.

A nurse with a clipboard walked in and looked at Skyler.

"Hello, Jude," she said. "You've changed your hair—very hip."

He tried to smile.

"What brings you here?"

Tizzie answered for him.

"Nothing specific, just a general checkup."

"Good idea. It's a smart thing to do," she replied. "Come with me."

Tizzie squeezed Skyler's hand, and he stood up, apprehensive. The nurse saw this, and on the way to the examining room, she turned to look him in the eye and said with feeling: "I hope it all works out okay."

An hour and a half later, after Skyler had given up every conceivable bodily fluid and had X rays taken of every bone and examinations of every orifice and protuberance, he was led back to Tizzie. He was shaken but in one piece, and he brightened visibly when he saw her reading magazines in the lobby, which moved her. They stopped off at a counter where a sign in block letters said: BILL MUST BE PAID AT TIME OF VISIT. Tizzie pulled out a check that Jude had already signed, and was about to fill in the amount when the Filipino woman behind the counter asked why Skyler didn't do it himself. So he did, writing the numerals and the zeroes in a fluid hand. Tizzie was struck, in fact, by how much his writing resembled Jude's.

An hour later, Jude and Skyler were riding in the subway. Lurching back and forth against the seat as the train screeched around a bend, Skyler could not believe that anything could make so much noise. But the people around him did not notice it or if they did, they gave no sign. He was fascinated by them—he had never seen anything like them, such a multitude of humanity and such diversity; he had never dreamed that people could come in so many different sizes and shapes and colors. Some of them looked like Kuta. And the clothes they wore were flamboyant and equally bounteous—T shirts with designs, flowered dresses, light jackets and short skirts, baseball caps and berets and earphones. But his fellow passengers did not seem especially happy; none of them were smiling. Across the way, a figure in short blond hair and dark glasses seemed to be staring at him; he looked back and realized with a start that he was looking at his own reflection.

The wheels screeched again and the train came into a station, and as it halted, the doors flew open, so that looking through them, Skyler could see walls covered in white tile and dark columns. Dozens of people got off and dozens more cleared a path for them and then stepped on board. Skyler was amazed that even children seemed unfazed by the noise and the crowd. One was asleep in a little chair that had wheels on it, the same device that he had seen on the sidewalks above.

He kept an eye on Jude and decided to stick close to him. Jude seemed so nervous, constantly looking around and even looking over his shoulder when he bought the coins that allowed them on the subway, that it made Skyler nervous. He began to feel that menace was lurking everywhere. Jude explained that he was on the lookout for the Orderlies, and he made Skyler promise to let him know the minute he spotted one.

Earlier, Jude had explained that he was taking Skyler to his own apartment, and he had assured him that he would be safer there, because no one would know where he was. Skyler was not so certain of this. He had developed an almost superstitious belief in the ability of the Lab to do whatever it wanted. Its power was unlimited, its tentacles reached everywhere. Surely, one of them could reach out and grab him no matter where he was hiding. And he was not too keen at the prospect of being on his own. It made him anxious, to think that he would have to make decisions and deal with this complicated city alone. He looked again at Jude, scanning the subway car.

He was beginning to trust Jude a little bit. But the trust was tentative; it came and went and he could drive it away by concentrating too much and thinking about all the possibilities. It occurred to him that if he was dead wrong and if Jude was planning to do away with him because of some conspiracy that was bigger than anything he could imagine, then this would be the way to do it. Jude would take him to some apartment away from everything, leave him alone and let him stew and then face his doom in solitude. Or perhaps there would be people from the island waiting there to take him away. Still, what option did he have but to go with him?

He felt a tugging on his sleeve—it was Jude, standing up. They had arrived at their stop. On the white tile wall outside, a sign read: ASTOR PLACE. The doors flew open and they stepped out, Jude first, Skyler right behind, stepping quickly lest the doors suddenly close and trap him and separate him from Jude forever. They exited through the turnstiles, Jude still scrutinizing the flow of people carefully, searching for a telltale forelock of white hair.

The air on the street above was stiflingly hot, but Skyler was relieved to be out of the underground tunnel. He followed Jude across the street and two blocks down. They went into a bar and immediately felt a rush of cold air. Air conditioning—he was getting used to it. A country tune played on the jukebox. Skyler pushed his glasses up on his head, but it was still so dark inside that he could hardly see. Jude sat on a stool and he sat next to him, and Jude ordered a beer for himself and a Coke for Skyler.

Jude took a long drink, set his glass down and wiped his mouth. He told Skyler to look through the window at the building across the street. That's where he would be staying. He must pick the key up from the super on the first floor and walk up to the third floor. He would have to lay low and wait for Jude to contact him; he could go out to buy food at the corner deli or emergency supplies, but that was about it. In the meantime, Jude would be working hard to figure out what was going on and to come up with some sort of a plan.

"Any questions?"

Skyler shook his head no, still feeling uncertain.

"Here, take this," said Jude, reaching into his front pocket and pulling out a wad of bills. "It's only fifty dollars, so it won't go very far, but it's all I've got on me at the moment."

Skyler put the money in his pocket. It was more than he had ever seen. He looked at Jude long and hard, which was easier to do through the dark glasses.

"You know," he said. "There are still a lot of things to tell you about the island."

"Like what?"

"Well, like about the people. I haven't told you about all the people. One in particular. She was in the Age Group . . ." He faltered.

Jude waited quietly.

"Her name was Julia. She was my whole life. She died. That's why I left."

"I'm sorry."

"I loved her—I still love her."

He stopped. There, he had said it. He couldn't say more anyway, not right now. That was enough for the time being.

Jude reached over and put his arm around him. It felt strange being touched by him like that—strange and comforting.

"Have a beer," said Jude. "I bet I know what brand you'll like."

He ordered two, and they finished them and got up to leave.

They parted, shaking hands, which struck Skyler as strange. He wondered if he would ever see Jude again. He adjusted his glasses, put his hands in his pockets and crossed the street to enter the building, just as Jude had told him to. He knocked on the door marked SUPERINTENDENT.

"Hot damn," said the man who answered it, holding one hand on the doorknob and looking him up and down, a cool appraisal. "It didn't take you long to change your look. I liked it better the old way."

The mattress Skyler was lying on was lumpy, and sagged so much in the middle that he could not turn to either side and still breathe. It made him even more claustrophobic, if such a thing were possible. As he lay there, with the windows open and the soiled curtains waving in the feeble wind, he sweltered. His body perspired uncontrollably, and he imagined he was suffocating. Yet when he stepped in front of the window, he felt a sudden chill and he practically shivered. He missed the equalizing breezes and balmy sun of his island.

The room was dingy and smelly, and it had depressed him the moment he opened the door. The cockroaches waited for all of five minutes before they began skittering across the linoleum in the kitchen. When he looked inside a closet, he found a trap with two dead mice. The windows were streaked with dirt, the wallpaper was starting to peel and the sink had bulb-shaped yellow stains under the faucets, which made him wonder if the water was safe to drink.

The sounds of the street flowed into his room and made him jumpy. From somewhere nearby, a radio was blaring Hispanic dance music. Again, he had that sensation of being overwhelmed by everything; it felt nauseating—too much noise, traffic lights, buildings that reached to the sky, people rushing about on the sidewalks. He had no one to talk to and no idea of what to do next, and he felt that he was in a vacuum and all the fears and uncertainties were rushing in from all sides and squeezing him so much, he wanted to scream.

He filled the time by spending it with ghosts, even though he knew that would make him even lonelier. And so, tossing about on the bed in his dismal room somewhere in the giant and heartless city, he traveled back to his earlier life on the island.

He thought about Raisin and how they used to run through the woods, wild with happiness at the sense of being free. He remembered once again how Julia used to trail after them, and the recollection plunged him into something akin to despair—had he only known how much he would come to love her, how differently he would have acted! He thought of the time she'd disappeared into the operating room and the panic that had gripped him, and he thought of how the two of them had discovered love-making and the memory raised him to a bittersweet joy.

And a curious thing was happening. Thoughts of Julia began turning into thoughts of that other woman. Tizzie. Tizzie—what kind of name was that?—he didn't even like it. A big question mark hung over her. She was not as beautiful as Julia, not as kind or as giving or as adventurous or as warm. Still, she had been tender and solicitous in the doctor's office—he had to give her that.

He did not know where she fit into the whole crazy puzzle. When he had awakened that first time and found her next to him in bed, he'd practically fainted. It'd been traumatic. And he could tell that she had been just as thrown at seeing him, which had made him feel even more agitated. Her reaction had made him think for a moment that she had recognized *him*, as he had recognized her, as if they *had* shared some earlier life together. But he knew, rationally at least, that she was shocked because he looked so much like Jude. She did not know who he was. She'd jumped out of bed, pulling the top sheet with her and wrapping it around her body, which had exposed his nakedness. He'd grabbed the bottom sheet and jumped up, too. They'd stood there, gawking at each other. Finally, she'd demanded to know who he was. He'd told her his name and how he had found Jude's picture in a paper and come to New York to find him. He had not had the presence of mind to ask her who she was. They had not said much afterward; they'd seemed embarrassed in each other's presence. Once they got hurriedly dressed, they'd sat in stricken silence until Jude arrived. She'd been extremely upset.

Since then, Skyler had felt so many conflicting emotions toward her he didn't know what to feel. When she was in the same room, he hung on her every word and her every movement, and he was hard pressed to pay attention to anything else. When she was away, he thought of her all the time. There were moments when she did recall Julia to him, the way she turned her head or sat curled up on her legs in the chair or sharpened the inflection of her voice. Sometimes the gestures were so vividly familiar that she seemed to be Julia reincarnated, and during those moments, Skyler had to turn away to contain himself. He felt elated almost, as if he had been given a second chance—like the time Julia had walked out of the woods.

Then there were other times when her gestures and intonation and all the little actions of how she presented herself to the world would be off. During those times she seemed such a poor counterfeit that it only caused him to ache for the real Julia, and it actually made him mad. It made him angry at the Lab and all those who ran it, and even, for some reason, at Tizzie herself.

He didn't know which was worse. At either extreme—whether she seemed to be like Julia or not at all like her—she aroused a confusion of passions that overwhelmed him. And it was even harder to shuttle from one extreme to the other—traveling from hope to despair and back to hope again. It was an emotional roller coaster that left him dizzy and exhausted.

But on a practical level, the level of his survival, what did her existence mean? What did it tell him about the mystery of the Lab and those who ruled the island? How could it be that there were two sets of identical-looking people whose lives were so interwoven? And if there were two, were there others? He needed to know more and to find out more, and until he did, he would not reveal the little that he did know. For the safety of the woman and perhaps for his own safety, too, he resolved to keep her resemblance to Julia a secret, no matter what—even from Jude.

Lying on the rumpled bed, lost in his thoughts and perspiring madly, Skyler came down to earth with a jolt. He heard something, a sound outside his door. Footsteps! And not a normal tread, but rather something lighter, as if the person was trying to sneak up to the door.

He rose steathily and crept to the door between the bedroom and kitchen, and he listened. He thought he heard the footsteps stop on the landing outside his door, and he thought he could sense a person there, thinking, waiting. Was it real or not? He decided not to wait to find out.

He ran across the bedroom and flung open the window. Right outside was a peculiar metal casing attached to the building, a series of ladders that led down. He turned and listened: did he hear someone knocking on his door? He couldn't be sure. He stepped out onto the metal grating, uncertain if it would hold him, and now there was so much noise outside he couldn't hear the knocking anymore. He hesitated no longer, but bounded down the metal ladder, feeling it shake madly with his weight. He ran along a platform on the floor below and then down another ladder and then to another floor and another ladder.

He looked up. Was that a dark shadow above through the metal strips, a head sticking out his window? He could not tell. He ran across another platform and felt the metal structure shaking. He made it to the lowest ladder, but it did not reach the ground, and just as he started down, he heard a ripping noise and felt a vibration that shook so strongly, he fell. He landed on the ground and, looking up, he saw that the ladder had slipped down and was resting in the air only a few feet above his head. He leapt up and ran as fast as he could, and as he rounded the corner and came into an alley, he almost bumped into the super, who looked at him with his mouth open.

But Skyler did not stop. He dashed out into the main street, filled with passersby who looked inquisitively down the alley and at him. He kept running, all the way up Astor Place, one block, then two, then three and four, running blindly and as fast as he could through the streets of the city.

McNichol sounded pleased with himself. He had come up with an answer for Jude, and he sounded like the man Jude had met the first time around—the effusive medical examiner who had given a guided tour of a corpse, not the one whose DNA test had fingered a living judge as a murder victim. He had insisted upon giving the answer to what he called "your little riddle" in person, which was odd. Why couldn't he just do it over the phone? He said he was coming to New York on business and would meet Jude precisely at four o'clock that afternoon. He gave an address on Foley Square, which Jude jotted down. It sounded vaguely familiar.

Jude was still trying to dodge assignments at the office. He hadn't written a story in days, and he was afraid he was acquiring that guilty hangdog look reporters get when they're not in the paper. It was worth a detour to avoid the bulletin board where the city editor had tacked up his favorite slogan: "You're Only As Good As Your Last Story."

Just as he was about to down a cup of coffee, his sixth of the morning, he heard his name out over the loudspeaker—the city editor was summoning him to the Metro desk. He took his time getting there, and when he did, he found Bolevil in a foul mood.

"What're you working on?" he demanded, in his grating Australian accent.

"The New Paltz murder. There're a lot of loose ends to it, and I think it could turn into something big."

"New Paltz— Shit! I thought you were told to drop that."

"No, not at all."

"I don't get it. Why are you still following that piece of shit?"

"Nobody told me otherwise."

"But I thought you were off that. Orders from—"

"Who? Orders from who?"

"Never mind. As of right now, you don't go near that story—you hear me? Jesus. New Paltz. Fuck me."

Like many of his countrymen, when Bolevil said "Fuck me," he meant "Fuck you." If the direction of his aggression was uncertain, the depth of it was not, and a small crowd had gathered at the nearby rewrite bank, enjoying Jude's discomfort. He couldn't blame them. Watching Bolevil chew people out was a favorite newsroom pastime. But it wasn't really a blood sport, because the city editor carried little authority—only what he could muster by invoking Tibbett's name, which he did increasingly during times of stress.

"We'll find something for you to do." The city editor shouted over to a clerk. "You got anything?"

A young man held up a piece of wire copy. "Construction workers acting up again, some kind of demonstration."

"Too good for him," bellowed Bolevil. His face turned red as a tomato. "I want something in East New York. Bed-Sty. Brownsville."

The red phone rang—the hot line from Tibbett—and the editor lunged for it. His voice transformed itself into something dulcet, and he promptly forgot Jude, who beat a hasty retreat back to his cubicle.

Jude called a friend, Chuck Roberts, the Sunday editor. Some years back, Jude had helped Roberts through a messy divorce, thereby incurring a debt of gratitude that was being paid off on the installment plan.

"Jim. Jude here. I need shelter. You got anything for me?"

"Who did you piss off this time?"

"The weevil."

"Aw, I was hoping it was something serious."

"Serious enough. He can mess me up."

"What's the problem?"

"I need the rest of the day free."

"Come on down to the Sunday department. I'll call the clerk on Metro. You've just become absolutely indispensable to us."

The Sunday department viewed itself as an ivory tower above the hurly-burly of the daily paper, turning out articles on timeless matters such as recipes for gazpacho and How to Train Your Dog to Love You. In its quiet corridors, which twisted and turned like an old English hedge maze, Jude found a small cubicle in the back. It had half of a window looking onto Fifth Avenue.

He turned on the desk computer, signed on with the password he had chosen years ago—"Luddite"—and went on-line. The machine was cranky and took a while, but eventually he got through. He clicked on Search and typed in "Institute for Research into Human Longevity." The machine took even longer than before. He went for a coffee refill, and when he returned, he found 984 hits.

Discouraged, he began scrolling through them. There were endless listings: research, remedies, anecdotes, case studies, stories, myths, superstitions, male, female, child, genetic antioxidants, caloric restriction, organ replacement, hormone therapy, life expectancy, gerontology. Almost at random, he hit one under the heading *drosophila.*

It began:

*Michael R Rose, a specialist in genetics who is obsessed with aging, thinks big but acts small. Since 1976, when he was a graduate student at the University of Sussex, he has worked on the radical idea known as the evolutionary theory of aging, and he has done it with the lowly fruit fly. He started with two hundred female flies in milk bottles, and every time they reproduced, he selected only the eggs from the longest-living ones. As he moved from university to university, Rose took his flies with him. Today, at the University of California at Irvine, Rose now presides over a population of flies almost one million strong. But it's not their number that's grabbed the attention of the scientific world—it's their age. They live as long as one hundred and forty days. That may not sound like much to you, but for a fruit fly, it represents a doubling of the life span. How would you like to live one hundred and fifty years instead of your predicted seventy-five?*

Jude found similar sites for worms, birds, goldfish and monkeys. He modified his search, adding *Jerome* and then he added *W.* He was linked to a web page. It appeared on the screen piece by piece, and as it took shape before him, he saw that it was a lizard standing upon a rock, looking enigmatic with a sleepy-looking hooded eye that seemed to follow the viewer. The site appeared to be an old one with only odd bits and pieces, but there was at least one reference to the IRHL, which Jude assumed was an acronym for Institute for Research into Human Longevity.

Down in the lower left-hand corner, he saw a box marked DISCUSSION GROUP and he clicked on it. There were four other people in the chat room, and he came upon a conversation already underway.

"every night i pray to God to let me live through the night and one more day. the next thing i do the same thing. and it always works. that's my secret."

"what's the name of that woman, the french woman who lived to some incredible age? she met some famous guy."

*"her name was jeanne calment. she died last year at age 122. As a child she met vincent van gogh, she sold him a box of pastel crayons."*

"that's it. so it shows whats possible, no?"

*"it does. but others have lived as long. they're going to have to change the record books because people are living longer and longer."*

"somebody's joined us. hello luddite."

"hello," Jude replied.

"we're talking about—what else?—getting older. and 'methuselah' here has been telling us not to worry—we're going to live forever ha ha ha"

*"no, not forever. but it's a matter of scientific fact that the human life span is getting longer and longer. at the turn of the century life expectancy in the u.s. was 46 or 47. Now it's about 76, though of course many people go way beyond that. it's going to keep going up."*

"but there's a limit, no?"

"there's no way around the basic facts. you get older and you die. the older you get the greater your chances of dying"

*"actually, that's not true. the opposite is true."*

"what do you mean?"

*"I mean that human mortality rates do not accelerate through the life span."*

"explain pls."

"that doesn't make any sense at all to me. why do you think I keep asking God for another day?"

*"your chance of dying starts to decelerate around the age of 80."*

"you mean accelerate."

*"no, just the opposite. if you make it to 80, the odds improve ever so slightly that you'll make it to 81. the human mortality rate levels off sharply at 110. So if you make it that far you might just be like madame calment—you'll coast along until 122."*

"but that doesn't make any sense."

*"it contradicts human reason, but science often does. Your surprise just shows how poorly we really understand the aging process."*

Jude decided to enter into the debate.

"Don't you think there are finite limits on how long we can live?"

*"yes, luddite. of course there are. but I'm saying we have not come anywhere near them. we've doubled the span within this century, and that's only by external remedy—diet, exercise, vitamins and so forth. we haven't even begun to manipulate the span internally by playing around with the genes."*

"can that be done?"

*"it's being done. And when that happens, there's no reason to think we can't live 150, 170, even 200 years. Imagine what you could do with your life if you had 200 years."*

"no wonder your name's methuselah."

*"there are no accidents. tell me something, luddite, you interested?"*

"certainly."

*"how old are you?"*

"thirty."

*"still young. tell me, what do you do?"*

Jude hesitated half a second.

"I'm a journalist."

*"aha. An honorable profession."*

"so what's the offer?"

*"offer?"*

"I thought you were going to recommend something."

*"yes. a good health club, eat a lot of fruits and vegetables containing carotenoids—that'll soak up the free radicals. run five miles a day."*

"that's it."

*"yeah."*

"let me ask you something else," wrote Jude, "what's the significance of Jerome?"

*"beats me."*

Someone else interjected, "could you explain that bit again about not dying after 80?"

*"sorry. time's up. must rush now and feed the cat."*

Jude typed quickly.

"one last thing—what's "W" mean?"

*"funny you should ask."*

"how so?"

*"I asked that same thing once on this same site. long time ago."*

"and the answer?"

*"i don't know what it means."*

"but what was it????"

*"double you."*

"double you?"

*"that's it. bibi"*

"bi."

Jude hit a button and the lizard came back on the screen. He hit another and signed off.

Jude was perplexed. He raised his eyebrows a tad—an invitation to continue.

"I recalled the story your paper did some years back on the ten best judges and the ten worst judges—very eye-opening, by the way—especially that trick of sending the same defendant before them. So I assume you are about to do a similar undertaking with respect to the forensic sciences—that you are, in effect, testing the various examiners in and around the city, to see who's the best and who's the worst. Or else your motivation is completely beyond me."

Jude did not deny or confirm. He didn't want to do anything that might upset McNichol, as they were approaching the critical juncture at which information is divulged.

"And what conclusion did you reach?" he inquired softly.

"Not so fast. Not so fast." He held up one hand, the traffic cop's signal. "Let me tell you about the journey before I reveal the destination."

He folded his hands upon the desk, as if he was settling in to tell a long story, and Jude sat back in his chair and waited.

"Have you ever heard of Leonard Hayflick?" he asked, as if it were the most natural question in the world.

Jude shook his head. He had his notebook out, but he stopped writing.

"Pity. He only happens to be one of the most outstanding anatomists of our time. He was a giant in aging research. Who said the world is fair? Everyone knows James Watson and Francis Crick, Cambridge University in 1953, the whole myth, going into a pub afterward and declaring that they had uncovered the secret of life itself—which of course they had."

"The discovery of the structure of DNA. The double helix."

"Precisely. The singular event that brought us into the modern era of genetics. Hayflick performed the analogous feat in the field of gerontology."

"What did he do?"

"He took some cells from a fetus and raised them in a petri dish. This was back in 1961—it's difficult now to conjure up the memory of how primitive the thinking was back then. In those days, aging was viewed as a straightforward matter of biological destiny. You got old because your body wore out, like a machine whose parts disintegrated under wear and tear. Your skin wrinkled, your hair fell out, your brain shrank, your arteries clogged. There was nothing you could do. A human was born, lived a certain number of years and died, and that was more or less all there was to it. Of course, you could cheat around the margins—depending upon whether you were an abstemious librarian or a Left Bank poet drowning in absinthe—but basically your life span was prescribed. One hundred years at the outside. It was the dictates of Nature. Now, of course, we know that all that is hogwash."

"So I've just heard."

"Well, you heard right. Believe me, the advances in life extension over the next fifty years are going to make your head spin. Future generations will look back at our pathetic span of eighty years and shake their heads in wonderment. Did you ever tour the *chateaux* of the Loire? When the guide points to those little beds five feet long and those tiny suits of armor, you're astonished that people could ever be so small. They'll regard our lifetimes like that. Remember your amazement upon learning that Alexander the Great died at age thirty-three? Future generations will feel that way when they discover that Einstein died at seventy-six."

He fixed Jude with a hard stare.

"And it began with Hayflick. You see, he tackled aging head on. He asked the pertinent question—why does aging happen? Does it happen because the individual cells give out, eventually incapacitating the whole human organism? Or does it happen because of an age-related deterioration in some part of the organism that shuts down the cells? When does an army lose a decisive battle? When so many soldiers are cut down that it can no longer mount an effective force in the field, or when a superior officer perceives a rout and gives the order to surrender? My metaphor, incidentally, not his.

"In any case, Hayflick designed a simple experiment—that is, simple in hindsight, like all great experiments. He put the cells in the petri dish to see how long they would live, left to their own devices. They didn't have to do anything—they didn't have to perform work on behalf of the nonexistent human. All they had to do was what cells do naturally, divide and multiply. Which they did. About fifty times. And then they died. He repeated the procedure with cells from a seventy-year-old person. They divided, but only about twenty or thirty times before they, too, died."

"So the answer is that the soldiers die?"

"Don't get hung up on the metaphor," said McNichol brusquely. "Real life is more complicated. Real life is not either/or. In real life, thousands of soldiers die *and* the general gives up."

McNichol stood up and began gesturing as he talked.

"The point is that the cells from the seventy-year-old were themselves older than the ones from the fetus. The point is that Hayflick had established that there is a natural limit to the life of a cell, that from the time it's a newborn, it divides fifty times and then turns senescent."

"If there's a natural limit, then there's no hope of overcoming aging."

"On the contrary, it means that there is hope. In biology, things don't just happen by themselves for no reason. In nature, nothing is so natural that it can't be undone by man. If there's a limit, that's because something is imposing a limit. Something is making it happen."

He was getting more and more excited.

"Don't you see? There's a clock, a clock inside the cells that tells them when their time is up. And if there's a clock there, it means we can find it and go in and tinker with it and eventually even learn how to reset it. We can make it last longer. Which is what we are doing."

"Where?"

"In laboratories all around the world. Scientists are discovering single genes that postpone senescence in simple organisms. There is only one tree of evolution, so the same gene sequences exist in us. Some of the most important work has been done on a one-celled protozoan that lives in ponds. It provided the key to the clock."

"What's the clock?"

"Telomeres."

"Telomeres?"

"Strips of DNA that cap the end of our chromosomes. As you know, chromosomes are long strands of DNA that contain the cell's genetic instructions. At the end of each one is a telomere. It's been compared to the little plastic tip at the end of a shoelace that keeps it from unraveling. And that seems to be pretty much its job here. Each time the cell divides, it loses a little bit more of its telomeres, so that the strand keeps getting shorter as the cell gets older. When the cell reaches its Hayflick limit of fifty divisions, the telomere is down to a nub. That's the point at which the cell switches over into old age and declines. That's the beginning of cell death.

"So the age of cells has nothing to do with chronological time, as we experience it. Which makes sense when you think of it—time is an artificial human construct to begin with. The age of cells is related to how much work they do, to how many times they have to divide. That is why the skin of someone who has spent his life tanning in the sun is so much more wrinkled than someone who stayed in the shade; the skin cells of the tanning fanatic have to keep reproducing in order to replace those destroyed by ultraviolet rays. They have to work harder—their telomeres are shorter."

"Fascinating," said Jude. "But for whatever reason, the cell still ultimately has to die."

"Ah, but does it? Or rather, does it have to die at such an abysmally early age?" McNichol drew his words out dramatically. "You see, living cells are extremely efficient. They are magnificent creations—they consume food, expel waste, perform work, and have a strong membrane for protection. A perfectly balanced world within a microcosm. So perfect that there is no reason to think they are cursed with a built-in limit to their longevity.

"That much we know from looking at cancer cells. Cancer cells replicate themselves endlessly, generation after generation, so much so that experiments to count the number of divisions virtually never end. There are cancer cells in laboratories that live on in petri dish after petri dish for decades. They are, for all intents and purposes, immortal."

"How do they do it?"

"How indeed? The secret lies in an enzyme called telomerase. It works like a little repair kit. Every time a bit of telomere is lost through cell division, it comes along and replaces it so that the strand never gets shorter. The shoelace never gets frayed, if you will, because it gets a new plastic tip. Telomerase is present in cancerous cells. It's also there in egg and sperm cells because, of course, these cells have to remain young—they're passed on to the offspring. But the enzyme is not in your run-of-the-mill normal cells even though normal cells could make it. They have a gene to make it, but the gene is switched off."

"So if the cells only had the enzyme, they'd live longer? That's the theory?"

"It's not theory. It is demonstrable fact. Scientists at the University of Texas Southwestern Medical Center have injected the core of the enzyme-producing gene into human cells. Incidentally, they were able to get the gene by studying our little pond protozoan, which happens to produce huge amounts of telomerase. After they injected it, the telomeres regained their youthful length and the cells kept on dividing happily way beyond their life span. The cells have been rejuvenated."

"So they've discovered the fountain of youth—Ponce de León?"

"No, aging is much more complicated. For one thing, not all cells follow the same rules—brain cells and heart cells, for example. But it's certainly an important start. It's confirmation of the fact that the human body, like all living organisms, has a remarkable capacity for self-repair. It turns out we are not machines after all."

McNichol sat back down, his lecture done. Jude was intrigued by all that he had heard, but he was at a loss to figure out what all of it had to do with him. He turned a page in his notebook—a sign that he wanted to get down to business—took a sip of coffee, which was now cold, and looked the medical examiner in the eye.

"Mr. McNichol . . . Dr. McNichol. All this is very interesting. But if you don't mind, what does it have to do with the two swatches of hair I left with you?"

"Background, my boy. Background. Without my little lecture—and I'm sorry if I went on a bit there—but without it you would not be able to understand what it is that I did and how I reached the conclusion I did."

"And what is that?" prodded Jude.

"As you might expect, all of this research has implications in my own little pond," he said with a false tone of self-deprecation. "The forensic sciences have grown by leaps and bounds in recent years, and we are doing things we never thought possible back when I was in medical school."

"Yes. Please get to the point."

"The point is, I did a straightforward DNA analysis, in which I compared the two samples of hair. DNA, as you know, is a matching of gene sequences that permits us to establish whether or not two specimens come from the same person. The likelihood of error is greatly reduced when compared to fingerprinting. We are usually able to establish ownership within margins that defy coincidence."

"Yes, I know. And you found . . . ?"

"Well, very simply, I found that the DNA matched perfectly. The chance that such a match would occur in two different people in this case is approximately one in four hundred thousand, which is to say, negligible. So that finding leads inescapably to the conclusion that the two hair samples came from the same person."

"Or," said Jude slowly, "they could come from identical twins—correct?"

"Yes, of course. Identical twins do not have the same fingerprints, since fingerprints form in a late stage of fetal development. But they do have the same genetic makeup, and so any DNA specimens from identical twins would form a perfect match. But in this case, I ruled out twins."

"What? Why?"

"Well, that takes us back to the telomeres. We have recently developed and refined a subset of DNA testing called RFLPS, which stands for restriction fragment length polymorphism. The procedure can differentiate between organisms by analyzing patterns derived from cleavage of their DNA. We can look at the length of the telomeres to come up with an estimate of the age of the person. It's not exact, mind you, but the technique is sufficiently sophisicated to establish a difference in ages between two samples. And that's what I was able to do here."

"And what was that? Dr. McNichol, please, tell me the conclusion."

"One sample—in the bag you marked A—came from a person who is five years younger than the sample in bag B. Give or take a year."

"But . . . but," Judd stammered. "That's not possible."

"Exactly. That's not possible if they were from identical twins. How could you have identical twins of different ages? And so I reached my conclusion, which you may feel free to print in your newspaper, provided of course that you do end up doing a story, and that conclusion is . . ."

"Yes."

"That the two swatches came from the same person, which I assume is you. You gave me two more or less identical samples of your hair, except that one was about five years younger. So you cut it off five years ago and preserved it."

Jude fell silent.

"What I can't fathom," said McNichol, "is why you would have saved it—surely you didn't have the foresight five years ago to know that you would be doing this kind of article."

Very slowly, Jude closed his notebook. He thanked McNichol for the work he had done, shook his hand and said he might be in touch with him if he had further questions. McNichol asked Jude when he thought the article would run, and Jude replied that he had no idea.

On the way out, a receptionist was sitting at the front desk that had been empty earlier. She was a young woman with sharp eyes who looked intelligent. Jude approached her and asked her the name of the agency that occupied the office.

"A number of agencies share the space—federal, state and local. It's spillover space."

"Law enforcement agencies?"

"Why, yes."

"Including the FBI?"

"Yes, the FBI among others. Why do you ask?"

He didn't answer, and when she demanded to know his name, and why he was there, he didn't answer that, either. Instead, he went to the elevator bank and, as luck would have it, got there just as the doors opened.

Jude called Tizzie from a phone booth on Astor Place and tried to keep calm. He didn't want his voice to sound as worried as he, in fact, was. She did not answer right away. He checked his watch—after five. The secretary would be gone. Was she still there? With each ring, he began tapping the side of the booth with a knuckle, and soon he was urging her to hurry—"C'mon, c'mon. Pick up."

Finally, she did.

"Tizzie. Listen. Skyler's missing. I came down to his place and he's not there. The super said he cut out."

"Why? Where would he go?"

"No idea. The super didn't know—he's not very helpful. At first he thought I was Skyler, and he started yelling at me for going down the fire escape. He said I almost wrecked it, it was illegal to use it, that he didn't want me there anymore. Then I told him we were brothers and my younger brother was a little slow and did he know where he went, but he didn't know anything. Except he said Skyler was scared of something. He said he looked like he was running away."

"What could he be running away from?"

"God only knows, but he was clearly spooked. We can talk about that later. I've got so much to tell you—you won't believe it. Some things are falling into place. But in the meantime, I've got to find Skyler. I'm going to go look for him. Can you wait over at my place, in case he calls? I think he's got the number, at least I hope so."

"Certainly."

"And keep your eyes peeled when you go in. Maybe he'd go there—if he's really scared I don't think so, he'd be afraid they'd look for him there. But you never know."

"Jude. Who are 'they'?"

"Later."

"Don't be so mysterious. You're acting strange, and you sound really upset."

"I'll tell you everything, but not now. I've got to get going."

Tizzie said she'd go right over.

Jude hailed a cab and told the driver to take him to Central Park.

"Whereabouts?"

That was just the problem—Jude hadn't the slightest idea. And since the park ran from Fifty-ninth Street to One hundred and tenth, he didn't have a hope in hell of launching any kind of thorough search. He told the driver to leave him off at Seventy-second and Fifth. He'd just have to take his chances.

He leaned back in his seat. *Now, where would I go, if it was me? After all, it almost is me, for Christ's sake. There ought to be some kind of advantage in being . . . so closely related.*

He could not bring himself to use—even in his own inner monologue—the word that had leapt to mind after his talk with McNichol.

❖

In the holding cell of the Seventeenth precinct, Skyler was allowed more than the traditional single phone call. After all, he was not, strictly speaking, arrested.

He had been brought in with all of the construction workers, burly men who had been screaming and cursing at the demonstration, but who had turned notably passive once they were in police custody, herded into a van. On the way to the station house, they'd joked with the cops and exchanged small talk, regular guys out on an adventure. Skyler, sitting in a corner of the van and staring through the wire mesh at the streets whizzing by, had been petrified. He had no idea of what was happening or where he was going or why. His leg throbbed and his head ached, and when he touched the wound on his scalp, he felt his hair caked in blood.

Even before they arrived at the station house on Fifty-first Street, the men in back pointed him out to the cops riding up front and said he had been picked up by mistake. The cops didn't pay them much mind. Once there, the men were herded into two large cells, greeting each other with laughter and whoops of joy, as if the whole thing were a lark. The metal doors were left open, and in no time, a union lawyer appeared on the scene to sort out the charges. He took the men's names, one by one, and when he got to Skyler, he asked him a few questions and then brought him from the cell out front to a white-haired desk sergeant, who listened briefly and told Skyler he was free to leave. Skyler was on the point of walking out the door, when the sergeant looked him up and down and said, "You got any place to go?" Skyler shook his head, and the sergeant offered him the use of a phone. Skyler could think of only one person to call, and the policemen looked up the number and dialed it for him.

"You want to get that head looked at," he said, moments before Tizzie arrived. When she walked in, breathless with her long hair and her white skirt flowing behind, the men who had been let out of the cells whistled and started acting up again.

Jude paced back and forth in his living room while Skyler and Tizzie sat on the couch sipping tea. Skyler told them about lying in bed in the rooming house and hearing someone on the landing, and his flight down the fire escape. He told about running through the streets and seeing the Orderly, or a man who looked like him, and ducking into the place with the naked woman and riding the subway and getting arrested. Jude remained skeptical that his enemies had tracked him down. He said it could have been anyone on the landing, and he doubted that of all the people in the city, Skyler had come across the very people who were hunting him. He said he thought Skyler's imagination was playing tricks on him.

Then Jude told them to sit back and listen. He looked at Tizzie.

"You remember I told you about these guys called Orderlies?"

"God, yes. They sound horrible."

"Well, Skyler says all three of them look more or less the same. I found out myself that at least two of them do when they were tailing me in the subway the night I met him."

"Ah, I see," said Tizzie suddenly. "If there really are *three* of them and they really are *identical*, then—then we're in a whole new realm of science."

"I don't get it," said Skyler.

"You can't have identical triplets," said Jude. "At least not in nature. There would have to be human intervention to create that."

Then he told Skyler about taking a sample of his hair to McNichol and providing one of his own and how the DNA testing results showed that they were identical in every respect except for age. And as he sketched the general outline of the theory that he was beginning to espouse, he found that it was not so hard to use the word that he had earlier pushed aside, that in fact he could not say what he was coming to believe unless he used it.

So he took a deep breath and just said it outright. Looking directly at Skyler, he said: "We've been thinking that we're related, that maybe we are brothers. But I think we're closer than that. I think you are my clone."

# Chapter 17

Tizzie led the way across the Columbia campus. To the students sunbathing on the steps they must have made an incongruous trio—her striding ahead in the pinstripe suit, Jude slightly disheveled in a corduroy jacket with a reporter's notebook sticking out of the side pocket, and Skyler bringing up the rear, looking oddly hip with his short blond hair and sunglasses.

They took rear seats in the amphitheater and looked at the portly man up front. Dr. Bernard S. Margarite. The science editor at the *Mirror* hadn't hesitated a microsecond when Jude telephoned to ask for a recommendation. When it comes to genetics, he said, Margarite's your man. Jude looked him up. He had written papers with daunting titles like "Nuclear Transfer in Blastomeres from 4-cell Cow Embryos."

Luckily, the lecture was for an introductory course. Several dozen summer students in various stages of undress piled their books on the floor and draped themselves across the chairs.

Margarite made a few announcements, warned about a test next week and cracked a joke or two. Then he looked over his notes, walked to the blackboard and drew five careless circles on it. A boy next to Jude opened a notebook and copied the circles.

"As any fool can see," said Margarite laconically, "these are eggs." He paused, as if to admire his handiwork.

"Frog's eggs. Why do biologists love frog's eggs? One simple reason. They're large—about ten times larger than human eggs. And they grow outside the amphibian's body, so you can observe them."

He tossed the piece of chalk across the room. Margarite had a reputation as a showman lecturer.

"Now, you all know what happens when an egg is fertilized. It grows and splits into two, and each of those halves grows and splits again, and so on. And eventually you have a ball of cells, an embryo. And as more divisions occur, the cells become specialized—some become skin, some become eyes, some turn into tail, some into spinal cord and so on. And pretty soon you have a baby frog that will someday grow up and may either be dissected by seventh graders or end up on a Frenchman's table.

"All higher animals go through the same process. We've all done it—though hopefully without the same denouement"—the remark brought some polite tittering—"and we humans do it to an extreme. In adulthood we have about a hundred trillion cells each."

The boy next to Jude wrote out all the zeroes.

"So the first question that the early thinkers had to face was, how does that pattern happen—how do some cells know to become muscle and others to become bone? How do they become *differentiated*? Why can't a brain cell, say, revert back to an embryo and then become something else? They believed—and it's a logical assumption—that the ability is lost through reproduction. When a cell divides, each of the resulting halves has less information. The original embryo cell can do everything, but its offspring cannot, and the further down the line you go, the less a cell can do. So by the time you're a liver cell, that's it—that's your lot in life.

"For fifty years, proving and disproving that basic hypothesis was the Holy Grail of biology."

And Margarite mentioned a half dozen names and ran through their theories and experiments—zoologists who had split eggs, punctured them with needles, shook them apart inside flasks. Even one—Hans Spemann—who had used tiny hairs from the head of his newborn son to strangle them into new shapes—"the way a clown squeezes a balloon into a duck or a rabbit."

"Then Spemann did something truly ingenious. He took a fertilized salamander egg and manipulated it into a dumbbell shape. The nucleus with the genetic material stayed on one side and began to divide and subdivide normally. While this was going on, Spemann loosened the stricture just enough to let one of the nuclei slip past and end up in the other end of the dumbbell. Then he pulled the noose tight until he severed the two sides. He was left with a developing embryo in one and a single cell in the other.

"What happened? Would the single cell grow into an embryo all by itself—even though its nucleus had already subdivided four times? Would it retain enough genetic information to do that? The answer—of course—was yes. It turned into an identical twin of the bigger embryo.

"Give me a name for what Spemann had done. Class? Anyone?"

No volunteers.

"It comes from a Greek word, and the word in Greek means 'twig.'"

A girl in the front raised her hand and said tentatively, "What he did was make a clone."

*"Yes,"* exclaimed Margarite. "He made a *clone*. It's crude, it's primitive, you have to use a helluva lot of baby hairs to do it, but he made a clone. He forced a salamander embryo to divest a piece of itself that then turned into an exact replica."

Jude and Skyler exchanged looks. The sound of the word "clone" was still jarring.

"Spemann, incidentally, had what he called a 'fantastical' daydream sixty years ago. What if you were able to take an egg and remove the nucleus from it? And what if you were able to take the nucleus out of another cell—one that was already well developed, that was truly differentiated—and insert it into the egg? What would happen? Would it grow? Would the egg proceed as if everything was normal, even though it was beginning life with an old nucleus that had been around the block a few times?"

"Well, in just another generation, the 'fantastical' was achieved. 'Nuclear transplantation' is its name, and it was done in the early 1950s by Robert Briggs and Thomas King at the Institute for Cancer Research in Philadelphia."

Margarite ran through a litany of scientists who had made advances in the field.

"Then, finally, of course, we come to five p.m., July 5, 1996. The world-famous Dolly is born. Ian Wilmut and Keith Campbell of the Roslin Institute in Edinburgh, Scotland, took a donor cell from the mammary gland of a six-year-old ewe and put it into an enucleated unfertilized egg. The key was sending the cell into a quiescent state, which Campbell did by starving it. That made it more adaptive to its new environment. Dolly will go down in history as the first mammal to be cloned from an adult cell.

"The message in all of this," concluded Margarite, looking at his watch, "is never say never. In science, if something can be done, sooner or later it will be done. And that's what I answer when people ask me: 'Will we ever clone humans beings?' I answer: 'If it can be done, it will be done.'

"As Robert J. Oppenheimer said before making the atom bomb: 'When you see something that is technically sweet, you go ahead and do it.' "

"So you're convinced that's it—you and I are clones," said Skyler, an undercurrent of aggression to his voice.

The three were sitting at a bar called the Subway Inn on Sixtieth Street. They had a booth, Tizzie and Skyler on one side, Jude on the other. It was dimly lighted, and the jukebox was playing an old Dave Brubeck piece, "Take Five." Tizzie was drinking bourbon. Jude was drinking a Beck's. Skyler had tasted Jude's and ordered the same.

"I'm not saying I know it for a fact," said Jude. "I admit it sounds far-out."

"Far-out?"

"Unusual," explained Tizzie. "Unlikely."

"All I'm saying is that it's the only explanation that makes sense and that accounts for everything. How else can you explain that you and I are so much alike—we look alike and we've got the same DNA, for Christ's sake—and yet we're not the same age."

"Maybe we are the same age. Maybe that guy—what's his name . . . ?"

"McNichol."

"McNichol. Maybe he messed up that test."

"Maybe, but that's not all," said Jude.

"What else?"

Jude took a long sip of beer before he went on.

"The physical exam you took. I called today and got the results."

"And . . . ?"

"And I spoke to my regular doctor, who was back. He was beside himself, totally confused—he thought there must have been some kind of mistake."

"Why?" asked Tizzie.

"First of all, he said"—Jude looked at Skyler—"you'll like this—he said I was in great shape physically, that I hadn't been this good in years. Lean and mean, body of a younger man, and all that. I pass the compliment on to you, since it's rightfully yours."

Skyler's mouth hinted at a smile.

"But he was thrown by my blood. He said that immunizing cells that I had built up from hepatitis, which I had three years ago, had totally disappeared. He found this strange. In fact, he said he first thought that there had been a mix-up of blood samples, but gave up on that because the blood matched in every other way. He was stumped."

"Yeah, well, we know the reason for that—I never had hepatitis. I don't think anyone on our island ever had it. So what?"

"The match of the blood in every other respect was strong enough to override his doubts. So there's one more indication that our makeup is the same, that our genes are the same."

"Which would happen if we were twins."

"Yes, but he also found something indicating an age difference. He spotted it on my X ray—"

"My X ray."

"Yes, your X ray, which he compared to my X ray from a previous visit. He said there was actually a reversal in bone density, that the natural thinning had stopped and reversed itself so that the bones were slightly thicker. As they would have been if I were five or six years younger than I am. He was so surprised, he called in a radiologist, who confirmed the finding. No wonder he's confused. He's beginning to think I'm one for the record books."

Skyler took the information in silence and finished his beer. He looked at Jude.

"You take my hair and have it tested behind my back. You send me to your own doctor. What other little tests do you have planned? What other surprises do you have up your sleeve?"

He stood up and went to the bar to get another beer.

"He's right, you know," said Tizzie. "He has every reason to be upset. He's probably feeling like a guinea pig. This can't be easy for him."

"It's not easy for me, either," complained Jude. "A week ago, I thought I was a normal person like anyone else on this planet. Now I find I'm some sort of freak."

"You're not the one who feels like a freak. He does."

Skyler returned and started talking even before he sat down.

"Ok, let's say it's all true. Why would anyone do this? Why would anyone make clones?"

"I don't know. But I do know that we had strange upbringings, you and I. Both of us. Me, raised up in some kind of group in Arizona, losing both my parents before I knew it. You, there on that crazy island where your every thought and practically your every movement was controlled. Neither of us knows our parents. We look alike. We act alike. But I'm older than you. For God's sake, you come up with an explanation!"

"I can't," said Skyler quietly. "And if it was done the way you say, I hate to think about why. I hate to think of the possibilities."

Tizzie's face drained of color.

"I think you know why," replied Skyler. "Let's not talk about the possibilities right now."

"Okay. I'll go along with that."

"For a while, at least."

Tizzie handed her empty glass to Jude.

"How about another drink?" she said.

"Sure."

When Jude left, Tizzie put her hand on Skyler's arm and smiled at him. He couldn't help himself—he lifted his hand and placed it on top of hers. He was afraid he was almost trembling.

"I know it's not easy," she said.

He didn't trust himself to say anything but looked at her full in the face. His stare was intense.

When Jude returned, they sat in silence for a while. Finally, Skyler spoke up.

"Let me ask you something," he said to Jude. "In your mind, am I your clone or are you my clone?"

"You're my clone."

"How so?"

"Because I'm older."

"I see."

"You don't agree?"

"Let's just say that's not the way I see it."

"How do you see it?"

"We both came from the same egg. You just got to use it first."

On the way out, Jude turned to Skyler and grinned.

"By the way," he said. "There is one more thing."

"What?"

"I have it on good authority that your wisdom teeth are going to come in over the next year or so. And I'd say you're probably going to develop what they call a 'dry socket.' And take it from me, it's going to hurt like hell."

Jude took the subway to South Ferry, and as he was climbing the stairs to the Staten Island ferry terminal, he took a detour. He had come to a decision—but he wasn't proud of it.

He walked to a newsstand and ordered a pack of Camel filters. He ripped off the cellophane, rapped the pack against his left forefinger, and pulled out a cigarette. Amazing, he thought, how all the practiced ancillary rituals of smoking live on. How long had it been?—two years almost.

Moving quickly, lest his conscience intrude, he lit up and inhaled deeply. He almost keeled over. He felt as if an invisible hand had grabbed his lungs and squeezed them. He was dizzy, then faint. A long-ago familiar light-headedness set in. He felt his blood racing though his system as if his veins had suddenly contracted. Then came the beautiful calm.

But it was followed by a paroxysm of self-loathing. How could he be so weak? He tried to keep it at bay with rationalizations: how often, after all, is a fellow's life turned topsy-turvy by forces beyond his control? Who could stop at a time like this? He flicked the cigarette down with his middle finger—another old habit—and heard it hiss as it struck the water. He boarded the ferry.

Raymond was nowhere in sight. He checked his watch: exactly ten p.m. No confusion there. He walked around the ferry twice on both decks and checked out the passengers sitting on the wooden slat benches or leaning upon the outer railings—the businessmen and blue-collar workers returning home, the secretaries staying late for a few drinks, lovers out on a cheap excursion. What a stupid idea to meet here. When Jude had called Raymond at home to set a place and he'd suggested the ferry, it had struck Jude as melodramatic. How many late-night movies had he been watching on television? But Raymond had insisted he needed to take the ferry anyway. Where could he be going at this hour? Maybe Jude was on the wrong one; maybe he should go back and wait for the next. He glanced back at the stern and, beyond it, the ferry slip. Too late. The thick tie lines were already off, and the boat was churning in the water, bouncing off the tires hanging from the wooden piers, which groaned.

He walked back to the passenger cabin, and something on the deck below caught his eye, a wiper washing the window of a black Lexus. Jude thought he saw a hand inside moving, beckoning. Of course, that would be Raymond. He always liked good entrances. And here was an added advantage for a paranoid FBI man: it's hard to bug the inside of a car.

"How're you doing?"

Raymond waited until he was inside with the door closed before he began the perfunctory formalities. Jude was in no mood to waste time.

"Not so good, to tell you the truth. I feel like shit, actually. I can't sleep. I can't work. I'm in the middle of something that I can't make sense of. I'm being followed by a couple of psychopaths, and I think I'm in danger."

"Yeah. And your health is going to suffer, too, if you keep smoking like that."

"So you saw me back there."

"Like I always say, being observant is just a question of being observant."

"You could have said something—I've walked around this boat three times."

"Four, actually."

Jude looked at him. He was a reasonably handsome man two years shy of forty with a narrow face, sad-looking brown eyes, cheeks slightly scarred by acne and tufts of white hair flowing around the tips of his ears. He was wearing an open-necked blue shirt, expensive-looking.

He looked back at Jude and bobbed his head. "Why don't you tell me about it? Start at the beginning."

"You know the beginning. It was that New Paltz murder, but how it figures in all this, I still haven't worked out."

"Remind me."

"It was a Sunday, I got the assignment and went up—"

"Who gave it to you?"

"What does that have to do with anything?"

"I've been doing this a lot longer than you. Just answer the goddamned question."

"Well, it was the weekend editor, a guy named Leventhal. What does that have to do with anything?"

"Let me be the judge of that. I notice the *Mirror* didn't play the story big."

"No, not at all, a couple of paragraphs in the back."

"They tell you why?"

"No, they just said another story was better. That's the editors' prerogative—deciding where the stories go, and they're, you know, jealous of it."

"Yeah, I can imagine. A place like the *Mirror*. And to think I always thought they just threw them against the wall to see which ones stick. Anyway, go on."

"Well, you know what I found out up there, which wasn't much. The guy McNichol picked as the victim turned out to be a local judge, which you told me. And he was alive and kicking. The strange thing is, when I walked into his court and he saw me, he practically had a fit."

"Hold on, not so fast. Why did you go back? Were you told to follow the story?"

"No, not at all. Here is where it starts to get weird. You see, I'd been hearing that a guy was walking around who looked like me, exactly like me, a double. And one night he turns up in my building, just like that, and that's what he is—an exact double. I thought at first that he's some kind of long-lost identical twin. Except that he's not—it turns out he's younger."

Jude looked at Raymond and expected to see a look of surprise or maybe skepticism on his face, but if it was there, he couldn't spot it.

"Do you mind if I smoke?" Jude asked.

"No, what the hell. But I thought you stopped."

"I did, but I hated being a slave to my willpower."

"Very funny. But you didn't answer the question—why did you go back to New Paltz?"

"You see, the corpse, the dead guy up there, had a strange wound on his thigh. I told you about it before. It was about the size of a quarter, and it looked like somebody had gouged it out, maybe because there was some kind of identifying mark there. At least, that's what McNichol thought. And my double, whose name is Skyler, by the way, it turns out that he has a mark in the exact same spot. So I made the connection."

"What was the mark?"

"It was a tattoo of Gemini—you know, twins, the zodiac. And that's what he—I mean, Skyler—said they were called on the island. Gemini."

"Island?"

"Yes. He said there was a whole bunch of them, just like him, and they were raised on an island by people who were doctors and who took care of them and kept them in really good health."

"I see."

Jude had the feeling, now that he was laying it all out, that the story sounded too ridiculous to be taken seriously. He felt faintly foolish, and half hoped that Raymond would make fun of him and that somehow the whole thing would just disappear. But Raymond didn't do that; he seemed to be paying close attention.

"And did he tell you where this island is?"

"No, believe it or not—he doesn't know. He got out by stowing away on a plane, and he doesn't even know what state he was in."

"And where is he now?"

"He's somewhere. It doesn't matter. It's not important."

"Maybe it is important. Maybe he's in some danger—have you thought of that?"

Jude was silent. He had thought of little else over the past few days.

"Go back to the judge a minute. You said he was upset to see you?"

"I walked into his courtroom while he was presiding. As I said, he took one look at me and practically fainted. He had to leave the bench."

"And he didn't look familiar to you?"

"No, not at all. I never saw him before in my life."

Raymond was silent for a while, turning on the ignition and pressing a button to lower the window on the driver's side to let the smoke out. He peered into the darkness of the car deck and, apparently satisfied that no one was there, back at Jude.

"So who else knows about this?"

A tiny alarm bell went off in Jude's brain.

"No one."

"No one at all? You've just been keeping this all bottled up by yourself?"

"Who would I tell? I mean, you have to admit, it sounds pretty crazy."

"No girlfriend, nothing?"

Jude shook his head no—a sort of halfway no.

"You said some guys were after you—following you."

"I don't know if it's one guy or two. If it's two, they look just alike—big guys with a white streak in the hair. Skyler says they're from the island. It sounds like they're some kind of enforcers. I saw them on the subway. I tell you, something about them makes my blood run cold."

Jude went to put the cigarette out in the ashtray, but saw that it was filled with coins and some kind of tablets.

"Zantac," said Raymond. "For my stomach ulcer. Days like this, I need it. Let's go outside."

They climbed the stairs and walked to the open deck at the stern. It was a magnificent night filled with lights—the blinking lights of stars, the warm glow of cabin lights on yachts and tugboats in the harbor, the tiny pinpoint lights in the skyline rising up behind like a cartoon cutout. The tiara on the Statue of Liberty glowed green.

"Raymond," said Jude. "I need to know what's going on. What can you tell me?"

"Not much."

Raymond was not looking at him, just talking off into the night.

"It's sketchy," he said. "There's a group, I don't even know the name—

the name seems to keep changing. It started sometime in the sixties, medical researchers and doctors, a bunch of smart kids. Most of them were connected to Johns Hopkins, Harvard and schools around Boston, N.I.H. They centered on a brilliant researcher, one of these incredible charismatic types. You know what I mean—once you meet them and you fall under their spell, you're mesmerized. You're convinced they can do anything and that they have the keys to the universe and you're willing to give up everything and follow them anywhere.

"This guy got in some kind of trouble at some medical school. We don't know what exactly—the records are missing, which is typical of this group, by the way, it covers its tracks. We don't even know the guy's name. Anyway, he was doing some pretty far-out research, stuff involving longevity or gene mapping or molecular biology. I don't know, but apparently he was pushing the boundaries with his experiments and ran afoul of some regulations that try to control all of this, and he either got the boot or picked up his tent and moved on. And a bunch of medical people moved with him. They ended up in Arizona for a while, and got tied in with some big-money people, mostly in California. In particular, one billionaire, a guy called Samuel Billington. He had it all, but apparently didn't want to lose it to the grave—one of those eccentric types who think they're above everything, they should even be above the laws of physics. So he bankrolled them sometime in the mid-seventies before he died. A lot of good they did him."

Raymond fell silent. Jude thought he was just pausing, but it seemed that he had come to the end of what he wanted to say.

"And then what?"

"Not much to say. The trail goes cold."

"It goes cold? You mean it just stops?"

"Not so much that. There was no one to really follow it. It wasn't a high priority."

"You say you don't even know the guy's name?"

"No. We know a name he uses later—Rincon. We assume it's an alias. There are no medical school records anywhere under that name."

"But the island—you know where it is, what goes on there?"

Raymond shrugged. "It's not really an active file. There're a lot of these groups around, cults of all kinds. There's no reason for an active investigation. We've got no indication anyone's breaking any laws."

"But those guys, the Orderlies . . ."

"A couple of guys on a subway. Got to do better than that."

"Raymond, for Christ's sake. Skyler looks just like me. But he's younger than me."

"Yeah, I know all about the tests."

Jude was surprised by this, but kept it to himself.

"What does that tell you?" he asked.

"What's it tell *you*?"

Jude was frustrated by his evasions.

"Somebody made him, for God's sake. He's a *clone*."

Raymond didn't blink an eye.

"And I know you know that. And I know you wanted me to figure it out. Why else would you have given me the ID on the judge? You wanted me to make the connection."

"Don't be crazy. How could I know that your guy would have some kind of tattoo?"

But Jude knew that he was close to the mark.

"You want me involved, right? You want me to do your work for you—the rabbit that gets the dogs running."

Raymond straightened up and looked toward the bow.

"Listen," he said. "We don't have much time left. Here's what we've got to do. You tell me where your guy—what's his name, Skyler?—you tell me where he is and maybe at least we can put him under some kind of protection. Make sure nothing happens to him."

"No, I can't do that."

Raymond shot him a hard look. "So you really don't trust me. After all this time, all we've been through, you really don't trust me."

"It's not that, Raymond. It's for his sake. The less people know about him, the better."

Jude could tell Raymond was not buying it. But Raymond didn't leave any doubt.

"Don't bullshit me," he said.

"Sorry. I've got to do what I think right."

Raymond looked over his shoulder again. "I see we're there," he said in a tone with a hard edge. He seemed to be trying to convey the sense of just how wrong Jude was. "I gotta run."

He turned to go, but Jude grabbed him by the arm.

"Raymond, c'mon. This is my life we're talking about here. I need something to go on. I need some help."

Raymond shook his hand off. His voice dropped low. "I can't. I don't really have anything to tell you. You're in the shit. You've grabbed a monster by the tail. You don't know what kind of monster it is or how dangerous it is or how big it is or how sharp its teeth are. But you should know this—be careful, be very careful. Act wisely. Think every move through. And don't trust anyone. Anyone—no matter how close."

Then he went below. Jude watched the line of cars pull out and drive off onto Staten Island, and then he waited fifteen minutes for the return trip to Manhattan. All the way back across the harbor, leaning on the railing that was rocking softly with the boat's movements, he thought about what Raymond had said and felt angry all over again.

Jude called the clerk on the Metro desk and said that he would be out for a few days, maybe longer. The clerk asked him what was wrong, and when he said he had come down with a cold or possibly the flu, he knew he didn't sound sick. Hanging up, he was convinced the clerk's "get well soon" was sarcastic. Screw it. He had bigger things to worry about.

He packed quickly for himself and Skyler, throwing a couple of shirts and pants into a bag, and drove across town to Tizzie's place, where Skyler had been staying after refusing to return to the room on Astor Place. The two of them were waiting on the front stoop, sunning themselves as if they hadn't a care in the world. What an incongruous sight, Jude thought, as he pulled up. Tizzie waved and stood up reluctantly and reached with her arms way above her head and stretched, arching her back. She was wearing khaki shorts and a blue workshirt tied at the midriff. Coming upon her unexpectedly like that, Jude was struck by her beauty. He got out and tossed her the keys. She opened the trunk, tossed in her small duffel bag, and plopped down in the front seat. When he turned on the ignition, she promptly spun the radio dial until she found some Mozart. Skyler got in the back, and Jude drove off.

He went down Eleventh Avenue and took the Lincoln Tunnel, reflexively checking in the rearview mirror to see if a familiar car was on their tail. Leaving the tunnel and climbing the winding ramp and then cruising the elevated highway through the New Jersey meadowlands, Jude felt better. The city was dropping away behind them. He looked at Tizzie, who smiled, and he realized that it was the first smile he had seen from her in a long time. She had been distant and peculiar since this whole thing began.

"It's good to get away," he said. "Arizona, here we come."

"Three people in search of a deep, dark secret," she said.

Jude peered in the rearview mirror at Skyler, who was gazing out the window at the oil refineries, looking preoccupied and worried.

"C'mon, Skyler. Cheer up. If you behave yourself, maybe I'll take you to see the Grand Canyon."

Skyler caught his eye in the mirror, and by way of response he gave a half smile. Jude felt a small but familiar emotional swell rise up within himself, the desire to take care of Skyler and protect him and make sure that no harm came to him. He was like a younger brother.

Jude drove fast, one arm resting on the open window and his foot solidly on the gas, moving smoothly in and out of the fast lane to pass every car in sight. He wanted to put New York far behind them, but it also felt good, therapeutic even, to command a machine and push it hard, concentrating on little else. They didn't stop for food until they were deep into the Amish country of Pennsylvania. They pulled off the turnpike at an exit and found a roadhouse that served large hamburgers smothered in onions.

Tizzie took over the wheel. She put on her glasses—she was nearsighted. On the way back to the turnpike, they passed a horse-drawn wagon with a rear lantern. Sitting up in the driver's perch was a solitary man dressed in a dark jacket; he did not look at them as they passed.

"Who is that?" asked Skyler.

Tizzie told him about the Amish and their religious beliefs that caused them to shun modernity. He asked her what religion she belonged to; she said she had been raised without any religion in a household of atheists. But lately she had begun to read the Bible, and felt more and more of an attraction to its teachings.

"But I thought science contradicted it," said Skyler. "How can you be someone who believes in science and also uphold religion?"

"There's no contradiction at all," she replied. "A number of great scientists are religious believers. Some of them say that the more they learn and discover, the greater is their belief. Their work reinforces their faith that there is a larger force than ourselves animating the universe."

Skyler contemplated the idea, and finally said: "I'm glad to hear you say that. On the island we weren't allowed to read the Bible ourselves. The only person who talked about it was Baptiste, and he sometimes read passages from the Book of Revelation. He said it depicted the end of the old world and the rise of science."

"It's an allegory. So people turn it into whatever they want."

Jude smiled at the exchange. Tizzie has taken it upon herself to be his mentor and guide, he thought. *And I have to admit, he seems to be a fast learner.* What was interesting about the thought, he realized, was how proud he himself felt.

# Chapter 18

Jude and Skyler waited on a bench in the Animal Services unit of the Agricultural School of the University of Wisconsin. The day before, they had driven straight through to Chicago. Tizzie wanted to see her ailing parents in Milwaukee again, and the two of them had decided to meet another scientist recommended by the science editor, so they had driven to Madison. Jude had called ahead for an appointment; he'd said he needed an interview for a magazine article.

The campus on the edge of Lake Mendota seemed to go on forever. The agricultural school at 1675 Observatory Drive was like a small farm, with a silo and a large red barn connected to animal pens—yet this farm was on the cutting edge of research that was pushing embryology into a new and unknown world.

A young man approached down a corridor, his hair long enough to brush his shoulders; he was wearing a checked shirt, black chinos and cowboy boots. It wasn't until he extended his hand that they realized this was the person they had come to see. Dr. Julian Hartman was an eukaryotic cell biologist so adept at transferring nuclei from one cell to another that he was known as "the man with golden hands." He was also said to have a lock on the Nobel Prize someday soon.

He must have read the surprise upon their faces.

"I know," he said good-naturedly. "Everyone thinks I must be older than I am."

Hartman gave them a quick tour of the lab, which was smaller than they'd expected, consisting of only three rooms. One contained a large freezer modified with twenty small doors and a computer-run temperature-control system. The other two rooms were for lab work. Each had two large double-vision inverted microscopes fitted with hydraulic manipulators for minuscule movements.

Across one wall was an illuminated panel, similar to those used by radiologists, but instead of X rays it displayed blown-up photos of eggs. Most were attached by suction to a blunt-nosed retainer. Some were pierced by a glass pipette sharpened to a point. The pipette looked like a vacuum cleaner hose, and the nucleus it was taking out looked like a ball that just fit inside it.

Hartman provided a narrative of the photos, explaining step by step how the nucleus was removed from an unfertilized egg and another nucleus put in its place, then given a tiny shock—1.25 kilovolts for 80 microseconds—to complete the merger and kick-start the process of cell division.

"Electric shock to start it off. Ironic, isn't it, when you think of Frankenstein? Maybe Mary Shelley was right, after all."

Nearby was a bulletin board pinned with photographs of animals. There were cattle, sheep, rabbits, even white rats. Many came in pairs or triplets or quadruples, and when Jude examined them, he realized that all the animals in each group looked exactly alike. Dates of birth were scrawled below.

"My children," said Hartman, following Jude's glance. "It bugs my wife to no end when I say that."

He pointed at a picture of two sheep looking up rather stupidly from a straw-filled pen.

"Mabel and Muriel. My first success. They're still kicking—in fact, they're mothers themselves now. I didn't produce all of these. There are four or five of us in this line of work around the world, and whenever we have a success, we send off a photo to the others. Bragging rights."

"But why?" asked Skyler. "I don't mean, why do you send photos. I mean, why do it at all? What do you hope to get?"

"The potential applications are almost too numerous to describe," Hartman replied. "For one thing, imagine being able to keep cells frozen to conserve genetic material in endangered species. You could bring them to life whenever you wanted, and create as many or as few as you needed."

He picked up a photo of a sheep. "This is Tracey. She was produced at the Roslin Institute, the same place that gave us Dolly. She has been made to carry a gene for an enzyme known as alpha one antitrypsyn, and she expresses this protein in her milk so you can milk her and extract it. It is extremely important, because it is the protein that is missing in people with the lung disorder emphysema.

"Lots of other work is going on to eliminate diseases and produce pharmaceutical proteins and allow trans-species organ transplantation. Pigs are in many ways ideal as donors, but the human body usually rejects their organs. If we could modify their cells, we would have an endless supply. Do you know that, every year, three thousand people in the U.S. die on the waiting list for organs, and another hundred thousand die before they even make it onto the list?

"Farmers have always had prize animals. A perfect cow. Imagine taking that cow and producing hundreds. Or maybe front-ending the process—producing thousands in a lab and selecting out the ones you want and maybe changing them here or there by adding or subtracting a gene. And then, when you get the truly perfect one, through cloning you could just keep it going and produce an endless number.

"The key thing is the number. Genetic modification is difficult. You don't know where to insert the gene, and you can't tell where it's going to end up. But if we can culture cells in a dish in the thousands or the millions, we don't have to insert it with precision. We don't even have to know exactly how it works. All we have to do is to be able to locate it. Then we just select only those cells which carry the modification we require. See, when you've got millions, you can modify them all in bulk and look for the ones you need."

"So basically," said Jude, "it's like imitating the conditions for evolution, but doing it all at once, all at the same time."

"Precisely," said Hartman, beaming.

"And you're the one who's doing the choosing, not nature or God or the environment or circumstance."

"Right again."

"But doesn't it ever go wrong?"

Hartman smiled. "Look, I won't pretend there aren't problems. It's a tricky business. Let's face it, you're subjecting that little cell to a lot of poking and prodding. You actually invade it and perform major surgery. You're implanting an alien set of chromosomes—maybe the chromosomes aren't in a resting state, maybe they'll divide out of synch with the embryonic cells. If you're lucky, the embryo will die. And they do—Doctors Wilmut and Campbell produced Dolly, but to get her, there were two hundred and seventy-six embryos that died at various stages."

"Are there abnormalities that live?"

"Of course. You don't hear about those, naturally. There are all kinds of reports and rumors about gigantism."

"Gigantism. What's that?"

"They simply grow too big. Sometimes too big for the surrogate mother to give birth to. Many of the cattle clones done by the Grenada company in Texas showed this abnormality. We don't know yet what's responsible.

"Look, life's not perfect. Mistakes happen even in nature—especially in nature. There comes a time when you just have to bow down before it. You know your body changes with age. What's that mean on the level of individual cells? They change, too. They reproduce over and over, and little mistakes creep in. Proteins misread or miscopy all those miles of DNA. It's like a Xerox machine that is constantly on the go, where the copies don't just fade but actually drop letters or add letters here and there. After a million copies have been run off, the document isn't nearly as legible.

"So now what happens if we take the nucleus of an old cell and put it inside a new egg? Do we really have a brand-new fertilized egg ready to take on the challenge of life? Or do we have a tired old nucleus inside a young egg? That's a question nobody knows the answer to.

"And you know when we'll know?"

Jude shook his head.

"We'll know if we start getting a lot of strange-looking human beings."

Hartman's tour had come to an end. He sat down at a wooden table near his desk.

Skyler, who had been quiet most of the time, spoke up. "And is it possible, Dr. Hartman, to clone human beings?"

Hartman smiled, the kind of smile that suggested he had been asked that question innumerable times before.

"Let me put it this way. All the prerequisites are in place. In vitro fertilization—by far the most essential—has been done since 1971. The ability to enucleate DNA—getting better and better all the time. Freezing sperm cells and egg cells—we've been doing that for years. So all the machinery's there. If we can do it with lesser mammals—and we have—we can do it with humans. In fact, there's only one barrier."

"What's that?"

"Public opposition. Ethics. A sense a lot of people have that it's a violation of nature or what nature intends."

"But if a group came along and didn't feel itself bound by ethical considerations, could it, say, produce a child, clone it, freeze the clone, and then reactivate it years later?"

"Sure. The science is there. You're talking about the merger of two already existing and well-understood procedures—cloning and cryopreservation.

In March 1998 a baby was born in Los Angeles from an embryo that had been frozen for seven and a half years. They thought it was a record until they learned that a baby born in Philadelphia had come from an embryo that had been frozen four months longer.

"Of course—for delayed cloning—you'd have to have a compelling reason to do it. I mean, who would want to have a child and then want to produce an exact duplicate years later? There's only one reason I can think of—or at least one acceptable reason."

"And that is?" asked Jude.

"Grief. If you had a child that you loved, and that child died, and the loss was so unbearably painful, you might want to try to re-create him. Of course, that would be hopeless—it ignores all the psychological and other physiological factors that form a personality. And anyway, the scenario presumes that the parent is already thinking about replacing the child before the birth, and even for total pessimists, that's a bit of a stretch."

"You said one *acceptable* reason," noted Skyler. "What's the unacceptable one?"

"It's too absurd even to talk about. It's the province of sci fi writers, and it could never happen."

"But for the sake of discussion, what is it?"

"Well, it would be to create a bank of spare parts. We were talking about organ transplants earlier. Despite all the advances, we're still in the Dark Ages. We still have to flood the recipient patient with immunosuppression drugs; sometimes they work, sometimes they don't. We set up elaborate computer files to search for that one-in-a-thousand match for bone marrow. We put people on lists waiting for other people to get into fatal accidents. Imagine being able to perform a transplant without fearing that the body's immune system will reject the organ. The organ wouldn't be foreign, because its genetic makeup would be identical to the one it is replacing. It would already rightfully belong to the host. All those wonderful tiny commandos that have been trained to hunt down intruders—the leukocyte antigens and T cells—they'd be disarmed. The body would welcome it with open arms. That's been a dream of surgeons for thirty years, ever since Christiaan Barnard put the heart from a twenty-four-year-old woman who died in a car crash into the chest of fifty-five-year-old Louis Washkansky and gave him an extra eighteen days of life."

Hartman had worked himself up into a speech and seemed a little embarrassed by it. Jude and Skyler remained silent.

The scientist took a piece of paper from a pad on his desk and unclipped a pen from his breast pocket, scribbling something. He handed it to Skyler.

"Let's talk more. Here's my address. Come for dinner tonight. Seven o'clock. Needless to say—informal."

"One final question," said Jude. "Is there a record of transplants? That list you spoke of, is it accessible and could someone go back and look at all the transplants that were done?"

"Certainly," replied Hartman. "The computer's database holds every transplant ever performed in every hospital in the country. If you want, I can gain access for you."

"I would appreciate that."

Tizzie took a taxi to her house, and as it drove along familiar Lake Drive, lined with oaks and green lawns, she felt a nostalgic tug. She knew every tree, every twist in the road. They all retained memories for her, even memories just beyond reach that she nonetheless knew were there. The world of her childhood, so secure and now so distant, never lessened its hold upon her.

She had been raised an only child, never understanding that tone of sympathy in people's voice when they learned of it. For her it was glorious to stand at the center of her parents' love, no competitor for their affection or even their attention. She was free to sulk like a child at the age of fifteen or to pretend to maturity at twelve. When she cried at night out of fear, they would come running, both of them. She tried it sometimes just to test them, and they never failed her. They both came, but when she replayed it in her memory, it was her father's hands reaching down to her that she remembered.

They had spent their first years out west, a time she was too young to remember, and then they had bought the house in White Fish Bay. She did not remember much about where they had come from, but she remembered the day they had arrived, the excitement of the moving van, their belongings looking so peculiar packed and jammed together all in one huge truck. Her doll carriage had been placed in its own cardboard box. The other children on the block had gathered on the sidewalk and examined the contents, while she had pretended to ignore them. But within a day, they had become friends.

Her father was a doctor, and for a while his office was in an annex of their house. She loved going there, the medicinal smells, his black bag, the stethoscope, the scales, and once or twice she snuck in and hid in a closet to watch while he examined patients. Some years later, when his practice grew, he moved it to a clinic of brick buildings and clipped lawns, and they gave the office over to her for sleepovers, to be plastered with posters of the Carpenters and Abba and, later, heavy metal groups.

Her childhood was idyllic except for a period of intense nightmares that made every evening a time of incipient terror as bedtime approached. "Night terror" was, in fact, a name she heard her father use once, in a hushed conversation with her mother. It came, she heard him theorize, from a child's coming to grips with the concept of death. Her uncle had recently died, and at his funeral he had been laid out in an open casket, his jowls gray and puffy and frighteningly cold-looking. Her father said the phase would pass, and so it did, but somehow she felt it had marked her.

The uncle who had died, Ben, had been her favorite. He would blow into town in a red convertible and take her for a spin, breaking the speed limit. It was like playing hooky. If Ben was the prodigal son, though, her other uncle, Henry, was the priggish opposite. He rarely spoke to her or even seemed to notice her, and on those occasions when he did, she felt as if she were in the principal's office. And yet he was of supreme importance in their household and a powerful influence in her upbringing. When he visited, her parents seemed to wait on him and to hang on his words. She was made to feel that she must never, ever be impolite to him.

Like many only children, she was coddled and protected. Health was paramount. She was given vitamins and diet supplements; her father examined her at the least sign of illness, and her inoculations were kept up to date. The pencil marks on the wall to record her growth spurts were not frivolous—they were read as signposts of a sound body. Her father offered her a gold watch if she would reach eighteen without lighting a cigarette, and threatened to ground her for a month if she did. She won the watch.

But her adolescence turned predictably and proverbially stormy. She began fighting with her parents, mostly with her mother but even with her father, sulking and slamming doors and bursting out in tears. She threatened to leave. And one day she did leave, having saved enough money to take a bus to San Francisco. She had visions of joining the flower children, except that, of course, she got there fifteen years too late. North Beach was a wasteland of druggies and wastrels, and one night, staying in a flophouse, she was mugged by two men. The next day she called home, and her father sent her money to come home. She didn't venture far after that, until Berkeley, and when she left for there, she had the queasy sense that she was abandoning her parents.

Now that they were doing poorly, she wished that she could do something for them, offer them what they needed—the little girl to care for. But she was too big for that, so all she could do was let them know how much she cared, and follow the dictates of Uncle Henry, who, as always, knew exactly what was required.

And this time she had some tough questions for them.

The taxi drew to a slow stop in front of her house, a white New England clapboard with green shutters that still somehow looked majestic to her eyes, despite the glaring imperfections, the missing gutter and blister spots on the paint and weeds poking through the flower beds.

They did not answer the door, which was not a good sign. And after she let herself in and put down her suitcase and found them resting in the bedroom at the top of the stairs, she was shocked at how much more fragile they looked, just in the few days since she had been there, and at how white her father's hair was.

Jude and Skyler could have picked out Julian Hartman's house from the beat-up rust red pickup truck out front and the face of benign neglect it offered Johnson Street. From the wide-open front windows, the strains of The Band could be heard, halfway through "Up on Cripple Creek." The house was of a piece with his persona—a man whose mind was on higher things than a haircut.

He welcomed them graciously and introduced them to his wife, Jennifer, a biochemist, who shook hands while a child dangled from her bent left hip. Three other children in various stages of undress ran wildly through the front entrance hall. The pungent smell of a roast filled the air. Hartman thrust drinks into their hands—margaritas in stem goblets with salt on the rim, no alternative offered—and ushered them into the backyard, where six men and women sat on folding chairs on a bald spot in the lawn. The two were introduced around.

"We were just talking about your favorite subject—what else?" said Hartman. "Bailey here"—he gestured with his head toward a thin young man in glasses—"was just getting raked over the coals for asking a silly question. He wanted to know if human clones would have souls. I explained that they would be exactly like identical twins, though not of the same age."

"Actually, they would be less identical than twins," put in a microbiologist called Ellen. Jude recognized her from the lab earlier in the afternoon.

"Identical twins have something in common that clones would not—they share the same womb. Those nine months are the first time the environment gets to weigh in, and it does it with a vengeance. Maternal diet, stimulants, hormones, the age of the mother, you name it—we're only beginning to discover how much fetal development depends on all these things. Even if the clones were born from the same mother, or surrogate mother, they would be there at different times, and so essentially occupy different wombs.

"And after birth, of course, all those other variables of time and place and culture come into play. Even if they stayed in the same family, their upbringing would be different. Birth order doesn't matter among identical twins—it's a joke to say that one is eight minutes older than the other—but if you extend that to eight years, you're talking about a whole new dynamic in sibling relationships. Imagine having a younger brother who has the same genetic makeup as you. How would you feel if he excelled, or for that matter if he failed? Imagine being the younger one—how could you possibly grow up without a huge inferiority complex?"

Skyler and Jude exchanged looks.

"I'm assuming that you two are brothers—that's why Hartman said you were interested in all this."

Jude nodded.

Hartman moved the conversation ahead. "The environmental influences are incalculable. That's why I hit the ceiling whenever people ask me if someday we'll be cloning a future Adolf Hitler or a future Albert Einstein. Believe me, it took a lot more than errant genes to create the monster of Hitler. I'm sure that someone with the same genes and a different upbringing would turn into a perfectly pleasant Viennese painter. As for Einstein, we could clone him from here to doomsday, and I doubt we'd get someone who even understands the theory of relativity."

"I suppose that's what I meant by soul," said Bailey, who, it turned out, was a psychologist. "Imagine Einstein without the genius or Hitler without the evil. Imagine a younger brother so desperate to become like his older brother than he imitates him in every way, or an older brother desperately trying to live again through his younger brother. Aren't we losing something here? Aren't we cutting down the mountains and filling in the valleys and ending up with something innocuous and homogeneous and faceless?"

"Nonsense," said Hartman. "Your use of the word 'desperate' in the examples you cite proves just how human they will be. They won't be automatons. They'll be capable of all the extremes of emotion, good and bad, just like the rest of us. And as for Einsteins and Hitlers, we'll have those in the future, too, but not because we breed them. Simply because the multiple variants inherent in both heredity and the environment are so vast that exceptional beings will continue to be thrown up on both ends of the spectrum."

"Don't forget mitochondrial DNA," said Ellen.

"What's that?" asked an older man whose name Jude had missed.

"It's DNA that is passed on through the mother alone. It's in the cytoplasm of the cell, not inside the nucleus. That means it is not affected by nuclear transfer. We're not talking about a lot of genes here, maybe sixty out of a hundred thousand, but they play a role in making enzyme proteins, which are important in development. So identical twins would have the same mitochondrial DNA, but clones would not. The more you think about it, the really strange aberration of nature is identical twins. If they had not existed and scientists had produced them, we'd be run out of town by mobs carrying torches as in the Frankenstein movies."

At that point, dinner was called. The group moved inside and sat around a long oak table piled with servings of potatoes and squash and green beans while Hartman carved a large chunk of meat.

The man to Skyler's right, Harry Schwartzbaum, hadn't yet said a word, and Jennifer Hartman turned to him.

"You've been quiet, Professor," she said. They were all professors, but she appeared to call him that in deference to his field, philosophy, which elevated him to the ranks of a deep thinker.

"I was thinking of a book I read two weeks ago," replied Schwartzbaum, "the diary of a sixteenth-century Spanish count, Don Jose Antonio Martinez de Solar. He wrote about absolutely everything of interest to him and his world, which was centered upon Seville in the year 1501. He wrote trenchant comments about mores and dress and high society and the Spanish church.

"But what he did not write about—and this is my point—is the event that had occurred less than ten years earlier, Columbus setting out from that very same city and discovering the New World. That one voyage ended up doubling the known world, but Martinez didn't include it, because he didn't see its importance. I think we can live through major events and major discoveries and not even recognize them for what they are.

"By the same token, I think that cloning—and by cloning, I include everything from the Human Genome project to genetic engineering—is the most significant scientific advance of the modern age. It surpasses by far the discovery of the atom. The atom allowed us to manipulate the external world. By zeroing in on isotopes, we were able to achieve nuclear fission and alter certain unstable compounds. But genes permit us to manipulate the internal world, our very selves, and there is no limit to what that can lead to."

Several nodded in agreement.

"Imagine, for example, the qualitative leap that would occur if we increase human intelligence by a factor of four. We know we only use a paltry part of our brain. You mentioned Einstein. What if he were able to tap into the full dimensions of his intellect? Or what would happen if we increased human longevity, so that the working lifespan of a creative mind becomes three times what it is today? Imagine if that same Einstein were able to work productively for one hundred years instead of forty. It would become possible for a single human being to become proficient in five or six major disciplines. You'd have someone conversant with, say, astrophysics and molecular biology and neurology, someone able to bring together all the divergent strands of human knowledge. Not since Samuel Johnson of eighteenth-century London has there been a person who could lay a claim to knowing everything worth knowing."

"You all keep talking about the advantages and benefits," said Bailey, "and you refuse to recognize the dangers."

"Such as?" asked Hartman.

"Such as the decline of diversity. Nature thrives on diversity and heterogeneity, and cloning moves in the opposite direction. In that sense, it is against nature. How about all those stories of genetically engineered strains of wheat and cotton? They're perfect. Each grain is extra-nutritious, each boll is packed with extra fiber. And yet when a new fungus or a new breed of insect comes along, the entire crop disappears overnight. The plants are identical, and so none of them have developed mutant variants to survive the onslaught and carry on to the next generation."

"But surely you don't think that will happen with people?" asked Hartman. "No one is talking about making every human on the planet like every other one."

"No, of course not. But if human selectivity is brought into the process, you can bet your bottom dollar all the interesting people are never going to be born. No more Franz Kafkas or Vincent van Goghs or Stephen Hawkings. If anything other than pure chance is involved, then the overall result will be a diminishing of the world's gene pool—for plants, for animals and for us."

Schwartzbaum finished his food and pushed his plate away from him.

"At the risk of sounding pompous, let me state my view," he intoned. "All of nature is a struggle between the species and the individual. The species strives only for procreation of itself, while the individual yearns for immortality for itself. One involves change and mutation, the other immutability and stasis. The conflict is irreconcilable."

"You sound like one of those wild-eyed evolutionary biologists," said Jennifer. "Those guys who say our only purpose in life is to pass on our sperms and eggs and then kick the bucket."

"Yes, Jennifer. There is a connection between sex and death. It's a common survival strategy—among lesser creatures with shorter life spans—to spread their seed as widely as possible and then pass into the night. Once you've procreated, nature has no further use for you. So we strut and fret our hour upon the stage and then are heard no more. Up to now, the game has favored the species. What could we do to achieve immortality, assuming we're not Shakespeare, except to have offspring whom we hope will in some way resemble us? But now suddenly the equation shifts. Now we can have offspring that *are* us. We can, as individuals, achieve a certain immortality. We do it by suppressing mutation and substituting replication. It's significant that cloning is the only form of reproduction that does not involve sex. We will have finally broken that age-old connection between sex and death. Women will be able to conceive children without men."

"Great," said Bailey. "Doesn't sound like much fun to me."

"Oh, I don't know," said Jennifer.

She and Ellen laughed.

"Are you familiar with the work of Adam Eyre-Walker and Peter Keightley of Britain?" asked Hartman. "They've shown that humans retain more adverse mutations in our genome than other animals. Something like 4.2 mutations *every generation* and 1.6 of them are harmful."

"It's a wonder we're still around," said Bailey.

"That's exactly right. And that points us, at least speculatively, to a theory on the purpose of sex. You see, sex is not an efficient way to reproduce. Face it, it's complicated—you have to bring two people together, the sparks have to fly, it's hit or miss. Why bother? We're here. Why not just divide all by ourselves like an amoeba? It would make life a lot simpler."

"Why not indeed?"

"To shed all those bad mutations. Sex is the only way to confront one set of chromosomes with an entirely different set of chromosomes to cancel out the bad ones. It's a way of shuffling the deck every generation."

"I knew there had to be a practical reason," said Jennifer.

The women laughed again.

"I think," said Schwartzbaum, "that asexual reproduction is narcissism carried to the final extreme, the ultimate ego trip. Nothing more counts than the continuation of Self. The direction is clear. Tomorrow, we'll have people giving birth to themselves."

"Good-bye, Eros," said Hartman.

"Hello, Thanatos," said Bailey.

"Speaking of tomorrow . . ." said Ellen, looking at her watch. "I have to get up early."

On that note, the dinner party broke up. The guests filed out into the bug-filled night, chatting as they went. Schwartzbaum moved down the front walk with a stately gait. Hartman had whispered to Jude and Skyler to stay behind, and he motioned them into a drawing room while Jennifer put the children to sleep. The house fell noticeably quiet.

Hartman poured himself another drink and offered them one. Both declined.

Jude looked at Skyler and decided to plunge ahead. He told Hartman part of the real story—how they had met only recently and believed that they were possibly brothers, but with an age difference. And so they were looking into the possibility—as incredible as it may seem—that they were clones.

Hartman simply laughed. "I thought you showed more than a journalistic attention to detail. That's all right"—he waved them silent—"you don't have to say a word. Why not let me talk?" He laughed again. "As if I haven't been doing enough of that.

"It hasn't escaped my attention that you two look alike, dyed blond hair or no. But let me put your mind at ease. What you're wondering about, what you're probably afraid of, if you have any sense—at least I would be if I were in your shoes—*cannot possibly be true*. Let me repeat that: it cannot be true. So eliminate it as a possibility, wipe it from your mind."

Skyler, stunned by the man's certainty, spoke. "How do you know? How can you be so sure?"

"For one simple reason: you're how old? Twenty-five? Twenty-eight?"

Skyler shrugged.

"Thirty," said Jude.

"Thirty, even more. Well, the technology for what you have in mind, for cloning, it exists today, no doubt about that. But it wasn't around thirty years ago. Not unless it was done on another planet, because no one on this one could have done it."

"No one at all?"

"Nope."

Hartman was quiet as he ran the names through a mental file.

"We all keep up with each other, you know. We keep an eye on what we're doing. Half out of comradeship, half out of anxiety. I mean, you saw those postcards and photographs in my office. I could tick off all the names for you and probably tell you where they all are at this very moment."

He seemed to stumble for a second; he had stubbed his toe, mentally speaking.

"There was one guy, years and years ago, but no one's heard anything about him for a long time. Dropped out of Harvard or maybe Chicago, or was sent away, I believe, for overstepping the bounds. Said to be brilliant and eccentric, all that. Went underground, did who knows what. This was a long time ago, in the sixties. He was rumored to have surfaced briefly in the early seventies, when he won a big award in the Netherlands. No one really knew if the fellow who picked it up was him or not. More than a little mysterious, as you can gather."

"His name?"

"Don't know the original name. The new one's odd. Ricard, or something like that."

"Rincon?"

"That's it. Very good. How did you know?"

"I've heard it around."

"Well, don't worry about him. No one's heard anything about him in ages. If he's done anything big lately, he's kept it a state secret. We scientists don't like secrets. We like prizes. So put your minds at ease."

He leaned back, gave them the once-over.

"I'd say, if you've just met, you're twins separated at birth. Nothing wrong with that, it happens from time to time—it should be exotic enough for you. You don't have to look any further."

They thanked him and moved to the front door. Jennifer came down the stairs to say good night. She kissed them each on a cheek, the opposite cheek, a mirror image good night.

"By the way," she said, "how did you like the meat?"

"Very tasty," replied Skyler.

"I'm glad. It's a sort of home recipe we like to spring on people. It's half goat and half cow. A chimera. My husband made it."

# Chapter 19

When they drove to Milwaukee to meet Tizzie, she seemed distracted, even troubled. She told Jude she didn't want to be picked up at home, insisting that it would be easier all around if they met her downtown at the old bus station. He took that as a bad sign, but shrugged it off. The way things were going, it didn't pay to overthink anything these days.

They drove his car, the windshield now streaked with crushed bugs and the backseat floor littered with maps and coffee containers, along the inner-city boulevards until they spotted the terminal. She was sitting on the curb waiting, with the small duffel bag by her side. She gave a half wave and stood. Skyler was eager to see her and leapt from the car as soon as it stopped. He gave her a hug, casually, and she hugged him back, and he reached down to put her bag in the trunk, and she let him do that, too.

Jude could tell at once, as soon as she settled into the front seat next to him, that she had been through a rough time.

"Things bad at home?" he asked.

She said yes.

"And your father—how's he doing?"

"He's aged," she said. "Every time I see him, he's aged more than I expect. My mother, too."

Jude nodded slowly. "It happens."

"I know," she said peevishly. "But that's not why I'm upset."

"Why then?"

She looked over, sorry that she had snapped at him.

"Sorry. I just don't want to talk about it—not now. Tell me about you. Did you find out anything?"

"Bits and pieces. Enough to know we're on the right track. Of course, I have no idea where the hell that track is leading."

He filled her in on their conversations with Hartman and related in detail all that they had learned about cloning.

"It's amazing," he said. "The cloning stuff seems so complicated at first, but when you hear him talk about it, it all seems straightforward and simple and doable. You can imagine sitting down and doing it yourself."

"That's the hallmark of a great scientist," put in Skyler.

"Pardon?" said Jude, surprised at the voice from the backseat.

"A scientist takes a complicated process or theory and strips it down to its essentials; he reduces it and experiments with it and makes it basic. And in trying to make it understandable, he may blunder into a fundamental truth. That's the way it works. Karl Popper said it—*science may be described as the art of systematic oversimplication.*"

"Karl Popper—the philosopher?"

Skyler nodded.

"Christ, you don't even know where the hell you were raised, but you know about Karl Popper."

"The simple things first," said Skyler.

They picked their way through Chicago and then to the west, where the Great Plains opened up and stretched before them, and their spirits lifted. They flew along the interstates, whizzing by small towns and fields dotted with cattle.

As they drove, they talked; Jude was increasingly impressed with Skyler, and he could tell that Tizzie was, too. He had learned quickly how to navigate the modern world; he had already mastered many of the minor everyday tasks that were second nature to them—placing phone calls, pumping gas, tipping in the roadside diners—and he was taking on new ones with gusto. His naivete had an optimistic strain to it that was appealing, Jude thought. He also thought it contrasted starkly with his own sometimes weary malaise.

They were barreling through Kansas on Route 70, when Skyler made a sudden announcement.

"I want to drive," he said. "Teach me."

"For Christ's sake," said Jude. "We're in a hurry. We can't stop for that."

But Tizzie, in the backseat, decided the issue.

"Why not?" she said. "It'll give us a break."

So they pulled off the interstate and found a back road between two fields of corn, waist high. Jude stopped the car in the center of the deserted road and walked around to the passenger seat; he felt the heat rising up from the concrete and heard cicadas buzzing in the heavy late morning air. Skyler slid over behind the wheel. Jude explained the controls, outlined the rules of the road, and helped him lift off the hand brake. The car moved forward slowly, tentatively. Skyler rotated the wheel to one side and then the other, and the car swayed gently, stuttering ahead as he gave it a bit more gas.

"Nothing to it," said Skyler, still gripping the wheel tightly. He concentrated on the road, then looked over at Jude and grinned.

"Way to go!" shouted Tizzie from the back.

"Not bad, just take it easy," put in Jude.

Skyler leaned into the gas pedal, and the engine leapt to life with a power that astonished him. He took his foot off, steered for a while, then gunned it, and the car took off at high speed, swerving madly. Jude was thrown into the door.

"Slow down! Slow down!" he screamed.

His head fell below the window, and he could see only Skyler, frozen in place. But he could feel the tires striking rocks and kicking up dirt, and he could hear grass slapping the undercarriage, and then suddenly the car rocked violently to one side, plunging downward but still moving ahead. Above, stalks of corn beat against the windshield.

The car stopped with a shudder. An ear of corn leaned in through the open window and dust circled inside. Skyler sat there, still with two hands on the wheel, stunned and white. Jude turned around to look at Tizzie, who was sitting on the floor, her eyes open wide in alarm. When she saw how alarmed Jude was, she began to giggle and then to laugh out loud, until Jude, too, began laughing. And then finally Skyler joined in, his laugh sounding an awful lot like Jude's, deep and resonant.

Later, they flagged down a farmer on a tractor, who hitched a chain to the car and pulled it out of the cornfield. They paid him ten bucks, then went to a diner for lunch, turkey sandwiches drowning in thick brown gravy. Halfway through, Jude looked across the table at Skyler and knew with an abrupt clarity what he was thinking.

"You want to try it again, don't you?" he said.

Skyler said he did.

"Not on my life."

And they all laughed again.

* * *

On the outskirts of Denver, they turned south on Route 25 and saw a blinking neon lasso, a Frontier Motel sign. They pulled up before a two-story lime green fake facade whose front entrance was flanked by wagon wheels missing three and four spokes. A young heavyset black woman in a checkered blouse with a gray cowboy hat sat behind the desk and slid registration cards over to them.

"Two rooms or three?" she said.

"Three," said Tizzie.

They filled out the small white cards with phony names—Skyler leaning over to crib the same surname as Jude—and carried their luggage down a claustrophobic hallway, turned a corner past an ice chest and Coke machine, and came to their rooms, side by side. Jude's was in the middle. Slipping the punch-coded cards into the slots at the same time, they heard three clicks in succession and opened their doors one after another—a sequence that struck Jude as vaguely comical.

"I'm beat," said Tizzie, looking at them. "See you tomorrow."

They exchanged good nights.

Jude's room was a standard L, built of cinder blocks painted a pale yellow. It contained a double bed without a headboard, polyurethane curtains of white and silver thread, and a long dresser of fake oak veneer under a mirror stuck to the wall with clear plastic fasteners. On the dresser, next to a metal beer bottle opener screwed into the wall, was a TV set. Light from a bedroom lamp cast an oval upon the ceiling.

Jude sat on the bed, reached for the phone receiver, and punched in a long sequence of numbers that he knew by heart. Six rings—it was slow this time of night in the city room—and a voice finally answered.

"Metro."

"Hello—who's this?"

A clerk paused—suspicious, but recognizing a certain authority behind the question—and gave his first name.

"This is Jude. I'm just calling to check in . . . to say, you know I've been out for a while, sick, and I'll probably be out for a while longer."

He thought he sounded a little too uncertain.

"I'll be in touch, when I'm feeling better, I just—"

"Jude." The clerk had finally cottoned on. "That you?"

"Yes."

The line went muffled, the sound of a receiver being covered. It lasted quite a while, maybe a minute or longer. Jude was about to hang up when the voice came back on.

"Where are you?"

"I'm here. Home. Still sick. I don't need anything. Just checking in, to let you know that, ah, I'm getting a little better."

The receiver was covered again, and this time Jude did hang up.

Afterward, he felt stupid. He shouldn't have called—or he should have called someone else, a reporter at home, to pass on the message. Could they trace the call? *Why would they do that? Now you're really turning paranoid.*

Still, the call preyed on him, made him feel exposed. Up to now, he had felt protected in that great anonymity of the vast American heartland, another piece of flotsam on that big prairie ocean. One phone call had ruined that—it had made him feel connected again to the whole damn nightmare.

He kicked off his shoes and lay on the bed to watch television. It didn't help. A vague depression settled over him, a mood of anxiety to which he was unaccustomed. He thought of knocking on Tizzie's door, or even Skyler's—inviting them out for a drink. He walked to the window, lifted an edge of the curtain and looked outside. A traffic light was blinking on a street across the parking lot—the night was gloomy, uninviting, a little threatening. He turned away, undressed and climbed into bed.

Night sounds came in from all sides. A murmur of conversation, the canned laughter from a TV. He strained to hear something from Tizzie's room, but without success. He shut the sounds out as best he could and then, mercifully, drifted off to sleep. But it was not a peaceful sleep because it was split with nightmares playing off his claustrophobia—long, harrowing dramas of running away from unspeakable horrors, crawling through tunnels, dashing across dark underground caverns. He awoke with a start, sweating, one sheet wrapped around his left leg.

Gradually, his heart stopped racing. He leaned over and looked at the numbers on the clock, gleaming like red cat's eyes: 3:00. He settled back, his head on the pillow, able now to distinguish shapes in the darkness, and he thought he heard something, a light tread in the corridor outside. He listened intently: was that not the sound of a doorknob turning slowly, a door creaking open? He leapt out of bed, put his ear to the door. Nothing. It was gone—but had it been there?

Jude dressed by the light of the bathroom. He opened his curtains, then checked to pat his pocket and make sure that he had put the door card inside, and slipped out into the hall. He paused before Tizzie's door to listen: nothing. He walked down the corridor, past the ice machine and into the lobby. The young black girl was still there, reading a thick book under a night light, surprised to look up and see him standing there.

"Forgot something in the car," he muttered, making for the door.

The air outside was pleasantly warm. He walked around the front into the parking lot, down the length of the building. The sky overhead was clear and glistening with stars. And as he walked across the tarmac behind the darkened cars, he counted the windows of the rooms and finally came to his own, the one with the curtains open. He stopped and looked at the windows on either side, glancing, as if casually, and saw that they both were dark.

Inside, in the lobby, he smiled at the girl, but she barely looked up from her reading.

They were passing through the town of Wagon Mound, New Mexico, on the way to Santa Fe, when Jude, driving, turned to Skyler in the seat next to him and told him to recount his life on the island.

"Everything you haven't already told us," he said. "From start to finish. Don't leave anything out. Tell us everything you can remember, no matter how small and unimportant it seems. There may be a clue in there, something we've overlooked that can point us in the right direction."

It was evening. For hours, the sky off to the east had been darkening with a gathering thunderhead, and now in the far distance they could see slanted gray steaks of rain pounding down on the plain. Tizzie was in the backseat, lying on her back with her feet propped up on the window jamb. Jude thought she was asleep, but he was not sure.

Skyler looked out the window, as if he were mulling over Jude's request, then opened the glove compartment and pulled out Jude's Camels.

"Mind if I try one?"

Jude frowned. "Don't be stupid. Why get started? They'll kill you."

"You're one to talk."

"Yeah, well . . ."

Skyler lighted up, drew smoke into his mouth and let it out in a cloud that enveloped his face. He tried again, this time sucking the smoke deep into his lungs, and was seized by a coughing fit. He looked at the cigarette in his hand.

"How can you smoke this?"

"It's an acquired taste."

"Christ," said Skyler, stamping it out in the ashtray.

Tizzie poked her head up.

"Not very smart," she said, lying back down.

Skyler stared out the window again, still coughing and clearing his throat. Then he began his narrative. He talked slowly and quietly and unemotionally, laying out the details of his life on the island as carefully as if he were putting down cards in solitaire. As he talked, he continued looking out the window, drawing a kind of strength from the foreign landscape of dark brown and red earth and rolling hills and scrub brushes.

He told of his earliest memories and Raisin and camping out and leaving the goats in the secret pasture to run through the woods. He told about the day they had met Kuta and Raisin's epileptic fit and the snake bite, and how Raisin had become a renegade.

He told about the bad things, too, the frequent physical examinations, the shots and the pills, the discipline and the Orderlies, and how members of the Age Group would suddenly disappear.

"Didn't it seem strange to you that all this was going on?" interrupted Jude. "That people could be perfectly healthy and then suddenly turn so sick that they would have to be operated on?"

"Not at all. That's just the way it was. I didn't know anything else. Don't forget—we didn't have much . . . much information. That was the way things happened. Growing up, I never had any reason to think my life was unusual. I never really thought about it one way or the other—not for a long time."

The rain caught up with them. It came in a sudden onslaught, falling on the windshield in loud, thick drops and making the roof rattle. They felt cut off from the landscape, snug in the car's interior. Jude switched on the wipers, which smeared the front windshield, but gradually cleared it, so that they could look out and see the raindrops pelt the road ahead.

It made Skyler think of his escape through the swamp.

Then he told of Raisin's escape and his death.

"At his funeral service, Baptiste and the others spoke with such feeling that it almost seemed like they meant it. But I knew they didn't. After all, they had practically caused it."

"Did you see—did anyone see—Raisin's body?" asked Jude.

"No, it was in a coffin. That would have been too cruel—I expect he was bloated and ugly."

Jude lighted a cigarette and cracked the window to let out the smoke; a spray came in and struck him in the side of the neck, but he ignored it.

Skyler talked about his disillusionment.

"It came gradually, like the dawning of an idea that won't go away. I can't tell you how upset I was. I remember reading about the late fifteenth century, when Europeans came to accept that the earth was no longer flat. I think it was like that for me. Gradually, the most basic assumptions of my existence—the very ground I was walking on—shifted beneath me. It crumbled and I felt like I was falling. I no longer knew anything."

For the second time, Tizzie spoke up from the back—which startled Jude. He hadn't realized that she was listening.

"Tell us about Julia," she said in a thin voice.

And so Skyler did. He told of what she'd been like as a young child and how he'd always looked for her in lectures without even realizing it, a quick once-over to make sure that that precious head of tousled hair was somewhere around. He talked about the bond between Raisin, himself and Julia.

"I think on some level I was secretly jealous," he said. "I thought she must love Raisin more than me—I mean, that made sense, he was so much bigger and stronger and smarter. So when she got sick, when she was operated on and got that big scar on her back and I snuck into the sick bay to see her and we held hands—that opened up a whole wonderful world to me."

He told how they had consoled each other when Raisin died. And then finally he told the story of how they had come to have sex—how they'd stopped taking the pills and felt a new vigor. He described the signal for a rendezvous—the rock under the oak tree—their secret meetings in the old lighthouse with the flapping of the birds' wings, the rush of excitement when they'd first touched each other's bodies. As he talked, an emotion welled up inside and closed off the back of his throat and so he had to stop.

He felt a hand on his shoulder—Tizzie's. Her touch was light, but it felt heavy, charged.

"But what was *she* like?" she asked.

Skyler drew a deep breath.

*A lot like you.*

He thought it but didn't say it. He turned to look at her and felt she could read his mind. He didn't answer right away, because he was afraid of what he might blurt out.

Then he told of the day Dr. Rincon and an assembly of dignitaries had come from the mainland. The Jimminies and everyone else had prepared for days. The Campus had been spruced up, the lawns mowed, even the Big House looked presentable. They'd been amazed as planeload after planeload had arrived and disgorged well-dressed guests who'd filed into the manor. Then Rincon himself had arrived—but the Jimminies were not allowed to see him; they were confined to their barracks. That evening, Skyler and Julia had formed a daring plan: they would sneak out and spy upon the gathering. They'd climbed a tree next to the Big House and looked in an upper-story window, but they couldn't see Dr. Rincon. Then they'd stolen into the basement. Julia had climbed into a dumbwaiter and ascended to the first floor, where the assembly was underway. She'd pried open the doors an inch or so and peered through as the founder was speaking, but she couldn't get a good look because of her poor eyesight. Skyler had cursed himself for letting her take the risk, but she'd soon come back down and they'd run back to their barracks.

"She heard him talking over and over about 'the Lamb.' And we thought he was talking about Christ—we had heard the expression 'the Lamb of God.' We thought he must have gone crazy with religion. Now I know he was talking about Dolly. They must have been afraid that the news about cloning was going to affect them."

The rain lessened and then stopped altogether as suddenly as it had started. Jude turned off the wipers. The black tarmac ahead was streaked with puddles and sent up puffs of steam.

Skyler told about their growing doubts and suspicions, the trip to the Records Room and the discovery of Patrick's body and how Julia had learned the computers and become convinced she had discovered the passwords to unlock the files.

And then at long last, he came to the part he had dreaded, the final chapter. Speaking haltingly, he told about Julia's death—how she'd disappeared and he had run in desperation from Kuta's shack to the girls' barracks and then to the Big House, how he'd found her body in the basement morgue, lying on the slab, serenely white and beautiful but grotesquely maimed, cut open, her insides missing.

And when he finished with that description, he finished with his tale and could not bring himself to talk about his escape or anything else.

The car was silent. Jude lighted a cigarette, and Tizzie sat with her knees raised, hugging them, her head to one side, staring through the raindrop-streaked window.

"Jesus, Skyler. I'm so sorry," Jude said finally, reaching over and patting his knee.

He was moved by Skyler's story and by the openness and vulnerability he'd displayed in telling it, and again he felt that sensation of brotherly protectiveness. The world was a large and dangerous place, never more so than now, and Skyler was ill-equipped to deal with it. Jude would have to make sure that no harm came to him.

But at the same time, Jude's gesture had a slight absentmindedness to it, because his mind was elsewhere. For he had heard something in Skyler's long account that set off a giant alarm bell—it appeared to confirm a suspicion that had taken hold in his mind like a tiny dark cloud on the horizon. It had been growing for some time now, and it seemed ready to burst, like the thunderhead that had clapped open upon their heads.

A smaller, minor suspicion had taken hold, too, and this one he decided to test as soon as they stopped for the night.

They drove into Albuquerque and found a small hotel on Central Avenue and took three rooms on the ground floor.

Jude took a hot bath, filling the tub almost to the rim, and soaked in it for a long time, thinking things through. Then he got out, dried himself, changed into a fresh pair of blue jeans and a clean shirt and walked down the hall to Skyler's room. He paused before knocking on the door, thought he heard voices inside, and gave two quick raps with his knuckles. Skyler opened it and Tizzie was there, sitting on the foot of the bed. She seemed embarrassed, and Jude felt suddenly awkward—though he quickly put that to one side and got down to the business at hand.

"Skyler," he said, looking into that face that so resembled his own, "I've got something to show you. I hope I'm wrong, but if I'm not, I don't want you to get too upset."

He reached into his pocket and pulled out a folded piece of paper, carefully opening it and smoothing it out upon the top of a table. It was the photograph of the judge that he had taken from the newspaper files.

Skyler stared down at it fixedly, his mouth dropping open slightly, and Jude could tell from reading his face and seeing the dawning realization begin to contort his features, that his suspicion had been correct.

The face in the photo was known to Skyler.

"Where did you get this?" he asked urgently, confused.

"It's a picture of the judge I was telling you about, the one up in New Paltz. I'm beginning to think the person who was killed up there, whoever it was, looked exactly like him."

"What's going on?" demanded Tizzie. "What's this all about?"

"He's older," said Skyler. "The eyes look a little different and the hair's not the same, but otherwise it looks like him . . ."

"I was afraid of that," said Jude, speaking softly.

Skyler sat on the bed, slumped.

"Come on," insisted Tizzie. "Jude, tell me, for God's sake. What's going on? Who are you talking about?"

"Raisin," said Jude. "He didn't die in a boat leaving the island. That was a lie. He made it to the mainland. In fact, he made it all the way up to New

Paltz, and he was probably there trying to track down his double, the judge. Maybe he even learned the name of his double before he left the island—maybe that's *why* he left. He might have cracked the code just the way Julia did."

"And what happened to him?" she asked.

"He probably made contact with the judge and they killed him."

Now it was Tizzie's turn to be dumbfounded.

"And who are *they*?"

"That's what we have to find out. But I'll give you odds it's those thick-necked thugs with the streak in their hair—the Orderlies."

"So they'll do anything," she said. "They'll even use the Orderlies as assassins."

Jude turned to her. "Who do *you* mean when you say *they*?" he asked.

But now Tizzie was worried. "What if these Orderlies are after *us*? What if they're on our trail right now?"

But Jude was still thinking about his own question to her and did not feel like calming her fears right now. He knew he would be thinking about it later, back in his room, when he replayed the exchange in his mind.

Skyler looked dreadful; the color had drained from his face, and his forehead had broken out in beads of perspiration that settled in the rivulets of the worry lines. He lay down on the bed and turned his face to the wall. Jude worried that he had broken the news about Raisin too coldly. Tizzie asked Skyler if he were getting sick, felt his forehead with her palm and said she thought he was running a fever.

But most of all, Skyler just wanted to be alone. He told them so, and they left the room, closing the door quietly behind them.

Out in the corridor, Tizzie walked, holding Jude gently by the elbow.

"How did you know the body was Raisin's?" she asked.

"I didn't know for sure. I guessed. But it was an educated guess. McNichol—he's the Ulster County coroner—initially identified the body as the judge's. The DNA was the same. So it was a clone. Not that many people have left the island. And I remembered that the judge was taking medication called Depakote. It's for the treatment of petit mal epilepsy. One of the organizations he joined as a board member raised money to study neurological disorders. But not until I heard Jude's story did I know that Raisin also suffered from it."

Tizzie looked at him, impressed.

"Don't you see?" he continued. "Everyone on that island is a clone of someone over here—that's what they're raised for. A whole legion of doubles. That's what this whole thing is all about—some kind of horrible experiment."

He could tell that what he was saying upset her, but he needed to air the questions that had been eating away at him.

"There 's one thing I don't get at all. When the judge saw me, he freaked out. He practically fell off his chair. I can't figure that out—I never saw him before in my life. What do I have to do with him or he with me?

"And another thing. When McNichol did the autopsy, he took samples of the organs and put them away for analysis and someone broke in and stole them. Why? You'd think it'd be to destroy evidence, so that nobody could prove the body was a double. But then why leave behind all the DNA evidence? That's the stuff that really established it. It doesn't make sense—unless they just didn't know what they were doing. And somehow I doubt that. They wanted those specimens for something."

The hand dropped away from his elbow. Tizzie looked almost as bad as Skyler. She said that she was feeling poorly and thought she would skip dinner. She turned and headed back toward her room, and as she walked away, Jude watched her receding figure, the shoulders uncharacteristically drooping. He wanted to go after her, but he knew it would be a mistake, and he felt a sudden sharp jab of loneliness.

Jude ordered room service—a ham and cheese sandwich, Diet Coke, potato chips and coffee—and while he was waiting, he opened his computer, plugging the modem into the phone socket. He went on-line and quickly found the web page for W in Jerome, Arizona, and once again the screen filled in with that strange image, the hooded-eye lizard clinging to a rock. He clicked onto the chat room. A discussion was underway.

". . . you remember tithonus?"

"who?"

"Tithonus . . . it's greek mythology. he was a handsome young prince. One day, Aurora, the goddess of dawn, falls in love with him. she wants him for a husband, but after all he's only a mortal with a short life span, so she goes to Zeus and begs him to bestow eternal life on him. Zeus does and she sweeps him off to her palace in the east. For years everything's fine, they live in bliss. But there was one thing she forgot . . ."

"what?"

"she forgot to ask that her prince stay young forever. And so he aged. He got older and older and lost all his strength and shriveled down and his voice turned into a feeble squeak and he ached everywhere and could barely move. he shrank so much that Aurora put him in a little basket in a corner of her palace and he was miserable he only wanted one more thing—to die. But he couldn't. so he just keep shrinking until he turned into a grasshopper and that's what he remained forever and ever."

"got the point but still i'd want to live a long long time. think about it—what's so bad about old age?"

"Everything. your teeth rot, your size shrinks, you walk like a cripple, you lose control of your bowels, your memory goes—what's to live for?"

"still, you're alive. you know the old saying: where there's life, there's hope."

"where there's life, there's dope. give me kevorkian anytime . . ."

"see we've got a newcomer. hello luddite. we're talking about old age. Machiavelli here prefers the live fast die young route. how bout you?"

Jude typed the first nonsense that came into his head: "i think it's too bad old age is wasted on the old."

"ha ha. you're as funny as your name."

Jude asked the question he had come there for: "any you guys talked lately to methuselah???"

"who he?"

"i know him but he doesn't hang out here anymore. havent talked to him in weeks. why?"

"nothing much. just wondered. another thing—why is this site called jerome arizona?"

"dont know."

"i think cause that's where it was when it began long time ago. but none of those people come on anymore."

"who were they?" Jude asked.

"dont know."

"me neither."

Jude didn't want to spend any more time on-line than he had to. "gotta run," he typed.

"ok. remember: a minute from now you'll have sixty seconds less to live. ha ha."

"and a minute ago you had sixty seconds more. ha ha"

Without a riposte, Jude signed off, and was about to shut down the computer when he noticed a blinking mailbox: someone had sent him e-mail. He clicked on the icon, and instantly the screen was swallowed by a message that popped up with an address he did not immediately recognize. At that precise moment he heard a knock on the door—it sounded soft, tentative—and his pulse quickened, because his sixth sense told him it was Tizzie.

He quickly read the name on the e-mail—it was from the University of Wisconsin, from Hartman.

Then he went to answer the door. A young man was standing there in a slightly frayed uniform, a tray hoisted on a bent wrist. Room service.

Jude let him in and watched him as he grandly lifted the silver warmer off the plate, revealing a small brown sandwich sitting in a pool of melted cheese, and fished in his pocket for a dollar tip. The man accepted it without a word and closed the door with the pantomimed sycophancy of a retiring butler.

Jude set the tray by the window and looked out into the darkened, deserted street. A car went by, rumbling with teenagers whose laughter penetrated the window, and then all was quiet again. The sandwich was cold and soggy; he ate only half of it and finished off the potato chips, swilling them down with Coke. Then he sipped his lukewarm coffee slowly, peering onto the street and thinking about their situation, turning the permutations and possiblities over and over. He felt he was groping in the dark, getting nowhere. The reference to Greek mythology played in his mind; he half dreamed that he was in a labyrinth, turning corner after corner, to the left and to the right, each one looking just the same, knowing that somewhere ahead or maybe behind was the dreaded Minotaur, the monster with the head of a bull and the body of a man, who fed on human flesh.

Then he noticed the laptop screen, still gleaming.

Hartman's message was brimming with Midwestern friendliness, but was nonetheless succinct.

*I've been thinking of you two and wondering how you're coming on your quest. Hope you remember my words of wisdom. The more I think about your situation, the more I'm convinced that I'm right. One more thing I thought you should know—a couple of days after you left, two men came by asking about you—FBI or at least that's what their badges said. We didn't tell them much, not that we had much to say in any case. And we didn't serve them any of my special concoction. All best, Hartman.*

# Chapter 20

They followed Route 40 into Flagstaff, Arizona, a town set behind long-needle pine forests high in the mountains. On the outskirts, three crude wooden crosses, each with a name stenciled in black, had been hammered into the ground.

The highway fed into a street of traffic lights and fast-food restaurants and hotels. In the first block were Burger King, Econo Lodge, Hilton, Hampton Inn, Del Taco, Sizzler and Denny's. A Texaco station sold clay cow skulls and bright pottery with Hopi geometric designs.

Tizzie was feeling better, but Skyler, in the backseat, spent most of the time sleeping. He was still ill.

Jude looked for a place to stay. He parked in front of a two-story house down the street from Sbarro's Pizza and Mountain Jacks burger house. A ROOMS FOR RENT sign was taped to the window of a back door. He stepped outside and looked up and down the sidewalk. They were on the campus of Northern Arizona University. Young people carrying books walked by—the boys in bowling shirts, Dockers and jeans, the girls in tank tops, bell-bottom pants and shoes with tire-tread soles. Their pierced ears and eyebrows glinted in the sun.

Jude got back into the car and started the engine.

"What's wrong?" asked Tizzie.

"Too cozy. I'm sure it's run by a landlady who sticks her nose into everybody's business and gossips with the neighbors. We'd stick out a mile away. We need a place that's anonymous, where so many travelers come and go that nobody pays any attention."

Fifty-four miles south on Route 17, he found what he had in mind in Camp Verde, a drab modern crossroads. On one corner was a Giant service station advertising gasoline at $1.05 and $1.25 in yellow letters two feet high; monumental self-service pumps sat in the dark shadow of a concrete canopy. Across the way was a Taco Bell with a long faux Spanish-tile roof, and next door a Country Kitchen, separated by two parking lots. On the other side of the road was a shopping mall—brown windowless structures under a forty-foot flagpole. Overhead was a jumble of traffic lights, telephone lines and highway lamps on huge stanchions with elongated necks.

A large blue and white sign with yellow letters—Best Western—caught Jude's eye. The motel restaurant advertised BREAKFAST, $2.99 on a green and white banner. Extending behind it was a two-story structure of brown brick, with wide brown doors and rectangular windows covered on the inside with heavy white blackout curtains. A staircase in the center, which had open slats between the steps, led to a walkway that lined the second floor.

Jude went inside to register. By habit, he asked for three rooms, and when filling out the forms, he checked a box for payment in cash. The woman behind the counter looked him over and stared across his shoulder at Tizzie and Skyler, now stirring inside the car. She asked for two nights' payment in advance. He reached into his pocket and pulled out a wad of large bills—the remains of a $4,000 withdrawal he had made in New York—held it below the counter and peeled off $200. She made out a receipt and directed him to a parking space at the rear.

They settled in. The rooms were stuffy, so they turned on the air conditioning and met in the restaurant for a cup of coffee.

"Now what?" asked Tizzie.

"I'm going to poke around," said Jude. "You get to take the rest of the day off. As for him"— he gestured toward Skyler with his chin—"he looks like he needs some time in bed."

"Don't you want company?"

"No. I'm just going to get the lay of the land," he lied.

Jude headed south. It was a nondescript town, a scattering of stores and houses and schools, except for a scenic backdrop of distant peaks covered with crowns of snow. He found the town hall and located the records bureau in the basement. A buzzer on the counter summoned a clerk from a back room. A middle-aged man, he eyed Jude as if he were a welcome diversion.

"And what can I do for you?" he asked cheerily.

Jude pulled out a photostated copy of his birth certificate and said he was passing through town and was curious to see the original. The man peered at it, then sat down at a computer and punched a seemingly endless round of commands; he stared at the screen, punched some more, waited, and repeated the process several times. Finally, he shook his head and came back to the counter.

"Well, you must have been born way up in the mountains. 'Cause at that time, looking at your birth date here, babies that were born way up past Cottonwood weren't registered here. They were registered on the Mesa, way up there on the Indian reservation."

Jude looked at him quizzically.

"So I'd say," the clerk continued, "you want to see it, you got to go way up there."

He gave directions.

Jude thanked him and left. He turned right at the next intersection on 260 West, a narrow, winding road gutted on both sides by dry gullies. He passed through rolling hills covered with patches of green grass and creosote bushes and bleached boulders. He came to Dead Horse Park and felt the road rising continually, twisting as it made its way up toward the Mesa. The wind was strong, sending tumbleweeds crashing into the guardrails.

For a spell, the road followed a dried-up riverbed, passing from one side to the other over narrow bridges, and when he looked down, he saw a frozen stream of rocks, rounded and gleaming white in the sun. He came upon a huge boulder that thrust out so far the road veered around it; it had a peculiar shape, almost like a giant fist. Approaching it, Jude had an odd sensation; it seemed so familiar. And when he passed the boulder and continued climbing, that feeling persisted.

Everything he saw—the shimmering heat, the sun glinting off bits of mica, the scrub bushes and tufts of grass and red brown earth gashed out along the roadside—it all combined to thrust him backward, into his childhood. He knew he had been that way before. He sensed a recollection slowly forming, a snapshot taking shape in his mind's eye like a Polaroid. He was in the backseat of a car, a convertible, for the wind was whipping his hair and the sun beat down so hard that when he touched the nickel fasteners on the collapsed roof, it scalded his hand. Someone was driving. His father. When he focused his inner eye, he could see the back of his head, the hairs waving in the wind, the sloped shoulders. He felt safe and protected and excited all at the same time. Where were they going? He had no idea, but he did not need to know, for he had given himself over into the hands of an adult in that childlike way of total trust. It was a feeling he had not experienced for as long as he could remember.

He turned a corner and the vision evaporated. But it left him light-headed. He hit the gas pedal and enjoyed the sway of the car as it snaked around the curves, still climbing. Finally, he reached a small plateau and there off to the right, where the clerk at Camp Verde had said it would be, was a dirt road winding off down a canyon. A dusty sign there told him it was the way to the Camp Verde Indian Reservation.

He took the road. It traversed the bottom of the canyon for a half mile, the ruts and stones rocking the car wildly. Giant promontories moved in toward him until they formed sheer cliffs on either side, just far enough apart for the road to pass through. Then the cliffs abruptly fell away, so that driving past them felt like stepping through a grove of tall trees to enter a meadow. Ahead was a dusty field and a cluster of wooden buildings.

The car stopped in a dust cloud before the main building. A burro with a colored blanket draped across its back was tied to a log fence, and it turned its head slowly to look at Jude as he stepped out into a puddle of dust. The air felt humid, and when he stepped upon the grass, it broke under his shoes as if it were brittle and petrified, like glass.

He heard flies buzzing around the burro; its tail flicked the rear right flank, which twitched. On the log directly in front of the car, Jude saw a foot-long lizard, sitting immobile in the shade. Its feet were splayed, clasping the fence in an embrace, and it cocked its head to one side and watched Jude with one large eye, rocking its head ever so slightly. As Jude walked around the fence the eye trailed him slowly. When he reached the threshold of the building, the animal scampered in a half circle and turned the other eye and resumed its deep, blank stare.

Inside were three Indians, two women and an elderly man. Only the man acknowledged him, nodding once. Jude explained what he was after, and without a word the man led him to a back room lined on three sides with old filing cabinets, and left him there. There was a single window of thick glass, obscured by dust, and the floorboards creaked when he stepped on them. It was stiflingly hot, and round patches of sweat appeared in no time on the underarms of his shirt.

He located the drawer he wanted and opened it. An array of thick cards, smudged gray with thumbing on the upper edge, fell before him. Each was filled in: names, dates, some with a child's footprint in ink. Most of the names were Navajo. He flipped through and came, surprisingly quickly, to his own. It was done in a florid hand, in purple ink. Date of birth: November 20, 1968. Place of birth: Jerome, Arizona. Weight: 7 pounds, 6 ounces. Attending physician: the name was scribbled. He stopped and stared; his given name was Judah. That was strange. Why did he think all these years that it was Judas? Who had told him that—his father? There was his father's name: Harold. His mother's name looked as if it had been obliterated. That was strange.

Jude closed the drawer, and searched in another one. He soon found that name too, Joseph Peter Reilly. The date of birth was five months later than his own. He had guessed it would be there, but still it was surprising to see it in black-and-white, in that same florid script, to realize that he and the judge both traced their early years up into these mountains. Still, that did not explain why the judge had been so upset when he'd seen him—it was hardly likely that the judge would have recognized him after all that time. Somehow, he'd known who Jude was, and he'd known they shared this childhood connection, both members of a desert cult.

Finally, with a heavy heart, Jude looked for the third birth certificate, the one he hoped he would not find—but of course it was there, too. He stared at it for a while.

He spent more than an hour combing the files, looking for more cards in that script, but there were simply too many to go through. The heat made him dizzy, and his discovery depressed him, so eventually he closed the sixth file drawer, leaving a dozen more unopened, and left the room. The elderly man nodded to him in farewell. He opened the door to step outside, and there was the lizard, still gripping the fence, looking inscrutable and almost malevolent.

He got in the car and drove back to Camp Verde.

By the time Jude returned, Skyler was feeling a little better and he looked better, too. He sat on his bed, watching reruns of sitcoms. Tizzie was pacing around and complaining; she said she was going stir crazy. So they decided to drive to Phoenix for the evening to "take a break," as she put it.

On the way down Route 17, plunging south alongside the Agua Fria ravine and losing altitude so fast they could feel it in their ears, Tizzie and Jude argued. It had begun in the Best Western parking lot when Tizzie had offered to drive them in her car.

"Your car?" demanded Jude. "Where did you get a car?"

"I rented one. You don't think I'm going to just sit around all day."

"And how did you pay?"

"Credit card."

At that, he exploded. "They can trace us," he said. "Why the hell do you think I've been so careful to pay cash everywhere?"

"Maybe it's not so easy," she retorted. "And even if they could, by the time they do, we'll be long gone."

"It was a dumb thing to do. They were watching me in New York. They'll be looking for me and Skyler everywhere. And now you may have just told them where to start. If they're looking for me, they're looking for you, too."

She was quiet.

"Only yesterday you were worried about the Orderlies coming after us. Have you forgotten?"

"No."

They passed a runaway truck ramp—a turnoff that led to a road looping up a long incline that stopped in midair like a ski jump. Then they came to the sign for the turnoff to Route 260 that Jude had taken earlier.

"Where did you go, anyhow?" asked Tizzie. "You just left us there for hours."

Jude ignored her question. He had to impress upon her how serious their situation was. He told her about Hartman's e-mail message.

"The FBI?" she said. "Why would they come after *us*? And how come they're involved in something like this—whatever *this* is?"

"I wish to God I could answer that. If I knew that, maybe I'd know what the hell we're in for. All I know at this point is not to trust anyone. *Anyone at all.* And not to make their job easier for them by leaving clues all over the place. Credit cards are the first thing they'll look for."

Tizzie had fallen silent, and Jude took that as a sign that his point had sunk in. Forty minutes later, they had crossed the desert and arrived in Phoenix. The transition from dirt and cactus to freeways and malls was so abrupt, it felt as if something in between must have been removed. They passed an Economy Inn and a Souper Salad and a succession of gas stations, drive-through banks and doctors' clinics. The streets all looked the same. There was no one on the sidewalks, and the bus stops were deserted.

Eventually, they found Mr. Lucky's, a country bar on Grand Street. It sat under a big neon sign of a joker, a two-story light blue building bursting with sound. They pulled into a parking lot filled with pickup trucks. When they opened the car doors, the heat struck them in the face like a wall. They walked past a couple necking in the shadows.

"Well, Skyler, now you're going to see the real America," said Jude.

They stepped inside, and the screeching fiddles of a country music band bounced off the walls and drowned out speech, and clouds of cigarette smoke billowed through the room. On a wooden dance floor, men in cowboy hats, tight pants and boots and women in halters and shorts were line dancing. A loudspeaker announced a drinks special in a drawl: "Fifty cents, long-neck beer." Stand-up tables were placed not far from the long wooden bar.

Jude lighted up a cigarette, grinning, and shouted: "My kind of place."

He pushed through to the bar and emerged sometime later, clutching the handles of three frosted beer mugs. They made their way to the rear and out a back door, where there was a corral encircled with a thick wooden fence. On it was written, WHERE THE PAVEMENT ENDS AND THE WEST BEGINS. They found seats in a grandstand and sipped their beers in the heat.

A placard with a name was displayed on a nearby wooden tower, a public address system mumbled the name of a cowboy, and on the other side of the ring a wooden door suddenly swung open. Out came a man with a number on his back riding a bucking steer. He held on with a hand between his legs while his other arm flailed at shoulder height, his body flopping in counter rhythm to the bucking animal beneath him. Five seconds later, he toppled onto the ground, a blur between the steer's legs, and then when two men ran out with flags to distract the animal, he leapt up and ran off, limping slightly only when he reached the fence. They finished the beers, and Tizzie went for refills. Another rider came out the chute.

Jude watched Skyler, who was totally engrossed in the spectacle.

"I know what you're thinking—that you'd like to try that," he said.

Skyler looked at him and smiled, and Jude knew he was right.

"Me, too," he said.

"You know, I'm not exactly like you," Skyler replied.

They downed the beers, and the next time Jude ordered a shot glass of whiskey as a chaser and then another. Soon he was having difficulty focusing on the people around him. When the next wrangler came out the chute, Jude's head swayed slightly as he looked at the spectacle; he felt it was incredibly moving and he wondered who he should root for—the man holding on for dear life or the animal desperate to throw him off his back. He bummed a cigarette from a man behind him. Shielding the match from the wind, he almost burned his fingers.

Tizzie was looking at him.

"You ought to take it easy, Jude," she said.

"Well, it's tough. This stroll down memory lane. Nostalgia for the past and all that. You ever feel that?"

His tone seemed freighted with meaning.

"You're drunk."

He took that as an invitation to have another round. They didn't join him, so he went inside to the bar alone and sat on a stool. He downed another shot and ordered another.

"Hold on there, friend," said the woman bartender, dressed in a flannel shirt in the air-conditioning. "You've had enough for one night."

He fixed her with a bleary eye.

"Enough celebrating for you," she said, not unkindly.

"Not celebrating," he muttered. "The opposite."

At that point, Tizzie and Skyler came and told him it was time to leave. They helped him to his feet and made their way back through the bar and the music and out the front door. Jude felt his head spin in the heat and someone fishing through his pockets for the car keys. He heard Tizzie say to Skyler: "I better drive."

They deposited Jude in the rear, and he laid his head upon the backseat.

"Don't trust anyone," he muttered. "That's the truth—no one."

The car started up and backed out of the parking space. Jude tried to focus upon the back of Tizzie's head, the top hairs glistening in the beams of an oncoming car.

He felt the fabric of the seat against his cheek and the weight of exhaustion. He wanted nothing more than to sleep for a very long time. In his drunken state, he had a wish-dream—that Tizzie slipped over the divide into the backseat, to hold his head in her lap and stroke his brow and tell him that everything was going to be all right. He didn't really expect it to happen.

Tizzie drove slowly and carefully and was bothered by the glare of headlights from a car behind them. She noticed that it took every turn she took, all the way back up Route 17 to the Best Western. She thought of her fight with Jude earlier. The disquieting thought that the car could be following them had proved him right.

---

Jude got up early and fought his hangover with two cups of dark coffee, then a breakfast of scrambled eggs and bacon. He borrowed a skeleton key from the front desk, let himself into Tizzie's room and found the car keys on a heap of crumpled bills on top of a dresser. She was deep asleep on her back, one arm bent across her forehead.

Outside, the sky was pink and blue with wisps of clouds. The heat hadn't started up yet.

He took Route 17 south and made the same turn on 260 West and passed the large rock protruding into the road, but this time he continued climbing past the turnoff to the Indian reservation. The road got narrower as it turned steeper and more and more trees dropped away, and huge clumps of tumbleweed collected in the gullies and embankments. He passed through the small town of Cottonwood—a food store, water-pipe outlet and a collection of trailers—and turned left on 89a toward Jerome. Still, the road was going up; in the distance he saw the humped peaks of the Black Hills mountain range.

He waited for that buried sense of familiarity to rise again and take hold of him, but it didn't happen. The landscape—humped hills of green and brown with occasional slashes of red earth—remained unconnected to him. He spotted gray trailings from a mine that had settled on a hillside like an ancient avalanche, and then another and another. The road began making hairpin turns, and the car fishtailed around them. He came to a gully with red tailings, the sign of an old copper mine, and then to a ravine with the frames of log houses.

Then to a sign, which read: ENTERING JEROME and underneath *Elevation 5246* and underneath that *Founded 1876.*

He recalled what he had read about the place: once a thriving copper, silver and gold mine, it had been home to fifteen thousand people at its peak in the early thirties. Then the price of copper had plummeted, and the population had dropped along with it to five thousand souls, mostly miners, drunks, gamblers, ruffians and whores. The miners had worked the old United Verde under Phelps Dodge until the ores were finally exhausted in 1953, and everyone had left. It had turned into a ghost town prone to landslides and sinkholes, but had recently come partly alive when hippies moved in, taking over the old houses and selling trinkets to tourists.

The road dipped to the right and then mounted abruptly, ascending a thousand-foot escarpment. The climb was so steep, his back pressed against the seat. Halfway up, the road deteriorated. The guard barrier was down for long stretches, and rocks and dirt from landfalls spilled out onto it so that he had to slow to a crawl to negotiate the narrow passage between the debris and a sheer drop-off to his left. Once, when the car rode over a pile of dirt and the front wheels rose up, he caught a glimpse of movement in the rearview mirror; it looked like another car behind him on a switchback at the foot of the mountain. He kept one eye on the mirror, searching for it, but it disappeared into an interior ravine. Finally, he reached the top, and as his car swerved onto level ground, he gave a kick to the accelerator so it seemed to land, as if coming off a wave, and before him he saw the shacks and streets of Jerome lying on a plateau.

The main street was cracked and gutted with potholes, but not totally deserted. He could see a half dozen cars and people moving about on the sidewalks. On one side it was lined with storefronts—some closed with rusted signs, metal gates, and shutters hanging by their hinges. But others were open—a pizza parlor, a bar, a coffee shop and a museum. The street doubled back and mounted to a second level, where the wooden structures had settled at odd angles. In the middle was the ancient three-story Central Hotel, the wooden railings on its triple balconies still perfect. Beyond, the road continued.

Jude took the road—out of instinct—driving up the mountain. It turned past leaning and toppled telephone poles and half-finished houses and abandoned shacks, black with age, that were cut into the ridges of the red-scarred earth.

Two more miles, and Jude came to a dirt side road. It was a mile long and ended at a tiny town. He parked the car and locked it, then walked down the center of the single street. No one was around. There was an empty barber shop with its front window broken, weeds growing under the old leather chairs. One whole section of storefronts had collapsed backward like a fallen stage set. Above it, he could see a sudden drop-off obscured by weeds, and then a spectacular view of green valleys and red hills as far as the eye could see.

He stepped inside a dry goods store whose empty windows were streaked with dirt. He walked upon creaking floor planks, and in the half darkness saw rows of empty wooden bins and racks and an old metal cash register decorated with filigree. Dust was everywhere, lying in a thick carpeting, broken only by the zigzag trail of lizard tracks. He stepped outside.

Next door was a bar; a faded sign out front said it had been owned by Thomas J. O'Toole. Here the dust was an inch thick. The bar itself, twenty feet long and chest-high, had rounded holders at the bottom where the brass rail used to be and a faded Western saloon mirror above. He spotted a wooden table upon which rested an uncorked bottle three quarters full of a brown solidified liquid. He left.

Two doors down was a house of faded green clapboards. The front windows were blocked by a sheet of rusted tin held in place with twisted wire. He pushed open the door and stepped inside. The front hall was empty, and there were footsteps in the dusty steps leading upstairs. He entered a side room where yellow-dirty lace curtains still hung. A foot-pedal Singer sewing machine and wooden chair sat in the glow of a large window. An old pair of shoes with turned-up toes lay underneath.

Out back was a wooden porch, its rotting floorboards covered with rocks and slanting precariously toward the escarpment. He decided not to test it and walked back through the house toward the front hall and went upstairs. His feet sank into the carpet of dust and sent tiny clouds billowing against the faded wallpaper. The ceiling was low and the hallway narrow and dark. He looked into the first bedroom. It was largely empty, except for a bookshelf with a dozen old books and a rocker; when he pushed it, the rockers left gashes in the mat of floor dust. The hallway creaked; he thought he heard a sound downstairs and froze for a full minute. He heard nothing more. The second bedroom had a broom, and one corner was swept clean; it contained a soiled mattress, and near it a plate with a candle held in place by melted wax. A rucksack lay at the foot of the mattress, along with an opened copy of *Penthouse* magazine. It was dated three months ago.

Suddenly, Jude flinched. A sound reached him, far away but loud, a pounding noise that seemed to shake the room. It got louder and louder. At first he thought it was a landslide that was going to bury him alive, but then he recognized the throb of engines. He rushed to the front bedroom and looked down just as the noise turned deafening: a group of motorcycles thundered down the main street, leather jackets flying in the wind, and clouds of dust spewing up behind. There were five or six of them, bulky men spreading their abdomens on the gas tanks, beards and studs and helmets and thick forearms gripping the handlebars. They were gone almost as quickly as they had come, riding off on the road farther up the mountain.

Jude looked up the road after them, leading up the mountain. And he suddenly knew that was the road he had to take. He could not have explained how he knew; the conviction just took hold of him. He walked downstairs, stepped outside and looked around. And he realized that he had been bothered by something since he had arrived, by the absence of something—that veiled sense of familiarity that he had first felt driving up Route 260. If he had grown up here, had spent his childhood here, then why did nothing that he'd seen here speak to him? Nothing did—until that moment when he knew that the road up the mountain was where he needed to go.

He walked to the car. Another one was parked farther down the road, a blue Camaro: was that the vehicle that he had spotted in the rearview mirror? He stared at it: Arizona plates, nothing distinctive. And no sign of the owner anywhere.

He got in his car, drove up the road, and after five minutes came to a turnoff on the right, a narrow dirt road rutted with holes and mounds. A beaten sign pointed the way to the Gold King Mine. Jude knew, even before he saw the dust still settling on the leaves from the motorcycles, that this was the turn to take; it was familiar and everything around it was familiar—the trees, the slope of the land, the look of the blue sky, as if he had suddenly stepped through a hidden door to his past. The sensation was frightening but energizing.

The road was short. It mounted a slope and then came to the crest of a hill, and he looked down, as if he were looking into the crater of a volcano, into an open pit mine and a cluster of wooden buildings. There were old warehouses and wooden dormitories, storage bins and a dozen outbuildings, piles of rock and railroad tracks. And in the center of it all, a large gray smelter with a giant red-brick smokestack. He knew the smokestack instantly; he had seen it before from all angles. He knew the entire scene, all of it—except that it now looked smaller, dollhouse size, compared to the tableau that had existed dormant and buried in his memory.

He drove slowly along the approach road around the rim of the pit. On the far ridge, higher up on the other side of the slope, was a narrow cabin where the motorcycles rested on their kick stands. A man in a black T-shirt sat side-saddle on one of them, smoking and watching him. Jude stopped the car before the road descended into the pit and parked on a narrow isthmus that separated the pit from the escarpment that fell off sharply into the Verde Valley below. He took a flashlight from the glove compartment.

Down the road he walked, at times so steep he had to turn sideways and dig his heels into the dirt. At the bottom, he knew to continue straight ahead, and entered a large building that had once been the mine office. The wooden steps were worn into concave bows by generations of boots. Had he not been there a thousand times? He turned to survey the layout from the doorstep—how strange to stand there, a giant returned to the homeland, looking at the buildings and at the tubular smokestack in the air, the only piece of the landscape that did not seem mysteriously diminished.

Abruptly, with the same certainty that had brought him there, he knew where to go next. He stepped outside and followed his feet, which took him through the encampment and up a rough road toward the hillside. He kept walking as the road curved, and finally came to an end before a gaping black hole in the side of the mountain, the entrance to the underground mine. He stepped inside and touched the rough rock walls with the palm of his right hand, then turned and took in the vista before him—the tops of the buildings, the smelter, the smokestack—it all fit so neatly into the mold of his memory. Unaccountably, he felt anxious.

He turned and walked twenty paces into the shaft until he was engulfed by darkness. He flicked on the flashlight and shined it around, up and down; the beam illuminated the roof of the tunnel, crisscrossing a mass of packed earth and rocks. From somewhere inside him came memories of warning of cave-ins and landslides, the childish terror of being smothered alive. Still, he walked on, and he managed to calm the fears as he made progress deep into the passageway. He came to a crossroads; to the left was a large tunnel in which he could see the rails for the iron cars, and in the hardened mud the sharp imprints of mule hooves. But he knew to take the smaller fork to the right.

Some ninety feet down, the tunnel sloped and passed under supporting timbers, which sagged. Then it narrowed until he could touch it on both sides, and as he did so, the fears returned with a vengeance. A wave of claustrophobia swept over him, so strong he decided to sit for a while. He waited a full ten minutes, then rose and walked on and came to another fork. This time he went left, and he realized he had followed a large white arrow that had been painted onto the rock face. He knew it from somewhere. After another hundred feet, he was stopped by an old cave-in. A support beam had split—half of it lay cracked in the middle of the tunnel—and above it the debris had tumbled down like sand, forming an impassable blockage. He felt a complicated rush of mixed emotions: he would be denied his destination, which attracted him with a force difficult to explain, but he was also almost secretly gratified that he would be forced to turn back and return to the surface.

But then he saw that the open darkness continued under the half beam. He shined the flashlight there. It was not just a beam but an entire wooden ceiling that had fallen, forming a kind of platform. Underneath was a stunted passageway about two feet in height. If he crawled, perhaps he could squeeze through. He inspected it thoroughly with the flashlight; it narrowed at the far end, which meant he could get stuck—or even worse, he might dislodge the precarious boards above, setting off another cave-in. He peered through it again, fighting down the panic that was pushing up from his chest. He got down on his hands and knees, then on his belly. He ducked his head and crawled forward, holding the flashlight ahead of him and pushing against the rocky floor with his feet. He closed his eyes as he moved slowly, feeling the dampness of the rock around him, the massiveness of the enclosing cocoon, breathing the stale air. Halfway through, he stopped to collect himself. He opened his eyes, which was a mistake: the wood above and the rock below seemed to converge into a thin envelope ahead; the wall on either side was less than a foot from his nose. He closed them again and squirmed forward—another six inches, another foot. Across the ridge of his back he felt a board; it scraped and he heard a sound, a slight shifting noise, and saw a trickle of dirt spilling down and forming a tiny anthill off to one side.

Then suddenly he was through. He pulled his legs out and stood up, breathing deeply. But he did not stay there for long, for he could tell, from a flick of the flashlight, that he had almost reached the place he was looking for. He walked another ten yards, and abruptly the tunnel opened up on all sides and he was standing at the opening of a large cavern. The floor was smooth rock, and the sides rose up like walls; there were electrical cables leading up to open light sockets on the ceiling, pipes to bring in water and, most surprising of all, furnishings. He knew the room from childhood.

He moved the beam of light slowly in all directions, and as he did so, it took in what little was left of the equipment that once had been there: long white enamel tables, double sinks, shelves for storage of flasks and test tubes and microscopes, even hooks for robes and masks. It was the ideal environment for a laboratory—sealed off underground from the outside world, no contaminants, constant temperature, almost hermetic conditions. It was also, he reflected, perfect for secrecy.

Jude examined the room. It looked as if no one had been there for a long time. He opened the drawers, checked the shelves, looked in the trash bins. It had been stripped of almost everything but the rudimentary furnishings. In one corner was a pile of rubbish that included empty cardboard boxes, a small sterilizing drum missing an electrical cord, used batteries and several pairs of latex gloves. He closed his eyes and tried to imagine it fully furnished and operating, tried to bring it all back, but the images remained just out of reach.

Then he heard a noise.

It came from the tunnel he had used, a small scraping sound—on second thought, it could be distant footsteps. He doused the flashlight, and when the cavern was plunged into total darkness, he saw a pinprick of light down the tunnel. It seemed to glow, stronger and then weaker, as if the wick of a lantern was being manipulated, but then he realized that it was the beam of a flashlight moving around the tunnel. He felt a tingling in his scalp, a twist in his gut. He moved to one side of the room and felt his way with his hands: there was the smooth surface of a table, then emptiness, then the rocky wall, until he came to a large cabinet. He snuck behind it and waited, still watching that little dot of light.

The sounds got louder. He realized that his pursuer, whoever he was, was negotiating the same narrow passage he had gone through. He had a split-second thought: shouldn't he run up the tunnel and catch him just as he was about to emerge? At a moment of vulnerability? But he stayed frozen where he was, in his hiding place, and he could hear grunts of exertion so close that he knew it was probably too late for that.

The light was brighter now and moving around, and Jude knew that the person was on his feet again. He flattened himself against the wall, and stood without moving, scarcely breathing, as the seconds ticked off. Then suddenly the light burst into the room like an explosion, almost blinding him before it flashed about wildly. It pointed away toward the other side, and Jude could see the round metallic edge of the flashlight and the sharp beam opening out in a V, and the dim outline of a hand clasping it.

And at that moment the person moved over to the wall on Jude's side and began slowly circling the room, holding the light before him almost like a protective shield. Jude held his breath as he came closer, until he was standing right next to him. Then Jude lunged. He grabbed him with both arms, knocking the flashlight to the ground, where it scuttled across the rock, the beam dancing wildly on the ceiling. A short sharp cry of surprise, a struggle. Jude felt an arm strike him under the chin, but he held on and dragged his pursuer down. He landed on top of him and grabbed an arm and twisted it behind with all his might until he thought it might break. The person froze. Then spoke.

"Jude, is that you?"

The voice sounded tiny, scared.

Jude reached with his other hand and found his flashlight. He turned it on, held it at arm's length and shined it down.

"Tizzie!" He almost screamed her name. "What the hell are you doing here?"

# Chapter 21

Jude let Tizzie up. She checked for bruises, bending over to roll up her left pant leg, revealing a cut on her knee. Two trails of blood trickled down toward her ankle, which she wiped with her hand, rolling the pant leg down again.

She still hadn't answered his question. He asked another one, simpler.

"You all right?"

She nodded yes, then added: "Frightened more than anything else. You scared me to death."

"Sorry. I didn't know it was you."

"I hope not."

Typical, he thought, that he should end up being the one to apologize.

"You followed me?" he asked, now with a touch of hardness to his voice. He didn't know how she was going to play it out.

"Yes. At least to Jerome."

"That was your car back there—the one you rented? The blue Camaro?"

"Yes."

"And then you followed me in here?"

She hesitated. "Not exactly," she said. "I knew you were coming here."

"And you knew the way—right?"

"Right"

"Why come after me?"

"I thought you might . . . get hurt. I thought they might be here. Or come after you."

"I see."

He looked around the bare room, almost absentmindedly, then realized he was looking for something to sit on. It was going to be for a long while.

"The time has come for a good long talk," he said.

"Do you want to go to our special place?"

The question rocked him. He had not heard or thought about that for a quarter of a century, but when she said the words, it came back in a flash—a cave that they used to frequent, hardly bigger than a closet. They'd liked going there because the entrance was small, not made for adults.

"You remember how to get there?"

She slid her hand in his—her fingers felt small and cold, and he realized she was frightened—and led him to a back passageway he hadn't seen earlier. The tunnel was narrow, so he dropped her hand and followed behind, shining his flashlight at her feet while she aimed hers farther ahead. She squeezed past a support beam and moved on, surprisingly quickly, so that he felt the need to hurry. He brushed the beam with his shoulder. It shifted a little, sending down a small shower of rocks and dirt.

She shined the flashlight back, and he could see her face in his beam, a worried look.

"I'll be careful," he said quietly.

"Almost there," she replied.

And they were. She ducked under an overhanging rock and he did the same, and they entered the small chamber that was instantly recognizable. There were shelves in the rock, and they sat on them, low down like adults in a kindergarten class. One wall was streaked with multicolored rivulets, and he remembered the candles burning there and dripping tears of wax while the two of them sat in these very seats.

Tizzie looked Jude in the eye—the first time in a long time, he thought, that she didn't seem to turn away.

"It's tough to know where to begin," she said.

"Try the beginning," he said tartly.

"I've only started to remember a lot of things lately—and there's still a lot I can't recall. But now I expect I remember more than you do. Some of my first memories are right here, in this room, with you. We used to come here a lot and play and talk. I remember the coziness of it and how we felt safe—or at least I did—safe and secure in the knowledge that not far away in the chamber just outside, adults were working, doing things, whatever it was they did—experiments in the lab . . ."

"Did you remember all that when we met? Did you know who I was then?"

"No. Not at all. Please, Jude. I know how you must feel—how suspicious all this seems. I swear I'm on your side. But let me tell you the whole story. If you keep interrupting, we'll never get anywhere."

"Okay. Go ahead."

"We lived right outside, in that building that used to house the mine offices. Don't you remember? I remembered it as soon as I saw it. Things are flooding back to me. When we lived here, the mine had been closed down for years. I guess somehow the group got the title to it. When we were little, we weren't told anything. I have a vague memory that we knew somehow that our parents were scientists, that they were doing great things, and that it was all very secret because the rest of the world wouldn't understand. They would try to stop it—whatever *it* was.

"My parents were involved. So were yours. And there were others—I don't know how many and I can't remember them. I can't really remember any of the important details, though God knows I've been trying this past week—ever since I went home. I always thought I'd just been too young to remember the years before White Fish Bay, but that wasn't it. I'd simply blocked them out. Until this week.

"I think I almost remember your father. Not your mother. As you said, she died some years before. But now if I close my eyes, I can remember the day your father took you away—I can almost see the car going down the road. I had a sense then that something horrible had happened, something shameful. When you described it, back when we first met, it seemed familiar, as if I had dreamt it. But after talking with my parents, I suddenly remembered it clearly. It was that sense of something bad happening—remembering that brought it back.

"My parents said we were all told never to speak of your father again. So your name just disappeared. There had been this huge argument, a fight among the parents, and that was why your father took you away. I don't know all the details because even now my parents don't like to speak about it. But I gather the split came because your father objected to something—something involving the research. I think I now know what it was—but we'll get to that later.

"The group was called the Lab. And they were working on research that they were convinced would change the world—life extension. And the center of it was this scientist, Rincon. When I heard Skyler say that name, I didn't connect with it at all. I don't recall him. But I do have a recollection of *someone* very important. You know how children have this almost innate sense of hierarchy among adults—who is above who. I knew there was this person that everyone worshiped. He was like the sun. I think he lived in that mansion in that town we passed, the Palmer mansion. I remember the grown-ups would traipse up there to meet with him.

"He had tremendous power over them in some way, I don't know what exactly. Anyway, we kids never saw him. To this day, I couldn't tell you what he looked like. But we *knew he was there.* And he was supposed to be good, benevolent, and extremely smart—brilliant—because he was the head of the whole thing."

Jude was burning with questions. So far, he realized, he had not learned all that much that was entirely new, though the pieces of the puzzle were beginning to fit together a little more snugly.

He took out a cigarette and lighted up. He saw a half candle lying on the floor, put it on the small, wax-covered ledge, and lighted it, too, dousing the flashlight. The glow made the cave come alive with shadows and seem even smaller.

"Go on," he said.

"There were a bunch of other leaders, Elder Physicians was what Skyler called them, and when my parents used the same word last weekend, I felt like screaming. Baptiste—I don't know who he is. There are others who are important, like my Uncle Henry. I don't know where he fits in, but he plays an emissary role for the Lab. I think he's like the group's contact point with outsiders. Now that I look back, I imagine that he and the others like my parents and your parents—they were probably the original founders of the group or something like that."

She paused and watched a drop of wax run down the candle.

"I don't know if you remember—I didn't, until I talked to my father—but even when we were young, they began our education. I think a lot of it was scientific stuff, and we felt special—we were going to be like little pioneers. And one day—this was sometime after you left—we had to go to a regular school down in the valley. I guess the state made us. I remember a yellow school bus would come all the way up the mountain to get us and then bring us home. It was exciting. But suddenly one day we had our own school right here—in some kind of old hotel. I recall being sad because I liked going down into the valley and meeting all these other kids. I thought of them as normal, and I liked something about reciting the Pledge of Allegiance and making cutouts of the state flower—it made me feel connected to the outside world.

"All that changed when we got our own school. And now here's why I remember all this. There was one day when inspectors came—from the state, I guess—and we put on a show for them. We prepared special classes ahead of time for that day and fixed up the schoolroom. We made paper cutouts of leaves or snowflakes or something and put them on the window—just like a normal school. It was to fool them. The whole thing was a charade to make them think we were getting the same education as all the other kids. But of course we weren't.

"And what I remembered was the feeling of lying—the shame of it. And my father said it was all right to do it. This weekend, when my father told me that he was dying and my mother was dying, he told me not to tell her. He said it was all right to lie. And just then, I had this memory breakthrough—everything about the school and playing here in the mines with you—it all came back to me in a single block. It was amazing."

"When you were growing up in Milwaukee, you didn't know about your parents?"

"No, not really. I felt they were different in some way. When I was young, I used to fantasize that they were scientists engaged in a supersecret project. Like the Manhattan Project, Los Alamos. That the research they were doing was invaluable and one day they would be famous for it, but in the meantime we had to keep quiet. That we couldn't talk about it, not one word, because there were benighted forces trying to stop them. It was a fantasy, but on some level it was real. I must have known about it."

"How much did you know about the breakthroughs they were making?"

Tizzie answered without hesitating, speaking now in low, urgent tones.

"Only some of it. I knew that life was important, that living long was desirable. I knew that it was important to expand my mind, to cram it with facts and research and scientific data. And I knew that taking care of my body was important. These were the values inculcated in me.

"Especially taking care of the body. Whenever anything went wrong—a cold, a cut, in the worst case, *a broken arm*—I was showered with attention. After all, my father was a doctor. Nothing was too much. Antibiotics were given freely."

She stopped for a second, now that she had come to the hard part.

"But if you're asking when I needed that kidney, did I know what was going on . . . where it would come from . . . the answer is no. What I told you before was true. When I was young, maybe fifteen or sixteen—funny how much of this I've repressed—I was ill. I got this urinary infection that went untreated for a while and turned serious. I was running a high fever, and it hurt so much when I urinated, I tried to hold back and that made it worse. I didn't want to tell my father, but finally he noticed. And he gave me this stuff, Gentamycin. And for a while I seemed better, but then I took a sudden turn for the worse. I recall going to a hospital in Milwaukee and being attached to a machine for dialysis. And then one day, I was operated on. It was done at a small clinic. I don't remember much about the operation at all, just that I spent days in bed and missed so much school that I had to have a tutor."

Tizzie paused for a moment, searching for the right words.

"I didn't even stop to think . . . to wonder where the kidney came from. I mean, why would I? I was just a kid. And the strange thing is, I don't think I've really thought about it since then. I must have questioned it at some point—I know now, obviously, that kidneys are scarce—and it struck me after the operation, much later, that I didn't have to take immunosuppression drugs and undergo that whole regimen, but I don't think I ever really came to grips with it. And then when I heard Skyler talk about Julia and about her operation, it registered somewhere. I still didn't take it in—not until my father told me. I was shocked. At least he had the decency to be embarrassed."

She stared again at the candle.

"But if I'm honest, I admit that I had a funny feeling—a feeling that I had known something about it all along on some level. The thing is, I don't know *how* I would have known. Because I was certainly never told. Imagine—telling a kid she's getting a body part from someone raised just for that purpose. So I didn't know about clones. I didn't know they existed. But on some level, I think I guessed that something horrible was going on."

"How many of you . . . us . . . I don't know what to call us . . . *prototypes*. How many prototypes are there?"

"I don't really know. Maybe twenty—twenty or thirty. Scattered all over the country. All are children of the original members of the Lab. I asked my father last weekend how they could have done it. As you can imagine, he didn't want to talk about it. What he finally said was that it was viewed as giving us a wonderful gift, the gift of extended life. They themselves couldn't live a long time, and back then—don't forget this was the late sixties—their own research was not that far along. They couldn't create clones of adults. In fact, most of them believed back then that couldn't be done, ever. But it wasn't all that hard to create clones of your children.

"As he explained it, he was almost proud. You take the fertilized egg, separate the cells out at an early stage, and put their nuclei into other eggs. You deep-freeze them and start them up whenever you want. Your mother gets the embryo implanted down the road. That's why Skyler is younger than you and Julia is . . . was . . . younger than me. If you think about it—and I've been thinking plenty about it—if you're raising clones to be organ donors, you'd want them to be younger. The organs would have to be vital and strong."

"But they'd be no good for inherited diseases. Because then the organ would eventually give out in exactly the same way."

"Yes, probably. But the organ wouldn't have any environmental component to disease. In that way, it would be stronger. And it would work for any disease caught by contagion. And of course for any accident."

She leaned closer toward Jude.

"You know, there's something else. There might even be still younger ones out there. You heard Skyler talking about the nursery, that place right next to the island. Maybe that's what that's for."

"Did your parents say that?"

"Not in so many words. But I inferred it."

"Why don't they tell you everything?"

"I don't know. They're scared of something. They've been scared for as long as I can remember. They had some kind of break with the Lab, too. It wasn't as dramatic as your father's and it wasn't a complete rupture, but they drifted away. It happened when I was maybe six years old. That's when we moved to Milwaukee. I don't know much about it, and whatever I did know, I've probably forgotten or repressed.

"But I recall some things. For one thing, there was suddenly money around. For another, my parents were distracted, bothered by things. They talked alone in their bedroom in low voices. And after we picked up and went to Wisconsin, we didn't lose all contact with the Lab. My uncle Henry used to come for visits, so I guess you could say it was an amiable parting. But it was definitely a parting."

"Tell me more about this uncle Henry."

"He's my mother's brother. He's been around as long as I can remember. I've never liked him—in fact, something about him is downright repulsive. I don't like the way my parents look up to him. I can't put my finger on it—but he seems to have something over them."

"What?"

"I don't know. I've thought a lot about it—he's on a power trip and they're on the losing end of it. They're ill and they seem to do whatever he says. He says they're working on a vaccination to cure them, and he uses that to pressure me. He came by the house last weekend and stopped me in the hallway. He said he had something he wanted me to do."

"What was it?"

"I'm not sure—he said we'd talk soon. But he was sneaky when he said it. I bet he's going to ask me to spy on you."

"To spy on me? And what will you say?"

She shot him a cold look. "No, of course."

"Tizzie, you said before that you were afraid that *they* had followed me here. Who are *they*?"

She looked into his eyes. "Jude"—she used his name for the first time—"believe me, I don't know. I've told you everything I know."

"Do you know where the Lab is? The island?"

"No, but we should be able to figure it out. We can piece it together from what Skyler knows."

"How has *he* taken all this?"

"You mean about me and Julia?"

"Yes."

"He's confused. He's angry. He knew from the first night he met you that Julia and I were exactly alike. He saw my photograph."

"He did? Why didn't he say anything?"

"I don't know. I guess he was afraid—he didn't know he could trust us."

"And now?"

"Now he knows that I didn't know about it—about her and how she was just like me—and that seems to make a difference."

"So you've talked about it?" Jude made an effort to keep his voice normal.

"Yes."

"I see. When?"

"Just yesterday. When you left us and drove off. And some before, bit by bit. Where did you go, anyway?"

"To the Verde Indian reservation. I looked up my birth certificate. Yours, too."

"And that's how you knew?"

"That's how I knew *for sure*. I'd been thinking about it for some time. Skyler acted strangely toward you from the start. When he's with you, he can't disguise his feelings, much as he tries to. He either never looks at you, or he looks at you all the time. And then there was your operation and Julia's—that was quite a coincidence. You weren't listed in the national registry of organ transplants—I got the information on that from Hartman—so I knew your operation had to be illicit. And some other little things that matched up—both of you being nearsighted, for example."

"I see."

"But beyond all that, there were two things that really disturbed me."

"What?"

"First, it was that you didn't tell me about it right off the bat, which indicated that you were probably in on the conspiracy. Then when Skyler told us the whole story as we were driving out here, he said something that stuck in my mind. Julia was killed because she had found something in the records—she knew too much and had become a threat. But as he described her body when he found her lying on the slab, he said all her internal organs had been removed. I asked myself: why would they have done that? Only one reason: they wanted to preserve them for some future use. They wanted them in case you needed them."

The horror of it all hit home, and Tizzie slumped against the rock wall.

"Jude, I feel so bad. I feel guilty about everything. What a grotesque, hideous thing to do, to make a clone. And I feel responsible for it. Julia was like a sister, a twin—only younger. I had nothing to do with creating her, but I feel that I did. It was done *for* me, so it's almost as if it was done *by* me. I took her kidney. I caused her to suffer. And then she died a horrible death, and I feel I'm responsible for that, too."

Jude went to her and knelt down beside her. She smiled up at him weakly.

"And you want to hear something strange? The whole thing is so upsetting I don't even want to think about it. But I want to know everything about Julia. When Skyler talks about her, when he describes her with such love, I could listen for hours."

Jude nodded.

"I think I knew, almost from the first time I saw him—well, not the very first, that was in bed, thanks to you—but from the first time I heard Skyler speak her name, I knew that she and I were the same."

"Not exactly the same. Remember everything you told me back when we first met."

"Right. Not the same. But similar—very similar, connected in some way. And I knew it from him. You're right—he acts strange in front of me. And when he looks at me that way—you described that look—it's a look of love. Just the way he must have looked at her. That's when I feel most connected."

They were silent for several moments.

"Anyway," she said. "I'm sorry—for everything."

He felt a rush of feeling for her and realized that it had been some time since he had felt like that.

"Let me ask you one thing," he said. "When we first met—that interview and everything—was that set up?"

"What do you mean?"

"Well, were you told to meet me? Were you operating under some kind of instructions?"

She put her arm on his. "No. You came to me, remember?"

"Yeah, that's what I can't figure out."

"I liked you the moment I saw you. But I'll tell you this—I think that somebody was pulling strings, that somehow it was arranged for us to meet."

"But why?"

"Maybe they were worried about you, maybe they wanted to keep an eye on you—after all, Skyler had already escaped. Maybe they knew he would try to contact you."

"I've thought of that. But it doesn't make sense. They could have just bumped me off—they don't seem adverse to doing that kind of thing."

"That's a pretty extreme step. And it's messy—it brings in the police."

"Okay. But then why send a spy who's ignorant of her mission?"

"What do you mean?"

"Why send a spy who doesn't report back? Unless, of course, you have been reporting back."

Tizzie looked at him, her eyes blazing.

"I suppose I deserve that. But I want you to know—it's just not true. I think that was their plan. But the moment I met Skyler and we all began figuring out the truth, there was no possibility. Don't ever think that—not for one moment. I would never do something like that."

Jude believed her—something in her tone convinced him. And he liked the fact that she didn't turn contrite but angry.

"That whole business about being a researcher in twins studies—that was true?" he asked.

"Of course. I couldn't bluff something like that. And I wouldn't."

"Quite a coincidence."

"Not really. I was always attracted to that research, lost twins and all that. And now, of course, I know why—somehow I knew deep down I had one."

He waited half a second before asking the next question.

"Tell me," he said. "When we went for dinner that first time, when we went to Brighton Beach, when we made love—all that was real, wasn't it? I mean, none of it was scripted?"

"Of course not. They just brought us together—like two little protozoa in a petri dish. They just let nature take its course.—*My God,*" she suddenly exclaimed. "I never thought of this. They had *reason* to think we'd fall for each other. Because that's what happened to Sklyer and Julia. They *knew* what would happen. We were like . . . puppets."

Jude looked at her; she was attractive, anyone would find her so. But he refused to believe that his feelings for her could have been determined by someone else ahead of time.

He thought he heard a sound way off in the distance, but he didn't mention it.

He took her in his arms. She yielded and placed her head into his shoulder. They stayed like that for some minutes, until she drew back, wiping her eyes with her wrist.

"You're right about one thing," he said. "The people we're dealing with here—*whoever* they are—they're powerful. They think they're invincible. We can fight them, and the odds aren't in our favor. But we've got one thing on our side."

"What?"

"They don't know what to make of us. They think you're on their side—or could be, with a little muscle. And as for me—I don't get it, but they seem to think I'm potentially of some use. I think that's why they haven't killed me."

He had another question, but he never got to ask it.

At that moment the sound in the distance grew; it turned into an ominous rumble, and the small cave they were in began to tremble slightly. He looked at Tizzie and saw his fear reflected in the pallor of her face. Then a little puff of wind extinguished the candle.

They felt for their flashlights and turned them on.

"What is it?" she uttered.

His answer came out in a single word: "Cave-in!"

They ran from the hideaway back through the tunnel they had used shortly before and came to the large research chamber and then the main tunnel. After two yards, they halted—ahead was a boiling brown cloud, a curtain of dust that swirled around them and out into the chamber.

'Stop! Go back!" cried Tizzie.

They leapt back into the room to wait for it to settle. Jude felt his fears grow and crystallize into the claustrophobe's panic: the unmentionable fear of entombment. His abdomen tightened, and he felt a wave of heat circulating through his bloodstream like bubbles of seltzer water.

"I can't believe that was an accident," he said. "Someone heard us. Or they knew we were in here. They made it happen."

"That wouldn't be hard to do. But that tunnel was shaky when I came through it. Maybe it just happened by itself."

He cast her a skeptical look. "You've become a great believer in coincidences."

The dust had settled into a thin blanket that covered the metal table nearby. Jude looked at the mouth of the tunnel, mostly clear now that the brown cloud had turned to a thin mist whose particles glittered in their flashlight beams. He dreaded going back in.

They stepped inside to investigate, careful not to touch the walls and trying to tread lightly, as if walking on thin ice. Tizzie went first and Jude made no effort to stop her—he was finding it hard to breathe and took gulps of air into his lungs. She stopped and he came up behind her, and they shined their flashlights over the debris before them, hoping to spot a hole. They didn't see one. The wall of rock and dirt appeared impenetrable, starting at the ceiling of the tunnel and slanting down at an angle to the floor. Tizzie poked it gently with her foot.

"Christ," he said. "We've had it."

"Maybe we could dig our way out, if we were careful. We could pile the dirt inside the room."

He shined the beam up at the roof, where a thin trickle of dirt was still pouring down through a crack.

"Maybe, but chances are we'd just make it worse. Once the ceiling is cracked like that, there's nothing to stop more earth from pouring through. It's like sand in an hourglass."

"Let's go back," she said. He felt relief to be leaving the tunnel.

Inside the chamber, they examined every wall, looking for an indentation, a crevice, anything that might hint at a passageway out. Again, they found nothing, except for the single tunnel at the rear that led to their cave. Tizzie went to investigate it, but Jude stayed in the chamber, watching her light bounce off the narrow walls and then recede, getting dimmer until it disappeared altogether.

He badly wanted a cigarette, and felt the pack in his pocket, but he knew that would be foolish and selfish—under no circumstances could he use up the little remaining oxygen. He looked around the chamber again, trying to estimate the size. How long would the air last?

For want of anything else to do, he paced in a circle, trying to think and to run through the possibilities. It was like examining the tunnels—there was none that led anywhere.

So deep in thought was he that he didn't notice Tizzie's return. He was startled when she spoke.

"Nothing," she said in a tone of resignation. "No way out there at all."

---

When Skyler awoke in the motel room bed, with the sheets twisted and damp with sweat, he knew that something was wrong—grievously wrong. His illness had taken a turn for the worse—more than a turn, he had entered a whole new territory. He was confused; he had been sick before, but never like this.

His head was burning and his chest was racked by pain. The violence of these fits of pain scared him; his teeth clacked together and the whole bed seemed to vibrate. He felt feverishly cold and wrapped himself in blankets, then suddenly so hot he had to toss them off. His throat was parched, and he was desperately thirsty.

Waiting until a shivering spell passed, he sat up, naked. He moved slowly to the edge of the bed and swung his feet to the floor. They fell like dead weights. Using the headboard, he pulled himself up and shuffled across the room into the hall. He managed to make it to the bathroom, flicked on the light, and turned on a faucet. He picked a paper cover off a glass and filled it with water, downing it in one long swallow. Then he took another. He was suddenly exhausted. His eyes lifted to the mirror, and he was shocked by the face that peered back. His eyes were lifeless, two glazed orbs set deep and rounded by blue-brown circles. His skin was loose and pallid; it hung in jowls from his sunken cheeks. His lips were cracked into pink and white strips, flaked with shards of skin.

A wave overtook him again—was it hot or cold?—he couldn't tell. But it was powerful. His knees buckled and he knelt on the floor, the glass falling from his hand and breaking in the sink. He fell and crumpled into a ball, lying like that until he felt the spasm pass. As the shivers subsided, his eyes fastened on a corner where there was a yellow plastic stand for a toilet brush. He stared at it, a fixed point, straining to regain equilibrium. A full minute passed.

He crawled out of the bathroom, sat for a while on the industrial carpet, regained some strength and finally made it to the bed, collapsing upon it. He lapsed into a half faint and then opened his eyes. The sheets were soiled—

spots of something. He tried to focus: it was dark, red. Blood. He looked down at his thin, pale legs, his thighs, his arms. There was blood smeared on his chest. It came from his hand, which he had cut on the glass. He held it up and watched the blood drip from his palm.

He looked to one side and saw the side table with a lamp and the phone. He moved across and reached for the receiver and brought it to his ear, pulling the phone off the nightstand. The line was quiet. He saw a folded card of instructions and picked it up, but couldn't read the blurred letters. He pulled the phone up by the cord and dialed numbers at random, and the receiver gave a strange buzzing. It was hopeless. He dropped it and rolled over to the wall, made a fist and began banging upon it. Surely Tizzie would hear him and come to help him. But she did not. He lay back and tried to think. He cocked his arm over his head, then felt the liquid running across his face and sat up and looked: the wall he had been banging had red smears upon it. He saw that it was connected not to Tizzie's room but to the bathroom he had just been in. He thought he heard the water running.

He fell back onto the sheets and drifted off to sleep. It was not a peaceful, nurturing sleep, but a wild, rocky sleep. It seemed to seize him and shake him. He awoke once, saw that the room was darkening, and fell off again. He tossed back and forth in the delirium of nightmares: he was back on the island, pursued by the Orderlies and the dogs. He was racing through the swamp, the water grabbing his legs so that he made little progress as the hunting party got closer and closer. He came to a clearing, and the dogs came at him from all sides. They surrounded him, backed him into a tree, snarling, their fangs bared, about to leap for his throat. . . . He sat up in bed, breathing heavily and sweating.

He looked around, getting his bearings. The light was on in the bathroom, shining onto the carpet outside and casting long shadows upon the wall opposite. He heard water running. He turned on the bedside light and saw red streaked across the wall, soaked into the sheets, smear-dried upon his chest. He held up his hand and examined a gash caked with thick blood. He must have lost a lot of it. Perhaps that was why he felt so weak.

He tried to stand, felt the chest pain, sat down and tried again. This time he was able to rise to this feet, and he stood there almost motionless for a few seconds, leaning slowly first to one side and then another. He managed to walk to a chair where he had thrown his pants. Painfully, leaning against the wall and finally sitting on the chair and lifting first one leg and then the other, he was able to put them on. He rested for a while, trying to remember what it was he wanted to do. His mind felt waterlogged.

He stood again, still wavering, and walked slowly to the door. It was locked with a chain and he tried to undo it, but couldn't fit the sliding guide into the open track. He turned the doorknob and pulled it, so that the door lunged open five inches and then jammed. Through the crack, he looked out and saw a slice of parking lot and felt a hot, dry wind. It was already growing dark.

He closed the door and leaned against it with his shoulder, using his opposite hand to move the chain slowly away from him. Then he jiggled it, and much to his relief, it fell and swung along the door like a pendulum. He grasped the doorknob again and turned it slowly, stepping backward so quickly that he almost lost his balance. He pulled the door open. The air hit him, hot and heavy. He stepped outside, grabbed a railing and bent over it, holding onto it with both hands and shoving them ahead like a man planing a wooden plank. The railing bent into a banister and slanted down the staircase. He followed it down like a drunkard, one step at a time.

It took him a long time to descend the steps. He stopped three or four times, when he felt faint, and he held on for dear life with both hands, knowing that if he sat down, if he gave in to that overwhelming desire to rest, he wouldn't get up again. He didn't give in, and he made it to the bottom, but then he was confronted with another dilemma. He was there in the open with nothing to hold onto. There was no one around. How would he make it across the parking lot?

He took a deep breath and lunged ahead. He felt himself toppling forward and keep pumping his feet ahead of him to right the balance until he was practically running, bent at an angle like a tree that wanted to crash down. In this curious fashion, he loped across the lot, barefoot and stripped to the waist, covered with blood. He mounted the curb, tore through a line of bushes and came crashing into the motel office, looking up just in time to see the mouth of the receptionist form into a perfect oval. The scream seemed to come from her diaphragm—it didn't come out right away, delayed like a sonic boom, but when it came, it was full-bodied. It was a bloodthirsty yell, and it rent the gathering dusk like an ax.

# Chapter 22

"You're sure you checked everywhere? Every crevice? Every hole?" Jude asked largely just to be asking, to be doing something, to be raking over all the possibilities together instead of sinking separately into despair.

Tizzie, seated upon the metal table, didn't answer. Instead, she just nodded in an absentminded way.

He was walking around the chamber, looking at every object there with a new eye, thinking of how it might be used for some purpose other than for the one for which it was built—for escape. He felt his movements were a little too frenetic.

Above all, he was trying to push out of his mind the idea that would not go away, no matter how hard he tried—the suspicion that breathing was actually becoming a little more difficult, that the oxygen was already noticeably depleting. He wasn't good at taking a mental measure of cubic meters or figuring out how much time they had left. But he knew one thing: they would die of suffocation long before starvation. The image of them thrashing about and gasping for air and pulling long drafts of poisoning carbon dioxide into their lungs was too horrific to contemplate.

He looked at Tizzie, sitting there, her hair tousled, her legs swinging slowly underneath the table. Her eyes rose to meet his, and she smiled a little, at first weakly and then sweetly. He smiled back and walked over and sat next to her and held her to calm himself as much as her. He felt a rush of feeling for her.

"I've got to admit, you picked a hell of a place for reconciliation," he said. She turned toward him and hugged him.

"I wanted your undivided attention."

"You got that, all right."

She became serious. "Jude, how much time do you think we have?"

"You mean, if we don't get out?"

"Yes."

"I don't know." He pretended to consider it for the first time. "Couple of days maybe, more or less." He knew it would be less.

"It's strange," she said. "As far as the world is concerned, we'll just drop out of sight, totally disappear. I guess they'd find your car eventually, maybe figure out what happened."

"Maybe."

"There's so much left undone. My parents. I don't know what they'll do. They need me. Skyler—he'll be lost without us. It's funny when you think about it—here I was supposed to live to a hundred and forty and I'm barely thirty.

"Me, too. 'Course I never thought I'd make it past sixty."

"I'm not leaving anything behind. There'll be nothing to show I even passed through. You—you're leaving Skyler. In a way, that's like leaving part of yourself."

"Maybe. It doesn't feel that way."

"But he's got all your genes, the same makeup. Maybe he'll pass it on to the next generation."

"That's something I'd rather do myself."

"But at least there'll be progeny of sorts. The line will continue."

"Some consolation."

It came out sounding bitter, and he hadn't intended that. He knew she was trying to salvage some ray of hope for him, and he appreciated the effort.

They lay back upon the cool metal table and stayed there side by side with an arm around each other, looking up at the rocks above.

"Hope this thing can hold us," she said.

Then she added: "Jude. I've got an idea!" She sat up excitedly. "I don't know if it would work, but it's worth a try."

She jumped off the table, and he did the same. Then she grasped the edge of the table with both hands and lifted it an inch off the floor.

"I remember reading that in old mines they sometimes built a second support system. It's like a second ceiling, with braces and beams right under the first one. We can use this table like that—it'll support the dirt while we dig underneath it."

He, too, lifted the table.

"If it's strong enough," he said. He let it go and it landed with a solid thunk. "We might as well try it. Anything's better than doing nothing."

He turned his back to the front end of the table and picked it up with his hands behind him. She picked up the rear. It was solid steel, heavier than he expected, which was good. They carried it across the chamber and into the passageway, stopping twice to rest. Once inside the tunnel, it was a snug fit. Not much dirt would fall through the cracks on either side—if only it was strong enough to hold. He continued walking, holding the lighted flashlight tightly under his left arm. When they reached the landfill, he set the table down gently. Then he scrambled back to where Tizzie was, and the two of them crawled underneath it. They arched their backs to raise it and moved it ahead another six inches, letting it come to rest at the foot of the pyramid of dirt. They backed out and returned to the chamber.

They selected a smaller table and carried it into the tunnel and placed it sideways on top of the other one so that it extended across the width of the passage, forming a backboard to catch falling dirt. Then they found some implements to dig with—a knife, a tin can, an ax handle and a large spoon—and two large cardboard boxes in which to haul the loose earth back into the chamber.

Jude went first. He crawled all the way under the table, stuck the flashlight into a small crevice so that the beam aimed forward, and pondered the wall of rock and dirt. Gingerly, he lifted the spoon and poked the wall. It was loose. He pried out a spoonful of dirt and pebbles that fell onto the rocky floor. Then another and another. Soon a little mound formed before him.

"I don't know," he said dubiously. "This is like Sisyphus pushing the rock up the damned hill. Every time I dig some out, more falls down to take its place."

"Try it higher," said Tizzie.

He did, and here the dirt was damp, so that he was able to burrow straight ahead and dig a hole about a feet deep. He then widened it and worked down, while Tizzie used the tin can to pour the loose dirt into the cartons. She dragged them into the chamber and dumped them against a near wall. After an hour, he had scooped out a cavity slightly taller than the table and extending two feet into the cave-in. He crawled out and they took up positions to shove the table forward, bending on one knee and digging their back feet in for support.

"Both together," said Tizzie. "That's the key. And keep pushing—all the way."

They pushed, but the table didn't move. The front legs were stuck against ridges in the uneven floor.

"I'm about to enter my worst nightmare," said Jude. And he dropped down, crawled under the table and rested on all fours. "Together," he said. "On three." And he counted slowly but emphatically: "One . . . Two . . . Three"

At that, Jude pushed up with his back with all his might, raising the table a half inch or so, and just at that moment Tizzie shoved it forward, so hard that she lost her balance and slammed into it with her shoulder. It lunged ahead and smashed into the dirt wall, setting off a shower of stones and rubble that fell upon the tabletop and trickled down the edges on both sides of Jude. It turned dark. His flashlight was dislodged, and he had to sift through a pile of dirt to find it. Then he jumped out from underneath the table. When Tizzie shined her light upon him, his face was pale under the smudges of dirt.

"Sorry," she said. "I forgot—you've got this thing about being buried alive."

"I'm strange that way."

"Well, we made some progress. If the dirt is damp enough, we can keep going. I bet there's an underground spring somewhere up there—maybe that's what caused the cave-in in the first place."

"Don't tell me you think it was natural. I could have sworn I heard something before—footsteps or something. I think someone was there."

"Maybe they were killed," she said sarcastically. "Maybe we'll find the body."

"Thanks. That's a hell of an incentive to keep going."

They switched places, Tizzie digging and Jude hauling the dirt away. She used the knife, which she hammered deep into the dirt using the ax handle, not at all fazed by the cascades of earth falling around her. Jude found that he could raise the table himself and carry it ahead a few inches at a time. Each time, it got harder to move, but their progress in digging their tunnel was much more rapid.

After four hours, they had penetrated so deep that the smaller table on top reached the upper wall of the cave-in. They went to the chamber, retrieved a third table, and set it in the passageway, end to end with the one they had been using. They rested for some minutes lying on the floor.

By now Jude dreaded it every time he had to crawl under the table. His phobia was rampant and he fell prey to the dark side of his imagination. What if the cave-in was so vast they couldn't tunnel all the way through it?

What if the table—already almost immobile because of the weight it was holding—simply refused to move? Or if the oxygen finally gave out?

Tizzie, on the other hand, seemed imperturbable. Jude was filled with admiration for her. He remarked upon it and she stood up to reply, wiping her hands on the rear seat of her blue jeans: "It's just because I've been blessed with a lack of imagination."

Again, he was struck by a new appreciation of her—of her energy, her confidence and resilience, her strength and raw-boned beauty.

"If we ever get out of this . . ." he said.

"Then what?"

"You're going to have a tough time keeping me away."

She smiled. "First things first. Back to the salt mines."

It was Jude's turn to work the cave-in face, and as he hacked away, the surface seemed more permeable. He was able to scoop out whole handfuls of dirt, and as he did so, he imagined he could feel the weight of the earth above shifting and straining. Reaching his arm into the recess, he tried not to think of what he was doing and of the protuberance above, the thin crust that could crumble at any moment, bringing down an avalanche. He pulled out a rock the size of a fist and dislodged a heap of sandy dirt that showered down to cover his knees. After that, he slowed down and worked more cautiously.

A half hour later, Jude thought he heard something like a distant groan. Tizzie was behind him, filling up the carton, and she reached over and put her hand on his back. At that split second the tunnel trembled and debris began crashing down, at first in thin streams and then in a flood. It poured down around all sides of the table and formed piles that hugged the walls and enlarged and spread toward the center. They instinctively ducked at the noise of the earth landing upon the metal inches above their heads. Jude grabbed the flashlight in one hand and clenched Tizzie's hand with the other. Everything about them shook, at first in small tremors and then a sustained, violent trembling. They froze and held their breath and waited helplessly.

Jude felt suspended. His mind was racing, but he wasn't thinking thoughts. He wasn't trying to think of something to do or planning an escape, because there wasn't any hope of that. He wasn't thinking about whether he was hurt or whether he was breathing. He was simply hunkered down, waiting in a half crouch, like an animal at the moment of supreme danger. Simply waiting vigilantly, poised to act, while the decision of life and death was being made elsewhere.

Clouds of dust filled their small subterranean hole. But at least the noise had stopped—the din of the earth coming at them from all sides, slamming down from above and inundating the walls so that it seemed to be pushing up from below. The noise had stopped and that meant, at least for now, that it was over. For the moment, they would remain alive.

Tizzie was the first to speak, and her tone—a frightened whisper, as if she were afraid that any sound could trigger yet another cave-in—said it all.

"Look," she said. "Behind us. We're trapped."

Jude shined his flashlight in back of her. There, instead of the tunnel extending under the second table, which had been their precious lifeline back to the chamber, was a solid wall of earth. It had crushed the table, a twisted edge of bright metal protruding at the bottom. The pile of dirt and rocks ran the full height of the passage and extended God knew how far beyond that. It was impassable. Their fate was sealed, as surely as was the space wherein they were now confined, not much bigger than a coffin.

The dust was settling; there wasn't enough air in the fetid enclosure to keep it aloft. Jude tried to form his thoughts, but was in too much shock to come up with any kind of a plan. And none was called for—their plight was elemental. They were trapped and they had to dig their way out or die. And they had to go forward rather than backward. That's all there was to it. From now on, survival was not a question of strategy but of endurance and luck—that and oxygen.

He picked up the ax handle and Tizzie picked up the knife, and together, squeezed side by side, they slashed and poked at the wall ahead. They no longer worried about causing more cave-ins. This was not a time for caution: they were in a race for their lives. They scooped the dirt out and thrust it behind them, working feverishly, each one trying to outdo the other, sweating, panting, piling the earth up behind.

Jude hit something with the ax handle, something hard. He cleared the dirt away with his hands, above and below. And then realized what it was.

"It's the beam," he cried. "Remember. You had to crawl under it to get here. Maybe we can do the same thing to get out."

"Unless the cave-in covered it, too."

"If it did, we've had it."

Now he dug under the beam, and the dirt was so loose he could reach through and pull it out by the armful. He thrust his hand in as far as he could and felt around—there was nothing but space, emptiness. He shined the flashlight; the beam did not hit anything. He put his face to the hole, and it seemed to him that it was easier to breathe. He widened the entrance to the passage and motioned to Tizzie.

"You first."

"No, after you."

He lay on his stomach and moved ahead, poking his head into the hole, wriggling his hips and digging in his feet for traction. Soon he had snaked his way deep inside the fissure. He felt the cold earth beneath him and the wood above him pressing down. It was much tighter than it had been on the way in. He found it impossible to fully expand his lungs. That damnable panic was taking hold of him again; he imagined the crevasse turning narrower and narrower until finally he got stuck. And just then he realized he could no longer move ahead—something *was* stopping him. He strained to pull ahead and felt a miniscule shower of dirt fall upon his face. He stopped. There was a snag: his belt was caught on a piece of timber above. He backed up several inches, exhaled, tightened his stomach muscles and slipped his right hand under his belly. Laboriously, he unbuckled it, and bit by bit pulled it out through the loops. Then he pressed his belly flat into the rock and tried slithering ahead. He moved an inch, then another. He made it—he was free! Another few minutes and he was out of the slender chasm and standing up in the passage on the other side of the cave-in.

He knelt to shine the light back inside, and the beam reflected off the top of Tizzie's head. She was already on her way, and he could hear her straining and grunting as she tried to fit her body into the narrow breach. The space looked so small, he couldn't believe he had just writhed his way through it; had it not been for the prospect of an agonizing death, he never would have attempted it.

Now he cheered her on, whispering encouragement.

"You're almost there, just keep coming."

Soon, her head was showing. She stretched out her arms and he pulled them, pulled them so hard that she popped right out. He hugged her and she squeezed him back, mightily. He held her at arm's length and looked into her eyes.

"I don't know about you, but I can't wait to get the hell out of here."

So saying, he led the way.

There was one final surprise, another cave-in that blocked their exit through the main tunnel. But Tizzie said she knew a detour, and she turned down a small passageway to the right. It sloped downward and seemed to be curving away from the direction in which they wanted to go. Jude was not certain that they should continue, and he said that to Tizzie.

"Trust me," she replied. "It's amazing—there are a lot of things I don't recall about my childhood, but these caves, I find I can remember almost every turn. They're imprinted on my brain."

The passage led to a small chamber. Its ceiling slanted downward at the far end, almost to the floor.

"Do you remember this place?" asked Tizzie.

"No. Should I?"

"Not really. But I do. We used to come here, too, I think."

"Right now, I'm more interested in getting out of here than anything else."

She led him to the rear, where the ceiling almost met the floor, and he saw that there was a space several feet high. They crawled through it and found themselves on the ledge of an adjoining chamber. They climbed down a rock face, jumped over a crevice and finally came to another tunnel, this time leading back toward the front of the mine.

In another ten minutes, they were standing outside, in the late afternoon sunshine.

"God, that feels good," said Tizzie, gazing upward.

"I have to say, I didn't think we were going to make it."

"And you believe that someone caused the cave-in?"

"I think it's a distinct possibility."

"If that's the case, then they must have overheard us. They know everything."

"Maybe."

Less than half an hour later, Jude thought he found proof. They had climbed up from the open pit to the narrow drive where he had parked his car.

It was not there.

He walked over to the edge of the escarpment and looked down into the valley. The signs were there to read: a deep gash on the red earth twenty feet straight down, brown indentations where rocks had been knocked out, some gashes in the trees farther down. His eyes followed the trail until they reached the bottom, where he saw, deep in the valley, a mangle of glass and steel.

"It could have been them, or it could have been anybody," said Tizzie. "Some antisocial types who want to keep out visitors."

Jude thought of the motorcyclists. He glanced up at the shack where their huge machines had been parked. They were gone.

They walked a mile down the road, back toward Jerome, to get Tizzie's car, parked beside the road on a turnoff. She pulled the keys out of her pocket, unlocked it, put their flashlights in the trunk and started the ignition. The sound of the engine made his heart soar.

They bypassed Jerome and instead took 89A toward Prescott across Mingus Mountain. A strong wind swept across the bald summit. It was chilly with pockets of old, dirty snow tucked into the shadows of rocks and hills and wafer-thin coatings of ice over mud puddles in the shoulder. There was an elevation sign (7,743 feet), a wooden ranger's station and a tree-trunk barricade over a gravel road, but not a soul in sight. The few pine trees were scraggly and bent over from the wind.

Going down the other side of the slope, the car kept gaining in acceleration, so much so that Tizzie lowered the gear and even then had to pump the brake from time to time. They fishtailed around the curves and felt the change in pressure in their ears, a clogged ringing.

They passed a sign facing the opposite direction, and Jude looked through the rear window to read it: JEROME.

Ten minutes later, they came to a pass that was scooped out of the mountains, and in it was a cluster of buildings. The structures were all of unpainted wood, leaning against each other like tombstones, with wooden porches and boardwalks. An empty riverbed, the banks eroded from flash floods, ran through it. There was no name that they could see.

One of the buildings was a roadhouse, and they decided to stop. They both wanted a drink. Half a dozen other vehicles were parked out front, pickup trucks and jeeps.

Tizzie looked down at their clothing, thick with dirt. "God, we're a mess," she said. "I've got a sweater I can put on, in the backseat. You're just going to have to do the best you can, I guess."

Inside, a fire was raging in a stone fireplace that took up one whole wall, casting a flickering glow. What looked to be elk antlers were hung over it, slanting to one side. Oddly, cut-off neckties were hanging from the ceiling.

Four men at the bar, separated by empty stools, looked up when they walked in but did not say hello or seem to find anything odd about their appearance. Tizzie was the only woman in the place, except for a waitress with frizzy hair and a short black skirt.

They found a booth and took turns washing up in the bathroom and brushing their clothes as best they could. When Tizzie emerged, her face scrubbed, two of the men stared at her. The waitress took their order: two beers.

Tizzie took small sips, but Jude drank half the mug in one gulp, set it down and wiped his mouth with the back of his hand.

"You know," he said, "there's a web site for Jerome. It's called W, which stands for *double you*. Get it?"

"I got it. What's on it?"

"It seems to be an ongoing discussion group about the horrors of old age. One guy in particular, Methuselah, he struck me as smart and plugged-in."

"Do you think he was a member of the group?"

"Well, he was certainly extoling the virtues of life extension—almost preaching."

"That doesn't surprise me. Face it, we're dealing with fanatics."

"Yeah. But they're also paranoid. That underground chamber we saw is like something the government would have constructed in the cold war to keep secrets from the Russians."

"So?"

"So, why would you go to such lengths to keep something secret and at the same time turn around and start a web site? It doesn't fit."

"Maybe they were engaging in public relations. You know, get the issue talked about, begin to raise consciousness, put their views across."

"Toward what end?"

"Sooner or later, they're going to have to go public. You can't have people living to one hundred and forty years without other people knowing about it. Maybe they wanted to clear the way."

She had a point, but it didn't strike Jude as convincing. He felt once again how little they knew about the Lab—how it operated and what its objectives were.

"You know, I was thinking while I was washing up—you said you thought this guy Henry was going to ask you to spy on me."

"Yes."

"I think you should tell him you will."

She looked at him, confused.

"You've got to get close to them. You've got to get them to trust you. It's the only way we'll ever learn what they're up to."

"Jude, you can't be serious."

But she knew he was. And she also knew, without stopping to analyze it, that he was right.

"You want me to be a double agent?"

"Not really. 'Cause, according to you, you were never a spy to begin with."

She reached across the table. "Jude, I don't blame you for being suspicious. But I wish I could convince you—we're on the same side."

"You, me and Skyler."

"Yes."

"Against *them*."

"Yes. Against *them*."

"Well—infiltrating the Lab would certainly be convincing."

When they left, the men on the bar stools did not look up. Outside, it was already getting dark.

Driving down the mountain, Jude became aware of headlights behind him. He noticed them because they came up so quickly, seemingly from nowhere—bright lights shining through the rearview mirror right into his eyes.

He pointed them out to Tizzie, who told him about the lights that had seemed to trail them back from Mr. Lucky's the other night.

"I can't say if it's the same ones," she said.

"Just don't call it a coincidence. There are too many coincidences happening around here."

Jude stepped on the gas, and the car behind did the same, keeping pace. He took a curve dangerously fast, sliding almost to the shoulder. The car behind fell back for a while, and then on a straightaway caught up again.

"Could it be somebody from the roadhouse?" she asked. "That was a pretty ugly group of guys back there. Did you see how they were staring at us?"

"I don't know. But I don't want to find out."

He pushed the pedal almost to the floor. The car was on a downgrade, so it leapt ahead. Below the steering wheel, he could see the needle on the speedometer rising steadily, but he didn't want to take his eyes off the road to read it. He looked in the mirror: the lights were trailing now, but not as far back as he would have expected. It definitely seemed to be on their tail.

Tizzie tightened her seat belt. The car was weaving across the road now, and on the hairpin turns, the wheels skidded to one side so that it came close to the guardrail. Once Tizzie looked down and saw the valley far below, the scattered lights gleaming in the twilight. She looked over at

Jude, clutching the wheel so tightly that his knuckles turned white, staring ahead. He gave it more gas.

Finally, they pulled ahead of the car behind them. Swerving down the snaking road, they gained so much ground that its lights were always at least one turn behind, no longer lighting up the rear window. At last, they reached the foothills on the outskirts of the valley, and the road straightened out before them, an unbroken ribbon of highway. Off to the right, a sign flashed by.

Jude suddenly doused the headlights, careering ahead in almost total darkness.

"What're you doing?" exclaimed Tizzie.

"Hold on," was all he said.

He suddenly swerved the car to the right. Tizzie felt it hit a flat stretch, then rise in a single stomach-dropping motion as if they were swinging on a loop-the-loop, the weight and momentum alone carrying them forward and up. Looking ahead, she saw the stars descend across the windshield, and she tightened and waited for the crash. Time moved slowly. Then she heard gravel kicking up on the undercarriage, and gradually, by force of gravity and friction, she felt the vehicle slowing down like a carnival ride coming to rest. Finally, it stopped.

Jude turned off the engine, opened the window and listened.

"We're on a runaway truck turnoff," he said. "I think we lost them."

And they had. They waited a few minutes at the top of the man-made mound, stepping outside to collect their nerves in the twilight. Jude smoked a cigarette, and together they watched the last rays of the sun expire in the west and the stars turn even brighter.

As Jude drove back to Camp Verde, his thoughts were unsettling. His first impulse was to keep them to himself, but then he reflected that he and Tizzie both had been doing too much of that lately; he was still feeling a glow from her confessional honesty in the mine shaft.

He stepped on the gas.

"Tizzie, something occurs to me. We have to face the fact that it's not likely that this was just a bunch of guys out to have a little fun by forcing us off the road."

"I know, I've been having the same thought."

"Which means that it was probably connected to the cave-in and my car going off the cliff."

"I'd say the odds of that are pretty good. And that means that they have decided to eliminate us. In which case that feeling you had—that somehow you've been spared by them for some unknown reason—is no longer valid. That's if it ever was, which I doubt."

She braced her hands against the dashboard and turned to him angrily. "Jude, for God's sake, slow down. We don't want to crash."

He was going close to eighty—on an unfamiliar road at night.

"We're in a hurry," he said.

"Why?"

"What I was about to say was: if they're after us, they've followed us up here. And if they've followed us up here, they know where we're staying. And that means Skyler's in danger."

Twenty minutes later, they pulled into the Best Western parking lot and swung around the back. Before the car stopped, they spotted the door of Skyler's room, open and swinging slightly in the breeze. Tizzie gasped.

By the time Jude had turned off the ignition, she was already out of the car, bounding up the metal steps, using the banister to take the steps two at a time. She stopped suddenly halfway up and looked at her hand, holding it up to the light to get a better look at the thick red substance that was on it.

Then she continued. She got to the door just as Jude reached the bottom of the staircase, and she rushed in, flicking on the light switch. She disappeared from view, but Jude knew that she had made some kind of horrible discovery. He knew it from the long, loud cry.

He raced up after her and saw her standing there, in the middle of the room, stricken, her mouth still open. She lifted one hand and pointed vaguely in the air, a gesture that took in the entire room—the tousled bed, the clothes lying about and the pale yellow walls, smeared with blood.

Skyler awoke in a haze to a strange, sterile room, all in white, and felt as if he were floating somewhere close to the ceiling. Although he was in fact drifting toward consciousness, he had the opposite sensation—he believed he was falling asleep. Not just asleep but dreaming, and not just dreaming but having a nightmare.

He looked out through a filter of white gauze; everything was blurry and unconnected to him. Sounds were muffled. People moved slowly, as if they were underwater, and talked gobbledygook They were adorned in sparkling white uniforms, which caught the light and seemed to shimmer.

A woman gliding soundlessly around the room had a halo of light brown hair underneath a little white cap. That particular detail arrested his attention, and he tried to marshal his strength and to focus.

For a dreadful thought had formed itself; it was so frightening that he wanted to abandon the nightmare right away, but the more he began to feel he was awake, the more terrifying the whole situation became. He did not want to come to and discover that the room was really there, that everything was really happening. Because the nightmare was that he was back on the island—in the basement of the Big House, in the operating room.

Why else would he be lying in bed like that with doctors around him?

*Doctors!* The mere thought was enough to send a jolt of fear up his spine.

He told himself to move a foot as a test. He did, and he felt the ankle joint bend, the curl of the toes, the movement of the sheets. He was not asleep. *This is really happening to me!*

The haze was slowly lifting now. He was beginning to see more clearly. Above him were ceiling tiles. He could see their joints and dots. A long white curtain hung down and cut the room in half. There in a corner was a blabbering television set, hanging from the ceiling.

*Where am I?*

A nurse had her back to him; her elbow was moving as if she was writing, and now he could see the bottom of a clipboard. She lowered it and turned toward him—so he quickly closed his eyes and froze, feigning sleep.

He could feel her bending over him—he could smell her breath, like almonds.

"Are you awake? Are you awake? Can you hear me?"

Her voice had a strange accent, one he had never heard before.

"Can you hear me? If you can hear me, open your eyes. Do you speak English?"

He played possum.

*"Habla inglés? Español?"*

He didn't move a muscle. He kept his eyes closed, trying not to squeeze them too tightly, and he made an effort to keep his breathing steady. It was hard to do—he wasn't sure he could stay perfectly still much longer—because he had an overwhelming desire to pull back and protect himself.

*What is she doing?*

Luckily, she moved away; he heard her footsteps retreating toward the foot of the bed, and he risked opening one eye. Her back was turned again. Her skin was light brown, and she was wearing a crisp white uniform.

Another blurry figure entered. A man, it seemed.

Skyler closed his eyes and wanted to leap out of bed and to cry out: *Who are you? Where am I?*

"He didn't come to yet?" *It is a man.*

"No." *That strange accent again.* "His signs are improving, but he's unresponsive."

"Damndest thing I've ever seen. Ambulance brings him in, no idea who he is, no ID. And on top of that, he's acting crazy."

Now Skyler began to feel things, a constriction on his chest, a weight on his right arm, which was lying on the bed out of his field of vision. In the distance he could hear other sounds, the canned laughter of a television show, the murmur of voices, and something else—something he had never heard before. It sounded like a series of blips and beeps.

"If I had to bet, I'd say it's a violent reaction to some new kind of narcotic. Whatever it is, I hope it's not widespread. That's all we need. A new drug plague." He sounded vaguely disgusted. "The crap people put into their bodies these days."

The man and the woman walked in a huddle to the door and left.

Skyler sat up. He felt a tug on his chest and looked down. There were wires attached to him, held on by white tape, and extending across the white cotton bedspread. And next to him was a contraption, a silver pole on wheels standing close to the bed, and attached to it was a large plastic bag—*it looks like blood*— and here was the truly scary part: the bag of blood was attached to a tube and the tube flowed down and was attached to him! He could see the red liquid moving down the tube and disappearing underneath a bandage. He raised his arm and the flow lessened.

*It's going right inside me.*

His eyes followed the wires, and he gathered them up in his left hand and lifted them, holding them high. They curved down and then up again and led to a machine. It had two green-tinted screens, across which white lines danced and squiggled in repeating patterns. It was the machine that was emitting the blips and beeps that had suddenly sounded loud.

He tried to calm himself. *You are not on the island. You've seen the operating room of the Big House, and it doesn't look like this. You are someplace else.*

He tried to recall how he had gotten here, what had happened just before. But he could not remember anything. He had been in the motel room, he thought. He tried hard to remember but could not; he saw Tizzie's face, then Julia's.

He knew he was losing it. He felt panic rising. He told himself he shouldn't give in to it, but he couldn't help himself—it was like a wave that started inside him and then moved outside. It grew all the time so that it became huge, as large as the room, and it turned against him, threatening to come crashing down upon him. Those doctors, those nurses, the uniforms.

*I have to get out of here!*

He pulled the wires violently, ripping them across his chest and felt the flesh tearing. The sounds! The pulsating blips merged into a continuous monotone, then turned into a high-pitched whine. Beeeeeep!

He grabbed the tube and tugged. It didn't give, so he picked at an edge of the bandage and tore it off—and looked horrified at the glass needle puncturing his vein. The whining continued. Beeeeeep! He grabbed the needle and pulled. It came spurting out, and now blood was pouring out from everywhere, from his vein and from the tube, suddenly flopping about like a loose hose, spraying red fluid everywhere, on the white bedspread, on the floor, on his arm, his chest. The sound seemed deafening.

*They'll hear it! They'll come!*

So he had no alternative but to flee. He leapt out of bed—he could see he was wearing some kind of pajama bottoms—and tried to stand, but suddenly he was feeling weak, very weak, or was it that he couldn't find his footing?—that he was sliding on the blood? He went down hard and landed on his rump. Then he lay for a moment on the floor, where he could see under the bed the feet rushing in and hear the sound of excited voices. He felt arms lifting him up, placing him back on the bed, people holding him down, those uniforms again and those faces, pushing in too close. A hypodermic.

A sudden quick pinch in his upper arm.

"There, that ought to do it."

The hands were still holding him down, but they seemed to be pushing, too, so that soon he found himself at the bottom of a well, sinking under the weight of the water. It turned everything blurry, the faces, the white cap. It muffled the sounds. He was going under, back to his dream, back to his nightmare.

Maybe he was, after all, on the island, in the basement of the Big House. Maybe—it was his last thought before he succumbed to unconsciousness—*maybe I've never really left it!*

# Chapter 23

Jude and Tizzie burst into the emergency room just as a young man with black hair and a scarred complexion was being treated for a knife wound. He was drunk and struggling, and it took two nurse's aides to pin him to a dressing table while a doctor swabbed the wound, blood covering the fingers of his latex gloves.

They had reached the hospital in no time flat, once the motel owner had calmed down enough to tell them what had happened. Scared out of her wits when Skyler had staggered into the office, bleeding on the reception desk and then collapsing on the floor, she had yelled at them as soon as she saw them.

"Your friend almost died," she said. "Turned out he cut himself. But he's sick, too. How could you leave him alone all day?"

She had called an ambulance and that had led to an unwelcome visit by the cops, and then a battery of questions and papers to be filled out—all of it complicated by the fact that she knew nothing whatsoever about her guests other than the names scrawled on the register. That Jude had paid for the rooms in advance—in cash—was of particular interest to the police.

But once the owner looked at Tizzie and read the distress on her face, she softened, going so far as to offer them a cup of coffee from an automatic percolator perched upon a bookcase. Tizzie had declined and took the directions instead, while Jude grabbed a fresh shirt and pair of pants.

Now, in the emergency room, they tried in vain to get the attention of the doctor. Tizzie cleared her throat.

"Excuse me," she said, loud enough to carry over the muffled grunts from the drunk, whose head was being pressed into the table by a bent elbow.

"Sorry, we're busy right now," the doctor shot over his shoulder. "You shouldn't be in here anyway."

Through a pair of swinging double doors, they found a nurse's station and asked if a man had been treated with a hand wound.

"Couple of hours ago," replied a nurse, punching a keyboard and searching a computer screen. "Here it is. 6:20 p.m. Admitted 7:10. No identification. We couldn't get a name out of him. So we listed him as John Doe."

She looked up and studied Jude. "Your brother, huh?"

Jude nodded.

"Thought so. You can go visit him if you want. Room 360—that's on the third floor, elevator down the corridor to the left."

They started to go.

"Wait a minute," she said. "I need a name. Address. Information on health insurance."

"We'll be back, settle it all up," said Jude, escorting Tizzie away by the elbow. "We've got to see him first, make sure he's all right."

The elevator door opened, and they ducked inside.

The door to Room 360 was closed. They opened it quietly and slipped inside. The room was dim, except for a night light above the closest bed, which was empty. Beyond was a drawn curtain, and behind it they could hear the piercing rhythm of a heart monitor. Tizzie went first, walking quietly and peering around the curtain.

Skyler was fast asleep.

His right hand was bandaged, a plastic blood bag was hanging from a stanchion and feeding a tube that went into his arm, and an oxygen tube was clipped to his nose. On the bedside table, the monitor chirped and sent its green blip dancing across the screen in waves.

"Doesn't look like the kind of guy who would trash a motel room," said Jude.

Tizzie approached the bed and took Skyler's good hand in hers.

"He must have been scared to death," she said. "What do you think is wrong?"

"Who knows? Raised on that island, there are probably all kinds of diseases he's never been exposed to. He could have anything."

Jude put his palm on Skyler's forehead, which did feel slightly feverish.

"The cut he did to himself," he continued. "There was a broken glass in the bathroom sink and a lot of blood. He probably panicked when he saw it, freaked out and ran outside."

He looked in the corner where a pair of Skyler's pants—Jude's, actually—lay crumpled on a chair. They had bloodstains.

"It must have been hard on him," said Tizzie. "You know how much he hates doctors, how much they frighten him—all those memories from his childhood."

At that moment, as if on cue, in walked a young man, nattily dressed, with a friendly-looking, freckled face. He put out his hand.

"Dr. Geraldi. I'm glad to see our patient here has visitors. We don't know anything about him. Not even who he is."

They shook hands. The doctor looked searchingly at Jude.

"Yes," said Jude. "We're related."

"Brothers."

"Yes."

The doctor looked at Skyler and, with a quick tilt of the head, summoned them outside into the corridor. They followed him to an office, where he gestured for them to sit down.

He peppered them with questions: Skyler's age, medical history, recent symptoms. Any known drug abuse? Any signs of strange behavior? They provided him with as much information as they could, which was little indeed, but they told him nothing about Skyler's true past.

Dr. Geraldi kept shaking his head.

"I've just never seen anything like this. I don't know what it is."

"He's lost a lot of blood," offered Jude.

"No, that's not it. He's got a mean little cut there on his hand, but that's not the main problem. I'm using the transfusion to give him urokinase."

"What's that?"

"It's for thrombolytic therapy."

"What?"

"The heart."

"Are you telling us he had a heart attack?"

"That's just it—it's hard to say. I'm not really sure."

"What do you mean?"

"Certainly some of the presenting symptoms were there—nausea, dizziness, pallor, shortness of breath and, of course, chest pains. At least from what I could gather. He was hysterical when he was brought in, by the way. I took an EKG—it showed Q waves. That's another sign."

"But you're not sure?"

"No. AMI is common in older people, but someone his age—"

"AMI?"

"Sorry. Acute myocardial infarction. A narrowing of coronary artery from atherosclerotic plaque formation—it's just not . . . well, common. You say he's twenty-five?"

"Yes."

"But when I look into his eyes, I can already see some signs of calcification. That leads to cataracts. Has he reported any blurring of vision?"

"No."

"And you say there's no history of heart trouble in your family?"

Jude squirmed. "Not that I know of."

"Well, you would surely know it. People don't just carry on."

"No, of course not."

Dr. Geraldi gave a wan smile. "But there are other symptoms I don't understand. It's as if his whole body is fighting off some raging infection, but I can't find what it is. I took a quick look at his blood and it's . . . it's just strange. I'll know more tomorrow—maybe. I've ordered a complete workup on it. In the meantime . . ."

"What?"

"We'll carry on with this."

"Will he be all right?"

"Oh, I think so. I see an improvement already in his vital signs. We may give antihypertensive and cholesterol-lowering agents, maybe antianginal drugs. I'd just like to know what it is. The symptoms are confusing."

"Will it reoccur?" she asked.

"It could. I can't rule out that possibility. You're sure he never had anything like this before?"

Jude shook his head no—but he was hardly sure at all.

"Well, I just can't say. I wish I could tell you there'll be nothing to worry about. Of course, it could be some obscure virus. These things happen, you know. They appear out of nowhere, make you sick as a dog for a while and then disappear."

That evening, Tizzie and Jude unwound over dinner at the Big Bull Steak House. The table they were shown to contained dirty dishes, and a Mexican busboy came carrying a plastic bin to take them away. Jude engaged him in conversation; they talked in Spanish before the place settings were laid.

Jude asked for a J&B as soon as the waitress brought them water, and another when they placed their order. Both drinks came quickly and did their work; before he had taken his first forkful of meat, he was feeling no pain. Tizzie was abstemious.

Skyler's illness cast a cloud over the dinner. But still, for the first time in weeks, they talked openly. No more secrets or unfinished sentences or long silences.

Amazing what honesty can do, Jude thought. And it did something else, too; as he looked across the table at her in the flickering candlelight, at her strong chin, her blazing eyes, her rounded shoulders, he realized how much he wanted her and how long it had been since they had slept together.

He reached across the table and she took his hand.

"I know how hard this is on you," she said.

He smiled.

"It all seems to fall on your shoulders. You're the one who figures out what to do, who plans ahead . . . you're the one who keeps us going." She looked him in the eye and added: "I want you to know that I see that."

She patted his hand—not a good sign, he thought.

She looked away and was silent, and he tried to imagine what she was thinking.

"I can't imagine another person looking like you," he said abruptly.

He had hit the mark. She leaned forward.

"Neither can I. That's what so strange about this whole thing. All your life you think you're unique . . . and then you learn there's somebody out there who looks just like you—or at least a lot like you. Somebody who maybe thinks like you do, feels what you feel. I would have given anything to meet her and to see . . . I don't know . . ."

"What?"

"I don't know. Everything. What I'm like from the outside. How I strike someone else. How I might have been different. What I would have been like growing up under totally different circumstances."

"I don't think you would have learned any of that. She wouldn't have been like you—*you* more than anyone should know that."

"I do, of course. But it's strange—all those twin studies. I've read them and understood them. But when it happens to you, it's different. It's not science anymore. It's *personal.* It goes right to the core of who you are."

She played with the wax from the candle, peeling it off and rolling it into a ball in her fingers. It reminded him of the cave—could that have been only five hours ago?

"You know what I've been thinking? My parents—they love me a lot. They would do anything for me. They clearly thought that what they were doing was wonderful—doubling my life span. But all those years, they didn't tell me the most important part—about Julia—and there was a reason."

She took a sip from Jude's scotch before continuing.

"They didn't know how to tell me. They were ashamed on some level. They were ashamed because they knew it was wrong. They're not . . . you know, they're not immoral people. They did leave the Lab. What's going to happen to them now?"

"Maybe they can help us somehow. They know more than they told you."

"They're not well. It's not going to be easy."

She threw the ball of wax down on the table. "God, why did they do it? Didn't they think it through? I feel so used, so *violated*. I feel like one of those primitive people you hear about—someone's taken my photo and I feel they've stolen my soul."

"But they haven't."

"But I feel it."

Jude's words came out in a sudden rush, like a declaration.

"It's not the same. There's no one else like you, Tizzie. You're unique, your soul is intact and . . . and you also just happen to be extraordinarily beautiful."

She looked at him and smiled—a wonderful smile that cracked wrinkles around her mouth.

"Well, that sounded pretty good. Is there more where that came from?" she asked.

"A bottomless pit."

He put his hand on her knee under the table.

The waitress came by with a pot of coffee, but they refused. Tizzie went to the bathroom, and Jude signaled for the check with air writing. He got it, and as he rose to leave, he spotted the Mexican busboy and walked over to him to say good-bye and talked some more, slipping him a twenty-dollar tip. The broad face registered surprise, and the dark eyes followed Jude on the way to the cash register, where Tizzie joined him. He paid the bill and they left.

"What were you two talking about?" she asked.

"Nothing much."

It was late now. Tizzie drove because she was the sober one. The gas station and fast-food signs were extinguished, and there were not many cars. The highway stretched before them like a dark river and the moon was up, and they felt as if they were the only two people still awake.

★ ★ ★

Every light in the motel was out. Their door cards were waiting for them in the office, sitting in mailboxes. Someone had closed Skyler's door, and the banister had been cleaned. It smelled vaguely of disinfectant.

"Want a nightcap?" Jude asked, opening his door.

Tizzie refused. More than anything, she said, she needed a bath.

They went to their separate rooms. But a minute later, he heard a rap at his door. His pulse quickened.

She was standing there, one hand on her hip.

"Wouldn't you know it—my tub doesn't work. Stopper's broken."

He let her in. Moments later, through the bathroom door, which was opened a crack, he heard water cascading into the tub. He turned on the television: a late night black-and-white movie. He let it roll on, but he didn't pay it any mind. From the mini-bar, he got a Budweiser and sipped it from the bottle.

Eventually, after much splashing about, she emerged in a cloud of steam, wearing two towels, one tied around her waist, the other draped across her breasts. She was carrying her clothes in a bundle.

Jude patted the bed and motioned for her to sit down. She did, without putting down her clothes. He leaned over toward her and kissed her gently on the neck, which smelled fresh and damp. He felt her wet hair on the back of his neck.

She pulled away slightly and sat upright. "Jude."

The sound of his name was the sound of a door closing.

"It's been a long day."

He nodded defensively.

"Mountain roads, cave-ins, a near-death experience. I'd say that's a lot for one girl. I'm ready to turn in."

"Funny—you didn't mention Skyler."

"That's because that one is still hanging. And I can't bear to think of it."

After she left, and he heard her door open and close, he sat up some more in bed, sipping the beer and watching the movie, whose plot he never quite caught.

The next morning, they got up early, had a quick breakfast and went to the hospital. Skyler's door was open, but the curtain was drawn. They saw a breakfast tray on the bedstand, a plate with half-eaten pancakes sitting in a pool of syrup. Tizzie pulled the curtain back.

The patient was sitting up in bed, looking alert. He was overjoyed to see them and gave them both hugs. It seemed clear from the reception he gave them that he had been through a harrowing time.

Skyler remembered almost nothing of his illness—only certain moments, he said, like staring at his blood on the motel room wall, stumbling down the stairs, the frightening wail of the ambulance.

"Has a doctor been by? Dr. Geraldi?" Tizzie asked.

"No."

He asked them where they had been yesterday.

So they told him what had happened to them in the Gold King Mine—how they had been trapped in the tunnel and dug their way out and lost the car and were then followed by a mysterious car.

"Christ," said Skyler. "I had it easy compared to you guys."

They also told him about their talk, about Tizzie's confession.

Skyler looked at Jude—uncertainly, but also a little defiantly.

"So now you know—about Julia?" he asked.

"Yes," replied Jude, thinking it strange that Skyler had said "about Julia" and not "about Tizzie."

Skyler looked away and said nothing, which bothered Jude. He's feeling half sad, he thought, and half guilty for keeping it a secret from me.

And it dawned on Jude that he was extrapolating from the way *he* would feel.

Tizzie fussed over Skyler, getting him an extra pillow and fresh ice for his water. Then she went off in search of coffee for herself and Jude, and while she was gone, the two of them felt awkward together, Skyler propped up against the headboard, Jude leaning back against a window ledge. They couldn't think of much to say, and the silence was uncomfortable.

Tizzie returned with two styrofoam cups containing black water with a hint of coffee. She had cornered Dr. Geraldi.

"He's gotten some of the tests back. He's less worried—though he still doesn't know what it was. He's convinced it was some sort of mystery virus and says the most important thing is if you're feeling better. He's going to stop by later—I think he'll discharge you."

Jude left Tizzie at the hospital to look after Skyler. He had things to do.

He stopped off in the lobby and found a bank of telephones with a phone book, in which he checked the government listings and the yellow pages. He scribbled the addresses. First, he drove to the Motor Vehicles Bureau and stood in line for a full five minutes, sizing up the operation. Then he stepped outside to have a cigarette, got back in the car and pulled away.

He found the photographer as advertised at a mall not far away. The studio was at the top of a staircase over a deli, a cramped office with a wall plastered with heavily airbrushed photos of smiling children and happy families.

The secretary was chewing gum with her mouth open. She took his name—a false one, naturally—and gestured for him to sit down. Five minutes later, he was posing for the photographer, a scrawny young man who couldn't understand why Jude passed up all the alluring backdrops—a bookcase crammed with leather-covered volumes, a bosky scene with a waterfall, a New England autumnal setting—in favor of a simple red background. That one, he remarked, was as dull as the Arizona licenses. He was doubly confused when, halfway through the session, Jude insisted upon exchanging shirts and combed his hair straight back.

While waiting for the photos to be processed, Jude had a cup of coffee in the deli and read the papers. Nothing much happening. But one brief item caught his eye: a body had been discovered in Georgia, maimed beyond recognition and with the visceral organs missing. It was the second such murder there within the week. Police were searching for what the papers had dubbed "the body-snatcher." Jude wondered: more maiming of dead bodies. Was it just one more coincidence?

He picked up the photos and drove across town, back to the Big Bull restaurant. Now for the hard part. He parked and walked around the back to the kitchen entrance. The door was open, next to an outdoor air-conditioning unit that was humming in high gear but not pumping cold air where it would do any good for the help. The cooks and dishwashers were pouring sweat. They watched him with curiosity, and when he stepped inside, no one stopped him and no one spoke to him. He found the Mexican busboy, and he could tell by the look on his face that he remembered him from the night before. Jude took him outside for a talk.

It lasted all of ten minutes. A cigarette offered and accepted, some chitchat and finally the request, gently but firmly made: surely you must know where something like that can be done—for a friend, you understand, someone perhaps in the same boat as friends of yours. The exchange was sealed with two more twenty-dollar bills, the new kind that still looked fishy.

An hour later, Jude was in a slum village on the outskirts of Phoenix. Dirt roads crossed other dirt roads and skirted trailer parks and dusty lots packed with shacks and lean-tos overflowing with children and chickens. It looked like parts of Mexico City.

He had to stop every five minutes to ask directions; he thought some of the locals were feigning ignorance. At last, he spotted the small handwritten sign he had been told to look for, reading DOCUMENTOS. He parked the car and started to walk inside, but his path was blocked by a heavyset Mexican who leaned across the doorway with a ham-sized forearm. Over his shoulder Jude spotted a large Xerox machine, incongruous against the chicken-coop whitewashed wall.

It took him forty-five minutes, six more cigarettes, a hundred and forty dollars and all the persuasive power of his inadequate Spanish to get what he wanted. He sat sipping a warm beer while the machine did its work and the man sat at a makeshift workbench like a master craftsman, wielding the knives and scissors and pieces of plastic that were his trade.

"But why two?" he had asked. "And why with the same surname but two different Christian names?"

"Family reasons" was all that Jude had replied, and that had settled the matter.

Driving away, Jude came to a small ravine that was banked on one side by rocky cliffs. He spied openings high up on ledges and wondered if they were caves once inhabited by desert Indians. They would have used them as the last redoubt, farming in the valley and then retreating up there with as much food as they could carry during times of siege.

Farther on, he came to civilization—a gas station and a cement factory. The road widened and turned to black tarmac. He saw a sign that caught his attention and started him thinking—thinking about something that had been bothering him, like a name he couldn't remember. He had been first struck by the memory, unformed but strong, when he'd gone up to the Indian reservation in the mountains. He had had it several times since.

He checked his watch. It was hours out of the way, but if he hurried, he would have time. When he reached the main highway, he turned south—toward Tucson. Farther on the rolling gray hills were dotted with saguaro cacti, their arms raised like hold-up victims.

The Sonora Desert Museum on Kinney Road was set in a valley down a steep, winding road through Gates Pass in Tucson Mountain Park. At the entrance was a landscaped patio with shaded spaces and *ramadas* made from saguaro ribs. Behind, like an adobe dwelling, was the terra-cotta stucco of the main building.

He parked next to a charter bus disgorging junior high school students. On the sidewalk, they formed into cliques self-segregated by sex. The girls skittered ahead whispering and conspiring. The boys hung back, lunging into one another and trading the occasional punch.

Jude paid $8.95 admission and waited for them to pass. He spent the time in the gift shop, looking at postcards, silver bracelets, beaded necklaces and Indian sand paintings. On a rack was a stack of papers; by reflex he checked the headlines. Nothing big happening.

He hoped the visit would be worth the money. He was beginning to worry about the bankroll. They would run through it quickly if Skyler had to stay in the hospital for any length of time. He could switch identities and put the bill on his own health insurance, but that meant he could be traced. And the longer they stayed there, the more clues they left for their trackers.

He went outside where the museum began, a series of paths connecting low-slung terra-cotta buildings. The coast was clear, so he headed straight for the tan building to the right with the flat roof and thick walls, clearly marked REPTILES & INVERTEBRATES. Inside, it was dark and he was momentarily blinded. His nostrils were assaulted by the acrid smell of urine and sweat. His eyes gradually adjusted. To his right was a glass-enclosed pen of worn, compacted earth interspersed with tree branches and barkless logs. Here and there were large turtles, motionless under their thick, humped shells. To his left was another picture window containing foot-long Gila monsters, their dull black bodies spotted with reddish-orange markings.

Then farther on came the snakes, sleeping or slithering around rocks and branches. A cluster of young children clutched the railing and stared, as motionless as the turtles had been, fascinated by the lure of a diamondback rattler splayed along a log. Its head was raised and poked in slow motion at the air.

Finally, Jude came to the lizards. There were scores of them, all different sizes, in browns and greens and speckled shades in between. Some were stump-tailed, others long-tailed. Some had spiny necks standing up like a row of teeth; others had thin, scaly flaps of skin hanging down from their chins like beards. Some disappeared against the mud, others stood out in silhouette, standing on logs like sentinels. The more he looked into the glass-enclosed cages, the more he saw. Most of them stayed where they were, as immobile as scenery, but others occasionally darted here and there, seemingly without purpose, moving with a speed that was somehow alarming.

He could stand close and look them in the eye. There was a Texas horned lizard (*Phynosoma cornutum*) with a flattened body trimmed around with spikes and a devilish cast to the skull. And a two-foot-long green iguana (*Iguana iguana*) clinging to a tree with delicate speckled fingers that ended in long black nails. And the iguanid chuckwalla (*Sauromalus obesus*), sixteen inches long, with a strange two-tone luminescent body, which as the sign informed him, had the habit of hiding in crevices and, when sensing danger, puffing itself up so that it could not be extricated. Not a bad defense, thought Jude.

Still he had not found what he was looking for.

He wandered outside and followed a winding path. He walked through a mineral gallery, under ground caves, an amphitheater. He passed by open pens separated by dry moats—mountain lions, black bears, porcupines, Mexican wolves, white-tailed deer.

Then, he saw it—on an island all by itself in a corner that was arid and hot as blazes.

The lizard was just like the one that had watched him balefully two days ago at the office on the reservation. It gripped a log, just as that one had, and it looked back at him with a single unblinking eye.

Jude stepped closer. He looked at the thick skin, the diamond-shaped scales piled in layers like shingles, the curvature of the mouth. The mouth looked cruel. He saw the sides expanding slowly, barely perceptibly. He looked straight into the eye, into the spherical black pupil. It seemed to spiral inward, bottomless in its blackness.

And suddenly it called to him. He knew it. He knew it from his childhood, had seen it close by for years. Of course, he said to himself. That was it. *We had lizards. We kept these lizards.* An image floated up from somewhere—himself as a young boy, his hands pressed against glass, staring at the lizards, at those deep black pupils.

His reverie was interrupted by a figure that appeared on his left, so suddenly he was startled. He turned to look at a woman in her thirties, blonde hair tied in a ponytail, a pair of large-rimmed glasses perched jauntily on her nose. She smiled.

"I see you're engrossed," she said. "They're my favorites."

He saw now that she was wearing a trim suit jacket. Above her left breast was a tag: CURATOR OF REPTILES.

She followed his eyes. "It's a better job title than 'reptilian curator,'" she said. "That's what they wanted to call me."

Now he smiled. "Why are they your favorites?"

He realized there were more than the one he had been looking at on the island, a half dozen or so of them. For the first time he read the sign attached to the railing, which said: DESERT GRASSLAND WHIPTAIL.

"Some peculiar characteristics," she replied.

"Like what?" he said. "What's he do?"

"*She,* actually."

"How can you tell? How do you know which one I'm talking about?"

"That's just it." Her smile had a triumphant edge to it. "They're parthenogenetic. That's the salient characteristic."

"And that means?"

Out of the corner of his eye Jude could see the horde approaching, the band of noisy, overly hormoned teenagers.

"It means she reproduces without fertilization of an egg. In other words, all extant members of the species are female."

Jude's mouth opened. "No males at all? How do they survive?"

"Quite well, in fact. They replicate themselves perfectly—through a primitive form of cloning. As a result, each one is exactly identical to every other one. In many ways it seems to make life easier. I'd say they have a happy little colony there."

She tugged the bottom of her jacket and leaned against the railing.

From behind came a giggling, a chorus of chuckles and snorts that grew louder as the boys and girls elbowed one another and pointed to a corner of the island. There were two whiptails, one on top of the other, clinging for dear life, locked together in a coital embrace.

Jude looked at the lizards, then at the curator.

"How do you explain that?"

She looked at the two lizards.

"And that's the behavior that's most puzzling. Every so often one female will mount another and they go at it. It's almost as if they retain a remnant memory."

"Remnant memory?"

"Of the sex act."

On the way back to the hospital, Jude couldn't resist cracking a joke to himself. *Remnant memory of the sex act,* he thought. *Just like me.*

In the hospital gift shop Tizzie picked out a package of disposable razors, a can of shaving cream, a bottle of aftershave lotion, a toothbrush and a tube of Colgate. She felt a need to buy things for Skyler. She looked through a magazine rack for something that might interest him. *Esquire? Vanity Fair? Newsweek?* Strange, she could have picked out magazines for Jude; she knew his taste in reading matter. But Skyler—what would he like? Would it be the same? Somehow, she thought not. She searched up and down. So many choices. Why were none of them appealing?

And where was Jude? He had been away hours. She looked at her watch—six hours, to be exact. What could he be doing? Not that she minded the time alone with Skyler. It was exhilarating to see him looking well again, back to his old self. She had helped him up for a walk up and down the corridor, and she could tell that when she touched his arm, he was responsive. He practically broke out in goose bumps. That was sweet.

The girl behind the cash register tallied up her purchases, bagged them, took her money and gave change, all in a perky manner.

"Thank you," said Tizzie.

"Thank you" came the reply, with a big smile.

Tizzie turned to leave, and at that precise moment her glance happened to fall upon the window, and she looked through to the street outside, where the sun was beating down and bouncing in silvery reflections off one or two car windows. And then her eye landed on something—or someone, rather, that caught her up short. She took a tiny gasp. Could it be? Or was it her mind playing tricks on her, a trick of the light like the reflections? For there, standing on the other side of the street and looking both ways as if to cross, was a large man with a bull neck and a streak in his hair. A definite *streak of white!*

She had never seen him before, but she had heard him described often enough, both by Skyler and by Jude. Could it be a coincidence? She knew, in her bones, that it was not. And she became more certain the more she looked at the man, at the impatient, arrogant way he waited, bouncing slightly on the balls of his feet.

She dropped the bag on the floor, heard a surprised "Hey, wait!" from behind the counter, and rushed into the corridor. She ran past the receptionist and past the ground-floor offices and up a side staircase, up past the second floor to the third, yanking open the door. She looked both ways quickly, then darted down the hall to Skyler's room and burst in just as he was drifting off to sleep.

She shook him violently.

"Get up! Quick! We've got to leave!"

He looked up startled, uncomprehending.

"I'll explain later!"

He was slow to move.

"Quick. I saw one of those guys downstairs—what do you call them, an Orderly. He's coming to look for you!"

Skyler leapt out of bed, grabbed his pants, put them on and was at the door. Shirtless, his pants stained with blood, he looked like a wild man. He would stand out a mile. That was dangerous.

The bed next to Skyler's was curtained off—a new patient had been admitted. Tizzie opened one of the lockers set into the wall. They were in luck. She grabbed a man's shirt and pair of pants and shoes and followed Skyler out into the corridor. They ducked into the staircase and he quickly changed, dropping his pants over the banister. They ran down the stairwell all the way to the basement, opening the door a crack and peering through. It was the X-ray department. Three patients were seated along the wall, waiting their turn. They looked up quizzically as they hurried by.

They walked to the front of the hospital, found another staircase and took it. On the ground floor, the door had a small rectangular window of wire and glass shoulder-high. Skyler looked through. He had been prepared for the sight, but still it shocked him—there was an Orderly, leaning against the receptionist's counter, apparently demanding information. The face turned in his direction, and instinctively Skyler withdrew, ducking to one side.

Skyler looked again. The man was walking now toward the main corridor. He was approaching them! Skyler pulled Tizzie to him, pushed her into a corner and stood before her. If the door opened, they would be behind it. He motioned to her to remain quiet, and they stayed there, frozen, as the sound of footsteps approached. The steps paused in front of the door. They could almost hear the man thinking, pondering a choice. Then finally, the footsteps resumed and grew softer. Skyler looked through the window again; he could see the back of the Orderly's head, the streak barely visible, as he moved down the corridor in the opposite direction. Only then did he realize that Tizzie had been squeezing his arm.

They opened the door and watched him walk to the end of the corridor, turn a corner and disappear. Then they stepped into the lobby. Again Skyler felt Tizzie's hand sliding through his arm, this time casually. Her arm hooked his own and he felt her moving closer, walking almost in step, like a couple out for a stroll. She steered him close to the receptionist and happened to catch her eye.

"Oh," said the woman. "There was a man here just now"—she glanced at Skyler—"asking for your brother. The one who has an identical twin, he said. I sent him up to the room."

She looked down the corridor, bustling with helpfulness.

"You can probably still catch him on this floor."

"That's all right," Skyler put in hastily. "We're not crazy about him."

"In fact," said Tizzie. "We don't get along at all."

"You could do us a big favor," added Skyler."When he comes down, don't even mention that you saw us."

"You bet. I know what you mean. I didn't like him at all. Pushy."

Outside, the sunlight was dazzling. It bounced off street signs and windows and even the pavement, so that at first they had trouble seeing. They didn't even spot Jude driving down the street, not until he honked the horn and then shouted across the intersection.

"Let's get out of here," Tizzie commanded, jumping into the backseat while Skyler took the front.

They told Jude about the Orderly. He hit the gas. They were already five blocks away by the time they finished describing their escape from the hospital.

Jude looked over at Skyler. "I'm not sure about your clothes. I don't think they're really you. We won't go back to the motel for our stuff—it's not safe."

Jude reached into his pocket and pulled out one of the Arizona licenses. He threw it across to Skyler.

"Here's your new identity."

Skyler looked at the picture. Not bad. It could pass for him. He read the name.

"Harold James?"

"Harry, for short. I'm Edward. You can call me Eddie."

"The James brothers?" said Tizzie. "Isn't that a bit thick?"

"Not at all."

"By the way," said Tizzie, as they roared past a sign for Pulliam that indicated an airport, "where are we going?"

The answer was soothing to her ears. "Far, far away."

They changed planes at Phoenix and stayed long enough to grab a quick bite. Jude bought the *Arizona Republican* and read it over a cup of coffee. Nothing in it of interest. Tizzie wandered off to buy some more toiletries—her second attempt of the day—and Skyler looked in a gift shop for some clothing but found nothing.

They bought the tickets using Tizzie's credit card. This dismayed Jude, but there was no other way to pay for them. Anyway, he told himself, her plane ticket was in her own name, too, so there was no way to cover her tracks. In for a dime, in for a dollar.

They killed a half hour wandering around the modern terminal, then headed for the check-in counter for American Airlines and stood in a long line. When their turn came, they were asked for identification and produced three driver's licenses.

"Luggage?" inquired the check-in clerk.

"We have none," said Jude.

The clerk registered surprise.

"We always travel light," Jude explained.

He was tempted to make a wisecrack, but thought better of it. No sense in drawing even more attention to themselves—they were conspicuous enough as it was.

They zipped through the X-ray line and headed for the departure gate waiting lounge, where they sat among all the other travelers. Anyone looking at them might have mistaken them for a modern typically atypical American family grouping—say, two identical brothers and a wife returning from a holiday in the sun. The only question that might conceivably be asked was: which one of the brothers was the husband?

Ten minutes later, the flight was called—nonstop to Washington, D.C.

# Chapter 24

The taxi passed the Washington Monument, drove along the Ellipse to the Capitol and continued on into the southwest sector, where they found a cheap rooming house called Potomac View. The name was misleading; the only view of the river was a badly-done watercolor that hung in the hallway above a stack of tourist brochures.

In the morning, Tizzie decided to call her office in New York. It was a calculated risk. She had to surface sooner or later, she figured, and the longer she was out of touch, the more suspicious her behavior would seem. Besides, she couldn't remain out of contact for too long. What if her parents needed her?

As a concession to Jude's burgeoning worry streak, she took a cab downtown to place the call from the Hay Adams Hotel. That wouldn't make it any harder to trace, but it would lead their pursuers no closer than a busy hotel in the political hub of the nation's capital.

As for Jude, he decided at breakfast to meet Raymond. He needed him. The three of them were out of their depth in tackling the Lab, that much was clear. They needed the resources of the FBI to get to the bottom of the whole murky business. And, frankly, it would be a relief to hand the whole damn case over to someone else.

But would the FBI be responsive? What were they dealing with exactly? Murder?—undoubtedly. For openers, there was that dead body in New Paltz. But they were a long way from being able to pin it on anybody. What else was there? Some kind of conspiracy to engage in illegal medical research? Most probably. But was that the kind of thing the government's prime investigative agency worried about? Raymond had said there had once been an active file on the Lab, but indicated it was all but closed.

Other priorities, he suggested. Then again Hartman had said that FBI agents had trailed them to Wisconsin. So at least somebody there was still interested.

Questions flitted through his mind. Would Raymond have enough pull to get the agency behind him? Maybe Jude would have to back him up in person in persuading his superiors. And come to think of it, how much could he trust Raymond? Raymond had warned him to be suspicious of *everyone*, no matter how close. In retrospect, that sounded like he had been talking about Tizzie. Did Raymond know about her? Or could the warning apply to Raymond himself? Don't forget, Jude told himself, from the beginning Raymond had been holding back information. But why would he warn Jude to be suspicious of himself? Would he say that if he *was* a part of it? On the other hand, what a perfect ruse—what better tactic to worm his way into Jude's trust? But then again, it was Raymond who'd provided him with the name of the judge that allowed him to take the first step on this whole long, crazy trail. That spoke well for him.

Jude decided to stop thinking so much. You just go round and round in circles and end up so spooked you're paralyzed. Take the bull by the horns. Just show up. Take Skyler. No advance warning, no time to spring a trap. And anyway, with these Orderlies and God knew who else after them, probably the safest place to be right now was the FBI Building.

Jude and Skyler grabbed a taxi.

"FBI headquarters."

The driver, a dark-skinned African wearing a bright print shirt, looked at them in the rearview mirror, first one, then the other. The bouncy rhythm of West African music came from a tape. Sounds like Sunny Ade, thought Jude, and he looked at the driver's name. Sure enough, he was Nigerian.

Tizzie was frantic. She left a note for Jude and Skyler—there was no time to wait for them—and took a taxi back to the airport. She pushed her way toward the front of the line and bought a ticket. A half hour later, she was in the air, en route to Milwaukee.

It sounded serious. She had tried to determine just how serious by gauging her secretary's intonation, but of course that hadn't revealed anything.

"They say you should come right away. She's doing poorly, and they don't know how long she'll last."

"When did they call?"

"Only a couple of hours ago."

Were they trying to spare her by giving her only half information? Would her mother be dead by the time she got there?

Strange, but she had always assumed that her father would be the first to go. He was the one who had always worked so hard, who had seemed so overburdened. Her mother had been secondary, someone who was there in the background. She was cleaning house or cooking meals while he was dealing with the world, seeing his patients or arranging trips or discussing weighty matters with Uncle Henry. Her mother always seemed to be expending less energy, to be going through life more or less certain of what she should be doing, and doing it at her own pace.

Tizzie couldn't bear to face the hard truth. She'd probably thought her father would die first because she feared that the most. Her mother—she loved her deeply. Her mother was a stalwart support, a nourishing presence. But her father was her whole world. The moon, the stars and the sun rolled into one. She could imagine life without her mother, but not without her father.

Guilt came next, and typically she was up to her neck in it. It was irresistible to her, like probing a wound to see how much it hurts. She called up as many fond memories as she could. A flood of images came on parade: her mother tending her when she was sick, staying up late to make sure she got home safely during high school dates, bandaging her foot at the seashore when she had stepped on a razor shell.

A new old memory came suddenly out of nowhere: sleeping in her mother's arms on a long car trip, being comforted by her. Where were they going? *Why, they were leaving Arizona.* It was the long journey to Wisconsin, and she was afraid, afraid because she was abandoning all her friends and was about to start a brand-new life. But also afraid for some other reason—what was it? Perhaps she was afraid because she sensed on some level that her parents were afraid. What would they have been afraid of?

How many other memories were there like that, waiting to be unlocked?

Tizzie was crammed in economy class. A man to one side of her kept falling asleep, his head tumbling upon her shoulder. Lunch came in a bag: a sandwich, piece of cheese, an apple and a plastic knife. A baby behind her was crying. But she scarcely noticed any of this.

She was too scared. More scared than any time since that car trip long ago.

And as it turned out, she had good reason to be. For when the plane finally landed, taxiing slowly from the runway to the gate and disgorging its passengers maddeningly slowly, she was met by a small delegation at the arrival gate.

She saw, and her heart gave out a sigh to see it, that the group included Uncle Henry. She could tell by their faces even before a single word was spoken that she had come too late.

She could tell that her mother was already dead.

The Hoover Building was large and impersonal, a nondescript bureaucratic monolith on Pennsylvania Avenue.

They got out a block early and walked the rest of the way, an old habit Jude had picked up when he went on important interviews. By now it had become a superstition, a bit of harmless ritual to make the interview turn out right. And considering everything, no interview in his life would ever be as important as this one.

There was a pay phone in the lobby, and Jude placed a call while Skyler walked around nervously.

He was put through right away.

"Raymond," Jude began.

There was a flicker of a pause. He imagined Raymond collecting himself to sound normal.

"Jude. Where the hell are you?"

He hadn't succeeded. His tone had an undercurrent of urgency.

"Right here. In D.C. I need to talk to you."

"Name your place. I'll be there."

"Maybe I'll come to you."

"Okay, fine . . . when?"

Jude thought Raymond sounded pleased.

"How about right now?"

"Good. Perfect."

A pause. Then Raymond added: "Are you alone?"

Why give him the satisfaction?

"Just me and my shadow." He thought: I hope that's ambiguous enough for you.

"Okay. I'll be waiting. How soon will you get here?"

"I *am* here."

"What? What do you mean?"

"I'm right downstairs—in the lobby."

"Shit. Why didn't you say so? I'll be right down."

"Okay."

Jude hung up with his finger, holding the receiver in his hand, suddenly uncertain. What the hell, the die was cast. At least he was back in the game. But then why did he feel so unsure of himself, so unconvinced that he had done the right thing? Why did he feel this little ball of nettles inside that he knew to be the onset of fear?

He looked around the lobby. Ahead was a security check, a walk-through glass booth manned by plainclothes guards. A little line had formed, people returning from mid-morning breaks. He was surprised at the dress of the men who whisked in and out of the front doors. It was normal and even stylish; he had half-expected to see the proverbial drab gray suits and short haircuts of the Hoover era. And there were a lot of women, too. Some people were even laughing.

On the other side of the metal detectors was an escort desk where badges were being handed out to visitors. Beyond was an elevator bank. On the other side was a newsstand with racks of magazines and newspapers on display. It was cool in the high-ceiling lobby and he could feel drafts from air-conditioning pumped in through vents.

Where was Skyler?

Jude scanned the lobby quickly. There he was, over by the opposite wall, still in that ridiculous shirt he'd gotten from the Arizona hospital. He was looking at some framed photographs on the wall.

Jude walked over and stood next to him. The photos were of agency officials, arranged in a hierarchical pyramid by title. Top ranking officials were at the top. At the summit was the FBI director, on the line below the deputy, then assistant directors, then division heads, and so on. Two out of the twenty were women. Skyler was staring at them. Jude turned around, looking behind the metal detectors for Raymond; he didn't want to be taken by surprise when he appeared.

Then he heard something—a quick intake of breath, suggesting shock. It came from Skyler. He looked to his side. Skyler was standing frozen in position with his arms hanging down and back. He was staring at the wall—at one particular picture on the wall.

Then he turned quickly and looked dead ahead at Jude, and his eyes said it all: he had seen something frightening.

He bolted for the door.

Jude went after him and saw him running across the lobby toward the front exit. Skyler bumped into a woman's shoulder so hard that she spun halfway around. People turned, their mouths open. No one made a move to stop him. Jude dashed after him, tried to catch him before he reached the doors. But he was not fast enough. He looked through the glass. There was Skyler outside, balancing on one foot, comical almost, as he was desperately deciding what direction to run in.

"Jude! Jude!"

The sound came somewhere from the distance behind him, but he ignored it, cutting it off by plunging ahead to the door. He pushed the door with all his might, and in another second he was outside, back on the humid sidewalk, watching Skyler running up the street.

He ran after him, but couldn't catch him.

Two blocks, three, four. Skyler wasn't slowing down. Jude watched the top of his head bobbing up and down among the crowd on the sidewalk. Several times, Skyler turned back to look and saw Jude coming and still kept running.

Strange, thought Jude. *He almost seems to be running away from me.*

But he wasn't. Quite the opposite. Skyler wanted to make sure that Jude, too, was running away.

Jude found this out a few moments later when he arrived at a park, stopped to catch his breath, looked around and couldn't see Skyler anywhere. Then he heard his name being called softly.

He joined Skyler, who was sitting on a bench partially concealed by two rhododendron bushes, breathing in great gulps of air.

"What happened?" Jude exclaimed. "Why did you run off like that?"

"The photo," explained Skyler. "The one of the deputy director. Eagleton."

"Yes."

"I've seen him before. On the island. He was one of those who came that day to see Dr. Rincon."

The funeral was tastefully done. It was held in a white clapboard Congregational church on Lake Drive.

The turnout was larger than Tizzie had expected—her parents must have known more people than she had realized. Many were elderly, sweet-looking women in bonnets and white Easter gloves, and men with wrinkled faces and perfectly pressed trousers; they knew by heart the rituals and protocol of funeral attendance. The odd thing was how few of them Tizzie knew.

Her father was too ill to come, which made it more difficult for her.

Afterward, the participants came back to her parents' house to pay their respects. A huge buffet was laid out—all kinds of salads, deviled eggs, bowls of tuna fish, sliced ham, coleslaw, loaves of unsliced bread and angel food cake—more than enough to feed everyone. Tizzie had no idea where it had all come from. She had the odd sensation that somewhere behind the scenes, professional funeral-givers were poring over plans and pulling strings.

She couldn't eat. It wasn't that food was totally repellent to her, just that she couldn't find her appetite. She had gone through the service flawlessly, standing and even singing the hymns at full voice. She didn't feel flooded with emotion and close to tears. She felt the opposite—empty, hard. Aside from those gruesome but uncontrollable efforts to visualize the cadaver inside the casket, her thoughts were not about her mother. She was thinking almost the whole time about her father.

And so that is why afterward, with the people coming and going downstairs, she abandoned her post of greeter at the door and ran up the stairs to what used to be their bedroom. How many times as a little girl had she turned that beveled glass doorknob to gain admittance to the inner sanctum? This time as she turned it, she could almost feel herself regressing, turning small as the years peeled away, like Alice in Wonderland.

Her father could be seen in the dim light, resting on his back in bed, a head propped up on a sea of pillows. He barely registered her presence. She sat down on the edge of the bed, more roughly than she intended, in part perhaps to shake some life into him. But there was precious little. She buried her face in his neck and caressed the thin yellow-white hair on his brittle skull.

It was at that moment that she became aware of someone else in the room.

He coughed slightly from the depths of the easy chair in the shadows in the corner. And it took no more than that for her to know instantly who it was—Uncle Henry.

"And how are you, my dear?" he asked. "How are you holding up?"

She thought the inquiry insincere and not deserving of an answer. Nor did she want to give him the satisfaction of having startled her. She sought refuge in silent stoicism.

Uncle Henry reached up and turned on a standing lamp. The light it threw struck her in the eyes and did nothing to illuminate him, as he sank back into the depths of the chair.

"I know it is hard on you. It's hard on all of us. Your mother was not the most"— he waved his hand in the air, searching for the right word—

"impressive person perhaps to the outside world. But to those of us who knew her, and loved her, she had her qualities."

Tizzie's father stirred a little, moving one leg.

"And it's especially unsettling when a member of the elder group goes, one of the original circle, so to speak. And so much before her time."

This last sentence was delivered almost in a whisper.

He paused, then picked up the tempo, almost like a preacher.

"Still, we must not look back. We must move on. We must think of the living. Those who have their lives before them, or who are still holding on to life . . ." She could feel his gaze shifting to the bed. "Like your father here."

"What are you trying to say?" she demanded, her eyes flashing.

"Nothing that you don't already know." His voice was harsh now, bracing in the face of the truth. "He is not in good shape. He is not doing well."

"I *do* know that."

"Do you really?"

She was puzzled by the turnaround. "Of course."

"Then why don't you try to do something about it?"

"I don't know what you mean."

"Why don't you help us? We're the group that is trying to help him. We're trying to find a cure for what killed your mother. Don't fool yourself—she did not die of old age."

"How can you be sure?"

"Come on, Tizzie. You saw how quickly she aged. She seemed to gain thirty years in just the last five. Have you ever seen anything like it?"

She remained silent, just shook her head.

"And your father has contracted the same thing."

"Is it a disease?"

"Perhaps. We have several people working on that question. A vaccine for what ails him. Someday, maybe, you will join them. You have skills in that department."

"Is that what you want me to do? Research?"

Uncle Henry coughed, bringing up some phlegm, which he removed with a pocket handkerchief.

"Not now. Right now there's something much more valuable that you can do. We have enemies. We need to know who they are and what they are doing."

Tizzie's heart sank.

"What can I do?"

"Very simple. You can tell us what they've found out."

"What they've found out?"

He suddenly raised his voice. "Don't play at being stupid—not with me."

"I won't. You want me to spy on people—on Jude."

"Now you're acting like your father's daughter. We want you to *report* on Jude . . . and others."

"Skyler."

"Precisely."

She looked over at her father, so frail in his bed, the brown of his freckles standing out against the white of the pillows.

"And it will help?"

"Without question."

"Then I will," she said.

"Fine."

"When . . . what do I do?"

"Downstairs in the study, you will find some paper. Simply write out everything you know—where they've been, what they've done, what they've said. Take your time, wait until the people leave, which will be shortly, in any case. I'd like it by this evening."

"I will."

"That's good, dear."

"I'll tell you everything. We were all together . . . out west . . . in Jerome."

"Fine. Write it all down. There will be more to do later."

Uncle Henry put two hands on the armrests and pulled himself up. He shut off the light, and the room turned dim.

"Will you help my father?"

"Yes, dear. Along with others. We must all do our bit."

He walked to the door and looked back.

"You should comfort him. I think he knows you. It's touching to see you two together."

"Good-bye, Uncle Henry."

"Good-bye, dear. I'm glad you told me about your gallivanting around the country with those two boys. It's good to reestablish trust with the gift of honesty. We already knew it, of course."

She heard his footsteps going down the stairs. It was hard to tell if his remark about trust had been sarcastic. He'd delivered it as if he were talking to a little girl, the very same one who had turned the glass doorknob.

Jude was excited by their accidental discovery. The implications were staggering.

He took Skyler into a small bar on K Street, where they took a corner booth, so they could think it through. He ordered them each a tall beer.

So Frederick C. Eagleton, the powerful deputy director of the FBI, an upstanding member of the establishment, was involved in this . . . this what? . . . this conspiracy.

Eagleton wasn't exactly a household name, but he was known to politicians and journalists and anyone else who followed the power game in Washington. Not since Hoover had there been a director with absolute power; some had even been figureheads. But the deputy director—that was a different matter. The deputy didn't come and go at the pleasure of the President. He was as constant and ubiquitous as the civil service, surviving from one administration to the next, accumulating more information, building the files, performing and receiving favors. If the director was a figurehead, then the deputy was the iron hand behind him, the one who pulled the wires and pushed the buttons. What some of those wires and buttons did, Jude didn't care to guess.

If Eagleton was involved, who else was? God only knew how big this thing was. And if it's a conspiracy, what holds it together? If there's a web, how far does it extend, and who is the spider sitting at the very center?

Rincon, of course. But how does he do it?

Jude sipped the beer slowly.

And exactly *how* was Eagleton involved? Had he been bribed to give the Lab protection? Was he in their pay? That didn't make sense. If he was on the payroll, why would he have made the trip to the island? That wasn't something an employee does. The way Skyler described it, it sounded more like a pilgrimage, a journey of faith. He went there with all the others to sit at Rincon's feet.

But why? What could Rincon offer them?

There was only one answer that made sense: longer life. Some people would do anything for it—especially people in power.

But the numbers didn't add up. Eagleton was middle-aged, sixty years old, give or take a couple of years. According to what Hartman had told them, he would be far too old to have a clone made at his birth. Sixty years ago was before World War II. The concept of cloning wasn't even dreamt of back then. The technology for it was nonexistent. The only people with clones were children of the Lab, in their early thirties.

Like me, he thought.

Jude was at a dead end. He pushed the question aside. It would have to be solved later.

He took another sip and looked at Skyler. He was getting used to seeing him across a bar table.

God, they had been lucky to spot that picture. That one little piece made a whole section of the puzzle fall into place. Eagleton's involvement accounted for the FBI's interest in the case. It explained the phone taps, the agents tracking them in Wisconsin, maybe even the tails he was convinced had been hounding them.

On closer inspection, the discovery raised a question. His old friend Raymond, where did his loyalties lie? He could be anything—friend or foe. Who knew what side *he* was on? Who knew which side *anybody* was on?

Jude had a sudden insight. He raised his beer glass and tapped it against Skyler's.

"You know," he said, "this guy Raymond, this FBI guy we were going to meet—he's been after one thing. All along he's been wanting to meet you. He wants to hook up with you. He asked me to bring you to him. And now we know why."

"We do?"

"Certainly. Don't you see? You're the key. You're a Rosetta stone."

"What?"

"It's a stone that helped them decode hierogly—"

"I know what the Rosetta stone is. I don't know what the hell you're talking about."

"You're someone who can help them break the code."

Now Jude was speaking faster in his excitement.

"If Eagleton's a member of this group, this conspiracy, then undoubtedly there are others. They're tied into it in some way and for some reason we can't fathom. But nobody on the outside knows who they are. They need to have some way to identify them. And you're it. You're the way. Because you're an eyewitness, don't you see? You saw them all together that day on the island. The whole congregation."

"No kidding. Don't remind me."

"I've been so stupid. Here you are, this font of information, so valuable the FBI is dying to get hold of you, and all this time you're sitting right next to me."

"I'm glad you finally see my value."

"C'mon, this is important."

Jude put down his glass with a bang.

"Don't go away. I'll be right back."

He was gone in a flash, out the front door. He soon returned, having visited a newsstand down the block, a stack of magazines and newspapers under each arm.

He spread them out on the bar and opened them at random. They were chock-full of pictures.

"Here, flip through these. See if anybody looks familiar."

"You're joking."

"No, give it a try."

And while he did, Jude read through *The Washington Post*, *The New York Times*, the *Mirror*, and some other papers.

One bit of news caught his eye. There had been another one of those "body-snatcher murders," the body found mutilated beyond recognition, the visceral organs missing. This one was the third. It had been discovered in a woods in Georgia, not far from the others. The story got good play in the *Post*, but merited only four graphs in the *Times*, and he couldn't find it in the *Mirror* at all.

I'll bet the odds are good that the mutilation includes a quarter-sized piece of flesh missing from the inside right thigh, he thought. And it's typical of the police not to let that information out—they're holding back something they assume is known only by the killer.

Just then Skyler found something of his own. He gave a little cry, not very loud but enough to turn a few heads at the bar stools.

"Here's one," he said, lowering his voice. "Look at this."

The heads at the bar lost interest and turned away.

Jude looked. Skyler's finger was resting on the forehead of an internationally known entrepreneur, an investment banker named Thomas K. Smiley. Smiley had reason to smile: at the age of thirty-five he had invested in a start-up software company. He wasn't the brains behind the company, he was the money behind the brains. It had done well for him in the rat race: it had gotten him out of the starting gate and given him a lead that he'd never squandered. He'd bought up companies left and right, carefully selecting the ones that needed an extra infusion of cash to bring home the prize. He had the Midas touch, and by sixty, his accumulated fortune was comfortably in the nine digits.

The photo showed a handsome man with a widow's peak and a tan, smiling at the opening of a charity ball at the Metropolitan Museum in New York. A long-haired socialite hung from his arm.

"I saw him that day. I'm sure of it. He flew down in a small plane. I'd recognize him anywhere—same cut of the jaw, same cocky smile. He expected everyone to wait on him—and they did."

"Bull's-eye. Two down—and God only knows how many to go!"

Two more beers and Jude was dragging Skyler off on his latest brainstorm.

They caught a cab. It was raining, the kind of late-summer halfhearted drizzle that doesn't cut the humidity but just seems to merge with it. Here and there on the sidewalks, umbrellas sprouted.

"So why are we going there?" asked Skyler.

"Oh, just a little stroll through the corridors of our nation's government."

They pulled up at the Capitol and took the tourists' entrance off the main rotunda. It was already late afternoon. A small line waited to go through the metal detector. They were sightseers, weary and short-tempered in dealing with their children, who were pulling on their skirts and pant legs, dangling from their hands and whining.

At first they had no luck. Skyler stared at everyone who walked by. They poked into offices and wandered around the hallways. They pretended to examine busts of famous lawmakers while eavesdropping on lobbyists. They found a reference room and searched the photographs in a bound volume called the congressional directory. They even followed a throng of representatives who led them to an underground electric train, which they took to the Samuel Rayburn Building and back.

Jude was ready to give up, when they noticed that the congressmen seemed to be hurrying though the corridors. A guard explained that a quorum call had been issued for a vote on a budget amendment, the last order of business before Congress would adjourn to start its summer recess. No wonder they were so eager to vote.

The two found their way to the visitors' gallery. Skyler took a front-row seat and peered down from the balcony, just as the speaker gaveled the proceedings to order and asked for a voice vote. A roll call was ordered, and the congressmen could be seen flipping switches at their curved mahogany desks to ignite a tally board off to one side.

Skyler elbowed Jude in the ribs. "That one, down there, fourth row back on the right."

Jude found him. A slightly rotund man with dark-framed glasses and a balding pate shining through a not-very-successful comb-over.

"I think so, but I'm not really sure. I need to face him directly."

They located the man's seat in the printed visitors' guide called "Know Your Congresspeople." It was a seat that belonged to the delegation from Georgia.

Ten minutes later, the people's business having been concluded, the gavel came crashing down and the figures below clamored out of their seats. They pumped each other's hand, gave a hug here and there, boomed good-byes in hearty voices and disappeared as quickly as children on the last day of school.

Jude and Skyler had to ask directions three times, but eventually they found the office. The door with a glazed window and the number 316 was closed. They passed it by and stood far away at the end of the corridor where it joined the rotunda, waiting. All up and down the hall, doors opened and men and women hurried past, carrying briefcases and magazines, a look of urgent expectation on their faces. After a good ten minutes, just when the place was quieting down, the door to 316 opened. Out scurried the small man with glasses. Seen from the same level, his body possessed an avocado-like shape.

He walked right at them. The two withdrew behind a pedestal bearing a marble likeness of William Jennings Bryan, standing in mid-oratory, one hand outstretched, the other clasped to his heart.

"Get a good look," exhorted Jude, remaining out of sight behind the statue.

The man emerged from the corridor, walking quickly, and veered on one heel. He headed for a door in the opposite direction.

*Turn around,* Skyler commanded mentally. *Turn around!*

The man continued on his way, reached the door. Just then Jude sneezed, a loud, rip-roaring sneeze that echoed deep into the corridor.

The man turned and Skyler got a good look. So good he was able to quickly turn his back and move behind Bryan's boot. When he stepped out again, the man was gone, the bang of the door resounding through the rotunda.

Skyler said only one word: "Bull's-eye."

"We've got one more port of call," said Jude, looking at his watch. "If we hurry, we can just make it."

In the taxi, he gave Skyler a lecture on the First Amendment, the freedom of the press and the glories of the Fourth Estate. When all else fails in a democracy, he said, when you're desperate and don't now where to turn, you can look to the nation's newspapers for deliverance.

"And that's why I'm already getting pissed off because of what we're about to find out," he declared.

The executive offices of Worldwide Media Inc. were the top three floors of a modern building on Connecticut Avenue. From it Tibbett and his executives could look down, figuratively and literally, upon the White House.

Once inside, Jude recalled that the lobby had an exit at either end. Hordes of people were already rushing out both of them. That was bad news: if Jude and Skyler door-stopped one exit, their man could slip out the other. There was nothing for it but to try to cut him off on the twelfth floor. Jude knew from a previous visit to Washington—when the bureau chief had for some reason invited him to the annual political roast known as the Gridiron—that the company had its own reception lounge there. The executives riding down from the top floors transferred elevators to reach the lobby.

He also knew there would be a receptionist on the twelfth floor who would demand to see their identification. He had his *Mirror* press card, but what would Skyler do? *He* was the one who counted. Maybe they could sweet-talk their way.

His worries were for naught. When they stepped off the elevator, the receptionist's chair was empty. So was the lounge. A TV set—tuned, of course, to Tibbett's broadcasting network, called "TB" by its detractors—played to itself in the corner.

Everything in sight, from the doorknobs to the curved hard steel of the chairs, was spanking modern. Floor-to-ceiling windows the color of smoke ran along one wall. All that glass lent an illusion of being suspended in space, like inside a cockpit. In fact, Tibbett was a fanatical pilot, and the aviation motif was picked up in knickknacks here and there, like model planes, propellers mounted on the wall and a crystal ashtray engraved with a photo of Lucky Lindy.

A couch rested on the wall opposite the elevators, and two deep leather chairs faced it at a gentle angle. Jude stationed Skyler in one of them. He handed him a newspaper from a pile behind the reception desk.

"Use this to cover your face if you need to. Don't forget: you have to see him, but he can't see you."

Jude waited in a small passage around the corner that led to the men's room.

They didn't have long to wait. Five minutes later, an elevator came down and a group of four men stepped out. They moved quickly to the downward bank. One was talking in the confident, preemptory manner of a CEO. Peering cautiously around the corner, Jude confirmed that it was Tibbett.

And Tibbett detached himself from the group and was headed right for him!

Jude beat a hasty retreat to the men's room. He heard the footsteps on his trail and ducked inside a stall. He stood upon the toilet and waited, holding his breath. He heard the door open. Then he heard footsteps approaching, a fly unzipping, a man relieving himself at the urinal, a loud flushing. He made not a sound. Finally, the footsteps moved again, the door opened and closed.

Jude waited a full two or three minutes before he dared to leave.

Skyler was in the lounge, standing.

"I was worried about you," he said. "He looked like he would have chucked you out the window."

"And is he one—"

"You know you don't even have to ask. I remember him clearly, because he flew his own plane."

The remark made Jude think. That evening back at the rooming house, he connected to the *Mirror*'s web site and culled through photos of Tibbett until he found the one he was looking for. It showed the real estate mogul dressed in a brown safari shirt, posing for the camera somewhere in the tropics. In the background were palm trees and the nose of a small aircraft.

"Take a look," said Jude. "Is this the plane?"

"Absolutely. I recognize the name—*Lorelei*. And I recognize something else. This is the exact same kind of plane I hid in to get off the island."

Jude looked at the name and saw a small insignia under it. He got closer to the screen so that he could make it out, and then he could see what it was—a tiny W.

# Chapter 25

Jude and Skyler made preparations for the trip south. Finally, after all this time of trying to devise ways to locate the island, they had a solid clue—the photo of the plane—that might point them in the right direction.

But first they needed money and a car.

Jude called Tom Mahoney, an old friend in the *Mirror*'s Washington bureau, and met him for a hamburger. Mahoney was a legend, and not just in his own mind. He had been on the political beat for as long as anyone could remember, and all those lobster lunches and steak dinners showed; he weighed in at about 270 pounds, and that before the first round of drinks, which began shortly after noon. But pound for pound, he was the best reporter around: good with anecdotes, loaded down with home numbers and able to pound out a banner lead—all on deadline. Jude had a lot of time for him.

He and Jude went way back, to Mahoney's slimmer days when Jude had been briefly trying his hand as a foreign correspondent for the Associated Press and Mahoney had worked for UPI. They'd met over a coup in Nigeria; both had seen the bullet-riddled body of the head of state in the back of a Mercedes, but Mahoney hadn't been able to file; he couldn't use the telex. Jude, a competitor but always the gentleman, sent the story for him, though not until his own was already on the wire. Mahoney never forgot the favor.

"What d'ya need?" he asked.

"Two thousand," said Jude, and he was grateful that Mahoney hadn't flinched. "And the use of a car."

"You in trouble?"

The answer to that one was hard to exaggerate.

They finished their hamburgers, talked a bit about the old days. When the check came, Mahoney said: "You pick it up."

They walked to his bank two blocks away, and he took out the money and gave it to him in fifties. Then he handed him his house keys and told him where to find the keys to an old Volvo parked around the back.

"Drop the house keys in the mail slot," he said. "Trudy will let me in—if she's not too pissed at me."

Mahoney wished him luck and shook his hand, then turned and walked away. Jude felt a rush of affection as he watched the broad shoulders recede down the sidewalk, without stepping aside for anyone.

After picking up the car, Jude made a quick call to Tizzie, just to tell her they were leaving Washington, and what they'd learned so far. Tizzie sounded tense, and they weren't able to talk long. Then they spent the rest of the afternoon at the Library of Congress. Jude used his real name and *Mirror* ID to gain access to the librarian's office, where, after a brief interview, he was granted the right to use the research room. They were shown to a large, windowless chamber deep in the bowels of the building. It was practically deserted, except for three scholarly-looking types who looked as though they had spent their lives there.

Along one wall was a series of cubicles. They worked out of one that had a plain, empty table and a computer in one corner.

First they ordered photostated copies of maps—nautical, topographical, all kinds of maps in all kinds of scales—anything that showed the coastlines of South Carolina, Georgia and eastern Florida. They spread them out on the table as if it were a war room.

Then Jude called up the photo of Tibbett and his plane from the Web, downloaded it and printed a copy. He propped it up next to the computer and went on-line, calling up dozens and dozens of files of small planes. Eventually, he found what looked like a match, a five-seater single-engine Cherokee. He called up the specifications and found what he wanted: fuel capacity, consumption rate, and top speed. He estimated the distance capability with a full tank of fuel at six hundred and fifty miles, more or less.

Jude borrowed a compass from an assistant librarian and, using the map key, set it to represent the maximum distance. Then he centered it on the dot that represented Valdosta—Skyler's landing spot—and swung it in a half circle, creating an arc that dipped out into the ocean and took in a large swath of coastline.

"The island's got to be somewhere within the circle," he said. He looked at the marking with a deflated air. It took in more land and sea than he'd thought it would, all the way south to the Florida peninsula and north almost to Washington.

"Now think. Think hard—anything you can remember, any landmarks, anything at all that will help us place it."

They sent for reference books on the barrier islands and eliminated the larger, better-known ones such as Hilton Head, Pawley's, Ossabaw, St. Helena, St. Catherines, and Sapelo. The odds of a medical cult coexisting with a resort or tourist island were decidedly low. Next they obtained books on plantation farming, Gullah culture and early Indian inhabitants, and they combed through them, looking for something, anything, that might trigger a recollection from Skyler. They found nothing.

"Damn it," said Jude. "There's got to be something. Try, can't you?"

Skyler was trying. He closed his eyes and remembered everything he could. He attempted to gauge the size of the island, its shape, even its distance from the mainland. But all he could see in his mind's eye was a flat expanse of a brilliant green and golden blanket of cordgrass around the edges, giving way in the center to luxuriant woods. His recollections weren't specific enough to convert into hard and fast estimates of acres or miles, certainly nothing befitting a map.

They took a break and went out for coffee. As soon as he took the first sip, Skyler's eyes lighted up.

"I think I've come up with something," he said. "Remember I told you about the abandoned lighthouse? That could be the landmark we're looking for."

They returned to the reference room and ordered up books on old lighthouses and mariners' routes and landmarks in the coastal marshes. They pored through them carefully, page by page, but found not a single image, painting or picture that resembled Skyler's memory of his precious hideaway.

"How about the hurricane?" said Jude. "You mentioned that a hurricane struck the island—not the one when you were in Valdosta, but one many years ago. Try and figure out what year it was."

Skyler tried to remember. He took a pencil and scribbled some notes. He thought some more and finally pronounced that his best guess was 1989. Jude called up Nexis and punched in the information.

"If we can get the name of the hurricane, we can call up the meteorological data," he explained. "Then we can plot the path of the storm on our maps. That might narrow it a bit."

He waited while the computer ticked, searching.

"Here it is," he said. "Hurricane Hugo. Struck Charleston, South Carolina. Sustained winds of a hunded and thirty-five miles per hour. Caused extensive damage."

"That's it," Skyler exclaimed. "Hugo. I remember it now from the radio."

"What did you say?"

"I remember, it was Hugo."

"But how?"

"From Kuta's radio."

Jude looked up at him hopefully. "And do you by any chance remember ever hearing the call letters of the station?"

Now Skyler caught on. "Of course! WCTB."

Jude closed the books and rolled up the maps.

"I'd say we've got enough to go on," he said. "What are we doing wasting our time up here?"

They drove the old Volvo to the rooming house to collect their few belongings, but couldn't get there. The block was closed off by police cars and fire trucks, their lights spinning and cab radios barking out squawks. Firemen in thick rubber boots and bright slickers carried hoses that unraveled out of the trucks like fishing line leaping out of reels. Jude parked the car three blocks away, and they walked back. A crowd had gathered, kept on the other side of the street by policemen. They pushed their way to the front.

"Jude—that's our place."

A cop stood four feet from Skyler.

"What happened?" he asked.

The cop looked him over a full three or four seconds before answering.

"Fire."

"Anyone hurt?"

"No."

"What caused it?"

"Hard to say. Could be a gas explosion."

They gaped at the damage. Smoke or dust hung in the air. The front of the building was blown away, its facade reduced to a pile of rubble. The roofs of the buildings on either side tilted toward the open cavity. The back was still standing, so that it was possible to read the layout of the missing floors upon it—a partial staircase, the white plaster lines of the walls, the wooden ceiling planks sticking out. It looked pathetically quaint somehow, like an overly large dollhouse.

It was entirely unrecognizable from the rooming house where they had spent the night only hours before.

Jude grabbed Skyler by the arm and pointed across the way to the other side of the throng. A large man was standing alone, looking at the damage with all the others, but from time to time he turned and looked at the people around him, surveying the crowd. That was peculiar.

Skyler held his breath and waited for the man to turn away. He wanted to see if he bore a white streak down the center of his hair.

The man turned. He did not.

Jude and Skyler slipped back through the crowd and walked quickly to their car.

They were shaken. They decided it was definitely time to skip town.

Radio station WCTB was little more than a whitewashed cottage in a weed-infested lot on Gloucester Street in Brunswick, Georgia. It had a dish on top and a thirty-foot-tall metal broadcasting tower that looked like something out of the 1940s. The windows were blacked out, and the front door, painted Ashanti colors of yellow, orange and green, was closed. A table and chair sat out front under a tree that had a tire swing.

As they pulled up next to a cyclone fence, Jude and Skyler could hear a distant steady thud, the beat laid down by a drum, coming from inside the building. The walls were practically vibrating, and as Skyler stepped outside the car, he imagined one of those anthropomorphic houses from the days of black-and-white cartoons, huffing and puffing and dancing so recklessly its shutters shook off.

It had been a quick trip. As they drove down Route 95 past Savannah and turned onto the old coastal road, Route 17, it was like moving back in time. The air had grown heavy with humidity and thick with the scent of magnolia and peach and, as they'd approached the coast, the pungent odor of the salt marshes. Skyler relaxed into the sounds and smells of a lifetime. He felt better now that he was back where there were peeling shacks raised on stilts, where Spanish moss draped from the branches and people moved as if they had all the time in the world.

They walked to the radio station. Skyler carried a cold six-pack they'd purchased from a convenience store behind a Texaco station. They had to bang on the front door for some time, and only then they were heard because a commercial interruption came along. The black man who opened it, in a loud printed shirt and with padded earphones hugging his head and leading to a cord that dangled by his side, peered at them from top to bottom and stepped aside to let them in.

Jude launched into an explanation, but it was quickly aborted. The man jumped behind a console, plugged in his earphones and flipped two switches, just as the commercial ended. The room was flooded with the languid flow of a D.J., caressing his words in honey tones. He was speaking a mixture of English and Gullah.

Through the picture window of a sound booth, they saw the man. He wore large mirror sunglasses, and he moved as he spoke, doing a little shoulder dance around the microphone but never touching it.

"Lissen now—de song comin op dey a good-good one fa dancin'," he said, giving a little shimmy.

When another record was put on, he stepped out of the booth. He was some six and a half feet tall, towering over Jude and Skyler, and his handshake was powerful. He didn't crack a smile.

"Bozman," he announced.

Jude and Skyler introduced themselves.

The man at the console turned the music down several decibels, and they chatted for a bit. The D.J. spoke perfect English.

He kept looking from Skyler to Jude and back again, and finally declaimed:

"Two white brothers, one raised in the North, the other down South. You could have your own little Civil War."

He whooped in laughter.

He slipped back into the booth, gave a peppy little talk, put on another record, and took his chair again, all done as seamlessly as a stage performance.

"Disya one fa all de oomen out deh"—this one is for all the women out there—he said.

When he returned, Skyler handed him a beer and said: "Dat de bes."

The man shot up in his seat and clapped him on the shoulder and came out with a grin.

"Now wheyside oona laarn fa taak Gullah taak?"—Where did you learn to talk Gullah?

"I laarn 'em right down yuh. I taak em only jes a lee-lee bit, dough. I a frien of Kuta, de jazz playa."

"Oh, yeah now, him a great musician."

Skyler translated for Jude: "He asked me where I learned Gullah. I told him down here, Kuta taught me a few words—he knows him, says he's a great musician."

"Ask him . . . Never mind, I'll ask him."

Jude turned to the Bozman. "Can you tell us where Kuta lives? What's the name of his island?"

The D.J. gave a basso laugh and pointed at Skyler. "But he should know—he was raised down here."

"That's just it, that's the strange part. He was raised here, but he doesn't know the name of the place, and—"

The D.J. slipped away back inside the booth. More chatter, another record.

Another half hour and three more beers and they still couldn't come up with the name. The Bozman, who didn't understand how Skyler could grow up not knowing where in God's creation he was, only knew *of* Kuta. He admired his playing, but didn't know where he hung his hat.

Then Skyler had a brainstorm.

"Bozman," he asked. "Did you ever hear talk of a slave rebellion—a whole band of Africans who stepped off the boat that brought them across the ocean, then walked right back into the ocean and drowned?"

The question found its mark.

"Why, *everyone* knows that. They were Igbo. May 1803, their boat pulled up Dunbar Creek. They sang a hymn to their god Chukwu and marched right back into the water toward Mother Africa. To this day, they call that spot Ebo Landing—that's how it got its name."

"But what island is it on?"

He gave them the name as if it were a present: "Crab Island," he said, smiling broadly and opening his hands palms outward. The answer was so obvious, he seemed to be saying.

He even pulled a frayed map out of a drawer and located it for them. It was the outermost island in a group of eight and it was not far, another forty miles down the coast.

What a prosaic name, thought Jude. How perfect as camouflage for an infernal undertaking. He looked at the shape on the map: it even resembled a crab, with a rounded body and a narrow peninsula leading to a smaller island that looked like a pincer.

Skyler and Jude shook hands with their hosts. The engineer sat down at the console, and the D.J. stepped back inside his broadcasting booth. He put both hands astride the microphone as if he were going to sing, but he didn't. Instead, he chattered, so quickly that Skyler couldn't catch most of what he was saying.

But he did recognize a word here and there, and he could have sworn he heard the Bozman utter Kuta's name. And the song that he then played on the air was jazz, hot New Orleans jazz, and Skyler also could have sworn that the trumpet was being played by Kuta, too.

They decided to spend the night at a Days Inn at Exit 11 on Route 95. The check-in clerk gave them the name of the best place to eat in town. They followed a back road, 99, for six miles until it petered out in the parking lot of a tumbledown wooden extravaganza called Pelican Point. It was tucked away in the marshes at the mouth of a snug harbor. Customers walked in the front door, and boats with fish swimming belowdecks pulled up to the back.

They ordered gumbo with crab cakes and extra helpings of fresh shrimp and swilled it down with beer. It was dark by the time they returned to the motel.

Skyler was too nervous to sleep right away. He stayed up late watching old movies on TV and finally dozed off about one in the morning. Jude raided the mini-bar and had two scotches that put him out. He awoke about five a.m. and had trouble going back to sleep.

He thought of Tizzie and felt like calling her. They hadn't spoken since he'd left Washington. But he didn't want to run the risk. He knew she was playing out her role as a spy; they had to be careful and smart. The best way he could protect her was to keep her in the dark about the important things. And this was important.

He let his mind wander ahead to the day before them. They would go to the dock behind the bait shop on Landing Road—Homer's, it was called. That was the best place to rent a boat, the waitress at Pelican Point had told them. They would pay cash. Then they would head out to the island and . . . At this point, whatever plan Jude had been formulating ran aground. It was impossible to predict what would happen. He felt a gnawing sensation in his stomach.

All this time they had been trying to find the name of the island, without any real thought given to what the hell they would do when they got there. Reconnaissance. Spy upon the Lab. Collect as much information as possible. Fine. But how? Sneak up through the bushes with binoculars? And then what? In the cold light of dawn, whatever grandiose plots he had been hatching over drinks the night before, plots of smashing the Lab and setting free the clones and apprehending Baptiste, or maybe Rincon if he was there—in short, of playing the hero and rescuing the whole situation—

began to look like pitiful fantasies. He had to face it: he didn't really have any plan at all, except to get there and play it by ear and find out what he could find out—all that while avoiding detection. What's more, he didn't harbor any illusions that if the two of them were discovered, they could escape.

The gnawing sensation in his stomach got stronger, and he knew it wasn't hunger. He tried fitfully to sleep for another hour or so, thrashing around upon the sheets that pulled out from the under edge of the mattress and got all balled up, and then finally, mercifully, he dropped off.

He awoke with a start and knew immediately from the light blazing in around the curtains that hours had passed. He grabbed his watch. Christ: it was ten o'clock. He leapt up, got dressed and knocked on Skyler's door. Skyler answered with a towel around his waist and steam billowing out of the bathroom behind him; he had been taking a shower.

That was annoying. He had probably been up for a while. Why hadn't he awakened him? They were getting off on the wrong foot, and they hadn't even left the motel.

Things did not improve once they did leave. They drove down to the shore and had trouble finding a place to leave the Volvo. At the first spot, along a wooded stretch of road, the owner of a faded green ranch house across the way came down and told them point blank to beat it. The next couple of places were more deserted, but the car looked conspicuous; sitting there all by itself, it seemed to invite trouble. Finally, they chose a road that led toward the marshes and drove to the end, where they found a semi-secluded area under a grove of pecan trees. They left it near a beat-up Buick with a rusted grille.

It was a longer walk back than they realized, and by the time they reached Landing Road, they were sweating and red-faced. Homer's bait shop faced the road. On the other side was a bay lined with waist-high grass and black needlerush. In the center of the bank, where it was worn smooth, a floating dock was set alongside four old piers that allowed it to rise and fall with the tides. Four boats were tied up. Off to the right, the road continued over a narrow wooden bridge that looked like it had been built from railroad ties. It crossed an inlet that fed the water on the other side, where it branched into channels separating dozens of marsh islands.

Three men sat on wooden chairs out front, under a sagging porch roof. One of them, with a grizzled face and a neck tanned the color of a peach pit, nodded slightly. The other two didn't look up at all or register Skyler and Jude's presence in any way; one was telling a long story about a trip to Mobile and he talked so slowly, with such long pauses, that Jude didn't know if he'd be interrupting or not.

Finally, Jude asked if Homer was there.

The storyteller looked up, let fly a small ball of saliva that formed a bubble in the dust, sized them up again and pointed behind him. Jude walked inside.

Homer was a young man stripped to the waist and wearing frayed blue jeans. On his right biceps he bore a tattoo of Mickey Mouse holding a dagger; from the tip of the blade fell tiny drops of orange-red blood. He was not unfriendly, even offering some small talk about the weather—that last hurricane had been one of the worst in memory, he said—but he became taciturn when Jude asked if he could rent a small boat. And when Skyler stepped inside, he looked from one to the other almost aggressively and acted as if he were dying to ask a question.

"I don't rent 'em," he said.

Jude pointed at a handwritten sign above a barrel of maggots. It said: BOATS FOR RENT. DAY RATE.

"We stopped," Homer explained.

"But we need to get to the island. Crab Island."

Homer was unmoved.

"Can you take us?"

"You want to rent my boat and me, too."

"Something like that."

Jude reached in his pocket and unfurled a bill roll. Probably not a smart thing to do, but he hadn't come this far to be stopped by a coastal cracker.

"I'll pay what it takes."

That seemed to alter the situation. Homer looked down at the money and quickly looked away.

"It'll cost you eighty bucks."

"Okay."

"And you'll have to wait till lunch." Homer gestured around the store. "Ain't no one here but me."

"I'll make it an even hundred if you take us now."

Homer scratched his head and looked at the old clock over the cash register. It was ten minutes after twelve.

"Guess I could close up early. Let me get my stuff."

He went through a door in the back. Jude and Skyler waited out front, but after a few minutes, Jude went back inside. He heard Homer's voice talking, then waiting, then talking some more. He was on the phone. Jude couldn't hear what he was saying. He hadn't heard the phone ring, so Homer had placed the call to someone. But who?

By the time Homer had shut down the place, putting lids on the barrels of maggots and worms, straightening up, puttering around and extinguishing the lights, it was close to twelve-thirty. He carried his fishing pole with him and put it in the boat. They pushed off from the dock at 12:35.

Skyler rode in the bow and leaned into the breeze as the boat left the inlet and picked up speed. He sniffed the air. A small egret flapped its wings and took off into the sky. Everything around him—the sky, the bleached look of the light, the smell of the marsh grass and mud flats—it was all so overwhelming, so familiar.

Jude, in the middle of the boat, was worrying about any number of things, like where they would dock and whether someone would hear the noise of the motor. He was amazed that Skyler was able to take everything in stride. Jude watched him from behind—you'd think he was out crabbing, he thought. Not a care in the world.

But he thought wrong. Skyler was barely able to contain himself. Wherever he looked, he saw something that conjured up a half-buried recollection. As it receded, the shoreline behind was beginning to look exactly the way he remembered it, as if the silhouette of the treetops was adjusting to fit a dotted outline branded into his brain. Everything called up deep and conflicting feelings of childhood—love and fear, desire and helplessness.

Homer broke the spell.

"So how you're gonna get back?"

"You'll have to pick us up," said Jude.

"Aw, I dunno."

"C'mon. You can't just leave us there."

"Depends what time. Maybe after the store closes. 'Course, it'll cost you again."

They fixed a time for a rendezvous—six o'clock. Jude had no idea if they would be able to make it.

They were let off near Kuta's place. They had to wade ashore, unable to tie up because the dock had collapsed, its wooden planks resting half in the water.

Skyler could see right away that something was wrong.

The shack was damaged by a large limb from an oak tree that had smashed into the roof. One window was entirely missing, and through it they could see a broken mirror hanging at a slant on the opposite interior wall. The old outboard engine had fallen from its stump and lay half buried on the ground, and a fishing net had been blown into the branches of a palm, wrapping it tightly. Broken branches and clumps of leaves were everywhere, and the grass was caked in dried mud that had been shaped into small curves and gullies by cascading water.

They were barely ashore, putting on their shoes, when they heard Homer's boat pull away. The sound from the outboard dropped off quickly and then puttered for a long while before it finally disappeared out of ear-shot, leaving behind a silence so profound that it seemed to be the sound of emptiness itself.

"This was Kuta's home," said Skyler, moving about as cautiously as if he were crossing a minefield.

He pushed open the front door and looked inside. The walls were streaked with water marks, and the floor was thick with mud. The bed was soaked and sagging, but the chest of drawers was still standing, with the old radio on top intact.

"I can't tell if he came back here after I saw the Orderly and left. For all I know, he never returned. Maybe—maybe he was killed."

"No reason to think that. This is all hurricane damage. He may have fled. It's hard to tell if he packed up before it struck."

Jude pulled a drawer, which was stuck. He yanked it hard and it flew open—it was filled with clothes, which he showed to Skyler.

"Well, maybe he left in a hurry," he said.

Skyler saw that the pegs for the trumpet were empty. That was a good sign—his instrument was the one thing he would be sure to take.

They went back outside.

"This way," said Skyler, moving through the trees toward the path to the Big House. He tried not to show it, but his heart was thumping against his chest and he felt his extremities tingling.

The path was blocked in half a dozen places by the trunks of downed trees. They had fallen in all directions, sometimes lying upon the ground, sometimes coming to rest in each other's branches, strange-angled protu-sions that broke the verticality of the forest and turned it into a jungle. The roots had pulled up giant clumps of rich brown earth that rose up eight and ten feet tall, like trapdoors of subterranean caves.

It took them a half hour to reach the Campus.

They moved into the shadows of the trees and waited for several minutes, watching and listening.

"Something's wrong," said Skyler. "This is strange. There are no sounds at all—just the birds and the cicadas."

Nothing moved. No one was around.

"It looks like the whole damn place is deserted," said Jude, whispering despite himself. "If you ask me, it's spooky as hell."

Skyler stepped out of the woods and into the sunlight. He felt it incumbent upon himself to be the leader. Jude followed him.

They walked quietly, following the treeline, until they came to the open meadow and the parade ground where Skyler and the other members of the Age Group had performed their daily calisthenics. Here, too, trees were down; huge slabs of earth and twisted roots tilted here and there like tombstones. The field was packed with a layer of dried mud from the downpour. They crossed it, leaving behind black footprints and several streaks where they slipped and almost fell. On the other side was the path leading to the barracks.

"What do you think?" asked Jude. "You think there's no one here at all? You think the hurricane drove them off?"

"Maybe. But I wouldn't bet on it. That never happened before, and there were big hurricanes when I was growing up. This is strange. I never imagined it could be like this."

A large oak tree had been uprooted and fallen parallel to the path. Instinctively, they moved behind the tree, keeping it between them and the Big House.

Skyler walked around to the door of the barracks, the door that he had entered tens of thousands of times throughout his childhood. He pushed it open, stepped up on the cinder block and walked inside. It was dark, but his eyes adjusted quickly. Instantly, he saw that it was the same and yet different. The beds and furniture were where they had always been, but they were stripped down. Everything that could be carried away was gone. In one corner was a pile of dirty sheets, in another socks, shirts and scraps of other clothing. The evacuation—if that's what it was—had been carried out hastily.

He walked over to a bunk and sat upon a bare mattress, which was damp. He saw that the window above was missing glass. How strange to look around and see the objects he had seen so often that he had stopped noticing them—how different they appeared, how rudimentary and crude. Was the difference in him? In his eyes that had now seen the world "on the other side"?

Jude walked in and looked around.

"I can't say you were raised in the lap of luxury," he said.

He walked to the other side of the room and sat on a bunk, which—by pure chance—happened to have been Skyler's.

"They may have given you the best medical attention science can provide, but they sure as hell didn't care if you were comfortable or not."

It felt strange to Skyler to hear Jude making pronouncements upon his upbringing. He felt an odd need to defend it; it hadn't all been misery and heartlessness. But he remained silent.

Jude stood up and kicked something, sending it scuttling across the floor. He walked over and picked it up, then handed it to Skyler, who looked at it with amazement.

"This was Raisin's," Skyler exclaimed. "This was his toy soldier. He always carried it with him."

He put it in his pocket. Then he walked to the door.

"Let's go to the Big House," he said.

Riding the subway to her apartment on West Eighty-seventh Street, Tizzie was lost in thought. She wasn't especially proud to admit it, but she was turning out to be a good spy—rather, a good *double* spy, which was twice as hard. You had to be always thinking in two heads at the same time.

Uncle Henry had been impressed by her "report" of their trip to Arizona. She'd included enough true events—like their harrowing visit to the mine, the cave-in and Skyler's illness—to make it credible. But she had not, she hoped, given away anything of importance that could tip their hand. That meant walking a thin line indeed.

For example: should she include the car chase from the roadhouse? It depended upon who she thought had been chasing them. If it turned out to be enforcers from the Lab and she omitted the chase—such a dramatic occurrence—then Uncle Henry would know she was duplicitous and never trust her again. But if the villains were some renegade FBI men—and happily she had talked to Jude since his near encounter with Raymond at the Hoover Building—then including it might be giving Uncle Henry some useful information. Why should he know about the FBI's involvement? Or if he already knows, why should he know that *they* know? Wheels within wheels.

Finally, she had left the incident out. And Uncle Henry, as far as she could tell, didn't seem the wiser. That, in turn, told her something—namely, that Uncle Henry hadn't in fact known about the car chase, which helped point the finger of suspicion away from the Lab. On such crumbs do double spies build their edifices of knowledge.

Certain things she never wrote about. Where Jude and Skyler were staying, for instance, or what their immediate plans were. They were too afraid of phone taps to talk about such matters, she explained. Another area that she shied away from—despite urging to the contrary from Uncle Henry—was her emotional life. He seemed to want to know a great deal about her feelings for Jude and for Skyler. But this was the last thing she wanted to put on paper. Partly, the reluctance came because she was revolted at the thought of that man poring over her innermost secrets, partly because she knew him well enough to fear what he might do with the information, and partly because she herself was confused about what she was feeling.

Her goal now was to turn active. She needed to move from information collection to operations. Uncle Henry had talked about research. That's what she wanted to do, and she had been pestering him to do it. She needed to find out about her mother's death and about her father's illness. If they were truly working on a vaccination, then she wanted to be part of that effort. He was right—she *was* good at it. And as any scientist knows, you can't come up with a vaccine unless you know what disease you're fighting. Maybe she could finally get some answers. And maybe those answers would help Skyler and Jude.

She got out at her stop, picked up some groceries and walked home. She had put the key in her mailbox, when she saw a figure waiting in the vestibule, and she knew at once that it was Uncle Henry. He was taking up more and more of her life.

She led him up two flights of stairs, noting how fatigued the climb made him. Once inside, she offered him a cup of tea or coffee, which he declined. He got right down to business.

"Your reports have been excellent," he said. "We have decided to let you into our laboratory. There is much to be done and little time to do it. There are three rules you must obey: Follow instructions. Do not ask questions. And remain at all times within your restricted area. Do you understand?"

She did. She also thought of many questions, but figured now was not the time to pose them. She imagined she'd be allowed one, though.

"When do I start?"

"Tomorrow."

Jude and Skyler did not approach the Big House by walking up the front drive lined by the ancient oak trees. That seemed too brazen. Instead, they walked in the shadows of the trees, keeping their eyes glued on the windows and door for any sign of life.

Not that they expected any. The place was a mess and gave every indication of having been abandoned. Most of the windows were knocked out, several metal gutters were hanging loose and swaying in the breeze, and a large tree had fallen on a section of the roof, collapsing it. One of the front columns had toppled backward, causing the small balcony above to sag dangerously.

The place looked used, decrepit, shrunken—not at all the majestic palace that Skyler had constructed in his memory.

When they reached the front steps, he went first. He treaded lightly upon the old wooden steps and tried the front door. It was stuck. He tugged, then took the brass knob in both hands and pulled with all his might. The door flew open, crashing against the outer wall with a force that shook loose a shower of rainwater trapped on the balcony above.

They exchanged looks and froze. When a half minute passed, they relaxed. If that sound didn't arouse a response, it was likely the place was deserted. They stepped inside, no longer worried about making noise.

First, they went to the basement room in front, the very one that Skyler and Julia had snuck into so long ago when they were spying upon Rincon and trying to hear what he was saying. Jude went down the staircase first and watched Skyler come after him, looking at his face, which was strained and breaking out in perspiration.

This has to be hard on him, thought Jude.

They went next to the Records Room, which was mostly empty. Two filing cabinets were there, but their drawers were missing. A table with nothing on it had been shoved into a corner. Half a dozen pieces of paper lay on the floor. Jude turned them over; they were blank.

"Nothing," said Skyler. "This is where it all was, all the records."

Jude's heart sank. What could they possibly hope to find now?

He barely noticed that Skyler had moved over to the other door, the one that led to the morgue. By the time he realized it, Skyler was gone, having disappeared through the door into the operating room. Jude tore after him.

Mercifully, this room too had almost nothing in it, nothing to indicate its former use. There were some empty cabinets affixed to the walls, a stanchion, and the floor slightly angled toward a central drain.

The stainless steel table, where Julia's body had been, was also empty.

They went back upstairs, searched the first floor and found nothing. The couches and chairs near the open windows were waterlogged, and branches and leaves had blown inside. Even the ashes and cindered logs in the fireplace were wet.

They climbed the stairs to the second floor, where Skyler had never been before, and split up. Jude walked through two rooms that were mostly empty, retaining only a few pictures on the walls and rugs. He came to a small hallway and knew he was entering the master bedroom.

And there inside was a four-poster bed, a bureau, and a night table. But what caught his eye was an object lying on the floor, incongruously on its side, spilling sand and bits of cactus onto the carpet.

It took Jude some time to realize what it was—a terrarium.

How bizarre.

Jude almost yelled out. He was tempted to share his find with Skyler, to ask him what it meant. But Skyler wasn't there any longer, for he had made a discovery of his own. He had run out of the house. For peering out a window on the second floor, he had spotted the old oak tree, the one that he and Julia had used for sending messages.

And looking at the base of the tree, he saw that the rock had been moved. It was positioned, according to their code, to arrange a rendezvous at the old lighthouse.

# Chapter 26

Skyler ran back into the Big House, yelled to Jude that he would be back, and disappeared under the oak trees. He ran across the Parade Field and past the barracks and into the meadow. He kept running even on the path on the other side that led to the woods, and then finally he had to slow down to catch his breath. From then on he mostly jogged, but when he came to a downhill stretch, he ran again.

He knew it was foolish to exhaust himself like that—he told himself to conserve energy, for he had no idea what awaited him in the lighthouse—but he couldn't help it. He felt driven by a force over which he had no control.

Then he rounded a bend, past the sand dunes and the ruts in the road, and he saw the familiar sight, the old tower rising up with its faded red and white stripes, so incongruous amid the brushed green of the loblolly pine and the pale blue of the sea. He stopped for a moment, squinting in the sun, looking at it. It hadn't changed—there was no outside sign as to what momentous surprise it might hold for him.

He reached the base of the lighthouse and pushed open the door, which sent the birds to flight, a frenzy of beating wings and loose feathers that drifted down slowly to the concrete floor. Then he mounted the spiral staircase, moving with a kind of hunter's stealth, as if he might scare away the prey above, whatever it was. He came to the gap in the stairs, stepped across it and moved higher, his eyes continually on the small passageway at the top. When he reached it, he paused, trying to calm himself.

Then came the moment. He tightened his muscles and pushed ahead, passing through the doorway and entering the glass room. It was hot and the sun's rays refracted from one lens to another in a dizzying crisscross, so that it was like stepping into a gallery of blazing light.

He looked around him. He looked at everything in sight, at first rapidly, sweeping the balcony with his eyes, and then slowly and methodically, so as not to overlook anything. He looked around the glass house and at the metal track, the circular walkway, the giant lens, the ceiling, the floor, the walls. He examined every inch of the place.

Jude had finished searching the master bedroom and a neighboring bedroom when he heard a sound coming from a narrow hallway. It was a grating noise, like something ripping, and it was magnified in the silence of the old manor house, so that it seemed incredibly loud.

Jude's first thought was that Skyler was behind it—he was opening something, cutting something—but he knew at once that that was impossible. Skyler had already left.

He walked to the entrance of the hallway and listened. The noise stopped for a moment and then resumed. It emerged from the darkness and seemed to come straight at him, as if it were directed at him. He felt around for a light switch—there was none. So he took a step into the hallway, feeling the walls on both sides, moving one foot slowly ahead. He continued in this fashion, sliding his feet before him as if he were walking on thin ice. Halfway through, he paused and cocked his head to hear better; the sound was irregular. It was not the sound of inanimate objects.

*Someone—something—is making it.*

He continued down the hall, and now he could see into the room ahead, which was flooded with light streaming through the windows. Still, the noise came.

Then it stopped.

Jude stepped ahead boldly now and found himself standing in a room. He looked around. Nothing was moving. The walls were covered in faded blue wallpaper, and a baby grand piano was standing in a corner, some of its keys missing. There was no other furniture in the room.

Part of the ceiling had collapsed from a toppled tree. A heap of plaster and broken laths lay on the floor, directly under a wide hole in the ceiling. Floorboards from the room above leaned down at the edges of the opening, and sunlight came in through a gap in the outside wall. It was most likely from there, Jude thought, that the noise had come. He waited quietly for a minute or so, and was soon proved correct. The noise started up again—a scraping sound—and the floorboards above shook lightly, bending under the weight of something.

Jude jumped back. Now, suddenly, the noise seemed very loud.

He went to a closet where he found a broom and brought it to the hole and raised it. He pushed hard against the loose floorboards and jumped back, and just as he did, something came crashing down. It was alive, squirming in midair, a creature with a long tail, scales on its back. It landed on its side awkwardly with a grunt, flipped over and scurried away, huddling in a comer. It looked at Jude with a baleful eye that he had seen before. A malevolent-looking, two-foot-long lizard.

They kept these things as pets wherever they went, he thought, as he turned his back in disgust and left the room.

After Jude left the Big House, closing the front door behind him and walking down the front stairs, he waited for Skyler under the oak tree that had been their message board. After a half hour, he saw him in the distance, walking toward him. As he approached closer, Jude could see that he looked odd, his face drawn and tense, his steps mechanical.

Skyler sat next to him and picked up the rock. He explained that he had looked out from the Big House and saw that it had been moved—that no one other than Julia knew that signal. He had run to the lighthouse and searched for a long time, until finally inside the glass room, over in a corner, he had found a note, held in place by a rock.

It was a note from her, written no doubt on the day she had died. A final message, delivered up in love.

She had discovered the passwords from observing the computer operators. She was providing them to him.

"Two words are needed to gain access to the files," said Skyler, talking like a man in a daze. "First: 'Bacon.' And then: 'Newton.' "

He explained about the ditty they had all recited for years.

> Nature and Nature's laws lay hid in night:
> Bacon said, *"Let Newton be!"* and all was light.

"Do you think . . ."—Jude tried to pick his way carefully—"that was why she died? Someone saw her or they found out somehow?"

"I do," replied Skyler.

He held the note in his hand, but he did not show it to Jude. Instead, he folded it up and carefully put it inside his pocket.

★ ★ ★

They spent two hours searching the rest of the island. They examined every building—the Meal House, the storage house, the women's barracks, the guest house, the airport hangar, even the old pump house for the unused swimming pool. And everywhere it was the same. Damage was substantial. Trees had fallen everywhere, crashing down on rooftops and buckling walls. Inside, the buildings were deserted and mostly empty, but with an odd assortment of things left behind in the water-damaged hallways and corners—socks, shirts, belts, batteries, sheets, pillows.

It was impossible to reconstruct what had happened with any certainty. Clearly, an evacuation of some kind had taken place; the members of the Lab had carted away most of their belongings and clothing and medical records and other essentials. Had it been done in panic—perhaps as the hurricane approached? That seemed unlikely. Too much had been taken away in too short a time. Had they returned after the storm? That seemed unlikely, too—the mud would have been covered with telltale footprints.

So the most likely scenario was a planned, methodical evacuation *before* the hurricane had even been predicted. But that raised as many questions as it settled. Why had it been done? After two hours of sifting through the debris, Jude and Skyler hadn't a clue. They didn't even know *how* it had been done—what kind of boats had been used or where they had docked. Never mind the ultimate unknown: *Where* had the boats gone?

One more mystery, thought Jude.

*Why do we always seem to be taking two steps backward for every one step forward?*

He stood next to Skyler on a small rise overlooking the Campus and checked his watch. Still two more hours until the meeting with Homer. From here he could see almost all the buildings they had searched. At least *they* had been methodical. They had looked in every building, in every room. There was nothing left to inspect.

Then Skyler reminded him of one place left to look

"We should check the Nursery. It's on an adjacent island—not far. I think it's easy to cross if the tide is right—though I've never been there."

It took Jude only a second to realize what he was talking about—the colony of small children raised by the Lab. He had assumed, when he heard Skyler talking about them weeks before, that they were another generation of clones. And, like Skyler, he had totally forgotten about them.

Skyler was already off, following a trail that ran north through the woods, and Jude was right behind him. The forest here was dense, and looking at the path they were on, he could see the prints of countless hooves.

After twenty minutes, they reached the northern shore. Jude was winded—they had been going faster than he realized—and so he leaned against a tree with one hand to breathe deeply. He felt his head clear and his heartbeat calm, and he looked around.

This coast was much wilder. The trees dropped away, so that ahead of them was a sea of waist-high grass, extending like a vast golden-green savannah. Beyond was the sea, coming upon them in breakers that washed upon a rocky shore. Off to the left was the island, no more than about two hundred yards away. But it looked like a treacherous two hundred yards. A rocky sandbar served as an isthmus, and it was almost completely under water. To reach the island, they would have to traverse that narrow bar of land. One large wave could sweep them into a channel, where the current, funneled between the two bodies, looked swift.

"Can you tell," shouted Jude over the surf, "is the tide coming in or going out?"

"I'm not sure. In, I think. Even so, we should be able to make it."

"Yes, but can we make it back?"

Skyler shrugged, and it was a gesture that indicated, with its fatalistic eloquence, how upset he was at thinking about Julia.

"I think so," was all he said.

He went back to the woods and returned a minute later with two large walking sticks. Then he undid his shoes, tied the laces together, draped them around his neck and rolled up his pants. Jude did likewise.

Skyler went first, moving sideways while facing the incoming water, feeling the way with his left leg to get a secure foothold before pulling his right leg up. He used the staff for support behind him whenever a wave came. Despite all this, he went surprisingly quickly.

Jude watched him and, once he was ten yards off, followed suit, imitating his movements as best he could. The water was warm and the rocks underneath were covered by seaweed, which made them slippery. Keeping his balance was harder than it looked, because the currents swirling around his legs kept changing direction and velocity. Twice, he managed to prop himself up with the staff just in time to avoid a dunking. At one point, Jude looked up and saw a fishing boat anchored maybe half a mile out to sea.

Soon they reached the halfway mark, and the water got shallower. Then they made rapid progress and reached the opposite shore quickly. Skyler sat down to put his shoes on, and Jude did the same.

"Did you see that boat out there?" asked Jude.

"Yeah. Just fishing. They're always out there."

"I guess."

Skyler looked around.

"I can't tell you how strange it is to be here, standing right here on this land. When we were growing up, it was prohibited even to come near the place. So naturally we had all kinds of fantasies about it—we imagined all sorts of things."

"Like what?"

"Mostly about the children. Who were they? What were they going to do?"

"This whole place must have filled you with fear."

"Not really. Though on some level, I think we probably feared they were going to take our places—"

"Which probably wasn't far off."

"I'd say it's right on the mark. Since we're clones, chances are they're clones, too—only younger ones. It all makes sense when you think about it. That way, their organs could be used further down the line, when ours wear out. Another great advance in extending life span."

Skyler said this with no effort to hide his bitterness, looking directly at Jude, as if he were holding him responsible.

"Anyway," he added. "All this is by way of saying that we don't know what we're going to find here, if anything."

Jude nodded. He had been thinking the same thing himself. Again, he was struck by the fact that his mind and Skyler's seemed to work in tandem. They were so much alike in so many ways—and yet so fundamentally different. He noticed that Skyler, back on his home turf, seemed more confident, more assertive. And again he was proud of him for that—proud and keenly competitive.

"You know," he said. "Now that I'm here and I'm actually seeing all this"—he waved one hand to take in the island they had just left—"I still have trouble getting my mind around it. I mean, it's just so incredible. This little colony existing off the coast of Georgia, the private laboratory of a madman, producing human beings for experimentation."

Skyler looked at him for a long time without speaking and then just grunted. He stood up.

"Better get going," he said. "Follow me."

The marsh grass was spread all around them. From where they stood it was apparent that this island was much smaller—they could see the shore on both sides where the grass abruptly dropped off. About fifty yards ahead was a line of trees. There the island widened, but it was still narrow enough to cross in five or ten minutes. There were no buildings visible, no sign of habitation at all, except for a thin brown path through the grass. Skyler found it and started off, and Jude followed.

Once the path hit the trees, it seemed to disappear, so they were forced to fight their way through the underbrush, which was thicker than on the other island. There were vines and brambles and thorn bushes that ripped their pants legs and scratched their arms. Their progress was slow, but eventually they came to a small meadow.

It was here that they first heard the sound.

A strange sound, like a low humming or even a moaning, distinctly human but unlike anything they had heard before. It carried on the wind, ghost-like.

They looked at each other, and without a word hurried across the meadow. Ahead was a grove of tall, smooth-trunked palm trees, rising up every which way to reach the sun. Through them they could see in the distance some sort of structure.

Drawing near, they made out a brick wall, about five feet tall, topped by razor wire. It looked solid and impregnable, without an opening. The sound was louder now—coming over the enclosure. They followed the wall to a corner where it formed a perfect right angle, and then to another corner and another right angle. Here the trees were sparse and there was a driveway, a small brick gatehouse, and in the distance a docking area, and beyond that, the sea. No one was in sight.

Skyler and Jude walked up to the entrance—two hinged wooden gates, large enough for a car to drive though, which were standing wide open. They walked through them and found themselves in the central courtyard of an old building, constructed in the French colonial style, with verandas, shielded walkways and slanting tile roofs. It had fallen on hard times; the walls were cracked, tiles had fallen to the ground, windows were broken. A large, spreading oak tree sat squat in the center, its limbs hanging so low that the Spanish moss brushed against the bare ground.

They knew right away that someone was there. Not from anything that they saw, but from the sounds—a mumbling, an echoing cough, a dry groaning, whispers—that seemed to come from the shadow of every window and every doorway.

The nearest door led to a sort of office, which was empty. A stool rested before a counter upon which a book lay, one page rustling softly in the wind. Sitting beside it was a mug whose bottom was coated with a brown layer of coagulated coffee.

Next door was a cavernous room. They paused at the door because the smell was overwhelming, a smell of decay and illness. They stepped inside, and as their eyes accustomed to the dimness, they began to make out shapes and movement—people lying upon bare mattresses that lined the wall. Not ordinary people, but small, wizened figures, turning slowly to look at them.

"Good God," said Jude. "What is this?"

They walked over to a small naked person lying on his back and staring up at the ceiling. He seemed to be a boy, but it was hard to tell. He was totally hairless—bald without eyebrows or eyelashes. The skin on his overly large skull was thin and crinkly, almost transparent, so they could see the veins throbbing underneath. He was about four feet in height, but oddly proportioned, with a bulging head and a small face and a small lower jaw and receding chin, protruding eyeballs and a huge beaklike nose. His skin had numerous yellow-brown blotches upon it. His chest was narrow, his belly stuck out, his knees were prominent and his sexual organs were large.

He was a strange birdlike creature. As they stood over him, his eyes moved and found theirs, and he looked from one to the other, silently. It was like looking into a bottomless well. He was beyond reach, gone. They had the odd sensation they were looking into the glazed eyes of an old man on his deathbed.

They realized they were in a ward of some sort, but no one seemed to be in attendance. There were no doctors or nurses. Their presence created no reaction. The moaning that had brought them there had stopped, and it was strangely quiet, except for the occasional dry cough. The only movement came from a ceiling fan, which turned slowly with a steady ticking. It churned the smells of vomit and diarrhea, spreading them throughout the sick bay.

"They've been left behind," Jude said to Skyler, whispering. "They've been abandoned."

Skyler did not reply. His eyes looked around, taking everything in furiously.

Many were lying upon the filthy mattresses. Sometimes their eyes flickered as Skyler and Jude approached, the only sign that they took notice of them. Others just lay there with their eyes closed, barely breathing, in a posture of exhausted resignation.

A few seemed to be quietly weeping. In the second ward, they again heard the moaning—the sound they had heard earlier beyond the wall. It came from a girl, and when they tried to help her, she withdrew into total silence again, a mummy with wrinkled skin and brown-rimmed eyes.

Many looked like the first boy, with that same birdlike body, except that some had hair which was wispy thin and white.

Skyler and Jude went into a third room. Here were some who could walk, but they did so with a wide-legged, shuffling gait, as if it were hard to move.

Skyler approached one who was pacing slowly in a circle.

"Who are you?" he asked. "What is wrong with you?"

The figure stopped moving and hunched its shoulders and furrowed its brow and looked up at Skyler, bewildered. Then wordlessly, it went to a corner and sat down and put its thumb in its mouth and slowly rocked back and forth.

In the fourth room were three corpses covered with flies. The smell was so putrid that Skyler and Jude could not stay.

Altogether, there were perhaps twenty or so of these poor creatures. None were over four feet tall, and most were under three feet. They had the look of exoskeletons, as if the being inside had shrunk inside a dried husk.

Jude took Skyler by the arm and led him to the center of the courtyard, under the oak tree. He was sick to his stomach and he felt a surge of vomit rising in the back of his throat, but he kept it in.

They stayed there for some minutes, too stunned to speak. Finally, Skyler collected himself and looked Jude in the eye.

"They seem to be children. They're no taller than children. But when you look at them, when you look into their eyes and see the suffering, they look like old people. What's going on?"

"I don't know. I've never seen anything like this. It's beyond horror."

"They're waiting to die—that much is clear."

"But from what?"

"God only knows."

"Do you think they were born like that?"

"I don't think so—why would they have been left to die? Somebody must have cared for them. Somebody must have fed them."

They fell silent again.

"We have to do something," said Skyler finally.

"Yes—but what?"

* * *

In the rear of the courtyard, they found a pump, and from it they drew a bucket of water. Then with glasses that they found in a pantry, they went from mattress to mattress in each ward, offering water to every child. Most did not take it—the water dribbled fruitlessly down their sunken cheeks—but some gulped it down greedily. Skyler tried to wash the glasses each time, worrying about contagion, but that took so long, he soon gave up and simply poured one after another.

They found a shovel in a tool shed and dug three graves out front, to the left of the gate. Then came the moment they had been dreading. They tied pieces of cloth across their lower faces and entered the last ward. The stench was overpowering; Jude opened his mouth and made retching sounds, but nothing came out. They threw a sheet over a corpse, capturing dozens of flies and causing dozens more to circle noisily in the air, and wrapped it tightly around the thin little body. Skyler lifted it easily and tossed it over his shoulder and carried it to one of the graves. He laid it carefully down, and they shoveled dirt in upon it, covering it quickly.

When they were going back for the second body, Skyler stopped Jude by the arm.

"Listen!" he said.

Jude could hear nothing.

"Voices," said Skyler. "I'm sure of it."

He led the way up an outer staircase to the second floor. There was a small tower here, and Skyler found a ladder leading to the top. From there, standing up, they could see part of the island spreading out around them, its lush foliage giving way to a perimeter of green grass and then beaches splashed by white foam.

Behind the compound, they saw six or eight newly dug graves. So someone had been here—maybe they fled when we arrived, thought Jude.

And looking back over the way they had come, across the isthmus to the larger island, they saw what Skyler had heard—four boats had anchored in the shallow water and men were wading ashore. It looked like they were carrying weapons. Others had already landed and had spread out, cutting off access to Crab Island. They were trapped.

"Who's that?" asked Skyler.

"Hell if I know, but they don't look friendly."

"Maybe the FBI."

"Maybe. Maybe not."

Skyler turned and looked at the ocean behind.

"That fishing boat is gone too. It was probably part of it."

They stood there for a couple of seconds, scared but fascinated.

"Well, we can't stay here," Skyler said with finality.

He pointed to the eastern end of the island, where the shoreline bulged and the woods of cypress, tupelo maple, holly and greenbriar ran closest to the water.

"We should head over there."

"That's where they'd expect us to go."

"'Cause that's what makes the most sense."

Jude stood there without moving, and Skyler shot him an irritated look.

"You can stand there and double-think this to death and get caught. Or you can follow me. I'm not waiting around."

Skyler turned and started back down the ladder, and as soon as his head disappeared, Jude went after him. They walked to the ground floor and through the courtyard, hearing the coughs and raspy breathing and low moans that echoed after them. They walked past the one filled grave and two gaping holes, back around the brick wall and razor wire.

As soon as they reached the woods, they felt more protected. The trees and honeysuckle and brush seemed to envelop them, though they knew they could not remain hidden forever. From the tower they had seen just how small the island was; in no time the men would divide it up and beat the bushes to flush them out. Even now, running on the path, they were actually moving *toward* the men, looking for a break in the forest.

About fifty paces in, Skyler cut to the left. When Jude caught up, he saw that he had turned to follow a broad stream. Soon it turned into a swamp—knarled tree trunks, hanging vines, banks of moss and black water skimming with bugs. Skyler stepped into the water and waded through it. Jude followed him, keeping an eye out for cottonmouths and water moccasins. He wondered, with his dread of snakes, whether it was more dangerous to forge the path first and stir them up or to follow behind when they were already riled.

It was hard to find steady footing and keep up with Skyler, who stopped from time to time, glancing back and waving him on urgently. Jude began to curse him under his breath and stopped looking at him, just concentrating on each step. He was sweating profusely. His legs were waterlogged and heavy, and he could already feel exhaustion nagging at him and beginning to sap his fear. He wasn't sure how much more of this he could take.

When next he looked up, Skyler was gone.

He blinked and looked again, then stood stock still. Ahead the swamp ended; the trees stood out in dark silhouette, and through them he could see the pearl blue sky. They had reached the shore.

Jude was about to step out into the grass when he saw Skyler bounding back at him.

"Get back," he said urgently. "The fishing boat—it's right here."

Jude turned, and they ran back into the swamp.

"I think they saw me," said Skyler, breathless. "They must have. I didn't even see them until I was right on top of them."

They went crashing through the water, heedless now of the noise they were making. They kept going until they came to a solid bank, where they hauled themselves out and stopped, the water draining from their pant legs. They listened. Far ahead through the trees, a murmur of voices—metallic-sounding. Someone talking over a radio—more likely, a walkie-talkie. They were hemmed in.

"We've got to find a hiding place," said Skyler. "That's our only hope—and it's not a good one."

They looked quickly around, and both saw it at the same time—a crater formed by the roots of an upended tupelo maple. The hole was partially filled with leaves and sticks and other debris, and they threw in more. Then they jumped in and burrowed down until they were totally covered, and they waited. They waited a long time.

At first they heard nothing, just the ticking and rustling of normal woods sounds. Then they heard the radio voices, snapping on and off across a frequency, barking orders and giving locations. It was impossible to tell how close it was, or what direction it came from, but eventually the sound receded. It got smaller and smaller until it disappeared. But then another sound took its place—the sound of footsteps approaching through the brush, steady, sure of where they were headed, directly toward their hiding place. The footsteps got louder and louder until they came right to the edge of the crater, where they stopped.

Jude and Skyler held their breath. Jude froze, his stomach seizing up. Skyler tried to stare up through the leaves. He thought he could see the tips of a pair of old shoes. A sound right next to his head, the debris being riffled, and suddenly he felt a pain in his side, a stick being jammed in.

It surprised him—he yelped.

Then he jumped up and grabbed the end of the stick and started to pull it down with all his might, until he saw who was on the other end of it, and then he just stood there, his mouth wide open. Jude, down below, had no idea what was happening.

"My God!" said Skyler, his voice flooded with amazement. "You!"

"Who oona spect fa see?" came back the voice, flowing in a familiar cadence.

Jude stood up, the leaves falling around him like scales. An old man was standing there, holding onto a long stick.

The old man looked at him with surprise.

"And who might this be?" he asked.

Skyler let out a laugh, a long low quiet laugh of relief.

"Jude," he said. "Meet Kuta."

He looked up at his beloved friend.

"Kuta, this is Jude."

Jude reached up and shook his hand. He was impressed by the power in the old man's grip. Kuta stepped back and examined him from head to toe, shaking his head slightly.

"If I didn't see it, I wouldn't have believed it," he said. "Well, I expect there're a lotta things that need explainin'," he added, turning and already walking back toward the shore. "But I think we oughta leave that to some other time and some other place. Right now we gotta get you boys outa here."

Kuta told the owner of the boat, a younger Gullah called Jonah, to head straight out to sea until they could no longer see the shore, before turning south for a spell and then moving back toward land. They were relieved to see that no boats were following them.

After forty-five minutes, they put in to a small village on the coast, peopled by Gullah fisherman. Kuta, Skyler was pleased to note, occupied a position of respect. He sent a young man off to bring back the Volvo, and the man obeyed him instantly.

They settled around a table set in the middle of an empty lot. Delicious smells of gumbo and frying fish wafted over from a house next door, where a feast was being prepared for them. They opened up beers, and as quiet settled on the neighborhood and fireflies lighted up the deepening blue of twilight, they told their stories.

First, Skyler recounted how he had left the island and his adventures in New York. Then Jude told about meeting Skyler and how shocked he was to encounter someone who looked so much like him. As he talked, the crowd around the table looked from one to the other, marveling at the resemblance.

Then, when the food was brought over in steaming potfuls and great heaps were piled on their plates and more beers opened, Kuta took the floor. He told about the night when Skyler had left the island, how he had heard a gang of Elders and Orderlies coming from the Big House and had run out to hide just as they arrived, pausing only to grab his trumpet. They'd ransacked his house and he'd assumed they were looking for Skyler, but he wasn't certain.

Then Skyler dropped from sight. Kuta learned that Julia had died, and he observed her funeral from a distance, sadly watching as her coffin was lowered into the grave. But he decided not to bring fish to the Big House anymore, and so he was cut off from any more news. Still, the rumors he heard from friends who still worked there suggested the place was in an uproar. They were moving everything out. For days and days they took boxes away by the boatload.

Everything seemed to come to a head with the hurricane. With the storm threatening to be the worst in decades, a boatload of policemen came to the island with orders to evacuate it. From what Kuta heard, the Elders refused. They insisted upon their right to remain there and barricaded themselves inside the Big House. But some of the Gemini—a small handful—took advantage of the situation and left under police protection and were escorted to the mainland. Skyler assumed that this must have been the small group that had appeared to take him seriously when he tried to warn them that the Lab was dangerous.

"And do you have any idea what happened to them?" Skyler asked Kuta.

The old man just shook his head.

Skyler shuddered at the thought that occurred to him, a thought so frightening that he was loath to say it out loud: perhaps these clones, who like him had opted to go to the mainland, were the "body snatcher" murder victims they had been reading about. It sounded a bit far-fetched at first, but the more he considered it, the more he was struck by the likelihood. Who else would be ghoulish enough to rip out their entire insides? Only someone who would let children like those on the island die of a horrible disease.

He tried to push the thought from his mind.

Kuta told of listening to the D.J., Bozman, and hearing his own record played and then the over-the-air announcement, casual and offhand, that an old "friend from the island" was back in town. He had known instantly who it was, he said, grabbing a beer bottle and raising a toast to Skyler and Jude.

Later, after a few more beers, he pulled out his trumpet and played a few licks. But Skyler and Jude didn't feel like celebrating. They were too upset by what they had seen earlier.

That night, with a full stomach under his belt, Skyler slept in the basement of a large frame house close to the water's edge. The air was fragrant and warm, just as he remembered it from his youth. Jude was sleeping in a bed on the opposite wall—he could hear the rise and fall of his breathing—and Kuta was somewhere upstairs. For the first time in a long while, Skyler felt secure, almost snug.

One thing that bothered him was something that Kuta had said before they'd retired for the night. It wasn't anything much, but it preyed upon the back of his mind, a nagging irritation that wouldn't go away.

After they had all told their stories, Kuta had looked at him and then Jude and then back at him and remarked: "You know, you two keep saying that you're younger than he is. But I gotta say, when I look at you side by side, you two look just the same. If I didn't know, I'd say you were the same age."

And the others who were crowded around all agreed: Skyler looked the same as Jude. What had happened to the age difference? Why couldn't they see it?

# Chapter 27

Tizzie had vaguely heard of the State University of New York branch at Purchase, but had always thought of it as an arts school. And sure enough, when she entered through the unmanned gatehouse on Anderson Hill Road, the first building she saw was the theater.

But the limousine sent by Uncle Henry, driven by a taciturn chauffeur who had raised the glass partition to seal off the front seat as soon as she stepped inside, passed the theater and continued to a wooded area at the rear of the campus. Set off by itself was a compound of nondescript buildings. From the outside it could have been a business school, except for the tall wooden fence that surrounded it. Sunk in the lawn out front was a sign in embossed metal letters: THE SAMUEL BILLINGTON SCHOOL OF ANIMAL SCIENCES.

Tizzie was dropped off at a locked gate in the center of the fence. The chauffeur popped the trunk, put her small suitcase on the ground next to her and motioned toward a buzzer attached to an intercom. Then he drove off.

A disembodied voice asked for her name and told her to wait. After several minutes, a portly man wearing a guard's cap came to the gate, checked her against a photograph that he carried and admitted her. He took her immediately into a small room off the main entry. A bank of monitor screens identified it as the security room.

"First thing, we gotta get you credentialed," he said, seating her before a Polaroid and snapping her picture. "You're going to be a *clearance three*."

"What's that?"

"Not very high, I'm afraid. In point of fact, it's the lowest. But it gets you into your building and the canteen."

She looked quickly at the monitors. There seemed to be four cameras—

three were trained on the outside grounds, the fourth inside somewhere, pointing at a door that had a keypunch lock.

He tossed over a laminated card with her picture on it, already strung with a metal necklace.

"You have to wear it at all times."

She was led out the back door and across a courtyard and into a three-story white stucco building. There was a peculiar smell of urine inside.

"That'll be the monkeys," explained the guard. "They're on the second floor, which is a restricted area. You'll be working on the first. Don't worry—you get used to the smell after a while."

It hadn't escaped her notice that in escorting her, the guard had left his office. Despite the cameras and the ID badges, security was not very tight, she concluded.

The guard knocked on a door; a sign outside indicated it was the office of Dr. Harold Brody—the head of the animal sciences laboratory. The guard left.

"Come in" said a soft voice.

She expected to find Dr. Brody reading scientific papers or going over lab reports, but instead he was seated at his desk, his back to the door and his arms folded behind his head, staring through half-closed venetian blinds at a desolate landscape—a lawn with bald spots leading to the fence. His posture was one of a man sunk in depression.

His handshake was weak, and his mind seemed elsewhere. After fifteen minutes of small talk—so small it was practically nonexistent—he took her up to what he called her "work station." There he introduced her to a co-worker—a young man with bright red hair named Alfred. He gave her some perfunctory instructions and left.

Tizzie took an instant dislike to the carrot-topped Alfred, who was about her age. He was both officious and sycophantic—he had all but prostrated himself before Dr. Brody. To top things off, he was hardly welcoming to her and quickly made it clear he regarded her as his lowly assistant. He kept looking at her badge, until finally she looked at his and figured out why: he had a *clearance one*, which allowed him access to every floor. She pretended not to notice. Why give him the satisfaction?

"How about a cup of coffee?" he said.

"I'd love one."

"No—I mean, how about getting me one?"

When she brought it, she was tempted to throw it in his lap, but she reminded herself that a good spy will do anything, even debase herself, for the cause.

Tizzie rapidly fell into a routine over the next three days. There were moments when she was not altogether unhappy, though why this should be was somewhat of a mystery—for the most part, she missed Skyler and Jude, worried about her father and wondered how she would ever figure out what was going on.

She worked hard and long and spent every working hour inside the cramped laboratory. The job itself was routine and tedious, far below her skills. She stained and classified cells on slides for hours on end, then passed them on for analysis to Alfred, who received them as if they were offerings from a peon. Everything about him galled her: the pens lined up so neatly in his pocket, the way he took notes in a book that he locked inside a drawer, the unctuous tone he used in talking with his superiors when they ate together in the canteen. She half expected him to rub his hands together like Uriah Heep, and once actually caught him doing it.

At dusk, she and the others knocked off and were taken in a bus to an old New England inn, the Homestead, in the nearby town of Greenwich, Connecticut. The lodgings were comfortable, but she rapidly tired of the food, which ran to large portions and heavy sauces. In the evenings, she strolled along the leafy streets past the manicured lawns of the mansions in Belle Haven or read in her room—Agatha Christie and Jane Austen.

Some of the co-workers, including Alfred, were also staying at the Homestead. When she joined them for dinner or a drink at the bar, they never talked about the job they were doing. When she asked them what they did, she got curt answers. Even with her medical background, they shed little light on the overall project; they said they worked in nephrosclerosis or hyperlipidemia or the accumulation of lipofuscin deposits in kidney and liver. That kind of thing.

Yet work seemed to be the subject on everyone's mind, and she derived the sense—as much from what was *not* said as what *was* said—that there was an urgency about it. They were all engaged in some grand overriding endeavor. Perhaps for that reason, conversations about every other topic seemed forced and unnatural, filled with long pauses. After a while, she stopped trying to socialize. It was less of a strain.

From what she was able to piece together, she had little doubt that the endeavor was what Uncle Henry had suggested—they were trying to come up with some kind of vaccine to conquer the illness that had consumed her mother and was eating away at her father. She suspected that others, too, were at risk.

And so, while keeping her eyes and ears open, she vowed to do her own bit, hunching over the high-powered microscope for so many hours at a stretch that her back ached almost all the time.

The slides appeared as if by magic in a box set in a wall. It had a sliding door on either side, and it mystified her that she never saw the opposite door open or anyone putting the slides in; she eventually discovered, when her door would not open, that the box itself prevented this.

She examined the cells—or more precisely, the fibroblasts, the basic unit of connective tissue fibers in humans. She dealt with them in assembly-line fashion, classifying them by appearance, photographing them, staining them with dyes, and, above all, testing the resilience and strength of their collagen, the protein that made skin thick and healthy, before passing them on to Alfred.

By the second day, she had become proficient. She also saw a pattern. The fibroblasts in the cultures divided roughly into two groups—healthy and sickly. She watched the healthy ones producing collagenase to expel the damaged collagen, enthralled by the ineffability of the process. Sometimes the fibroblast was forced to divide to do its work, to produce new collagen. She saw that each time, inside the fibroblast, as the chromosome lined up to split so that it could form two new cells, a little piece at the end of the chromosome got just a little bit shorter. The telomere.

The unhealthy cells were old cells—so perhaps it was a misnomer to call them sickly; they were just tired. The problem was not that they were inactive; quite the contrary. They seemed to turn out huge amounts of collagenase, but instead of clearing out only the collagen in need of repair, the strange part was that it seemed to attack all the collagen directly. Their telomeres were badly shrunken.

She dyed the healthy cells red and the sickly ones blue, and passed them on to Alfred, who conducted his own analyses and tests and wrote the results down in the notebook that he kept locked up.

Working was not the only thing she did. She would leave the room for brief periods, telling Alfred that she needed to use the bathroom. On her first excursion, she went up the staircase to the forbidden second floor, prepared to look lost and ingenuous if anyone discovered her. From the top step, she saw the locked door with the keypunch lock and, trained upon it, mounted on the opposite wall, the camera.

On the second day, she learned the code to unlock the door.

Through the window, she had seen that the guard was out of doors. She left the lab, went across the courtyard and slipped into the security room. There on the monitor was the view of the locked door. She opened a drawer, found the tape machine that corresponded to the monitor and pressed Rewind. The tape fluttered until the image of a person came on, moving backward jerkily. She put it on Play and watched carefully: the figure approached the door, raised a finger and punched the keyboard four times. She played it back and looked again closely at the keypunch until she got it: 8769.

She moved the tape ahead, restarted it and left, checking her watch. She had been away six minutes. Not bad; it had felt like fifteen.

"Where have you been?" demanded Alfred. "The work's piling up."

"Women's problems," she explained, looking down. That usually took care of male curiosity.

He shook his head, but said nothing.

Bending back over the microscope, she reflected that obtaining the code had been the easy part. Using it to get inside the restricted laboratory—and out again in one piece—that would be the trick. She was more than a little scared, and glad that Jude had given her Raymond's phone number—just in case.

Jude waited for Raymond near a grove of pine trees inside the entrance to the park. It was dusk, which was good. That way, he would be able to see the headlights of Raymond's car as it approached. And the parking area was divided into lots separated by trees, which was good, too. Raymond wouldn't be able to tell that he hadn't parked his car there.

He lighted a cigarette and pulled the smoke deeply into his lungs.

Jude had tried to plan everything ahead of time. He knew he was running a risk in showing himself. There was always the chance that the FBI would snatch him as soon as he was out in the open—there wasn't much he could do to prevent that—but he was operating on the assumption that it wasn't him they were after, but Skyler. *He* was the one who could identify the conspirators. The FBI wanted to use Skyler; the Orderlies wanted to eliminate him. Either way, Jude had to ensure that he could extract himself from a meeting without leading them to Skyler—in other words, without being followed.

He could tell on the phone that Raymond was eager. His old friend had sounded desperate for a meeting; he'd made no effort to conceal his excitement at hearing Jude's voice or pretend that everything was normal.

"Where are you?" he said, giving each word its own emphasis. "I need to see you."

"That could be arranged," said Jude, warming up to a role he had seen countless times in the movies—the hunted man calling the coppers on a pay phone. "But it's gotta be on my terms."

"Name them," replied Raymond, falling into the same familiar patter—the gumshoe leading the dragnet.

No tricks, no weapons, no backup, Jude insisted.

No problem, said Raymond—he'd even come without his partner. Jude named the time and place, a spot he had carefully chosen, the Delaware Water Gap, an odd bit of untamed nature only an hour and a half west of New York.

Of course, he'd already been there when he placed the call.

He took another drag on the cigarette and tried to quell that little voice inside that told him he was being foolish.

There was nothing else to do. He and Skyler and Tizzie couldn't take on the Lab alone. They needed allies now. They had done all they could by themselves, and that was a lot: they had tracked down the origins of the cult in Jerome. They had found the island. They had even discovered some co-conspirators. But now they needed help. They didn't have evidence; they didn't know where the group had gone or what it was planning. They had a password that could open up the files, but they didn't know where the goddamned files were.

The discovery of Eagleton's involvement had changed everything. They were up against some powerful people. Who knew how high up this conspiracy extended? Or what it was capable of? Or what could explain that ghastly sight of suffering and dying children back at the Nursery? And meanwhile, if the victims of the killers in Georgia were who Jude thought they were, the group was still murdering people.

The evening was warm, almost muggy, but still Jude felt himself shivering. Nerves. He would have to control himself in front of Raymond—the agent did not overlook weakness in others.

Fifteen minutes before the appointed time, a car pulled up. It was a black Lexus, Raymond's own. He'd probably made a point of using it, knowing that Jude would recognize it from the ferry.

A lanky figure got out and looked toward the pine grove. Jude pulled on the cigarette to make it glow, signaling his presence, and the figure walked across the tarmac.

"I keep telling you, but you don't listen," said Raymond. "That stuff's gonna kill you." He was back to his old self.

"Yeah, and I lead such a healthy life otherwise."

Raymond looked around. "Quite a spot you picked out here."

Jude knew Raymond was registering everything—looking for other cars, another person, something out of place. He thought of a wisecrack, decided against it.

Jude gestured up a pathway that led into the woods behind him.

Time to deal.

"Let's take a walk," he said.

Raymond shrugged. "It's your dime."

They were silent, trudging up through the darkness. The pine needles softened their footsteps and warmed their nostrils with a pungent smell. Jude led the way and, nervous with Raymond behind him, began to breathe heavily as he made his way up a slippery incline. His body took over its own defense, listening intently to the night sounds around him, a rustling here, a small animal darting across the leaves there.

They walked for a good ten minutes, following the path. Twice, Jude had to pull out his flashlight to find the way.

"Don't forget, we gotta find our way back," complained Raymond. "I'm a city boy. Put me in Central Park and I'm helpless."

Jude grunted.

At the top of the slope, they came to a flattened ridge that ran in a straight line in both directions; in the darkness they saw two parallel bands disappearing over the horizon—railroad tracks. Jude stepped on the bank of coal and then onto a wooden tie between the steel tracks. Raymond followed him and looked up and down as far as he could see. It was pitch-black except for what looked like a green signal way off to the east.

Raymond reached into his pocket, pulled out a bottle of pills and tossed one into his mouth. He took out a hip flask and swigged it down. When he turned, Jude got a whiff of whiskey.

"Like I say, a helluva spot," said Raymond. "I hope you checked out the train schedule. What tracks are these, anyway?"

"A freight line. The old Pennsylvania."

Time to end the small talk. Jude started walking west on the railroad ties, with the FBI man at his side.

"I need your help, Raymond. I'm in so deep in this thing, I don't know which way is up."

"You're right about that. Don't say I didn't warn you." He stopped in his tracks. "By the way, that day you guys came to the Bureau, why did you run away?"

"I thought I'd be the one to ask questions."

"You ask some, you answer some. It's called give and take."

"Fair enough. I'll answer it. But first I'd like to know something—those were your guys on that island, right? Crab Island. You were after us, right?"

"Let me repeat something I tried to get through to you last time, on the ferry. You're at a disadvantage here. You don't have a lot of information. You're caught up in something that's big, very big. It's complicated. You don't know who you can trust. So if your question is: were those guys FBI, the answer is, yes, they were. But you asked if they were my guys, and the answer to that is no."

"What are you saying? The agency is split? You have some guys on one side and some on the other?"

"Split is one way to put it. At war is another. Spying, phone tapping, betrayal—you name it. Look, this thing—this conspiracy, whatever you want to call it—I suppose you've figured out by now that it involves some pretty well-connected people. It goes way beyond a couple of crazies who dropped out of medical school because they were convinced they found the fountain of youth."

"Tell me about it."

Raymond sighed. "In a nutshell, there's an inner circle of scientists who have mastered new techniques. Big stuff. Genetic research. They're in league with various high-placed, wealthy individuals. These constitute a conspiracy—I call them 'the Group,' for lack of anything better. It's made up of big names from various power centers—business, politics, the government, the media. They've got millions of dollars at their disposal. Their aims are not altogether clear—other than to keep the work secret, to hold on to the levers of power and to live for a very, very long time."

"How did it get so big?"

"I'm only guessing the general outline. There's this brilliant doctor, right? Rincon. He's loaded with charisma, one of those types who comes along every so often—you just want to follow him, do whatever he says. He's talking about a brave new world. And he delivers—a small investment, a couple of smart medical researchers in an underground lab, and they hit a major breakthrough. They figure out how to clone. First time in history. Mucking about with basic nature—turning two cells into two identical people. That's heady stuff. Now you're prepared to follow this guy anywhere.

"So what do they do with it? The procedure they developed only works at the very earliest stages of life—the fertilized egg. So it has only one application for humans—you can clone an embryo, and that's it. So they cloned their own children shortly after conception. Like you. Like your girlfriend. That much you've already figured out. The original impulse was parental love, mixed with a healthy dose of narcissism. If you can't live forever, at least fix it so your children can. Part of you will endure. Which brings us to what the clones are for. That's the gruesome part—and not incidentally, the illegal part. They're there to supply organs for transplant. You need a new liver, you've got one—your own private stock. So basically, you're creating a whole subclass of humans who are just there to serve you. They're grown to be harvested. Like plants. And you space them out—you have some born five years later, some twenty years later. You keep going."

"The kids on the Nursery. What happened to them?"

"I'll get to that. Don't interrupt. You may learn something. Where was I? You raise the clones on an island. You treat them well—up to a point, because you need them. Your only concern is to isolate them from the general population. Because whatever happens, you can't let them meet up with the originals. That's disaster, because that's when the cat gets out of the bag. As you proved only too well."

"Skyler proved it. He's the one who escaped. I didn't do a damn thing but accost him in the hallway of my building."

"Whatever. Anyway, these scientists are under the spell of this Rincon. He's directing their research. Things are going along okay. They're way ahead of anyone else anywhere in the world. Partly because no one else is really going after it like they are—fanatics, very shrewd, very methodical. Here and there, some legitimate scientists are busying themselves in university labs, but for the most part those guys are regarded as cranks. Sometimes our guys even plant one or two of their own at universities. They do phony experiments on cloning—pretend they've done it, mess it up and end up being disproved. Throw people off the track. Disinformation experiments. Smart, huh?

"Meanwhile they keep working away like busy little beavers in the secret lab. And at some point they succeed beyond their wildest dreams. They are able to clone an already existing adult. We think they made this breakthrough at the underground lab in Jerome—nice work in getting there, by the way. Anyhow, that's really big stuff. That takes it to a higher level. Now you're in the Big Time. Suddenly you can clone anyone. You can clone the President, the postman, your favorite cousin. You can even clone yourself. And that means that *you* can live forever. Well, not forever, but maybe another fifty, sixty, seventy years. Not bad—a whole second life. All you need to do is raise your clone up some place safe and get him old enough, get him through adolescence."

Jude interrupted. "But these guys, the original scientists—they're already old. They couldn't use a clone as a donor until it was old enough to have full-sized organs."

"You're right. We don't know if the original scientists made clones for themselves. You're not so dumb for a reporter. But you still have to learn something."

"What?"

"Don't interrupt when you're finally getting the story."

"Sorry. Go ahead."

"Back to the Lab. The breakthrough is important in another way. It provides you with what you need more than anything else—money. Because now, you see, you can sell your little experiment. It's a dream. Who wouldn't want to buy a longer life? So what if it means you have a clone somewhere—you never see it, you never even really think about it. Maybe you're not even told about it. All you know is you've got your own private little organ bank. It's like insurance. So Rincon and his boys are operating in a sellers' market. They become choosy. They sell it to people of influence. Very hush-hush. A discreet visit to the office. And once they're hooked, they're in your little net, and then they'll use their influence on your behalf. So now you have both money and influence. There's no stopping you."

"So the people they sold it to had clones, too?"

Raymond shrugged. "Who the hell knows? We're talking way-out stuff here."

The railroad track came to a bridge over the Delaware. There was a walkway to one side, and Jude crossed the tracks and took it. Raymond looked out over the expanse of water beneath them.

"Christ, where we going? Across the river?"

"Why not? It's a nice walk."

Jude started across the bridge and, reluctantly, Raymond followed. They could feel the wind whipping down the ravine.

Raymond fell quiet. Jude wanted to keep the conversation going.

"So what are they really after?"

"That's a hard question. I'd say this group—the Lab—they made all these important scientific breakthroughs. That's quite a kick, I'm sure. Must make you feel like you're God or something. Playing around with the cradle of life. They're convinced they really can extend human life—and more important, they've been able to convince others that they can, too. They're selling it. Starting at ten million bucks a pop, from what we hear."

"My God. People would really pay that?"

"Are you kidding? You're talking about some of the most powerful people in the country. People at the top of the world—they've got power, money, fame, access. They've got all that, but they're missing something. What is the one thing they all want from life? To be able to hold on to it. If you could offer these people an extra fifty, seventy years—good, productive years—you don't think they'd take it? You don't think they'd do anything to get it?"

"So you know what they're up to. Why don't you arrest them?"

"It's not so easy. For one thing, you've got to know who they are—all of them. If you screw up and you get only some of them, no good. Then you've just driven them underground and made them even more dangerous."

"For another?"

"Another what?"

"Another *thing*—you began by saying 'for one thing.' "

"Oh. Well, for another . . . a lot of what I'm telling you is conjecture. It wouldn't stand up to a clever defense attorney."

"Sounds to me like you've got a lot."

"You haven't seen the file. It's pretty thin. A lot of field reports, some transcripts from phone taps, newspaper clippings. A lot of blank spaces. If I didn't know better, I'd say somebody's been cleaning it out."

Jude didn't need any interpretation. Somebody within the FBI was working the other side of the street.

"These other guys—in the Bureau—they're the ones who almost killed me in the mine and chased me afterward?"

"Check."

"And blew up the rooming house in Washington?"

"Check again."

"Why don't you stop them?"

"Easier said than done. I think they're more of them than there are of us."

"Who do you trust?"

"I trust nobody. Just myself. And my partner, Ed—that's Ed Brantley. I almost brought him, but I figured you'd freak."

"Why not arrest somebody?"

"Who?"

Jude was quiet for a while.

"How about this multimillionaire you talked about? What's his name?"

"Billington. Sam Billington. Yeah. He was critical. He bankrolled them at some point. Got them out of Jerome. Gave them enough money to buy that whole little island you explored. Not a bad setup, is it? Without that, I don't think the whole scheme would have worked."

"Who is he?"

"Who *was* he. He's dead, remember. He made a lot of money in plastics. Made a good life for himself—didn't want it to end. He became obsessive about it, attended conferences, sponsored research, even advertised. So when he met up with the Lab, it was a natural match. He gave them millions and millions, even on his deathbed. The breakthroughs didn't come in time to do anything for him. But they froze his body, like Disney. So he figured someday science would catch up and they'd thaw out their benefactor. He died happy, from what we understand."

"Let me ask you something else—that web site called W—all about life extension. Did they run that?"

"Maybe. Don't know for sure. I figure they started it, probably as a way to attract clients. But you get too many kooks and freeloaders. It wasn't worth the effort. So they probably dropped it and it just kept going on its own."

"So how did they get clients?"

"Dunno for sure. Maybe super-expensive health clubs. Maybe word of mouth. You get one top guy in there, he's gonna want to tell his friends. They all know each other anyway, these guys who run the world. Like kids in a clubhouse."

"Do you know who they are?"

"Frankly, no. We know one or two. But we need the complete roster. That's why we're hoping to meet your buddy. We wondered if he could identify them for us."

Jude did not want to go down that path, not right now.

"Do they have a name?" he asked.

"Not that I know of. That's why I call them the Group. The way I figure it, there are the original scientists and their kids—that's the Lab. Then there're the rich people they sold their little secret to—that's the Group."

"So the two are separate?"

"Yeah. Probably."

"Did you ever hear of something called the Young Leaders for Science and Technology in the New Millennium?"

"No," replied Raymond. "Quite a mouthful. Who are they?"

"Just a name I heard. Probably doesn't mean anything."

There was a pause as Raymond looked down at the swirling currents below. He seemed suddenly reflective.

"We think there's been some kind of screw-up," he said. It seemed to be bait. Jude took it.

"What do you mean?"

"We're really into conjecture here. But I think something's gone wrong."

"What?"

"Dunno. But maybe they've screwed up something basic."

"Why do you think that?"

"A couple of reasons. One: there's been a flurry of activity lately—phone calls, meetings, that sort of thing. I wouldn't be surprised if they all congregated. Something's going on, some urgent business. We know some of it from the few taps we have. Of course, they don't spell it out; you have to read between the lines. Like I say, we're really into conjecture here.

"And the second reason—that's the Nursery. Yes, we found those kids. They've been transferred to a hospital in Jacksonville. But I can't say the outlook is good."

"What do they have? What's wrong with them?"

"Progeria. Vastly premature aging. Technically, it's called Hutchinson-Guilford syndrome. The key thing about the disease is you take these kids and they're just like somebody who's ninety years old. That's what the doctors say."

"Christ. To die of old age at twelve. Those poor kids."

"It's extremely rare. Those kids on that island are more than all the cases that have been reported worldwide to date. The doctors are stumped."

"You're right—something must have gone wrong."

"Weird things have been happening. Like McNichol's autopsy lab in New Paltz. You went up there. Did he tell you somebody broke in there, actually stole some of the samples? Why would anyone do that?"

"Raisin."

"What the hell is raisin?"

"That's who was killed. He's the clone. He was trying to reach the judge."

"Well, he succeeded. And they killed him for it. And whoever did it suddenly wanted a piece of him back—at least that's my guess. Where'd he get a name like that anyway—Raisin?"

"Doesn't matter. But tell me, the judge—"

"He's been ill lately, hasn't been to work."

"That's not what I was going to ask. Why did you give me his ID? Was it that you wanted me in the game?"

"Yep: I always thought you were a pretty good reporter."

"But why not tell me he was still alive?"

"You may not believe this, but you got to that particular piece of information before I did."

"And why did he freak out when he saw me?"

"Good question. He's about your age, he had a clone, so he was in the Lab. Maybe he recognized you from those happy days back in Jerome, though that's unlikely. Or maybe the whole group knew that your guy Skyler had escaped. Maybe there was an all-points bulletin out for him. Maybe his picture was circulated. Maybe the judge thought *you* were Skyler. Anything's possible, if you think about it."

Raymond hunched down in his jacket for warmth. The wind had a chilling edge to it. They were almost across the river now.

Jude's mind was churning with questions.

"Those guys who came when we were on the island?"

"They were after you. You were lucky to get away. Otherwise, all I can say is—we wouldn't be talking like this."

"And those other guys who've been following me—the Orderlies—what about them?"

"You know as much as I do. All I can say is I've seen them, and they look like psychopaths to me. I'd stay out of their way. They may be the clones of somebody who is . . . how shall we put it? . . . undesirable. You've seen horror flicks, you've read sci fi novels. Once these mad scientists begin brewing things up in the lab, they start thinking about security. If you were in their shoes, you'd probably want a Boris Karloff around—or two or three."

"Tizzie."

"What about her?"

"Whose side is she on? Can I trust her?"

Raymond looked at him hard. "Look," he said. "I'm not a goddamned oracle. You've gotta rely on your own instincts for some of this."

"Tibbett?"

"What about him?"

"Do you know he's a member?"

"I do *now*. What can you tell me about him?"

"Not much. Skyler identified him. He was part of a group that went to the island for some kind of big meeting. Rincon was there, too, but they didn't get a look at him. Anyway, Skyler's sure Tibbett was there. I can't figure him out. The strange thing is, when I look back, I see he's been doing things for me all along. My book was published, it was given a big push. And somehow it was arranged—at least I think it was—for me to meet Tizzie. And the couple of times I've met him, he's always treated me as if *I* were the one who was special, not him."

"Maybe he's just an old-fashioned gentleman."

"Somehow I doubt that."

"So do I. And that brings me to the point of this meeting."

Jude felt his guard go up. They had reached the riverbank and were standing off to one side. They heard a distant rumble—a train approaching. They stepped farther away from the tracks.

"Go on."

"I thought maybe you could help me."

Jude looked at his friend, who appeared suddenly helpless, almost pathetic.

"*Me* help *you*?"

"Look—we don't have time to putz around anymore. We're working against a deadline here. You're in the middle of this thing. You've got Skyler, who can pick them out. You've got Tizzie, who's almost infiltrated the goddamned group. And you are—as you say—*special* for some reason. We need you three."

"But where is the Lab?"

"That's what I'd like to know."

"But didn't you track them to the island? Didn't you follow them when they left it?"

"Jude—this is what I'm talking about. I didn't even *know* they were on an island until they'd already left it. And I got no fucking idea where they are now!"

"Christ!"

"I know. It's pathetic."

"Do you know *why* they left the island? Was it the hurricane?"

"No, that one's easy. The way I figure it, they were all packed up and ready to go. They knew they'd have to leave the day Skyler got away."

The noise of the train was getting louder, so that Raymond practically had to yell.

"So what d'ya say? You gonna help us?"

Jude had time to contemplate the question. The train rushed past, stirring dust and rustling branches and making their clothes flap. It was too loud to talk.

When it had passed, Jude looked at him.

"I may be able to do something," he said. "You want to know who's in the Group? I can get you the list of members, and I can get into their medical records, if we can just find where they are. But I'm telling you—I'm going to demand something in exchange. We'll talk about that later. To start with, I need to see your file."

"That's illegal. FBI files are classified."

Jude just stared at him.

"Okay. I'll see what I can do."

"Okay."

Jude looked off into the woods beside the track.

"Be careful. You were lucky to get off that island, you know. And by the way, there's an all-points bulletin out for you."

"Thanks for telling me. That comes from the other FBI, I take it."

"Right."

"Okay. I'll be careful. You can stop telling me that."

Again, seemingly out of nowhere, Raymond seemed compelled to speak up. His voice seemed full of genuine concern.

"There's something else you should know—these clones. They're not the only ones getting killed. We've lost some guys, too."

Jude started to walk toward the woods. He had hidden his car there, parked along a dirt road that ran for almost five miles before it joined a highway. He could see the surprise beginning to dawn on Raymond's face.

"Hey, where the hell you going?"

"This is my stop," Jude replied.

"Fuck."

Jude was pleased to note that he sounded angry.

"You can find your way back, Raymond. And here's something else. Think of it as a down payment on the information I'm going to give you. One of the top conspirators—it's your boss. Eagleton."

By now, Jude was practically shouting.

"That's why we ran away in Washington. So remember—trust no one."

On Friday, Tizzie decided to make her move. That afternoon, she told Alfred that she wouldn't be taking the bus and would have to leave early because her uncle Henry was picking her up. His name would be enough to stop Alfred from asking questions, she had assumed, and her assumption proved correct.

Instead, Alfred just went into a sulk.

At six p.m., she put away the equipment, picked up her purse and paused at the door.

"Don't have them hold dinner," she said. "We'll be eating at Maison Indochine. I'll bring you a doggie bag, if you like."

The sulk turned into a slow burn.

Maybe it hadn't been wise to rub it in like that, but it sure had been fun, she thought going out the door to the courtyard.

Instead of going to the front gate, though, she looked around and then slipped behind the garage into a four-foot-wide dead space that separated it from the fence. There she waited—and waited. It seemed like hours, but it was only forty-five minutes when she finally heard the sounds of doors opening and people heading out—their voices lightened by a sense of release on Friday evening. She heard the bus pull away, then other sounds of people in ones and twos walking toward the gate and slamming it behind them and starting up cars in the lot outside.

Finally, all was quiet. She was about to emerge from her hiding place, when she heard another sound—someone entering by the gate. Was it a night watchman? She hadn't counted on that. She waited for another half hour, listening intently, but didn't hear anything more. Could the person have left without her knowing? Maybe through a back entrance?

She had to risk it.

Slowly and stealthily, she crept out from behind the garage. In the gathering shadows she crossed the courtyard, used her badge to open the front door and climbed the stairs to the restricted area, the second floor. There was the door—and the camera. Was it functioning at night? She couldn't take a chance. She took off her shoe, rose on tiptoes, and slipped it over the lens.

Then she approached the keypunch. 8769. Immediately, there was a responding buzz; the door clicked open. She was inside the restricted area. The smell hit her full in the nostrils.

Light in the first room came in through the windows, just enough to cast a dim pallor over everything. There were rows and rows of metal cages stacked to the ceiling, and inside were rhesus monkeys, one to a cage. Some grabbed the wire mesh with both hands and shook their cages loudly as she walked by. Others sat almost motionless, as if in a stupor. She noticed that these monkeys were stooped and grizzled, with gray hair on their chins and lining their temples.

She moved quickly past the cages and into the second room, the inner laboratory, a clean, windowless chamber where computers regulated the temperature of the dust-free atmosphere. Microscopes and lab machinery told her this was where she wanted to be. She closed the door and turned on the light.

There on the desk was a pile of reports and lab notes. She sat down and skimmed them, and then kept skimming through daily records, charts and graphs, and computer printouts. Gradually, a picture of the research began to emerge. She went to the counter, switched on the microscope and sampled the slides. They were of cells much like the ones she handled—in fact, some of her stained handiwork, red and blue, were stored carefully to one side.

But most of these cells were different.

She looked closely. Before her were dozens, hundreds, of diseased cells that, like the others, mimicked the symptoms of old age. They looked as if they had simply reached the end of the line—the Hayflick limit. That in itself was not peculiar; what was strange was that *she could see it happening right before her eyes.*

She couldn't believe it. She put in another slide and then bent down to the eyepiece again. There it was—happening again. These cells were in instantaneous terminal crisis. It was as if they passed from the bloom of youth to senescence in the blink of an eye—with no middle life whatsoever. As she peered through the microscope, she had the sensation that she was watching the stages of life play themselves out at high speed—breathtaking in the brutal way that death took the cells at half bloom.

It did not take her long to identify a major part of the problem. The diseased cells were flooded with telomerase, which was odd. Telomerase was supposed to keep cells youthful, by capping the chromosomes with protective sequences of DNA so that the chromosomes did not shorten with replication. All cells had a gene that produced telomerase, but it was switched off and inoperative except in two cases—the cells of the germline, which were passed on from parent to child, and the cells of cancerous tumors.

And yet these other cells, these ordinary cells for skin or bone or organs, were drowning in telomerase. And far from making the cells live longer, the enzyme seemed to be killing them.

It was too much of a good thing. Germ cells and cancer cells. The beginning of life and the end of life.

She turned off the microscope, closed the books, and after a look around to ensure that nothing appeared disturbed, she extinguished the light. It was darker now in the outer room, and as she walked past the cages, her footsteps sounding loud, the monkeys began to stir. One leaned into the cage and screamed at her. Then another. Soon the whole room was in chaos, and she fled between the rows. When she reached the door, she flung it open and quickly closed it behind her. Still the chorus of screams resounded through the building. She reached up behind the camera, retrieved her shoe and ran down the staircase.

Then, as she was crossing the courtyard, she heard another sound, and looked behind her. It was a guard dog, tearing around the building from the rear, coming straight at her. She ran as fast as she could, flung open the door and ran through the entryway to the opposite door. She knew the dog would come around the building after her.

She was right. But she had gained precious time. And now she ran flat-out for the gate. She could hear the low growling, the sound of its paws hitting the ground. Ahead was the door latch. She lunged for it. If it was locked, she would be dead.

It was not. She was through the door and safely on the other side before she knew it, listening to the beating of the paws on the other side, the growls and barks. Only now that it was over did she begin to feel fear overcome her, making her legs tremble. She had to sit down.

She was still sitting when a figure loomed up before her, almost indistinguishable in the growing darkness.

"I knew you were lying," the figure said.

It was Alfred.

# Chapter 28

So how do you want to do this? I call them up right now, we go over there, I denounce you and we see what happens—or we talk first and then I denounce you? Your call."

Alfred was enjoying his position of power. That's the trouble with a sycophant, thought Tizzie. You give him a little leverage and it goes right to his head. *A little leverage*—hell, he thinks he's got me totally at his mercy.

They were driving on Anderson Hill Road, which dipped and turned around the hills and threadbare lots of Purchase, then merged into King Street and entered the multi-acre estates of Greenwich. They passed a small roadhouse with a red neon beer sign beckoning in the window.

"How about a drink?" she ventured.

"Very good. She picks option number two," he said, in the pseudo-resonant voice of a quiz-show narrator.

What an asshole, she thought.

They took a wooden table in a corner. She ordered a vodka straight up and he, not to be outdone, did the same. When it came, she drank it straight down, and so did he.

"Okay, why don't you tell me exactly what you happened to be doing in the restricted lab after dark with no one else around? I'm sure there's a perfectly credible explanation, now that you've had five minutes to think it up."

"What makes you think I was in the restricted lab?"

"The monkeys. They make quite a racket when they see a stranger."

He had her there.

"Not all of them. Some are too old to do much of anything. I wonder why that is?"

The redhead scowled. She had to find a way to play for time. She finished her water and hid the glass under the table. Just then, their second vodkas arrived, and while he downed his, she poured hers into the glass.

"Let me ask you something—why did you suspect me?"

"Give me a break. I've been on to you for a long time. Always leaving. Sneaking around. *Women's problems.* Christ's sake—what do you take me for?"

She was tempted to tell him. Instead, she ordered another round of drinks—it would begin to affect him soon, she thought.

Time for the calculated risk. Sooner or later, all spies—all *double spies*, at least—reach the point of no return.

"I might as well tell you," she began. "I don't see what there is to lose."

She saw that she had his attention. He was leaning forward over the table.

"You figured it out quickly. Not everyone would have."

The appeal to vanity—the oldest trick in the book.

"You're wondering who I am working for, aren't you? Who's behind me?"

He nodded.

"I wish I could tell you specifically because it might be important for you—*very important.* It's crucial for you to know what you're up against—just as it was crucial for me to know what I was up against. These people are playing for keeps—on both sides. Understand?"

He nodded again, a little uncertainly.

This time he ordered the drinks.

"I have to admire the Lab, when I think of all they've done—the breakthroughs, the underground research in Jerome, that island, the colony of clones. It's remarkable stuff."

She raised her glass in a toast. Albert did the same, looking confused.

"It would have been twice as remarkable, don't you think, if the Lab could have done all that without attracting the attention of . . . certain agencies. But in a way, I suppose they are victims of their own grand design. I mean, it's just too ambitious, too big. The web site. All that equipment. It's quite impressive, really, but how do you think for one moment that it was possible to keep it all a secret? People talk, word gets around. You following me?"

He was. She could tell by a tiny gleam of fear that had crept into the corner of his eye.

"I was trying to think just the other day how many laws have been broken. Murder one—multiple times. Conspiracy. Conspiracy to commit murder. Some of these states have the dealth penalty, you know. Organized-crime statutes. RICO. Federal laws. Violations of civil rights. Conspiracy to inflict bodily harm."

She looked off, as if she were contemplating the marvelous scope of the law enforcement system.

"This one starts at the top with capital punishment crimes and goes all the way down to income tax violations and probably even mail fraud. They usually throw that in just for laughs."

"And, of course, these people I'm working for, they know what I'm up to. They know what I'm doing. They even know about you."

"About *me*?"

"Of course—you don't think they're just going to send me there all by myself and stay out of contact. Why do you think I've been taking those walks at night? Anything happens to me and there's going to be hell to pay."

He definitely looked concerned.

"A person could do a lot of time for something like that. You're already in enough trouble as it is."

"Who are you working for?"

He was slurring his words. Time for another drink all around, she thought, signaling the bar maid.

"I wish I could tell you. I really do. They make us sign things, you know. We're pledged to secrecy. But I see a certain doubt in your eyes. I have a number you can call to check it out. The contact's name is Raymond. You don't have to talk to him. Just see who answers the phone. See if there's anyone there by that name."

On a cocktail napkin, she copied Raymond's number. It was time to twist the knife.

"Things could be pretty tough for you in prison, you know, with your red hair. Hair color like that attracts attention. Gets you a reputation. Some of those guys in there—it'll be like waving a flag at a herd of bulls."

He staggered off to the men's room. When he came back, he looked dreadful.

I think I've got him, she thought.

"You know," she said. "Maybe you were the lucky one tonight. Finding me there might have been the best thing that ever happened to you."

He stared at her, angry, confused, uncertain.

"I may just turn out to be your lifeline," she added.

She stood up, almost knocking over the water glass of vodka on the floor.

"There's no need to do anything, no need to say anything," she added, in a voice that had a certain element almost of solicitousness. "Let's just go back to the Homestead and sleep on it. Maybe in the morning, when you've got a clear head, you can call that number. Then we'll get together—see what we can work out."

They left the roadhouse, and she held her hand out for the car keys.

"Alfred, I better drive. You've had too much."

At breakfast the next morning, she was happy to see that Alfred looked horrible. His hair, ordinarily so meticulously combed, was disheveled, and his clothes, usually crisp and pressed, looked as if he had slept in them. She looked closely; he *had*—they were the same shirt and pants he'd been wearing last night. His eyes were bloodshot.

She let him eat in peace and then suggested a Saturday morning outing. He meekly agreed. They drove to a tiny harbor downtown filled with bobbing sailboats. On a pier, they purchased two tickets and boarded a ferry that would take them to Island Beach, a mile out in Long Island Sound.

It was a glorious July day. They sat on the upper deck and felt the sun warming their skin. The sky was a crystalline blue, speedboats purred by heading for the open water, and on both sides of the harbor, Gatsbyesque mansions dominated hills that sloped down to rocky jetties and were covered with lawns the color of billiard felt.

She looked at her fellow passengers. There were teenagers stalking the opposite sex, gray-haired couples engrossed in books, and families out for a barbecue, the men guarding heaps of utensils and grocery bags, the women chasing after children. Not a suspicious-looking person among them.

She felt a tug at her heart. The sight of the families filled her with an unsettling loneliness. Time was speeding along—almost like those cells in the lab—and passing her by.

She fixed her eyes on Alfred. "So. Up late thinking?"

He turned to her with a look of something akin to hatred.

"I tried the number. I didn't talk to the guy. But it was what you said it was."

"Good. Let's start."

"I don't know anything about that other stuff you were talking about. I only know about the science."

"All right, then, let's talk about the science. Do you have a clone?"

When she put the question starkly like that, on the top of a ferry boat cruising through Long Island Sound on a perfect Saturday morning, it couldn't help but strike her as surrealistic.

"No."

She couldn't tell if he was lying or not.

"Tell me about this, then. You and I have been looking at cells. Some young and healthy, others old and dying. Last night I saw a third kind. They were dying so fast, they looked like they were committing suicide. They were flooded with telomerase. Someone altered these calls, didn't they?"

Albert looked out over the water and sighed.

"You're speaking hypothetically," he said finally. "Understand?"

"Yes."

"We're just talking science here. Abstractions."

"To explain how the telomerase got there. Someone put it there. Someone is working on life extension."

He looked at her blankly, so that she felt compelled to continue.

"It's a natural idea. The idea of adding exogenous telomerase into cells is bound to be appealing. I mean, if cells die because their chromosomes get too short, why not put in extra enzymes to keep them long?"

"Of course," he replied, in a hollow voice. "As a way to restore the normal balance or homeostasis which healthy cells maintain."

"Exactly."

"And how—since we're speaking hypothetically—would one get it there?"

So he wanted to be the one to ask the questions. Okay.

"Injection, probably. That would be the simplest method. That's what doctors do when patients are missing something. Like insulin to treat diabetics. Since the pancreas doesn't produce enough of it, the patient gives himself an injection every day, and so replaces the protein his body doesn't produce.

"It wouldn't be that hard to do," she continued. "First, you'd isolate the gene for the protein. Then you'd put it into a bacterium, which starts making proteins from all of its genes, including the new DNA. It divides, you purify the stuff, and you put it into a serum for inoculation."

"Too unwieldy. Daily injections might work for a while—in fact, they do work—but they're a pain. Don't forget, you're trying to get people to sign on for the long term."

"Sign on?"

"Sign on," he repeated irritably. "Sign up. Agree to pay a lot of money in exchange for the prospect of unparalleled health and life extension. If you want to attract customers, you need something a lot sexier."

"I see," she said quietly. "So what is the answer?"

"Hypothetically?"

"Of course. Hypothetically."

"Gene therapy. Use nature itself. Let the cells do the work."

"How?"

"It's simple enough, if you know what you're doing. The technique of polymerase chain reaction can be used to replicate DNA in a test tube. You make millions of copies from a small segment of DNA. Then you need a vector to deliver the DNA into the cells. Viruses are natural vectors—that's what they do. They make proteins by injecting their DNA into cells, using the cells to make virus proteins and then repackaging the viral proteins. So, you put the gene for telomerase inside a virus, have the virus infect cells, and then the cells will take up the gene and start making telomerase."

Tizzie smiled encouragingly. "You make it sound easy."

"It *is* easy," he said, looking out at the water and then looking back. "It's very basic. The problem is, it's so basic that if one little thing goes wrong, it throws the whole thing off. The consequences can be devastating."

"Like what?"

"Like mutant telomerase. Something that goes wrong in the isolation of the original protein or in the creation of hundreds of thousands of copies. Some little flaw, a change in one building block—a base pair substitution or a base pair deletion—and it becomes magnified a thousandfold, a millionfold. You end up with a wild-card enzyme that does the opposite of what you want it to. Instead of adding to the telomere cap, it just sticks there, causing the chromosomes to clump together. The daughter cells don't come out younger and vital with all their DNA. They come out like freaks, with chromosomes missing or, even worse, extra ones added on. And then things really go crazy. The mutant enzyme turns into a cannibal. It actually starts chopping up the DNA, cleaving it in two like a butcher's blade."

Tizzie stopped a moment, to take it all in. It was monstrous.

"That's what I was looking at," she said.

"And then, of course, you can't stop it, because you've created the damn thing to keep going and going. So it goes on and on, until finally there's only one thing that stops it. Cell death. And when you have massive cell death, you have progeria."

"Progeria?"

"Premature aging. Hutchinson-Guilford syndrome."

Alfred turned away, so that his back was to Tizzie and he was staring out at the island now approaching.

"Ironic, isn't it?" he asked. "You set out to increase the human life span and you end up creating Hutchinson-Guilford. You know the average life span of a person with Hutchinson-Guilford?"

"No," said Tizzie. "What is it?"

"From birth to death—12.7 years."

She whistled softly and pressed his arm to make him turn around and face her.

"And have you discovered anything to arrest it. Any vaccine, anything?"

"No."

"So the Lab—the scientists, their children, my father—they're all dying from this."

He nodded yes.

"You bastards."

He was quiet for a while.

"Of course," he said finally, softly, "we're just speaking hypothetically."

"Yes, of course."

"Do you think that's enough?"

"Enough?"

"Enough information. To save me?"

For the first time, she actually felt a flicker of pity for him.

"I think so. Especially if you keep your mouth shut now. Don't tell anyone anything about me. Right?"

"Right. I promise."

Albert looked at the beach, already filled with blankets and people.

"Do you mind if we just take the ferry back?" he asked. "I don't feel like swimming."

Tizzie returned to New York feeling anxious and restless. She didn't know what to do next. She felt it was too dangerous to go on working at the Animal Sciences lab, and besides, she thought she had learned everything she needed to know. She doubted the researchers would get anywhere in the search to tame the mutant enzyme. The stench of failure hung over the place. When she had told Dr. Brody that she thought she'd go back to the city, concocting a cover story about research results she wanted to check out back at Rockefeller University, she wasn't even sure her words registered. He was in the cafeteria, reading a novel, and he waved her off in a distracted way.

She felt herself in a kind of precarious semi-hiding. She didn't want to go back to her apartment. She remembered all too well how Uncle Henry had simply turned up there with no warning. On the other hand, if she didn't go back there, and the Lab checked on her, they'd immediately suspect something. And then they'd hunt her down. So she decided to hide in plain sight—to go home, go to her office, just as she'd told Brody.

And that's where Skyler found her. She'd only been home a few hours, when there was a knock at the door—the sound practically made her jump out of her skin. When she opened it, there was Skyler, smiling shyly. She ran to him and threw her arms around his neck.

"God, it's good to see you," she said, with a depth of emotion that even surprised herself. "How are you? How's Jude?"

Skyler explained that he and Jude had just gotten back to New York the day before, and were staying downtown under false names at the Chelsea Hotel, hoping to lose themselves among the drifters and rock musicians. Skyler had staked out her apartment and seen her arrive, but waited a few hours to make sure she hadn't been followed.

He told her everything about their trip to the island and meeting Kuta and discovering the shrunken aging children in the Nursery.

"I think I can explain that," she said. "We'll meet with Jude and go over everything together—everything that each of us has found out."

Then she told him about the Animals Sciences lab at SUNY and how she'd escaped from the dog only to fall into Alfred's clutches.

She noticed that Skyler looked pale sitting there, and he put his right hand onto his chest and grimaced.

"You're getting sick again," she said, and it was all he could do to nod.

She led him out of the kitchen, through the windowless study piled with books, and into the bedroom. There, she took off his shoes and put him to bed, puffing up the pillows behind him so that he could get a view of the street through the iron grille of the fire escape. She felt his forehead—perhaps a slight fever.

She leapt up and went to the bathroom. Looking in the medicine chest, she found aspirin and gave him three, then leaned over to kiss him gently on the forehead and covered him with a blanket up to his chin. She went out for supplies, bringing a prescription pad with her. Down the block was a drugstore, where she got more aspirin and a thermometer, cotton swabs and alcohol, and a bottle of nitroglycerin tablets. At a grocery store nearby, she bought two bags of food, including four cans of chicken soup.

When she returned, he was asleep. She woke him, gave him the nitroglycerin, took his temperature—it was one hunded—and then brought him a bowl of steaming soup and crackers on a tray. She fed him spoonfuls.

Afterward, he felt better. He sat up in bed and smiled at her.

"I don't know what I would have done without you," he said.

She felt good, better than she had felt for a long time, and she hardly knew how to explain it, given the desperateness of the situation.

She stood up with the dishes and gazed down at him. "Just lay back," she said, "and get some rest." Something was poking at the back of her mind. What was it?

A few minutes later, while she was washing the dishes, she walked back into the bedroom, holding a dish towel in one hand and the soup bowl in the other.

"Skyler," she said. "When you were on the island, growing up, you said they gave you inoculations."

He said they did.

"Did they tell you what they were for?"

"Not always."

She finished drying the bowl and went back into the kitchen.

Jude hadn't expected to hear from Raymond so soon. He found a brief message on his answering machine. No name—Raymond was counting on voice identification. Jude never called from the Chelsea. He checked the machine in his old apartment from various pay phones around the city. He hadn't seen anyone tailing him since he'd returned from the Delaware Gap, but he didn't want to get cocky.

"Call me, quick," was all Raymond said.

From a phone booth ten blocks away, he called Raymond's office. The secretary gave him another number and told him to call it in ten minutes. On the first ring, Raymond picked up. Jude could tell he was at a booth, too, from the sounds of Washington traffic in the background.

Raymond cut to the chase.

"You win. Let's meet. I'll bring the file, you give me whatever other names you have. Right away."

"I thought you said the file was hopeless."

"Not hopeless, just thin. Plus, I've got something new on your friend Rincon that I think will interest you."

They fixed a time that evening and a place in Central Park.

"Don't be late," chided Raymond.

"Yeah, I know. The park's dangerous at that hour."

"Very funny."

He hung up.

Jude entered the park off Fifth Avenue, south of the Metropolitan Museum. The sky was a deep dark blue, and the streetlights were coming on. The footpaths at the edge of the park weren't deserted, but everyone on them was leaving, walking briskly. No one, other than Jude, was entering.

He took the wide walkway that curved north, passing Cleopatra's Needle, and soon the foliage blocked out the twilight and made him feel as if he were in a forest. There was no other soul in sight. It was amazing how quickly the city dropped behind; even the sounds were at first muffled and then seemed to disappear altogether. His footsteps echoed. He felt a breeze come up, rustling the leaves overhead.

The path narrowed a bit and curved gently southwest, aiming for a tunnel that went under the East Drive. As he approached, he could hear the cars humming above and the clip-clop of a horse-drawn hansom cab. At the other end of the tunnel was a circle of light.

But then within the light, he saw something move, a shadow disturbing it, something vertical wavering from side to side. It was a person inside the tunnel, striding toward him. The movement of darkness against light seemed exaggerated, which made the figure appear large and phantasmagoric, like a specter bursting out of a starry well.

Even from a distance he could tell it was a man, and he knew his reaction was crazy—it could be anyone, after all—but Jude retreated. He drifted to the right side of the path, where there were some bushes and a tree, and slipped behind them, moving slowly. He hid, hoping the man had not seen him, and waited, barely breathing. The footsteps resounded against the pavement, getting louder. Seconds later, the figure loped into view as it passed him. It was running, carrying something in one hand.

Jude did a double-take. Something about the man was menacing—his build, the way he carried himself, a look of cruelty. Jude froze in fear. *Was that a file folder the man was carrying in his hand?* Then, involuntarily, he backed away behind the tree, gliding backward like a shadow. He leaned against the trunk and felt the bark against his hands, not looking anymore but only listening, waiting for the footsteps to fade. It seemed to take a long time.

He waited until his heart stopped thundering in his chest, then stepped back out on the pathway and looked carefully in both directions. No one in sight. He listened—only the whirring of the cars overhead. He took a deep breath, released it slowly, and set out for the tunnel. He ran through it, his footsteps sounding doubly loud to his own ears, and felt a burst of relief when he came out into the blue-black air on the other side.

He decided to keep running and followed the path as it skirted Belvedere Lake and mounted toward the castle way up on a bluff. Just the way Raymond had told him. The steepness of the grade slowed him, but he kept running, not caring now about the noise he was making, wanting only to arrive and find Raymond there. At the top of the rise, he came to a narrow path off to the left, hemmed in on both sides by bushes, just as Raymond had said, and he took it. The path curved and straightened, opening into a small bower with a bench to one side. Raymond was sitting on it in the shadows.

Jude felt the flush of fear leave him, the warming glow of relief. He looked again. Raymond was out of his FBI suit, wearing a suede jacket and a scarf or maybe an ascot. He pretended not to notice that Jude was there, remaining seated.

Jude sat down next to him, caught his breath, was about to speak about the man he had seen. Then it struck him—the odd fact of it, Raymond not talking like this, not moving. He poked him with his elbow. Raymond seemed to stir, rise upright a bit more, then, teetering in slow motion and lunging downward, he fell face forward into Jude's lap. Jude looked down. *Not a scarf. It's blood!* Raymond's throat was covered with sticky red liquid, and for a moment Jude just stared in disbelief. When he raised the head gently, straightening the body, he pulled his hand away and saw that it, too, was covered in blood. He saw a knife on the ground.

Raymond was dead! *He's been murdered!*

Jude stood. Raymond's body began to slide again, and he stopped it, propped it back up. He didn't want him to fall on the ground. He wanted him to remain upright in a sitting position. And then he heard a sound in the dark, someone coming behind him on the pathway. He bolted. He ran straight through the woods, into the bushes, past the briars that ripped his sleeve. And when he was out of the underbrush and past another pathway and running across an open field, he turned. And he saw that he was being pursued. A man was just tearing out of the bushes, coming after him. A streetlight cast a funnel of light downward, and as the man ran into it, Jude could see him better, and the sight made panic well up inside him like an explosion in his gut. *An Orderly!* That hideous whiteness glowed under the light like a snowy top.

Jude darted across the field, flying so fast that his feet barely touched the ground. He did not turn to look behind him, but he knew that the man was still there, still coming after him. The field gave way to a grove of trees, and then another pathway, which he took. He ran so hard that his feet slapped the pavement and began to ache. It seemed to him that he heard an echo of footsteps, the banging retort of his pursuer. He turned and looked. He was right. But the man had not gained on him; if anything, he had fallen behind. He was slower than Jude. This made Jude run even faster.

He came to a waist-high wall of stone that bordered the street, and vaulted it, landing on the pentagonal cobblestones of the sidewalk. Two or three pedestrians looked at him, startled. He ran across Central Park West and down a side street, and just as he turned the corner, he threw a look back. The man had spotted him. He was still coming.

Jude had thought that he would feel safer out of the park, that the sidewalks would be bustling with people. But the side street was riddled with shadows; it was anonymous-looking and frightening. The few people he saw recoiled from him, and he knew they would not help him; he was very much alone. He ran up the street, came to Columbus Avenue. This was a little better, some stores, more lights, bigger sidewalks.

He dashed across the street just as a wall of cars was beginning to move forward, and he instinctively leveled a football straight-arm to hold them at bay. He made it to the other side just in time, past a line of blaring horns. He was totally winded. A door was open, a Korean grocery, and he tore inside, swiveling to look through the window. There on the other side of the street was the Orderly, bouncing up and down, looking for a hole in the traffic. He spotted Jude. The sight made him spring forward onto the street, dodging cars, his arms upraised. He looked lost, confused by all the vehicles speeding by, the horns sounding. He spun around, stepped back just as a car swerved to avoid him, then scooted ahead into the path of another. There was a screech and a thud, a scream.

People mobbed the front of the store, looking out onto the street. The cars stopped, a crowd sprang up out of thin air, a circle of babble. Jude stepped outside. He walked over and waited several minutes, then pushed his way through to the front. A woman in a suit was bending on one knee, holding the wrist of the downed man. Another man was talking into a cell phone, calling for an ambulance.

But it was clearly too late. The figure sprawled on the street, his arms akimbo, was clearly dead. Blood was rushing out from behind his head, a little fountain of red that poured into a widening puddle. It had already reached the woman's shoe, and she replaced the victim's arm upon his chest and stepped back.

Jude stared at the inert body, the feet pointing outward, the puddle of blood. What struck him, what intrigued him, was the face and the head. For the body appeared to be the body of a youngish man. But the face was already wrinkled, like an old man's, and the top of his head, where there once had been a streak of albino hair, was now totally white.

That's why he couldn't catch me, thought Jude.

*He's aged.*

# Chapter 29

Jude was badly thrown by the killing of Raymond. He came back to the Chelsea shaking, and he had trouble telling the story coherently. Skyler had never seen him like that and went down the hall, where some musicians were staying, and came back with a bottle of Jack Daniel's.

"Here, take this," he said, pouring Jude a stiff drink.

He took one himself.

Jude told the whole story again. He said it was strange, how natural Raymond looked on the bench, what a shock it was when his body fell forward.

"The thing is, I should have trusted him. I doubted him—I admit it."

"You think it was an Orderly who killed him?"

"No. I think it was the first guy I saw. *He* took the file. The Orderly was probably following me."

Jude took a healthy swig.

"And that's another thing—tell me why the Orderly looked so old all of a sudden, when he was lying there dead. I got a glimpse of him on the subway—or at least one of them—and I promise you, that one was years younger. Somehow it all fits in with those kids on the island—but damned if I know how."

"Tizzie knows—or thinks she does," said Skyler.

Jude was taken aback. Emotions flooded through him.

"You've seen her? How is she? Is she all right?"

"Yeah, she looks okay—tired, though. The important thing is, she's found out some stuff. She wants us to meet at her office tomorrow. To go over everything."

"Her office—at Rockefeller? I don't know, is that safe?"

"She says the place will be quiet. We just have to be careful how we get there, make sure we're not followed."

"Okay. Tizzie! Christ, it'll be good to see her." He looked at Skyler. "You were gone a long time. Were you with her the whole time?"

"Yes. I, uh, I had a little relapse."

"What? What happened? Skyler, are you okay?"

"No, no, I'm fine. It wasn't much. In fact, the timing was good, as it turned out. Tizzie made some calls, and arranged for me to get some more blood. They put that medicine in it—what's it called?—urokinase."

"Did you have to give your name to get the blood?"

"No. We went to some clinic in Brooklyn. The doctor called himself an alternative medicine practitioner. He said he was willing to bend the rules 'for the sake of my health.' He also wanted to be paid in cash—in advance."

"But you're okay now? You certainly *look* better."

"Best I've felt in days."

"Good." Jude lay down on the bed.

"Christ. What a day."

Jude closed his eyes to go to sleep, and Skyler stayed up for a while, watching over him.

Jude and Skyler traveled separately to Tizzie's office, and arrived within five minutes of each other. Tizzie didn't have any trouble signing them in; because of her twins research, the guards were accustomed to look-alike visitors.

She unlocked her office.

"I believe this is the time to put everything on the table," she said. "Everything we know. We can analyze it, think about it and then hopefully come up with some idea of what to do to get out of this mess alive."

She fixed them coffee. As Jude sat in a chair, looking at the African sculptures, he couldn't help but think back to the first time he had met her. The memory carried a small ache, like an echo of a happier time, which didn't surprise him. So much had happened since then, so much had changed, things that he never would have believed.

He felt like laughing to himself. But they were real: just look how his life had been turned upside-down. Back then he had been worried about intangibles like career and relationships. Now he was worried about being knifed in the street.

He looked at Skyler. Again, he was struck by the thought of how much he had grown, how much older and in command he seemed.

Skyler and Tizzie sat side by side on the couch. They looked natural together. To Jude, it suddenly seemed obvious that they had reached a new intimacy. He wondered if they had slept together. He wondered, too, if he was fighting back jealousy—he thought of probing his emotions to find out, like jabbing a tooth with a tongue to check for a cavity. The problem with looking for emotions was you had to know what to do with them once you found them.

But the new situation, whatever it was, did seem to make for a certain awkwardness. It struck him that both of them appeared overly solicitous of him—she poured him coffee and he brought it to him. And Jude kept noticing little things he didn't particularly want to—like how they seemed to lean toward each other ever so slightly when they talked on the couch.

He caught himself. I've been a little off ever since Raymond, he thought. Next I'll be looking for her handkerchief in his pocket.

Tizzie took charge. She moved over and sat behind her desk and asked Jude to tell her everything from start to finish—the trip to the island, meeting Raymond on the railroad tracks, finding his body in Central Park. He recounted it all, including fleeing from the Orderly and seeing him dead as an old man on the street. Then she told them about her reports to Uncle Henry and her time in the SUNY lab and her ferry ride with Alfred.

"Let me ask you something," said Skyler. "What did he look like?"

She made a face. "Repulsive-looking."

"Beak nose—right? Flaming red hair?"

She was astonished. "How did you know?"

He laughed out loud. "I knew his other half—on the island. A Gemini named Tyrone. He was just as bad—he was a snitch, too."

"Christ," said Jude. "We ought to check all these people out with you. You grew up with them, so you know what they're going to do before they do it."

It occurred to him that the remark applied to Tizzie, too.

After coffee Tizzie turned serious, got up and walked around and then sat down opposite Skyler.

"Yesterday, when I asked you about inoculations on the island, you said you didn't always know what they were for. I want you to explain that."

Skyler leaned back, cleared his throat.

"Well, there were the regular weekly injections. Everyone got them—vitamins, I think. At least, that's what we were told. Sometimes gamma globulin, things to keep you generally healthy. Plus all kinds of vaccinations against disease.

"But at one point—this goes back some years, a long time ago—a group of us were given some kind of special treatment. We got injections once a week. It lasted quite a while. Maybe a couple of months—I don't know exactly. I remember the experience, though, vividly, because we got excused from regular activities. But I hated the needles—they were large. And there were a lot of follow-up exams, probing and prodding, that kind of thing."

"How many got this special treatment?"

"I think there were six of us. The group included Raisin and"—Skyler looked down uncomfortably—"Julia. Me and three others."

Jude looked at Tizzie. "What are you getting at?" he asked.

But she didn't answer directly.

"I want to show you something."

Her voice was grave.

She led them out of her office and down the hall, where she unlocked a door. Inside was a laboratory, banks of workstations with thick Formica tops, computers and thin hoses for gas and water. The overhead lights were already on—she had been there only minutes before they arrived.

She led them to a corner, where a microscope was set up. Next to it was a tray of slides. She slipped one in and turned on the power, looked through the eyepiece, turned some knobs and made other adjustments. Then she stepped back and let them look.

It took a while to find the focus point through the long cylinder, but soon they saw it clearly enough—a blob of jelly-like substance contained in a near-perfect circle. A single human cell. She then showed them three more slides, highly magnified so that it was difficult at first to figure out what they were looking at. She provided a narrative.

"The first one shows the chromosomes of a normal average-age cell. Look at the tips. Those little squiggles you see there are telomeres, which shorten each time the cell divides. The next one is an old cell. It has divided the requisite fifty times and is approaching senescence. See—the telomeres are practically down to nothing. The last looks much the same. The telomeres are short, the cell is dying. The difference is that, in this one, the aging is premature—it comes from a boy who is, in chronological years, only thirteen. He has a disease that is causing his cells to die."

"The kids on the island—the Nursery," said Jude.

"Precisely. See how dark the last slide is. That indicates a superabundance of telomerase. Telomerase is supposed to be beneficial. Its job is to cap the chromosomes with protective sequences of DNA. But put it in cells where it doesn't belong, and put in a mutant variety to boot, and you've got a problem."

"And that's what they did?"

"Yes. Think of it. They've already established a procedure for organ transplants, which is the first step on the road to longevity. But old age involves much more than your organs breaking down. It's the whole system giving out—your blood, your cells, your brain, the marrow of your bones."

"I understand."

"You don't have to be a scientist to figure out that human life is complicated. The whole is greater than the sum of its parts. You can't just plug in one organ for another and sit back and think you've solved mankind's quest for immortality. You have to do something more. And these guys are top scientists—they've already solved cloning."

"So what do they do?"

"Once they've created clones, they've got access to a bank of organs. But they need to take it to the next level. So they go back to primary research. The structure of cells, cellular immortality, telomeres. A lot of legitimate research is going on in these areas as it is. The journals can't keep up with it all. So it makes sense that the researcher in the Lab would be attracted to it. And, of course, they've got one great advantage that other researchers don't."

"Which is . . . ?"

Tizzie looked at Skyler.

"Which is that they have a group of ready-made guinea pigs. Human guinea pigs. I'm sorry for this, Skyler, but you should know."

Skyler nodded.

"What do legitimate researchers do when they want to test a vaccine? They use it on a prison population. And that's what happened here. They achieved a breakthrough. They isolated the enzyme telomerase. And they had to test it. Don't you see? Everything was falling into place for them. If cells die because their chromosomes get too short, why not put in extra enzymes to keep them long? How do you do that? The simplest way is by injection. And who do you inject it into? The clones."

She paused for a moment to look at them. Then she resumed.

"They chose three subjects. One was Skyler. He was disposable, in a sense, because he was your clone and you had already left the group. The other was Raisin. We know they devalued him because he was an epileptic. The third was my clone, Julia. Why? I don't know, but one reason might be that my parents had already made it known that they were opposed to inoculations. So I was already marked down—in their minds, in Rincon's mind—as someone with a lesser life span The other three were a control group. They probably got placebo injections."

"I have to admit," said Jude. "What you say makes sense."

"It's the most natural thing in the world to them. They were used to thinking of the clones as objects, to dehumanizing them. Skyler said they would sometimes give them shots against disease. What for? Why protect them from diseases if you know they are never going to leave the island, which is presumably disease-free? The answer is that they wanted their parts and their blood to carry immunization for the day when they would be used by the prototypes."

"Prototypes?" asked Jude.

"That's you."

Tizzie paused.

"One thing I can't figure out is why the regime of inoculations ended. Skyler said they did it for a while and then stopped."

"What's your theory?" asked Jude.

He knew her well enough to know that she would have already come up with an explanation.

"They achieved another breakthrough. This one was a breakthrough of tremendous proportions. It's called gene therapy, and it's brilliant. You don't inject the protein or enzyme directly. Instead, you give the DNA that encodes it. Once you get the DNA into the cell, the person's normal protein-production machinery takes over. The new DNA is read, along with the preexisting DNA, and the sequences are converted into proteins."

Jude watched her in admiration. Skyler was riveted on every word.

"Gene therapy is used now for a number of diseases, particularly genetic diseases. One is cystic fibrosis. Children who have it lack a protein that allows normal functioning of the lungs. Biotech companies are using aerosolized DNA to try to get the necessary gene into the lungs of CF patients.

"That guy, Alfred, up at Samuel Billington virtually admitted that they used it. The advantage of gene therapy, if it works, is you only do it once. The disadvantage is it's hard to control. It's more likely to go haywire."

"What happens then?"

"For one thing, you'd probably end up with a mutant protein. Normally, cells make mistakes when they read their DNA and convert it to proteins. The mistake is usually discovered during what's called the 'proofreading' phase of protein synthesis. But the novel genes inserted during gene therapy probably wouldn't undergo such proofreading, so that mutations wouldn't be caught.

"What happens then? There're a number of possibilities. One is that the mutant variant attaches to the end of the chromosome and just sticks there without adding the cap. This would prevent the so-called good telomerase from doing its job—keeping the ends long. So you have a paradox: instead of extending life by keeping the natural degradation at bay, the mutant would speed the chromosome shortening and trigger premature aging.

"There's another possibility that could affect offspring. Let's say gene therapy leads to an excess of telomerase in the germline—the cells that reproduce to create new life. The mutant enzyme seems to make the ends of the DNA sticky, causing the chromosomes to clump together. During replication, the chromosomes must separate into the daughter cells. If the mutant causes the ends to stick, the daughters might end up with missing chromosomes or extra chromosomes."

"So the offspring could be freaks?" asked Jude.

"Well, they could be damaged in some way."

Sometimes Tizzie was alarmed at how insensitive Jude could be.

"Your theory explains why they stopped giving me injections," said Skyler.

They both looked at him.

"Why?" Tizzie asked.

"If they made a breakthrough using gene therapy, they would surely want to measure it the best way possible. Why use young men and women? It would make more sense to use children. They would show the results more clearly, because the aging process is more visible, and so, more measurable."

"That's it," said Jude. "They switched to the Nursery. And it backfired and caused that disease—what's it called?"

"Progeria," replied Tizzie.

"It might explain something else," continued Skyler. "If Raisin was a member of the original experimental group, then they would certainly want to analyze his tissue after death. They would need to know if anything was going wrong. That's why there was the break-in at the autopsy office in New Paltz."

"Yes," said Jude. He remembered Raymond reaching the same conclusion, but this was more compelling.

The recollection triggered another one.

"How about those bodies that have been turning up?" he asked. "In Georgia and elsewhere. They're mutilated, so no one can identify them—so we can assume they were clones. But their insides are missing, too."

"There is a possible explanation," said Tizzie. "But it's pretty damn gruesome, and it would take a monster to think of it and carry it out."

"Go on," said Skyler.

"It's possible that the organs are required for something. Let's say the prototypes of the clones got the original rejuvenation treatment, that they underwent gene therapy. For a while, everything was going along great. They've arrested aging—they're feeling younger than ever. Then it started turning bad—it triggered premature aging. They try everything. A crash program in research, experiment with monkeys, experiment with child clones—you name it, they'll do it. The people they've sold this bill of goods to are turning ugly. But they come up empty-handed. One way to try to stop it, a last-ditch desperate measure, would be some kind of massive replacement of body parts. Not just heart or lung or kidney, but everything. It's called an organ block transplant. It's rare. The chances of success are not good. But . . . if you're desperate enough—"

"Christ," exclaimed Jude. "Is that really possible?"

"I'm afraid so."

"Then we've got to find the rest of them," said Skyler. "That's why they've taken the clones with them. We've got to find them before they're killed, too."

Tizzie turned off the microscope, straightened the lab, and they walked down the corridor back to her office.

"There're a lot of loose ends," said Jude. "For instance, these guys in the Group, like Tibbett and Eagleton—do they have clones?"

"Who knows," replied Tizzie. "My guess is that they do. But the clones would be too young to help them. You can't transfer an organ from a young child into a sixty-year-old man and expect it to work."

"Do you think"—Jude lowered his voice a notch—"that I have another clone? A young one?"

She was amazed that Jude could be thinking about himself at a time like this, that he'd missed the subtext of the conversation back in the lab. He should have been more concerned about Skyler.

"I think you probably *had* one. The question is: did they give him the treatment? Did he come down with progeria? If they didn't, he's probably alive somewhere. If they did, he's dead."

Jude fell quiet, then went off to the men's room.

Standing before the door to her office, Skyler looked directly into Tizzie's eyes.

"So the bottom line is, if I just got inoculations, maybe I have a chance. If it was gene therapy, I've had it."

She couldn't speak, so she just nodded—yes.

On Monday, an unaccountably pleasant day for mid-July, Tizzie walked to work across to the East Side, feeling a glimmer of hope. Maybe, somehow, things would work out all right. Maybe they'd find the clones somehow and call in the "good" FBI. Maybe Skyler's sickness would lift, like those strains of malaria that recurred with less and less severity. Maybe they'd discover a vaccine and save her father.

Her thoughts darkened: that was a lot of "maybes."

She resolved to visit her father soon. It was hard on her, because he was failing so rapidly, and she didn't know what to do or say, standing there in his gloomy bedroom. She had never felt that kind of awkwardness in his presence before, and she knew where it came from: she couldn't forgive him for all the secrets that had been uncovered over the past two months. Still, she could pretend for his sake. In any case, she shouldn't let two weeks pass without seeing him. He needed her more than ever, now that her mother was gone.

The receptionist greeted her warmly, and her secretary brought her a steaming mug of coffee and placed it next to a stack of mail on her desk, fussing over her.

Five minutes later, the secretary poked her head in the door and said: "You've got an important call."

She picked up the receiver. It was St. Barnaby's Hospital in Milwaukee.

The woman on the line had that kind of compassionate but straightforward voice that is accustomed to dispensing bad news.

"Ms. Tierney. I'm calling because your father was admitted to our hospital early this morning. He is not doing well, and I think it best—if you would like—for you to come see him—as soon as possible."

She added—unnecessarily, "He *has* been asking for you."

The secretary came in with an airline schedule as Tizzie scribbled down the address. It made her want to scream: St. Barnaby's. Room 14B. *The Samuel Billington Pavilion.*

She barely had time to call Jude before she left for the airport. He didn't want her to go—too dangerous—but she wasn't going to risk arriving too late, the way she had with her mother. She promised she'd be careful.

At the hospital, they seemed to expect her. She walked in, holding in her hand the scrap of paper with the room number on it, and before she spoke, the receptionist gave her complicated directions, involving a change of elevators and walkways through atriums filled with potted palms. The Billington Pavilion was lavish, with a chrome-covered elevator bank and a nurse's station done in travertine marble of rough-hewn edges. Fourteen B occupied a full corner at the end of a corridor, and it turned out to be not a single room but a three-room suite that looked like hotel accommodations. A woman in a sky-blue uniform showed her the way and motioned her into a sitting room with easy chairs done up in chintz.

She didn't sit down. She threw her jacket on the chair and opened the door to the adjoining room, which was dim, the only light coming through the slats of blinds drawn across the window. The bed was at the center of the wall, so imposing that it seemed to be the only furniture in the room. She could hear machines going, and also the thin, reedy sound that she took a moment to identify—her father's breathing.

There was no one else there—only him.

His eyes were closed, their lids seemingly quivering. His head was sunk into a large pillow, and the indentation made it look heavy, like a small, hard melon submerged in a canopy of white-tufted milkweed. He looked so frail and even *puny*—that was the horrible word that kept intruding into her mind.

She pulled a chair up and sat next to him and watched him. That might have been a mistake, looking at him like that for such a long period of time. Her thoughts began to drift. She didn't know what she felt, now that the time had come. He didn't look like himself, this wizened pile of flesh and bone. Was he really her father? Could he really have been part of that whole horrible scheme—he who used to tuck her into bed at night and keep the monsters at bay by telling her stories in a loving monotone until she fell asleep? Was the monster—in fact—him?

Something touched her hand, and she jumped, startled. It was his hand.

She held it and looked at him—his pink, watery eyes open, staring at her. He looked lucid. He licked his lips—he wanted to talk.

Was this it? Deathbed communication. The stuff of literature, the time for honesty and absolution. It felt so strange, sitting there, holding his bony hand, feeling so much and so many contradictory things, loving him and despising him for what he'd done. She felt outside the whole situation, outside everything that was happening. It scared her to feel so cut off.

His labored breathing made it hard to understand him. She poured him a glass of ice water and lifted it to him in a bent straw, holding him up gently by the back. He weighed so little, it was like lifting the pillow.

His lips moved, so she leaned down and put her ear to his mouth, feeling his hot breath as he formed the words.

"You know everything."

Was it a declaration or a question? She couldn't tell.

"Yes," she said. "Everything but *why*."

He was quiet so long, she wasn't sure her answer had registered.

But then he began to talk, at first slowly, and then with more urgency as he rallied to tell her everything.

"It was for you. All for you. We wanted to give you a gift. We gave you life, and we wanted to give you more life. It was going to be so beautiful, so perfect. The first ones ever. You were going to *live* it—not wish for it, not dream about it. But *live* it."

She listened then, as he described the Lab in its early days in Jerome, trying to make her understand how exciting it had been to stand at the threshold of scientific discovery, to "do things that had never been done before." He told it as a narrative from the beginning, but, drifting in and out, he came back at different junctures and left great gaps, so that the story was disjointed and spliced out of sequence. She had to re-edit it back as he spoke.

He described Rincon, the mesmerizing power of that person. He told of the first great discovery in the underground chamber in Jerome—how to pull cells apart in the blastomere and keep them alive and make them grow separately. The long discussions about doing that to their own offspring, the endless debates in bed at night—what was best, what was right and what was wrong, the dictates of science. The fertilized egg had looked so small under a microscope, it was hard to believe it came from them. And so finally they had agreed to create what he called her "reserve"—he said the word three times before Tizzie understood it. Not once did he use the word "clone"—or, for that matter, the word "sister."

"We were able to not think about them. They were away on that island. We didn't visit, we didn't see them, we didn't talk about them. Only Henry—he was the only one who went there."

He talked about creating the trio of Orderlies from the embryo of a sociopath. He talked about the break with Jude's father, which came because of his attack of conscience, his opposition finally solidifying on the day Skyler was "activated" as a fertilized egg. And he talked, slowly and sadly, about the car crash that had killed Jude's father, which had not been an accident at all. Finally, he recounted his own break years later with the Lab, which had not been total—they were not stupid, they had learned from what had happened to Jude's father—and how difficult it was to stand up to Rincon. It was all out of love for Tizzie. They did not approve the use of the inoculations; it was too experimental, too risky for them to subject their only child to it.

"And I was right," he gasped, with a hubris that Tizzie thought unseemly.

He talked about the discovery of how to clone from an existing adult—almost ten years before Dolly—and how this had opened wellsprings of money, as the lure of life extension was sold to what he called "the high rollers." By that time he was out of the group, working quietly in Milwaukee, in touch only through Henry, who dropped by to keep an eye on him and make sure that he did not betray them by cooperating with law enforcement authorities.

Her father began suddenly to fade away again. She tried asking him questions.

"Do you know where they are now? Where is the Lab now?"

He frowned, his head moved—but was he saying yes or no?

She asked him about Rincon.

"Where is Rincon?"

He tried to talk, but was seized by a sudden coughing fit. His eyes widened in seeming alarm. Then the coughing subsided and he closed his eyes and he didn't reopen them. He fell back into the pillow in a deep sleep, and then later lapsed into a coma. About three hours after that, he died—more or less peacefully.

Walking down the corridor, Tizzie was too stunned to know what she was feeling. Here she had been waiting weeks—months, really—for him to die, and yet when the time came, she was feeling so many different emotions they seemed to cancel each other out, leaving her simply exhausted.

She was nearly at the elevators when she passed a large examining room with its door open. Something out of the corner of her eye made her glance in, and what she saw stopped her. A large woman was seated imperiously on an examination table, dressed in a hospital gown, and a doctor and several nurses were buzzing around her. Illumination from behind caught the woman's gray hair, as if in a spotlight; it sparkled and radiated wildly in all directions and seemed to cover her head like an aura.

Tizzie almost gasped, so powerful was the sight. The grouping was arranged like a Renaissance painting, *The Adoration of the Magi* or Giotto's frescoes at St. Francis in Assisi, the nurses attending with their heads lowered, almost bowing, the doctor holding his stethoscope to the woman's belly like a blessing.

Then Tizzie noticed something. The woman was elderly—perhaps in her sixties. Her physique was large and her face was strong, with elongated features and a strangely thin and sensitive mouth. But most riveting of all were her eyes, which shone like two lumps of luminous coal pressed into clay. The woman felt Tizzie's gaze, and as she stared back with those black eyes, she seemed to look deep within her.

So engrossed was Tizzie that she almost missed the most striking feature of all—the woman had a huge belly protruding upward, a rounded hill of tightly-stretched skin that she was exposing to the doctor. My God! She was pregnant. She had to be at least twenty-five years past the normal birthing age.

The doctor turned, looked at Tizzie and frowned. The name on his badge flashed at her—Gilmore—and then the door flew closed. Tizzie stood there a moment, the vision of those coal black eyes fixed in her mind. Then she shook her head, left the hospital and went immediately to the airport. She would not stay for the funeral this time. She did not want to see Uncle Henry.

⁂

She met Jude at the coffee shop near the Chelsea Hotel, crowded with the usual morning clientele—unshaven old men nursing cups of coffee, and long-haired and shaven-head rock musicians nursing hangovers. Couples of all types and sexual configurations shared tables.

Jude and Tizzie sat at the table in the corner, waiting for Skyler. She'd passed on everything her father had told her before he died. Now they were feeling stymied.

"So where do we go from here?" asked Jude.

"Hard to say. I can't think of anything. Back to the judge in New Paltz?"

"I doubt he'd be much help. Anyway, Raymond said he was ill."

"Maybe he'd talk to us. Tell us something."

"You mean a deathbed confession? Not likely."

Tizzie wondered if that was meant as an oblique reference to her father. She decided it wasn't. She had told Jude what her father had revealed: that his father's death had not been an accident, and the news had upset him greatly.

She had also described in great detail the bizarre sight of the pregnant woman with the coal black eyes and the doctor who was examining her with reverent caution.

"How about the other FBI guy? What's his name?"

"Ed something. Ed Brantley."

"You could call him."

"That's a crap shoot. Who the hell knows what side he's on?"

"Yes, but you came to trust Raymond. And Raymond trusted him."

"And Raymond's dead."

"Okay. I take your point."

She took a sip of coffee.

"Jude, we've got to do something. We can't just sit here."

Jude was about to answer, but a young man sat down at a table across from them within earshot. He was wearing a black leather coat, tight black chinos, black leather gloves with the fingers cut off and a panoply of silver rings and necklaces; his black hair stuck up in clumps, and his left ear was studded from top to bottom with safety pins and silver earrings. He jangled when he sat down.

He didn't look like a federal agent, Jude told himself. But you never knew. Raymond's death had gone a long way toward reigniting his paranoia.

Out of the corner of his eye, he saw a familiar figure through the window. It was Skyler. Seeing him just appear like that, walking down the sidewalk, Jude was able to make a split-second, halfway objective appraisal. It was like gazing in a mirror. The walk was very much like his own, a casual stride, head up. What impressed him was how much at home Skyler looked on the city streets now—how quickly he had adapted. Jude wondered, were the situation somehow reversed, if he would do as well.

When Tizzie saw Skyler, she looked at him closely. She had been examining him lately every time she saw him, trying to see if he looked older in any way. She couldn't tell.

Skyler entered, spotted them, waved and came over and sat down. He was carrying a copy of the *Mirror*, and he wore a self-satisfied smile.

"I got something," he announced.

"What?" asked Tizzie.

"First things first."

He ordered a cup of coffee, and when it came, he took a big sip.

"I can see how you get used to this stuff. They never let us have it on the island."

"Okay, wise guy," said Jude. "What's up?"

"Have you seen your paper today?"

"No, and I hate it when people call it 'my paper.' What's the big deal?"

"Page sixty-four. Check it out."

Skyler handed the paper across the table. The front-page headline was about a pornography shop that had opened two blocks from Gracie Mansion. It read: PORN MAKES MAYOR HOT.

He turned to page sixty-four and quickly found the item sandwiched inside a gossip column:

EGGHEADS TO MEET

> New York—Young Leaders for Science and Technology in the New Millennium said yesterday it was going to hold its first meeting ever. The group of big-think heavyweights is going to hold forth at the DeSoto Hilton in Savannah, Georgia, next Tuesday. If you've made your vacation plans there and your IQ is below 150, you may want to rethink.

"Holy shit," exclaimed Jude. "That's it."

The young man across the way looked up at them, startled at his outburst.

"They've called a meeting and used Tibbett's newspaper to do it."

"Let's go up to your place," said Tizzie.

As they squeezed past the tables, the young man caught Jude's arm and looked at him through bleary eyes.

"Hey, man, you dudes look just the same," he said, slurring his words slightly. He seemed to be trying to focus on a question. "You in a band?"

"Yeah," replied Jude.

"What's the name?"

"Xerox."

In Jude's room on the Chelsea's fourth floor, Tizzie and Skyler sat on the bed, while he worked the laptop at the desk. In the mirror on the wall above his head, he could see them, their lower halves, headless, side by side on the bedspread. He heard the musical sign-on, typed in his password, and connected to Nexis. The search box popped up.

First he tried to link *Savannah* and *Young Leaders*. Then *DeSoto Hilton* and *Young Leaders*. Nothing. The group had not met there before, or if it had, it hadn't made the papers. Anyway, the *Mirror* article said it was the first meeting.

For the next twenty minutes, he tried various combinations, but without success.

"So what's the problem?" asked Skyler. "We know where they'll be on Tuesday. We just go down there."

"Of course," said Jude. "But then what? We're looking for their headquarters, for the whole nest of vipers. We're looking for a colony of clones, for Christ's sake. We're not going to find that at the Hilton."

"And you think it's somewhere near Savannah. We'll follow them."

"But which ones? There're three of us and two dozen of them. They're coming from all over the country. We won't be able to keep tabs on them. And they know what we look like—remember the judge. So we can't let them see us. We have to spy on them without being seen."

Jude went back to the computer. He tried various combinations of words for another half hour, then began cursing as the computer answered each time the same way: zero files.

He turned in exasperation, and as he looked at Tizzie, he could see an idea take shape, the inspiration dancing into her eyes.

"I've got one," she said. "Try *Savannah* and *Samuel Billington*."

He knew it made sense even before he punched it in, but he still cheered when he saw the file come up. It was a single short article from the *Atlanta Journal and Constitution* dated September 12, 1992. It was about the sale of an old army base sixty miles from Savannah. A Georgia congressman, P. J. Clarkson, had put through a special bill permitting the base, which had been abandoned for years, to be sold into private hands. The buyer was Samuel T. Billington.

"Clarkson, he's that guy you spotted on the floor of Congress," said Jude. "He's a member of the Group. And once again, Billington is putting up the money. He gave it to the Lab."

"It all fits," said Tizzie. "We've found your nest of vipers."

Jude's excitement was mitigated somewhat, though not too much, by a sight that he saw in the mirror overhead. Lifting his eyes to the headless bodies, he saw that Tizzie had placed her hand on Skyler's knee. Not his knee, really—closer to his thigh.

In fact, thought Jude, her hand was probably resting just over his Gemini tattoo.

# Chapter 30

Tizzie rented a car at the Savannah airport, and they headed out of town, threading their way through a countryside of military bases. They took Ogeechee Road across the wetlands that skirted Hunter Army Air Field. Twenty miles later, they picked up Route 144 past Wright Army Air Field. At Route 119, they turned right, toward Fort Stewart.

"Roads may be closed," the map warned, and it was correct. Twice, they passed barricades. They were aiming for the base annex, known during its army lifetime as Stewart II, a secret area that for years was not to be found on any document available to the public. Since the base had been decommissioned and sold into private hands, however, the plans were available through the Army Corps of Engineers. Earlier that morning, Jude had obtained a set, as thick as a village phone book, and he sat up front, guiding Tizzie.

They had to drive twenty more miles north to 280, then west through the small towns of Pembroke, Groveland and Daisy, and finally south toward Midway. They were coming into the military region through the back door.

"Turn here," said Jude.

There were no signs, but the sharp left angle of the turn was a giveaway—and so was the slightly elevated tarmac, suggestive of solid design and good drainage: a road built to carry weight, like military trucks. It was straight as a gun barrel. After a mile and a half, the road entered a grove of tall pines. A dirt road cut off to the left and disappeared into the trees. They took it, hid the car and walked through the pines, until they came to a vast field of foot-high grass.

In the center stood the army base. They could barely see the buildings themselves, because the perimeter was protected with a cyclone fence topped by an angled overhang that was ringed with concertina wire.

"Now what?" said Tizzie. "If they have any kind of security, we won't even make it as far as the fence."

Jude grunted. He pulled out a pair of binoculars and peered through them, moving slowly, left to right and back again, up and down.

"From the little I can see, it doesn't look like there's much activity," he said. "There's a guardhouse at the front gate, but I can't tell if it's manned."

He focused on the razor-sharp teeth of the concertina wire.

"The fence looks strong. No holes."

"Are there lights?" asked Skyler.

"Not sure. There are no lamp posts. But there could be spotlights on the ground. For that matter, maybe the fence is wired to an alarm. I saw a security center on the plans, and it said something about an alarm."

"Great," said Tizzie. "Any ideas?"

"There's a back gate marked on the plans. And if I remember right, a control panel for it about twenty feet in from the fence. That's on the far side, so I can't see it from here. But if we could just get one person inside, he could open it up."

"Getting one in is as hard as getting three in," she said.

"I know that. We'll figure out something. We just need a little time."

"We don't have time. Today's Monday. Tomorrow the Lab meets in Savannah. They'll undoubtedly come here. And once they're inside that fence, they can do anything they want. We won't be able to stop them."

"Tell me something I don't know."

That was something Raymond would say, Jude thought. He missed him—especially at the moment. It wouldn't hurt to have a trustworthy ally in the FBI right now.

"Let's go back to Savannah," Jude said. "We can go over the plans and check out that hotel."

No sooner had they turned back into the woods than they heard a sound coming from the road—a car. They ran back, threw themselves on the ground and watched. The car, a Ford Taurus, moved slowly along the approach road and stopped at the front gate. A man came out of the guardhouse and stooped down toward the driver's window, talking. Then he stepped back and the car door opened and a man got out. The two walked to the back of the car, and the driver opened the trunk for inspection. The guard reached in and touched something.

Tizzie tugged at Jude's binoculars.

"Give them to me. Quick."

She grabbed them and raised them, just as the driver was starting back to the door.

"Show me your face," she urged. "Show me your face, damn it."

The guard opened the door, and the man stepped forward to sit down. Then, as luck would have it, he stood leaning against the open door while they talked some more.

When they left the woods and were walking on the dirt road, Tizzie explained why she had suddenly become so excited.

"I recognized him," she said. "That's the doctor, the one who examined that old pregnant woman in the hospital. His name is Gilmore."

She stepped between Jude and Skyler and grabbed an arm of each.

"And just when I thought it couldn't get any stranger."

They spent the night at the Planters Inn in Savannah. The next morning, after a breakfast of bacon and eggs, Tizzie went off to look for a medical supply store, while Jude and Skyler staked out the DeSoto, a fourteen-story brick building on Liberty Street. They didn't dare enter the lobby, but took turns from various locations across the street.

Skyler was sitting in a coffee shop, sipping cup after cup and swiveling around to keep an eye on the hotel entrance, when he saw a car pull into the circular drive. Out stepped the judge, whom he recognized immediately; he was an older version of Raisin, startlingly frail as he moved slowly through the front door. Skyler went to a pay phone on the wall and called Jude on his cell phone. Jude was three blocks away, and he hurried back. He missed the judge, but he arrived in time to watch a parade of other arrivals.

They don't really look like young leaders anymore, Jude thought, as cars and taxis pulled up at the entrance and disgorged men and women who appeared to be in early middle age yet youthfully dressed.

Tizzie returned in the car and parked across the street from the hotel. They slipped inside and waited there, Jude hunched down in the passenger seat behind a pair of dark sunglasses and Skyler sitting in the back. Seeing Raisin's double had made Skyler quiet. Now he picked up the plans of the base. He located the one building he had been looking for, the hospital, and he began studying it in detail. If they could get one of them inside, there was a way. . . .

A black limo with tinted windows moved grandly down the street, paused for a second and turned quickly up the circular drive, depositing an entire entourage. Then the car drove down the street and turned quickly toward a garage around the corner. Tizzie leapt out of the car, hurried across the street and disappeared inside. A few minutes later, the front door opened and she reemerged.

She gave a hidden thumbs-up as she approached the car and got in.

"That's it," she said. "She took the presidential suite. Was I right or was I right?"

"Okay," replied Jude. "But I still don't understand it. Why in hell is a sixty-year-old woman about to give birth? What's the big deal? Aside from the fact that she belongs in the *Guinness Book of Records*. And what does she have to do with the Lab?"

"Who knows? But if we're patient, I've got a feeling we'll find out."

She looked over at Jude.

"Loan me your cellular phone. Skyler, is the phone number for the base on those papers?"

They sat in the car an hour and a half, conversation at an end and their attention wandering, when suddenly the front end of the limo sprang into view, rounding the corner. Tizzie was so surprised, it took her some seconds to shake off her thoughts and find the ignition. She pulled out two cars behind.

"She must have gone out a back way," she said. "I hope she's in there."

They followed the limo at a respectful distance, and as it took the route they had traveled the day before, moving swiftly and with assurance as if its driver knew the way, their confidence grew. They were reasonably sure now that they knew where it was going and who it was carrying.

The question was: could they get inside the perimeter fence?

When the limo turned onto the base road, they held back until it was out of sight. They waited a full ten minutes, then took the turn and peeled off onto the dirt road into the trees. Tizzie stopped the car, opened a package and put on the white lab coat she had just purchased. Then she produced her badge from the SUNY lab and placed it around her neck. Jude and Skyler stepped out. Each of them hugged her.

"Good luck," said Jude. "I'm still not sure about this."

"It's our only chance. I've got the coat, the badge. If I can convince them I'm Gilmore's assistant and let me in, then we can follow Skyler's plan. What other choice do we have?"

They turned and walked into the trees as she pulled away in the car. They took up the same position on the edge of the field and watched as her car pulled up to the gate. A guard stepped out to speak to her. He was carrying a clipboard and he looked at it.

"Shit," said Jude. "Let's hope Gilmore *has* an assistant. Or she'll have to do some fast footwork."

The guard peered at her badge. She held it up for him to get a good look. Then he went back to the list and made a check mark.

It seemed to them that they were talking a long time—too long. But finally, Tizzie stepped out and opened the trunk. As the guard looked inside, Jude peered through the binoculars and spotted her hand behind her back, the thumb raised once again. In no time, she was back inside the car and the front gate yawned open to admit her. Then she disappeared—inside.

"We should get in position," said Skyler. "She might make it to the control box and throw the switch right away."

He didn't tell Jude, but he was beginning to feel ill again. It came upon him suddenly, starting with a feebleness in the legs. He knew the symptoms that would soon follow: a heaviness in all his limbs, then a weakness and a horrible pain in the chest that might lead to a blackout.

He prayed that he would be strong enough to do what he had to do.

They followed the line of the trees around the field. Skyler went behind Jude and found it hard to keep up; he felt as if he were walking through knee-high water. Twice, he had to stop to catch his breath. Jude walked ahead without realizing that he was alone, then stopped to wait for him.

"C'mon," he said. "We've got to hurry."

When they finally reached the rear of the base, they lay on the ground while Jude reconnoitered through the binoculars. Skyler was breathing heavily. Jude poked him with an elbow, still looking through the field glasses.

"There's a drainage ditch over there." He pointed to a spot about twenty yards away. "It looks like it leads right up to the fence not far from the back gate. We can take it. It'll give us some cover."

He was off again, moving back through the woods. Skyler found it difficult to get up, pushing himself off the ground with his arms.

Jude positioned himself behind a bush, lowered his head and ran in a half crouch across the field until he reached the ditch, throwing himself into it headfirst. He didn't disappear—Skyler could see his back and the top of his head—but he was harder to spot. If they have lookouts, they'll catch us, Skyler thought as Jude looked back and waved him forward urgently.

Running was hard. He felt weak and exposed, both at the same time, and when he reached the ditch, he flung himself down and just wanted to stay there. But Jude was already ahead, crawling on his belly with the weeds on either side partially concealing him. Skyler felt a surge of adrenaline and followed, wriggling painfully, digging in with his knees and elbows. It felt as if he were pulling himself bodily up a cliff.

By the time he arrived at Jude's feet and looked up, the fence looming over him with its sharpened wire coils silhouetted against the sky, he was exhausted.

"Stay here," Jude whispered. "I'll try the gate."

And he was out of the ditch, hugging the fence until he reached the cast iron gate with a metal handhold. He tugged it, then pulled harder. Skyler could see him mouthing swear words as he tried to heave it outward with both hands, straining with his arms and shoulders. No success—the gate was solidly closed, locked. He looked over at Skyler helplessly, then darted back to the ditch.

"We're screwed," he said.

Skyler's heart sank, but he knew there was another possibility.

"Maybe not."

Skyler pointed dead ahead where the ditch dipped a bit and disappeared into a culvert at the bottom of the fence. The opening was under two feet in diameter, a tight fit, and it disappeared into blackness. But it might work.

"I hate that," said Jude. "You go first."

And Skyler did. A few feet in, his way was blocked by a metal grate. He squeezed his fingers through the grid and tugged. It gave a bit, but remained in place. He undid his belt, pulled it out and threaded one end through a hole near the periphery. He backed up and pulled, with Jude helping him, until the grate popped out, crashing to the ground. They pulled it out, and Skyler set out again.

He pulled himself forward again until he felt the concrete cylinder enclose him on all sides. He wanted to lift his head so that he could face forward, but there was no room and he kept banging it. He extended his hands ahead of him, for protection as much as anything, and squeezed himself ahead inches at a time. He felt something cold and clammy on his elbows, then his chest and belly and thighs. It seeped into his clothes. Rank water. If it rises, he thought, six inches—it's all over, I won't be able to breathe.

He halted for a minute to fight down a rising panic. Behind him, he could hear Jude, grunting and straining. He felt even more trapped with him trailing behind.

Then came the sound—high-pitched, excruciatingly loud, a ringing. It seemed to scream, almost inside the pipe itself. Skyler's heart pounded. The sound stopped, dying out in an echo. Then it started again, as loud as ever, and stopped again. Finally, it started and cut off abruptly.

Jude cursed.

"Goddammit."

Skyler heard him struggling, the noise of arms flailing about, a tiny splash.

"Goddamned phone."

Jude whispered into it. It was Tizzie.

"I know it's locked," he said. "We're underground, dammit. Why the hell did you call? The noise is deafening."

Jude was silent for a while, then spoke softly.

"Okay. And for God's sake, don't call again."

He clicked off. Then he whispered to Skyler.

"She says she thinks she knows where this ends. There's a manhole or something inside the fence. Just hope this leads there."

"She's okay?"

"Sounded okay."

His voice echoed underground.

Skyler kept going in the darkness. He felt that if he stopped, he would be unable to summon the strength to begin again. Progress was measured in inches, and they were harder and harder to come by. After ten minutes, his hand reached a pool of water. He pulled himself forward, and he entered a different kind of space. He could raise his head and see thin beams of gray light shooting down from above. The pipe led into a vertical cylinder about three feet wide and four feet high. He squeezed his way into it and stood bent over. Water covered his feet. Above was a thick manhole cover.

Either way, he realized, they had come to the end. Either they could remove the cover and get out, or they would likely perish where they were. There was no retreat: the cylinder was too narrow to turn around in and fit back inside the culvert.

Jude's head emerged from the pipe, then his shoulders. He grunted and finally extracted himself, standing up next to Skyler. They were crammed together inside the concrete tube.

"I'm here."

The voice was a bare, disembodied whisper. It came from above—Tizzie.

Skyler took his belt and poked one end through a hole in the cover.

"Put it back through the other hole. Then when I say *three*, lift the belt with all your might," he directed.

The tip of the belt reappeared. Quickly, he fastened the buckle, gave it a tug and he and Jude straightened their legs until they felt the manhole cover resting against their upper backs.

Softly, Skyler counted: *one . . . two . . . three!*

They stiffened and heaved themselves upward, straightening their backs to carry the weight in their legs. Above, Tizzie grabbed the belt in both hands, straddling the cover and lifting with extended arms.

It lifted. It moved. It hovered several inches in the air, as all three of them strained to keep it there. Then Tizzie jumped to one side and pulled the belt from an angle, as hard as she could, so that gradually the cover slid over, scraping against the ground. She stopped, pulled again, and the cover was halfway off, leaving enough room for Skyler and Jude to squeeze past. First one, then the other, leapt up, grateful to be above ground again.

Quickly, they looked around.

No one was in sight. They were midway between two squat, rectangular buildings painted in peeling army gray with black shingled roofs. They looked like barracks or maybe offices.

"Come. Over here," said Tizzie, leading them around a corner to a doorway. It was up a few wooden steps, painted gray, and set under a small eave. A faded sign on the door read: QUARTERMASTER.

They stepped inside. There were four desks, venetian blinds on the windows, filing cabinets—some with empty drawers opened—lamps and wooden chairs.

Tizzie talked breathlessly.

"I found the control box for the gate—no trouble. But when I opened it, it was empty, just some loose wires. I came in here and found the phone, so I called you."

"That much we know," said Jude.

"Sorry about that. But it's okay. No one knows. There's no switchboard. In fact, there's not really much of anything. It's bizarre—the whole place is strange. Half-deserted, things falling apart, a bunch of people walking around looking lost. No one stopped me. No one's even spoken to me. It's unreal. I had this strange thought when I was walking around—this is probably what it felt like to be in some city under siege, one of those walled cities in the Middle Ages. Except no one's doing the sieging."

"No one but us," replied Jude.

Skyler slumped into a chair.

"You don't look good," said Tizzie.

He shook her off. "Don't worry about me. I'm fine."

"I hope so."

She looked at Jude.

"So what now? What's the plan?"

"We look for the records."

She shot him an exasperated look. "Any thoughts on *where* we look?"

"These people are scientists, right? Methodical. Organized. The records are very important to them. We saw their last headquarters, and there they kept them in the basement of the Big House. Chances are, they would do the same here. So I say we go to the main building and look there."

They all agreed it made sense. She insisted on going first. After all, she said, she knew the base somewhat, having parked the car near the front entrance and walked across it. And she was wearing the lab coat, which she felt served as a sort of protective coloring—it and a lot of bluff had been enough to get her inside the place. Jude and Skyler could follow behind and keep out of sight. She would let them know when the coast was clear.

Jude didn't like it, but before he could think of an objection, she had opened the door and slipped outside. They watched her through the quartermaster's window, striding boldly away on the pavement as if she had every right to be there.

If anyone can carry it off, she can, he thought admiringly. It's all a question of attitude.

He was about to open the door, when he felt Skyler's hand on his shoulder.

"Listen. You go after her. You two get the records. I can't. I've got something to do."

Jude knew what it was. He had seen Skyler examining the plans, memorizing the layout of the barracks and the hospital. He knew also that he did not have a chance in hell of dissuading him.

"Okay."

Then they did something neither expected—they embraced each other, tightly, and drew back and looked at each other squarely in the face, and wished each other luck. Abruptly, Skyler turned and stole out the door and disappeared behind the building across the way. When he was gone, Jude left and hurried in the direction Tizzie had taken.

He went around a corner and saw her up ahead, now turning casually to make sure he was there. She continued on, and he followed, trying to look inconspicuous. He did not dodge from building to building—that would have looked absurd and caught somebody's attention—but he tried to stay in the shadows and walk slowly and shrink into the landscape. Tizzie was right: there were not many people around, thank God.

First they tried the general offices, which dominated a cluster of buildings set around an oval driveway. They entered by a side door, and Jude waited in a basement stairwell while Tizzie went from floor to floor. No luck. On the way out, she asked Jude where Skyler was, and when he explained that he had gone off on his own, she frowned and shook her head. Next they tried the supply center, kitchen and the mess hall—four cavernous rooms now unused, marked with falling plaster and white dust on the long tables bearing the delicate footprints of rats.

Then they came to the assembly hall. Three or four people were congregating on the front steps and inside the vestibule, so they slunk around to the rear. They found a pair of double doors—but they were locked. Jude took a credit card from his wallet, slipped it between the two doors so that it hit the catch, and rocked them slowly until it slid open.

"One advantage of a wasted youth," he said.

Instinctively, they went down the stairs to the basement and knew at once that they had found what they were looking for. Through the window of a door, they saw neatly arranged desks and cabinets—the only clean room they had seen so far—and four computers lined up side by side upon a long oak table. The door was unlocked.

Jude sat down at a computer and switched it on. The screen jumped to life, casting a ghostly glow over his chest and forearms. He punched a few keys, and the screen responded instantly in a one-word demand: PASSWORD. Carefully, his fingers almost shaking, he typed in the word that he had learned on the island, the word that Julia had given her life for: B-A-C-O-N. The screen blinked and flipped, turned blank and flashed again with a second request: 2ND PASSWORD. Jude typed the second name: N-E-W-T-O-N. And in no time, a file menu came up. Jude quickly read the items: medical, match-up, doctors, Group members, Lab research, child placement, experiments, births, deaths, journals, history.

He tabbed down to MATCH UP and clicked the mouse. A few more blips, a second of hesitation and there it was—two lists. One to the left, headed *Prototypes*, consisting of names, addresses, professions, families, blood types, capsule medical histories. One to the right, marked *Geminis*, with names, dates of implantation, dates of birth and medical information. Here the address under each name was the same: Crab Island.

Tizzie was standing watch at the door.

"I'll be damned," he said. "Look at this!"

She rushed over and bent down over his left shoulder.

"God."

That one word said it all. It was uttered with a sense of awe. They knew the master list existed, they had traveled hundreds of miles to find it and endured hardship to attain it, but still, once it was there in black-and-white, they were amazed.

It was like taking a course in theoretical physics and then watching an atom bomb explode.

Tizzie resumed her post at the door. Jude scrolled down to his own name and saw a notation: INACTIVE. *See individual file.* Across the screen he saw the match-up with Skyler. Underneath it said: Escaped from Crab Island. Marked for retirement. *See individual file.*

"Jude."

She was calling to him softly from across the room.

"Listen. A lot of people are coming. I think they're coming into the building."

He was too engrossed in the file to pay much attention. She opened the door and left, and a few minutes later, she was back.

"Jude, listen to me. People are gathering upstairs. Cars are pulling up. They're all coming here—from all over, all of them. The Young Leaders, the prototypes. There's some kind of big meeting about to happen—right upstairs."

He had pulled up on the screen a name on the left that meant nothing to him. But on the right, under the Gemini, the lengthy medical record ended with a date and three words: ORGAN BLOCK TRANSPLANT. That was one who had run away from the island and was killed, he thought.

"I hear you," he said. "But we can't leave this. We've got to copy it. Look around for a disk."

"I'm not saying you should stop," she insisted. "I'm saying we've got to know what they're up to. I'm going to the meeting."

She opened the door and she was gone.

A second later, what she said sank in, and Jude knew that it was a mistake, that he should have stopped her. But having finally found what he was looking for, having finally found the fountain of knowledge and imbibed, he was loath to break off.

He scrolled down until he came to her name: ELIZABETH TIERNEY . . .

Skyler peeked around the corner of the building and saw the hospital about twenty yards away. It was off by itself in one corner of the base, which made sense—the patients would have a view of the woods to soothe their convalescence, and in case they bore infectious diseases, they would be isolated from the general population.

The isolation suited his purposes, too.

He had already searched the barracks. There were ten of them, low-slung buildings of concrete floors and bunk beds in various states of disarray. It was obvious that they had not been occupied for some time, and as he inspected them, walking as quickly as he could, considering the weakness that was overtaking him, in one door and out the other, he felt an unbridled sense of anxiety. He knew at once the source of the anxiety—the barracks aroused memories of his own past, waking and sleeping years on end in a similar structure, growing up with the Age Group in a solitary world.

But one of the barracks, closest to the hospital, he could not examine because people were inside. He had heard the voices just as he was about to turn the doorknob, and he stole around the corner just as the door opened. A nurse stepped out, carrying a tray of implements to the hospital. A minute later, out came another, carrying blankets. He found a window and looked inside. Far from being dirty, it was clean and sterile. Hospital beds were made with crisp new sheets. There were stanchions for IVs, bedpans, call buttons on cords and all kinds of medical monitoring machines. It looked like a recovery ward.

Now, peering around the corner, he realized that the base had come alive. In the distance he could hear cars arriving, doors slamming, voices calling out. People were moving about; they were entering what seemed to be a large assembly hall. Some of them looked over in his direction, toward the hospital. One figure—dressed in a doctor's scrubs, he realized with a spasm of fear—was walking toward him.

He didn't have much time. And he was feeling none too good.

Skyler took a deep breath and ran across the gap to the hospital. When he reached the wall of the building, he leaned against it to catch his breath. He stayed like that for some time, recovering. Finally, through sheer will, he pushed forward. He was shaky, but feeling a little better.

He told himself he had to do this.

*You must.*

He walked around the building, leaning against the wall, until he came to the rear. There he found what he was looking for—a large picture window. Inside were chairs and tables—it appeared to be a sun room—and looking through the room and through an open doorway, he could see the ward.

And what he saw there jolted him. He felt his senses spring to alert, the blood coursing through his veins.

Upon the beds, one next to another, he saw his Age Group, his fellow Gemini. He recognized them, each and every one of them. And his heart went out to them. They were strapped down on their beds, lying there looking at the ceiling and at each other, in poses of barely controlled panic.

Jude was relieved that Tizzie's file substantiated her story. It was all there—the childhood disease, the transplant of the kidney, her family's departure from Arizona, and finally the death of her clone, Julia. This latter event was noted in a rare bit of bureaucratic poetry: GEMINI DEMISE.

What was reassuring was that Tizzie's file had terminated in the same phrase as his—INACTIVE.

He hated to admit it, but his relief told him something. Since their meeting at the mine outside Jerome, he had trusted her, but only up to a point. He had been badly burned by her initially, and although he had held his suspicions at bay, he had been unable to banish them altogether. Now, he could. That single word—INACTIVE—spoke volumes.

As Jude scrolled through the records, reading hungrily, he was too excited to be afraid. He heard people assembling in the hall above—the sounds of their shoes thudding and scuffing against the floorboards was magnified by the concrete walls of the basement office. He knew he could be caught at any time. All it would take was one person who decided to come downstairs. He played the scene over in his mind: the sight of him typing away at the keyboard, a shrill cry, those footsteps turning back and thundering down the steps, the crowd grabbing him and hustling him off. Still, he could not stop. What he was turning up was too valuable. It was worth the risk.

Those two passwords had opened the cave, like an open sesame. They had enabled him to tap into the mother lode of information. Almost everything was recorded in the computer: how the Lab operated, its original membership, the scientific breakthroughs, the births of its children and their clones, the financial records, the outside contacts. There was even a narrative; it told how the early researchers, including his father, had come together. It told how they had stepped over the line of what was permissible at their medical schools, how they'd become obsessed with cloning and gone underground in Arizona, and finally how they'd transformed themselves from a cult of brilliant scientists into a conspiratorial web that used the lure of immortality to reach into the power centers of the country.

What the records did not tell—and the omission was conspicuous—was anything about the spider at the vortex of the web, Dr. Rincon.

It was like a puzzle with a single piece missing—a piece right smack in the center.

Still, there was more than enough for the FBI to go on and for prosecutors to break up the Lab. Most important was a listing of the outside conspirators who had agreed to join the Group. Jude wanted to whistle as he read through the list of names, twenty-four in all. There was Tibbett. And Eagleton. And the Georgia congressman. And others equally prominent. They represented people at the height of the professions, movers and shakers in politics, finance, the media, commerce, and retailing. Raymond had been right: they'd paid ten million bucks a head for the right to participate. In return, they got a regime of gene therapy—weekly injections of DNA inside enucleated viruses, targeted at the bone marrow, where blood is manufactured. They also got a clone. In a backup file Jude found their names and addresses—foster children who had been placed in homes around the country. The oldest, he noted with disgust, was seven.

In another file, Jude found the account of what had gone wrong, how the complicated medical process had backfired and actually triggered off premature aging. For those who had received gene therapy—including most in the Lab and the Group—it was most severe, leading to illness and a painful death. But even those who had received only the early experimental injections—like Skyler, he thought—were susceptible.

The solution was a desperate one. The prototypes of the clones, the children of the original scientists, were to undergo radical surgery. With a sense of dread, Jude saw that the operations—spelled out in bold uppercase letters, ORGAN BLOCK TRANSPLANTS—had been already scheduled. He looked at the times and dates, then at the clock. Was it possible? According to this file, the first block transplant was about to begin.

Jude left the computer and searched through the cabinets and desk drawers. Behind a stack of stationery and yellow legal pads, he found what he was looking for—a plastic container filled with disks. He chose one, shoved it into the computer and began copying. He watched as, with horrible slowness, the tiny symbols of a file copying itself floated across the screen. He hit the keys, did it again, then hit them again and again. He could not copy everything—that would take too long—just the basic files on the Lab and the Group.

Seven long, agonizing minutes later, he was through. He ejected the disk and put it in his pocket.

He had one more thing to do.

Hurriedly, he called up the Eagleton file. From somewhere behind him, or maybe up above, he thought heard something, footsteps perhaps. Undoubtedly Tizzie coming back to join him.

He couldn't break off, for this was more important than anything else. He had to locate the backup files. He had to see who else in the FBI was named as a conspirator or who was working for them. He had to know whom he could trust.

The sound got closer. It seemed right behind him, and he was preparing to turn around just as he found the one file he was looking for, and started to read it . . .

He jumped as the hands landed on his shoulders and his arms, roughly. The hands lifted him out of the chair and twisted one arm behind his back until it hurt. They grabbed his cell phone. Then they trundled him away.

Tizzie slumped down in a chair near the back of the auditorium. She was not in the very last row—that, she thought, might draw attention to herself—and she hoped she was far enough from the front to be hard to spot from the stage. She wanted to blend in, and wished that someone would sit next to her or talk to her so that she would seem to belong. But no one did. She'd also put on a pair of sunglasses she'd had in the pocket of her coat. She didn't know who would be here, but the last thing she wanted was to be recognized.

She was beginning to feel that she had behaved recklessly. She had simply mounted the stairs and joined the flow of people entering by the front door. They'd gone straight ahead and she had followed them, entering the hall, which had a vaulted ceiling high above and a wooden balcony at the rear. Faded color banners of some sort hung from the rafters, left over from the former occupants. The room was large enough to make them feel small.

There were perhaps fifty people altogether. They were prosperous-looking, and they could have been an upper-middle-class group anywhere—say, parents at a get-acquainted evening at a private school. Except that they did not come in pairs. About half were the prototypes, she thought, the beloved offspring. They were roughly her age—or seemed to be, though in truth, they looked older. Some of their parents were there, too, the original scientists in the Lab. These are the true believers, she thought, the ones who'd started it all. They looked old indeed, wispy-haired, withered and frail, with liver-spotted skin, and they were scattered through the crowd like white mushrooms. Here and there were other men and women in nurse's uniforms and scrubs and lab coats like her own, which made her feel a bit less conspicuous.

The crowd was strangely silent. What was odd was how everyone in the audience appeared separate and isolated. She could not put her finger on it exactly, but never before had she sat in a group that felt so atomized, less than whole. Everyone, she imagined, was thinking of himself. Maybe this is the way it is, she thought, when a group of men are about to go into battle.

The reason that she did not want to be close to the stage was that Uncle Henry was sitting upon it. He looked stiff in a straight-back wooden folding chair, looking out upon the crowd as if he were a captain surveying a rough patch ahead in the ocean. He was about to speak, she could tell, because he took an envelope out of his breast pocket and jotted a note upon it.

Sure enough, he stood and approached a lectern at stage left. He cleared his throat. It was not a gesture to capture attention, for no one in the crowd was talking and all eyes were already upon him.

"You know why we have gathered," he began, dispensing with an introduction.

"There is no need for me to recall the road that brought us here. Let me just say on behalf of all the Elder Physicians—and on behalf of Dr. Rincon—that we regret this temporary setback in our journey, though temporary we are confident it will prove to be. There is no road worth the taking that does not double back upon itself at some point. This is not going backward. This is going forward in a different direction."

A man sitting near her in a three-piece suit scoffed under his breath. The sound did not carry far, but it created a slight stir that caused the speaker to frown.

"What went wrong? you might ask. Let me remind you of the first axiom: Science does not know right and wrong. The double helix has no moral content. We are, each of us, a universe unto ourselves—just as profound, as benighted, just as shallow, as lighted. 'Each living creature,' wrote Darwin, 'must be looked at as a microcosm—a little universe formed of a host of self-propagating organisms, inconceivably minute and as numerous as the stars in the heaven.'

"Do not worry. The pendulum of the historical-cultural cycle is swinging to our side. May we all recite Rincon's First Law: 'Human life alone is sacred, its preservation and extension is our mission.'"

Tizzie noted that most people had not joined in.

Uncle Henry lifted the envelope out of his breast pocket.

"We have already begun the heroic measures. We will perform ten operations a day—three surgeons working full time. They are our own. From start to finish, the operations will take three days. The schedule will be posted upon the bulletin board outside this hall. If you do not keep your appointment, you will not be rescheduled. Is that clear?"

His hatchet gaze swept the hall.

"Are there any questions?"

There was a rustling of discontent, a cough here and there. A hand shot up—only one.

"Dr. Baptiste. What are the chances?"

"The chances?"

"Of survival."

"I would say the chances are not inordinate. But neither are they insignificant."

That man called him Dr. Baptiste, Tizzie thought.

*My God! Uncle Henry is Baptiste!*

The realization frightened her more than she would have thought possible.

The man in the three-piece suit complained in a stage whisper to no one in particular. "One hundred and fifty years," he said. "I'll be lucky if I see the other side of forty."

She looked at him; he appeared to be about forty-five.

Another man glared at him and said: "Be quiet, Judge."

From on stage, the voice of Uncle Henry—Baptiste—boomed out.

"You will all be happy to know that the clones are in good shape. They have been prepared their whole lives for an event such as this. It truly is their finest moment. They have weathered the travel well and have adapted readily to their new environment."

His voice dropped a notch, now the stern schoolmaster.

"Obviously, you should not encounter your clone while it is still alive. That would be a violation of protocol of the highest order. It is recommended—required—that you stay here indoors."

Tizzie tried to shrink lower in the chair. His gaze was moving up and down the rows, like a whip.

It settled on her. He seemed to squint, as if trying to make out her face but not quite succeeding.

"And you," he thundered. "You there in the lab coat. Did you have a question?"

She felt the blood rushing to her head, a numbness spreading up from her legs. She shook her head no.

"But surely I saw your hand. Tell us who you are. Why are you wearing a lab coat? What are you doing here?"

Tizzie was vaguely aware of people turning to look at her, a buzzing beginning throughout the auditorium. One of them was a red-haired man, whose eyes widened. Alfred. He began to open his mouth.

"The birth," she said, faltering. "I'm here for the birth."

"The *birth*," repeated the man on the stage with false mirth. "The birth. I would say you have come to the wrong place if you're expecting to witness a *birth*."

The audience laughed, too, but it was not a jovial sound.

Out of the corner of her eye, Tizzie saw two men coming toward her—men with white in their hair. She felt their hands roughly grabbing her arms, lifting her out of the seat and hustling her out of the hall. In the process, her sunglasses were knocked off. Tizzie looked back and saw Uncle Henry looking at her, his face suddenly, unexpectedly sad.

They took her outside and frog-marched her across the yard to another building that she hadn't noticed before. It had an outside staircase running up one side, and they dragged her up it and through a thick wooden door. By the time they started down a long corridor lined with doors, she realized where she was—in the military prison.

They put her in a small room. She had been there less than a minute, when she heard a voice from a next-door room call out her name. She recognized the voice instantly—Jude's.

# Chapter 31

Skyler knew from the plans he had memorized that the hospital had a false roof. The question was how to get inside it.

He went to the short back side of the rectangular one-story building, stepped away and looked up. The two sides of the roof came together in a gradual peak. In the center of the triangle underneath was a round object—a vent for an attic fan. It was not far from the outstretched branch of an oak. Instantly, a flashback vision seared his brain—the memory of him and Julia clambering up the tree to spy on Rincon, so long ago.

As he climbed the tree, his own agility surprised him. No more than ten minutes ago, he'd felt barely able to run the distance between two buildings, and now here he was, pulling himself up branch by branch. He came to the limb he had spotted. Leaning over, holding onto it with his left hand, he stretched out the fingers of his right hand and fastened upon the blade of the fan. He pulled, hard, but it would not budge. He tried three times without success. Then he climbed higher, stood upon the branch sideways and edged his feet out until he was within striking distance. He leaned outward and gave the fan a swift karate kick. It fell inside and hit the floor with a thud. He waited breathlessly to see if anyone came. No one did. He disappeared into the hole.

Inside, the attic was no bigger than a crawl space. It had apparently been built for storage, though it appeared that it had never been used. The darkness was cut by blades of light shining up through the floorboards from the room below. A sliding ladder was pulled up in its resting position next to a trapdoor. It looked as though it would descend into the ward where the Gemini were. That was a stroke of luck. It would save him from having to climb down the tree and break into the room from outdoors.

The attic gave him a perfect vantage point to reconnoiter the hospital. Through the cracks he could see into every room. He leaned over and put his eye to the sliver of light. Directly below was the ward with the clones. From here he could see the thick belts that bound them to their beds, their fearful, uncomprehending looks. They made no noise, and he wondered if they had been sedated. If they were heavily medicated, he realized, his chances of saving them, remote enough to begin with, were practically nonexistent.

The beds were lined headfirst against the wall, but one was out of place. It had wheels on it, and he could only see the foot. Moving quietly on his hands and knees, he positioned himself above it and bent down to look again. It was not a bed but a gurney, he saw, and lying upon it—the knowledge struck him like a slap across the face—was Benny. His friend was instantly recognizable, though he looked small and wan and was swathed in white with sheets and pillows surrounding his round face. An IV stood beside the gurney, feeding his veins with liquid of some sort, but he was not unconscious, not yet. And his eyes darted around nervously, even at one point passing by Skyler's, so that there was briefly an illusion of contact.

Skyler tore himself away and moved on, crawling to another position. He looked down and saw a room with no one in it. It had swinging doors on both sides and banks of monitoring equipment and five empty beds, ready for occupancy. Clearly, a recovery room. He crawled on and came to the point where a second, smaller ward joined the room he had just seen. Looking through the crack, he saw something that he had already feared seeing, something that was pointing him toward a conclusion his mind resisted. There, right beneath him, was another gurney, and lying upon it was a patient who looked exactly like Benny.

*The prototype.*

They're going to perform a transplant, thought Skyler. *They're getting ready to take out Benny's organs and put them into the prototype.*

He knew he was right even before he looked down into the next room. But what he saw there confirmed the hideous realization. For he found himself looking down upon a fully equipped operating room, in which surgeons were washing up and preparing for surgery.

"Jude—is that you?"

Tizzie talked at a half whisper, even though she had heard the jailers leave.

"Yes."

"So they got you, too."

"I was at the computer. I had just downloaded the files when they grabbed me."

"The phone—do you have it?"

"No such luck."

"So you know what's going on—about the operations?"

"I saw a schedule on the computer. They're going to do all of them right here. We've got to figure out some way to stop them."

She looked around her cell-like room. It was sparsely furnished with a tiny window high up on the wall, covered with wire mesh embedded in glass and beyond that metal bars. The door was thick, but it was not metal, and it did not quite touch the threshold.

"That's not going to be easy—from in here," she said.

"Where did they get you?"

"In the auditorium. They recognized me. Even that guy Alfred was there. I was stupid to go. And you want to hear something amazing? Uncle Henry—it turns out he's Baptiste. All that time Skyler was talking about him, it never occurred to me that he was the same person."

"Me, neither."

"It was unbelievable—all those people, my age, they look like normal people, like yuppies. And they're about to kill off all these other people, just like themselves, without a second thought."

"They're desperate. Their whole lives have been dedicated to a single proposition—that they'll live twice as long as anyone else—and now they're dying twice as fast. It's enough to make you believe in a higher power. I always thought God had a highly developed sense of irony."

"Jude. What about Skyler? Do you think they got him?"

He was sure they had by now.

"He's probably all right. He's a pretty smart guy. Hopefully, he's kept himself hidden."

"What do you think they're going to do with us?"

He was tempted to lie again, but then again, he thought, she deserved to know what he really thought.

"I think—if you really want to know—that we're dealing with fanatics. With people who will do anything to achieve their goals. And like I said, they're desperate. I think they're going to kill us."

She didn't answer right away, not only because what he said was frightening to her, but also because she was partly occupied examining her cell, inspecting every inch of it—looking for a way out.

* * *

From his vantage point Skyler could see and hear almost everything that was going on in the makeshift O.R. There were five people, three men and two women, dressed in faded green scrubs, moving around the room in a complicated choreography. Some were checking instruments, others taking readings from machines or taking inventory. At first, Skyler couldn't tell which were the doctors and which the operating assistants.

The room itself was small and packed with equipment. Beside the operating table, an impressive array of tools had been laid out, ranging from minute knives to saws and mallets. There were four-foot-tall cylindrical tanks for the anesthetic, a white cabinet with sliding tray doors for surgical implements, drawers filled with large swaddling bandages, bins for trash. One bin, mounted on wheels, had a thick white plastic liner, which he realized—with a rush of horror that almost caused him to shudder—was probably for discarded body parts.

When they talked, their voices were so clear that Skyler felt as if he were in the room with them.

"This year I did two of these at Minnesota," said one of the men. "I thought I needed the experience."

"How'd it go?"

"The operations themselves, okay. The patients—that's a different story. One lived for a while and the other died. The one who lived—I don't like to tell you this, but it wasn't easy. Poor son of a bitch didn't know whether he was coming or going. Eating, crapping, pissing, you name it—it was done by someone else's organ. With all those wastes backing up, he blew up like a beach ball. Eventually, his body rejected the organs. Or the organs rejected his body—it's hard to say which."

"That won't happen here."

"True. But you should know—it's no picnic."

"I've done three," said one of the women. "They're tricky, but not impossible. Believe it or not, the hardest part is lifting the organs out all at the same time. There's always some little connection or other you forget about. And their viability times differ. So you have to reconnect them in the right order and do it fast. Once I forgot to connect the urethra. That didn't work out so well."

"There's something I've been meaning to ask," said the third surgeon. "Which one of you two is going to do me?"

"I thought I would," said the woman. "And Dr. Higgins"—she gestured at the first surgeon—"he can do me."

"But he's the best."

She smiled. "I know."

"And then who does Higgins? Nobody's left. We'll all be recovering."

"I'm going to have it done on the outside, obviously," replied Higgins. "It'll have to be finessed. Timing's important. My clone will have a car accident just the right time. And of course his face will have to go. We don't want any questions asked."

"Another damned car accident. You'd think we'd be more imaginative by now."

"I don't see why. If it works, stick with it."

"That's right. If it's not broken, don't fix it."

"And if it is broken, pull out every goddamned organ and start over."

They chuckled, but it was not a jovial sound. At that moment Higgins walked over to the basin and washed his hands. He removed his green cap, and as he splashed water on his face, he tilted it upward toward the ceiling. As a result, Skyler got a good long look at it.

He recognized it instantly—or rather, he recognized the clone who was the surgeon's double. That was no great feat, considering that Skyler had awakened some six feet away from him every morning for two and a half decades.

Gradually, a plan was forming in Skyler's brain; it didn't leap there all at once, but sort of crept up and settled in. It was audacious and hardly foolproof—still, it was a plan; it was better than doing nothing. And who knew . . . it might just work.

He was feeling much worse. He took a deep breath and tried walking quietly back across the attic. He made it about halfway when his legs would no longer follow his commands, when he started to hobble painfully. He reached the ladder and sat down next to it to catch his breath. His chest was on fire. The pain was mounting.

He stayed like that for some time, recovering. Finally, through sheer will, he pushed himself up again and stood, a bit shakily but nonetheless standing, which made him feel slightly better. Now all he had to do, he told himself, was lift a ladder that weighed about a hundred pounds.

Jude hadn't expected them to come for him so soon. He had barely had time to inspect his cell when he head the footsteps in the hallway. At first, they sounded like a single person walking with a heavy tread or maybe an echo. Then he realized that the footsteps came not from one person but two—marching in lockstep. That should have been a clue, but he did not grasp it. He didn't comprehend who his visitors were, until the cell door swung open and he was face to face with the two remaining Orderlies.

Jude was shocked to see them in person. They looked older than he expected, but now that he was confronted by them, he felt fearful—more than he would have anticipated. It was something in their demeanor, the glint in their eyes underneath those disfiguring swatches of white hair.

They smiled, both of them. But not seemingly because they were overjoyed to see him—or rather, not because they were cheered to be in his presence, but for the simple reason that they were gratified to be holding him prisoner and powerless. One grabbed him by the throat while the other held him from behind, squeezing his arms together roughly and slapping on a pair of handcuffs. The first one looked him in the eye steadily, with an unwavering hatred. He leaned back like a discus thrower winding up, and then abruptly straightened, swinging his fist in a round arc and smashing it against his chin. Jude felt his head snap back, pain slicing through his lower jaw, back across his neck and into his vertebrae. The Orderly grabbed his fist and shook his hand in a little dance of pain.

The two Orderlies switched places. The second one leaned back, held the pose for a long half second, and brought his fist up straight up like a hammer. Jude turned his head, and it struck him in the left temple, so hard that he gasped for air and lost his balance. He was held up from behind.

They blame me for their brother's death, he thought. And he knew then that that was why he had feared them.

*They've come to kill me.*

And that knowledge struck him as a cold ache in his stomach and spread through him, through his whole system, like thickening oil. His mind raced: they were not open to dissuasion; there was no help at hand. *This is it.* He stopped thinking, only feeling. And he was surprised by something. He had always feared dying—with a cold dread impossible to describe. It was not death that he had feared so much, but the moments preceding it, the knowledge that it was imminent. That is why he had always thought he would crumple into a helpless coward under torture. But now that the moment had come and was actually upon him, he felt a cool detachment. Not bravery, exactly, but a disassociation from what was happening that could pass for bravery. He was watching himself. And he was surprised—how well he was holding up and also at how slowly everything was unfolding around him.

So he was puzzled by what one of them said next: "Don't hit him in the face. Baptiste will see it."

To emphasize the point, this one spun around quickly, delivering a fist in Jude's solar plexus that knocked the wind out of him, sending him to the floor.

"What's going on?" shouted Tizzie from next door.

"Shut up," said one over his shoulder. "You'll get yours soon enough."

And they brought Jude into the corridor. One held him by the belt while the other went to open her cell door. But no sooner was the key in the lock than Jude made his move. He raised his foot and swung the sharp point of his heel against his guard's shinbone. The man grunted and doubled over, releasing him. He bolted down the corridor, running awkwardly with his arms pinned behind him.

He had almost reached the end when they caught him, bringing him down with a rain of blows. They struck him in the head, the neck, the back, and the kidney. They picked him up—raising him from behind by the handcuffs, holding him helplessly with his feet off the ground like a trussed turkey—and dropped him again. And when they stepped outside and stood at the top of the flight of stairs, he was convinced they were going to throw him down the steps.

But they didn't. Instead, they escorted him down, one on either arm, as if he had suddenly become a precious package.

Now that we're outdoors, he thought, they don't want witnesses. But did that really make sense? Who was there to see except for members of their own conspiracy?

They reached the ground and kept going, not toward the assembly hall, which he expected, but in the opposite direction. With the Orderlies leaning against him, the threesome walked unsteadily but purposefully, like a trio of drunks.

"Where are we going?" Jude demanded.

They did not reply.

The threesome made its way around the mess hall and followed a path that cut between two deserted barracks. Jude looked up at the sky, already beginning to darken. In the west, he could see red and orange hues gathering. He couldn't help thinking: it would be a spectacular sunset.

They came to a circular driveway that led to the only handsome structure on the base, a three-story white clapboard house that had once been the residence of the base commander. They marched Jude up the front steps. He noted that the Orderlies were breathing heavily, and for the second time he felt a secret pleasure at their weakness. They, too, were aging. They might do away with him, but their end would come soon. One held him tightly while the other turned the knob and swung open the front door.

Stepping into the entrance hall was like stepping into another era. The decor was tasteful Victorian, with thick hand-woven carpets, a silver umbrella stand filled with walking sticks and a grandfather clock, whose pendulum swung slowly with a stately annunciated click. Ahead was a staircase with a Persian runner, held in place by thin brass bars mounted in the crevice of each joint.

There was a peculiar scent in the air, almost like musty flowers, except that it was more medicinal than stale.

They did not go upstairs. They turned to the right and walked through a doorway into what appeared to be a drawing room. It was lavishly furnished with Victorian couches and love seats piled with pillows, woven hassocks and Pembroke tables. The walls were covered with gilded framed paintings of romantic landscapes and hunting scenes.

Shadows rent the room, which made it difficult to see, so that Jude did not notice right away that someone else was there—sitting in a chair. Instead he felt the presence of another person, intuiting it from the way his escorts let go his arms and turned toward the chair, backing away slightly.

Then Jude saw him. Sitting in a high-back chair, which gave off the pretentious grandeur of a throne, was an elderly elegant man with a strong hatchet face.

Jude knew instantly that this was the man he had heard Skyler and Tizzie speak of so often—Baptiste. Uncle Henry.

The phone rang in the operating room at the most inconvenient of times. Still, with the first operation about to begin, they thought they should answer it. Who knew what kind of problem could have arisen?

"Dr. Higgins, it's for you," said the assistant.

The doctor took the call, annoyed and frowning at the interruption, and put the receiver down none too lightly.

"Wouldn't you know," he said peevishly. "Problem in the ward. I'll straighten it out and be right back. Don't do anything until I get back—I won't be long."

He pushed through the double doors into the prep room, took off his green cap and smock and slippers and threw them into a bin, angry that he would have to put on fresh ones and scrub down all over again. He quickly put on his clothes, a pair of chinos, a striped pink and blue shirt, and loafers. He looked over at the gurney where the clone was lying in a daze, ready to undergo deep sedation. Expertly, his eyes sized him up, those parts that were visible—skin, muscle tone, eyes. No doubt about it, a good specimen.

Then he pushed through the second set of doors and walked into the ward, like a stern headmaster.

Dr. Higgins was as good as his word. He came back into the operating room in no time, scrubbed, clothed in green and ready to go. He was pulling the gurney with the clone behind him, and the others rushed to assist him.

They readied the instruments, counting them and placing them in correct order on the tray. They adjusted the overhead lights and moved the clone from the gurney to the operating table. They took his readings, attached the electrodes to monitor heart and brain, swabbed his trunk thoroughly with antiseptic, shaved him, covered his mouth with an oxygen mask, and gave him a huge dose of anesthetic.

It was a routine they had all done hundreds of times in their careers, separately, and yet they knew that all those times had only served to prepare them for this time.

"You do the first one," said Dr. Higgins grandly. "You take the first honor."

The female surgeon was taken aback, but pleased by the professional respect she felt was long her due.

She quickly stepped into place beside the body while the others took their positions, the anesthetist at the top of the table, the top assistant at her right elbow next to the tray of instruments. The surgeon held her right hand out as if for a tip. She didn't have to say a word—the assistant placed into it the thick, crisscrossed handle of the first cutting knife.

"All right, gentlemen. Let's do it," she pronounced, almost with a touch of melodrama.

And then she placed the blade under the sternum, in the center of the rib cage, and pressed down squarely so that it penetrated the pale skin. The first trickle of blood rose like a tiny fountain.

Baptiste told the Orderlies to leave and gestured Jude toward a chair with a languid air. He tipped the fingers of his hands together and contracted them so that they looked like two spiders touching the legs. For a long while, he was silent, almost as if he were waiting for Jude to speak. But then he did.

"This is a meeting I have imagined many times," he said.

"And why is that?" Jude asked.

Baptiste sighed. "It's a long story," he said.

"I know most of it," Jude declared.

"Do you?"

The question was swathed in a patronizing tone that Jude found hard to bear.

"Yes."

"Such as?"

"I know about the Lab. I know about Arizona and how it got started there. I know about the island, Crab Island, and the clones and how they were raised as nothing more than banks for spare parts. I know about the scientific breakthroughs and how you sold the knowledge to rich people and how you all expected to live one hundred and sixty years."

Baptiste was listening closely, but he did not appear to be impressed.

"I know about W, the conspiracy"—here Jude paused for effect. "I know the names of everyone who's in it."

Baptiste cut him off. "No matter. They won't be in it for long."

"You mean because they're aging. I know about that, too. Progeria. They all have it. The members of the Lab have it. Their children have it. *You* have it."

Baptiste nodded and shrugged.

"I know that you've killed people.'

Baptiste shrugged again. "Clones," he said. "We killed clones, not people."

"Clones are people."

Baptiste looked at him again with a patronizing air—as if to say, you have so much to learn.

"And Raymond. How about him? You killed him?"

"*We* most certainly did not. That was the FBI. My boy, please learn to tell your various conspiracies apart."

Jude was aghast at the man's equanimity, but also fascinated.

"No, Raymond was not ours. We can't claim him. There was one—a long time ago—but that was all." He did not elaborate.

"My father."

"Your father, my boy, was killed in a car accident. And there was no one who grieved more than myself. I loved him deeply."

"That's not what I heard."

"Well, you heard wrong." Baptiste looked up solicitously. "Say," he added suddenly, "would you care for some coffee? Some tea?"

Jude was totally flummoxed. "For Christ's sake. You jail me. You beat me up. And you invite me over for tea? What the hell is going on? What are you up to?"

Baptiste allowed himself a thin little smile.

"I thought you said you knew everything."

"Not everything. Almost everything."

"Evidently, not the most important part. The puzzle with the missing piece—and that one piece contains everything of significance in the puzzle. Do have some tea."

Jude relented. He was quietly seething. Baptiste rang a small bell. An elderly black man appeared, took the order and left. Baptiste settled back in his chair. He had the air of a man about to divulge a matter of great importance, and he was enjoying it.

"You say you were beat up? The Orderlies?"

"Yes."

He nodded gravely. "That's most serious. They are not allowed to disobey instructions. Still, they've been very upset. You did—at least in their eyes—kill their brother. And they were bred for aggression, so to speak. And then they were the first to get the treatment—it was still in the experimental stage back then—and the counterreaction struck them first. It's hard, when you're bred for strength, to be losing it so rapidly."

"The treatment—you mean, telomerase?"

Baptiste simply nodded, looking at his watch.

Jude wanted to know exactly how the Orderlies had been bred, along with other things, but even more, he wanted the key piece of the puzzle. He remained silent as the tea was brought in on a tray, taking a cup with two sugars. Baptiste did the same, stirring it in a thoughtful silence and then looking over at Jude.

"A minute ago, you accused us of killing people. If you were under that misimpression, did you never wonder why we didn't kill *you*?"

"I wondered about it. I'm sure you had chances."

"Many times. At least nine of them, by my count."

Jude remained silent.

"Did it never occur to you that these Orderlies, whose wrath you've just experienced, were perhaps not out to eliminate you? That perhaps they were actually *protecting* you?"

Jude was too stunned to speak.

"Or why we never killed Skyler? After all, he caused us a lot of trouble. His escape put us all in great jeopardy. In fact, it brought down the whole edifice—forced us to abandon the island."

"Why didn't you?"

"We didn't kill him because of you. Because you might need to live one hundred and sixty years yourself. You might be required to. You have been marked out to play a very special role in our great and historic drama."

"The drama of your death?"

"No, quite the opposite."

Baptiste was suddenly animated. He stood and walked in a circle, and as he came into the light, Jude saw for the first time that his hair was not black but gray.

"What is the opposite of death? Why, birth—of course. And that is why I am here, I and a few others, the select few who have assembled in this drab locale. I hasten to add that I am not speaking of those who are undergoing operations, who think only of themselves and their own lives. I am referring to the select few—those of us who are ready for the next stage, the final breakthrough."

"And what is that?"

"Don't worry, you shall witness it."

"But why me? What is this special role you're talking about?"

Baptiste just looked at him, long and hard, and finally said: "You poor boy. You simply have no idea—do you? Why don't you come with me? We'll go upstairs and you can see for yourself. But first, more tea."

He rang, and the black waiter returned and poured another cup for each. As he handed a cup to Jude with a strong hand, the waiter looked at him and said: "Tie yuh mout. Study yuh head."

"Cornelius," Baptiste said. "Our guest does not speak Gullah."

"What was that? What did he say?"

"Cornelius is my cook. He is such an artist in the kitchen, I bring him with me wherever I go."

"And what did he say?"

"A bit rude, I'm afraid. Literally, it would be: 'Keep quiet and use your head.'

The old black man leaned over and whispered something in Baptiste's ear. Baptiste stood up quickly, suddenly keen-eyed.

"He informs me that we do not have time to finish our tea."

"But where are we going?"

"Upstairs." He paused a heartbeat. "I think it's time you met Dr. Rincon."

The surgeon was worried by what she saw. At first, the operation had gone well. She had cut through the skin neatly and peeled it back with a symmetry that was undeniably the work of an expert. She had moved on quickly to the next stage, opening the chest cavity and widening the slit to expose the upper and lower abdomen.

It was then that she noticed that the organs did not look good. The color of the stomach was a little off, the texture of the liver was wrong, the feel of the intestines was flaccid.

"I don't understand it," she said through her mask. "I expected a clone to be in perfect condition. That's what he was raised for. How can we transplant these organs with any chance of success?"

"Something's wrong," said the second surgeon.

"Wait a minute," said the assistant, in a tone that overstepped her authority.

She removed the instruments that had been lying upon the sterile white sheet across the patient's lower body. One by one she placed them upon the tray, leaving a little trail of blood.

"What are you doing?" demanded the female surgeon.

"Checking," she replied as she began to roll down the sheet, exposing first the pubic hair, then the genitals and finally the thighs and legs.

They all saw it more or less at the same time and found it hard to speak for the shock of it—of what wasn't there on the thigh. There was no Gemini tattoo. It was not a clone they had been cutting into. It was a proto.

The assistant dropped the sheet.

"Higgins," shouted the surgeon, turning around. "You've made a mistake. A horrible mistake. You brought the wrong one."

She looked around the room, but Higgins wasn't there. He had slipped out at some point. She dropped the knife she was holding, ripped off her mask and ran through the double doors. She ran through the prep room and tried to get into the ward, but the door struck something. It was difficult to open, and she had to push it with her shoulder. When she did, and when she finally stepped inside, she saw what had been blocking it—Higgins's body. He had been knocked unconscious, lying there dressed in a pair of chinos and a pink-and-blue-striped shirt. She bent down to take his pulse. So involved was she in checking his condition that she did not know why those who rushed in behind her had lost their heads and were yelling.

But when she looked up, she saw why. She saw that all the beds that had been occupied by the clones were empty. The sheets were scattered upon the floor, the door at the end of the ward was wide open, and the thick belts that had strapped them in place were hanging down toward the floor, some of them still swinging gently.

★ ★ ★

Tizzie had been struggling with the key that the Orderly had left in the lock for almost a half hour. She took the unused safety pin from the back of her badge, bent the sharp end into a straight line and inserted it, trying to turn it so that the key aligned with the keyhole. Then she unscrewed her ballpoint pen and used the point on the plastic shaft to try to push the key outward. It was hard because she could not see—she needed two hands, which blocked the view of the keyhole—and because the key kept sliding back to its original position.

But eventually she got it—she felt the pin push forward and immediately heard the key hit the floor. The sound was softened a bit because it landed upon her blouse, which she had slipped under the door, spreading it out as best she could. Now, slowly and carefully, she reeled the blouse back in, praying that the key had not bounced away. She did not dare believe she had succeeded until she saw its rounded metal head peeking up at her.

It fit perfectly from inside and turned the lock in no time.

She ran down the corridor, past the open door of Jude's cell, and outside onto the staircase. It was getting dark. In the distance, she thought she heard muffled noises, the sound of people, vague shadows running. She would have to be careful.

She crept down the stairs and ran to the perimeter of the base, following the fence until she came to the quartermaster's office. She rushed in, grabbed the phone, and dialed Washington, D.C., information. She got the number of the FBI.

*What's the man's name? What is it? Jude mentioned it.*

The phone was ringing.

*Oh, no. It's late. He won't be there. No one will be there.*

But someone picked up. The name came to her.

"Brantley. Mr. Brantley. Ed Brantley. It's urgent."

"One moment, please."

And then, to her amazement, she was talking to him. And if he sounded much closer than Washington, D.C., that's because he was much closer.

At the top of the stairs, Jude was assaulted by a smell. It wasn't a good smell. It was strong and medicinal.

Baptiste had led him up the staircase, pulling himself up with his right hand on the banister and guiding Jude under the elbow with his left—which was curious considering that he was the feebler of the two. The old man was excited. They turned a corner, down a corridor, and now Baptiste seemed to be hurrying, as if he feared being late. They came to a door. Baptiste leaned one ear toward it and listened for a moment; Jude thought he could hear strange sounds inside, a moaning perhaps. Then it was quiet. Carefully and slowly, Baptiste turned the doorknob. He went in first. Then Jude.

The room was flooded with light, so much so that at first Jude could hardly see. In the far corners were strong lights, mounted on stanchions, pointing toward the center of the room. There was a large bed, king-size, draped in sheets so white they seemed to be blazing. In the center of the bed, propped up halfway, was a large figure, a woman drenched in sweat, her hair spread out in long tangles on the pillow behind her like Medusa. Four people attended her, one wiping her brow with a cool rag.

It was a bizarre sight. To one side was a tripod upon which was set a video camera trained upon the bed. Against the wall to the right of the door was a large screen that showed the same view in color. Along the far wall was a sink and table spread with a receiving blanket and medical equipment, including an incubator. On the wall opposite, visible from the bed, was a four-foot-high terrarium filled with sand and branches and a cactus. To Jude's amazement, one of the branches moved—and he realized it was a large horned lizard.

The woman moaned and clenched her teeth. Jude's first thought had been that she was dying, but then he saw the gigantic belly that seemed to protrude from her chest all the way down to her thighs, a huge, hard mound of flesh. And it all fell into place. She was pregnant, in the throes of labor. This was the woman Tizzie had seen. And there was the doctor she had described, nervously checking the woman's pulse.

The woman looked at him. She did not smile, but she narrowed her aged eyes and furrowed her brow in recognition, and motioned to him to come closer. He stepped toward the bed, and now that haunting antiseptic smell grew stronger, and just as he got within two feet, suddenly the woman's body seemed to lunge upward as if an invisible wire were pulling her navel, and she screamed. She let out a long, hideous scream that began as a howl and rose in pitch until Jude's ear ached. He stepped back. The attendants moved closer, wiped her brow, touched her arm. The moment passed and the scream died away.

He stepped closer again. She looked up at him and their eyes locked, and suddenly Jude remembered something, Tizzie's description of coal black eyes that seemed to pierce to the very recesses of the soul, and he felt he was undergoing the same mesmerizing power. And it was then that the first rays of comprehension began to dawn and that soon he knew he was to see the whole sky light up with the horrible truth—and the magnitude of it would be blinding.

A voice behind him spoke. It was Baptiste's, heard dimly, as if he were far away.

"Jude, you are in the presence of Dr. Rincon."

*This was Rincon.*

"Come closer," said a deep, resonant voice from within the heap of flesh and sweat and pain. "Come closer, so that I can get a good look at you. It's been so long."

*Rincon is a woman.*

He did. His thigh rested against the bed. She reached over with a hand, a wide, thick hand, and touched his own. Her touch was not cold, but warm, almost—he thought—hot.

There was a strong smell—pungent, almost antiseptic.

"Do you understand?" she asked. Her tone was warm, almost loving.

He shook his head no, unable to speak.

"I'm glad at least that you are here, that you are witness to this moment."

Another wave of pain seized her, and carried her up and held her suspended in the air for another long, ghastly scream, before it dropped her back on the shore, exhausted. She waited a few moments, then opened her eyes again and talked to him as if nothing had intervened.

"You were to have a special role, you know. All along, I thought of you and I planned it. That is why we reached out to you. That's why I protected you even when you were outside. That is why I wanted you with me now."

He was still confused.

*Why me?*

"I wanted you to witness the virgin birth."

Another paroxysm came and sent her away into the island of pain that seemed to be moving further and further away from the bedroom. This time she took even longer to open her eyes again.

"I don't like this," said the doctor. "I don't like the way this is going."

He attached a monitor to her heart and another to her belly. The sounds of the two machines beating separate rhythms filled the room. Jude turned and saw the movement of limbs and arms on the video screen, focused on the woman's abdomen.

They settled down, and now she held Jude's hand to her cheek.

"Why me?" he asked.

She looked up at him. "Because you were the first. Because you were my prince. I hated it when your father took you from me."

And at that moment the whole truth came crashing down upon him, like a wave. He had seen it coming in the distance, but he had refused to look, and now it rose up seemingly out of nowhere and knocked him off his feet.

"My son," she said. "You were such a lovely baby. Your hands were so small then—I loved the way your fingers curved around my own."

She lifted a single forefinger into the air.

"Hold my hand again."

He did, horrified.

She started screaming again. He felt her hand dig into his, the fingernails cutting the back of his hand. The monitors banged like drums.

The doctor pushed him to one side.

"Move away. This is serious."

He stepped into a corner and looked at the backs of the doctors and nurses huddled around the bed and the blur of movement on the screen. Baptiste stood beside him.

"So now you know."

He was looking distracted, worried.

"She said virgin birth. What did she mean?"

"Just that. There is no father. She impregnated herself with an embryo containing her own DNA."

"What! That can't be. It's impossible."

"Not at all."

"But that means—she's giving birth to . . ."

"Go on."

"She's giving birth to herself."

"Precisely. An exact replica. Another self. She is going to start all over again. It will be a wonderful moment for the Lab—the supreme moment."

And at that moment Rincon groaned and heaved again and was suddenly quiet as she puffed out her cheeks and dug in her heels and pushed with all her might. Nothing happened.

"She's too old," the doctor yelled. "The baby's too big. It's huge."

Jude looked at the screen. Between her wrinkled legs, a darkened crest appeared, the top of a head. It fell back, and out came waves of blood and water. Rincon made a strangled, gasping sound.

Baptiste grabbed Jude's arm.

* * *

Five minutes later, the doctor decided to operate. They gave Rincon an anesthetic and cut her open and lifted the baby out as carefully as if it were a bundle of dynamite. Jude could not bear to watch on the video screen, and Baptiste was slumped in a chair, holding his head between his hands.

The large monitor slowed and then stopped. The room sounded strangely quiet without it. The doctor tried everything to save Rincon. He gave her extra oxygen and shots of adrenaline. He even tried thumping her chest to revive the heart, but that proved gruesome, since it sent more blood streaming from her open cavity.

"Turn off the camera," shouted Baptiste.

Ricon was not yet dead.

She opened her eyes, halfway now, and looked once again into Jude's eyes. There was more there than pain. He tried to read the look. The mesmerizing stare was gone, replaced by something else—simple and more human. But what? Regret? Shame? Pride? Fear? Love?

Maybe all of them.

The eyes closed, there was a final shudder, the head fell to one side.

The doctor looked down, his eyes wide now. She was gone. He gave up.

The nurses were gathered around the baby. It was obvious from their movements—a sort of reluctance to get too close, quick glances and then looking away—that something was terribly wrong. Jude went over and caught a hurried glimpse, but his view was blocked by a nurse's uniform and he did not try a second time. He had seen enough of the large, misshapen thing that had emerged, its eyes closed as if in fury.

And he thought it odd that no one paid any more attention to Rincon, even though she was dead.

He looked at her for a while and thought she had a certain beauty. Then he raised the sheet and placed it over his mother's face.

The clones followed Skyler's instructions to the letter. They ran to the assembly hall and barricaded the doors, holding the protos inside. They piled so many things upon the doors—desks and chairs, logs, cinder blocks, car engines from the dump—that escape was out of the question.

Some of the clones climbed up the side of the building to look through the windows. They tried to pick out their prototypes, and when they found them, they pointed excitedly.

When Tizzie and Jude appeared, walking out of the evening shadows from different directions, they created a sensation. The clones gathered around them, staring at them and talking among themselves.

They were still doing that when sirens screamed and cars speeded into the base with their lights flashing and stopped with a screech of brakes. Police in uniform and men in suits jumped out.

One of them walked over to Jude and Tizzie.

"You two all right?"

"In a manner of speaking," replied Jude.

"I'm Brantley," said the agent, sticking out his hand.

"I'm Jude."

"I figured."

"And I'm Tizzie."

"I know. Good thing you called."

"How did you get here so fast?" asked Jude.

"We were in Savannah when she called," he said, gesturing toward Tizzie. "We saw that thing in the paper for the Millennium group. Good thing you mentioned the group's name. You told Raymond and he told me."

"He didn't miss much."

"No, he didn't."

"And the other guys?" asked Jude. "The Eagleton group."

"After they killed Raymond, they tried to lay low. But we got them now, I'm sure. The records will tell us who they are and put them away for a long time."

He added an afterthought: "And New York's got the death penalty now. I'd like to see it used—I'd like the guy who murdered Raymond to be the first one."

The police took apart the barricade, opened the doors and made the arrests. One by one the prototypes came out, hands in cuffs, to be placed in squad cars. There were so many of them the cars would have to make several trips. A group of them sat under an oak tree, including the surgeons and nurses, all chained together. They looked strange there, as if they were getting ready for a Sunday outing.

An ambulance carried away Rincon. Baptiste required a stretcher. The two Orderlies submitted meekly and sat together in the back of a squad car, handcuffed together, mirror images.

Brantley went into the basement and came back looking concerned.

"They raided the computers," he said. "They erased everything, whatever files there were. They even smashed the machines. That'll make it harder to build a case against them."

Jude smiled—for the first time in a long while.

"I've saved the important stuff on a disk. But it'll cost you."

"Name your conditions."

And so he did. Then they shook hands, and he reached into his pocket and pulled out the disk.

Tizzie was worried that Skyler had not turned up. She looked for him everywhere—in the barracks, the hospital, the mess hall, the offices. Jude helped her search, and the FBI joined in, but they could not find him anywhere.

It was dark now, with a large yellow moon rising in the sky. A thin sheaf of clouds swept across it from time to time.

Jude had just lighted a cigarette, Brantley was talking over a cell phone and Tizzie was standing next to them nervously, when the figure of a large man appeared out of the darkness and motioned to them to follow him. It was the Gullah cook.

He led them along a pathway to the base commander's house, then around back, where there was a basement door set in the side of the building. Down a flight of concrete steps, they entered the basement and followed him across it to a door. Inside was his room, neatly furnished, and against a wall was a bed with a quilt upon it. Lying in the bed with his eyes closed was Skyler.

Tizzie rushed over to him. Jude felt his forehead and Brantley took his pulse. Then the FBI man pulled out his phone again and dialed a number. He called for the ambulance.

"He don't look too good," he said.

Jude had to agree. Tizzie just sat on the edge of the bed, holding Skyler's hand and making a silent prayer.

When the ambulance came, she got into it with him and sat down on a bench in the rear as it drove off. Brantley drove Jude to the hospital.

He stayed that night and the next night, side by side with Tizzie, as the doctors gave Skyler heavy doses of heart medication. They didn't know what would happen, the doctors said. It was all too new to them. They could only wait.

In the middle of one of the long hours, Jude looked at Tizzie, her face drawn, her eyes closed. He wanted more than anything for Skyler to recover. But he also knew there was a question he had to ask.

"Tizzie," he said.

She opened her eyes.

"I'll have to go back soon. Do you know what you're going to do?"

She shook her head, but her shining eyes told him the answer.

Jude thought he'd feel worse, but somehow he didn't. It was no surprise, after all. In fact, it was only fitting. He had always known she was drawn to Skyler. He had hoped it was because Skyler was so much like him.

It had turned out it was because he was different.

# Epilogue

Two years later, Jude's life had returned to a semblance of normality. Like many people his age, he'd moved out to the suburbs—to Larchmont in Westchester, New York. He could be seen leaving Grand Central every evening on the 6:40 or 7:20, one of that army of commuters who scrambled for seats in order to sleep on the way home. His house, on a tree-lined street, was within walking distance of the station. It was small but tidy, and on weekends he enjoyed puttering around the garden, planting and weeding and, most of all, harvesting vegetables—except for the tomatoes, which invariably failed him. He was becoming a more than passable cook.

He was still at the *Mirror*, not traveling as much as he used to, but it was partly through his choice. He was halfway through his second novel, this one called *Double Exposure*. Pure fiction, but the subject—a pair of identical twins who run a detective agency—drew on what might reasonably be called firsthand experience. His agent seemed to be enthusiastic about what he had written so far, but Jude was still worried—in darker moments, he was convinced that his first book had succeeded only because the full muscle of Tibbett's empire had been behind it.

Tibbett himself had died of a rapidly advancing disease that had been mysterious to all but Jude and half a dozen others. Rumors among the uninformed said it was AIDS. He'd spent his last days in prison, where he had been consigned for insider trading. A surprising number of other big names in politics, finance and science had found their way behind bars for crimes whose sheer variety was surprising; they ranged from political corruption to—in the case of a thirty-year-old redheaded medical researcher—mail fraud. So many of them had died that the *Mirror* was nervously updating its obits on just about everyone. Jude, of course, could have told them which ones to concentrate on, but he derived a secret pleasure in witholding the information. After all, he'd never gotten to write the big story. That was a condition that had been set down by the FBI.

The agency had insisted upon his silence as the price for meeting his demands, which were straightforward enough: punishment of the Lab members and the W conspirators, and seizure of the Group's assets for the establishment of a huge trust fund. The fund was held on behalf of recipients in two categories. One was a group of bright but unsophisticated young people in their late twenties who needed special education to adjust to the fast-paced modern world. The other consisted of young children who had been placed in foster care around the country—and who, a gifted observer might have noted, bore uncanny physical resemblances to those movers and shakers who were doing their moving and shaking in prison. These youngsters were adopted by good families and slotted to eventually receive Raymond La Barrett scholarships to elite Eastern prep schools.

The FBI itself underwent a mysterious and dramatic shakeup. It followed the abrupt resignation and suicide of the powerful deputy director, Frederick C. Eagleton. Some fourteen men and one woman were booted unceremoniously out of the agency—all of them ending up behind bars. Acres of newsprint were devoted to explaining the "house cleaning," but the root cause—something to do with a wiretap scandal—remained vague in the public mind.

Promoted in Eagleton's place was a relatively unknown agent, Edward Brantley. Shortly before taking over, Brantley himself traveled to Prairie du Chien, Wisconsin, where a five-year-old boy who bore a certain physical resemblance to Eagleton was living. From a list of schools for him to eventually attend, Brantley chose Phillips Andover Academy—whether as a reward or punishment was hard to tell.

The FBI cleaned up Crab Island. All the children who had been abandoned on the Nursery died, but a handful of healthy ones survived. The coincidence of so many victims of progeria provided a major boost in research on the disease, culminating in a major conference at Berkeley at which several important papers were delivered.

Baptiste—whose real name turned out to be Henry Burne—fell into a coma and expired two weeks after the mass arrests at Fort Stewart. Once the case was closed, Jude was given partial access to the FBI file based upon debriefing of the Lab members and learned all about him, including his early years as the son of a Bible-pounding fundamentalist preacher. Jude also learned that Burne was the driver of the car that had killed his father and left the scene of the accident. This tidbit came from someone close to Baptiste who had become an informant—the Gullah cook, who, it turned out, had been primed by Kuta to keep a watchful eye over Skyler.

Jude never did find out a great deal about his mother, and what he did learn showed how wrong he had been about her. The original members of the Lab, before dying, insisted that she had loved Jude's father very much. It had not been an arranged marriage; they had met years ago at school. Why she had been expelled from Harvard Medical School—it *had* been Harvard, after all—when she'd gone by the name of Grace Connir was never determined; the records had been lost. Half a year ago, while playing Scrabble, he suddenly realized that Rincon was an anagram of her earlier surname.

The medical records, notebooks and descriptions of the W experiments were all classified and remained in possession of a special unit set up by the National Institutes of Health and the National Security Agency.

As for Tizzie and Skyler, Jude saw them whenever they came to New York from Raleigh, North Carolina. She did research there at the Duke University Hospital, and Skyler was going for his B.A., studying social work—he was interested in working with the homeless. When they'd gotten married a year ago, Jude had, of course, been best man, and the wedding had attracted people from around the country who had grown up on Crab Island. Since then, Tizzie had written to Jude once a week or so. Her last letter had told him she was pregnant.

Skyler had been lucky when it came to his health. Because he had received injections of telomerase instead of gene therapy to keep producing it, his version of the aging disease had been less severe. He needed to continue taking heart medicine and to watch for atherosclerotic heart disease. Replacing his blood supply had been only a temporary measure, of course. What he'd needed was a new kidney; his had been damaged by their heroic attempts to flush the pathogens out of his system. Jude could hardly have refused, and the donation had constituted, as he'd joked with Skyler afterward, a certain poetic irony. The operation had not been as difficult as he had imagined, but the recovery had been long. At least, he had been forced to cut back on booze and to give up smoking once and for all.

Jude admitted that sometimes, when the days were long and slow and hot, he thought of Tizzie and what might have been. What if the cards had been shuffled differently? He wondered sometimes if he would have loved the other one—Julia—and if she would have loved him in return. Life, as he had certainly learned, was strange. You spot someone in your entryway one evening, and it can change you forever.

But he was not unhappy. Nor was he totally alone. One of the handful of young clones to survive the Nursery had turned out to be his own—after all, the boy had not been a candidate for the telomerase treatment, since Jude had not been a Lab member in good standing. Meeting him for the first time at JFK airport, this little, lost-looking lad holding the hand of a hulking FBI agent was a memory he would take with him to the grave.

So now he came home in the evening, on the 6:40 or the 7:20, to a housekeeper and a young boy, Harold, named after Jude's father. When he picked him up at school after Saturday soccer practice, or attended a third-grade play, people said the boy looked amazingly like him. A real chip off the old block. Who knew what would eventually happen? Jude didn't think about it. Maybe when the boy reached the age of twenty-one, he'd go off on his own. Maybe he'd get it right for both of them.

In the meantime, he loved his company. Their life together was almost cozy and suburban-perfect. Except for Sundays, when they went to the institution in order to visit the little girl—if that's what she could be called—the huge one who was kept in a separate room, because her presence made all the other orphans cry.

## Acknowledgments

Many people contributed advice, support or the fruits of their research to this book, some knowingly and others unknowingly. Among them, I would like to thank personally:

Dr. Keith Campbell of the Roslin Institute, the co-creator of Dolly, for patiently explaining cloning procedures.

Steve Jones, author and Professor of Genetics at the Galton Laboratory at University College London, for his inspiring ideas.

Jason Carmel, medical student, for his superb and indefatigable research in cloning, DNA, telomere work, autopsies and aging.

Arthur Kopit for his friendship and editorial contributions and suggestions.

Doctors Paul Skolnick, Daniel Lieberman and Stephen Ludwig for generously sharing their medical knowledge.

Malcolm Gladwell and Lawrence Wright for articles in *The New Yorker* that provided essential material, and Gina Kolata, science reporter for *The New York Times*, for the material in her ground-breaking book, *Clone.*

Larry Lieberman and Trisha Harper for on-the-ground reporting in Arizona.

Gilly and Harry Leventis for providing gracious company and contemplative lodgings in Barbados.

Catherine Mullally for material on the Gullah culture.

Stephanie Hughley for her travel advice and Nancy and Caesar Banks for putting me up at their homey Weekender Lodge on Sapelo Island, Ga.

Linda Lake, researcher at *The New York Times*, for her assistance.

Joe Lelyveld, executive director of *The New York Times*, for alowing me to take a leave, and Martin Gottlieb, deputy culture editor, for enabling me to do so.

Peter and Susan Osnos for their sage counseling.

Kathy Robbins, my agent, for her always invaluable advice and editorial comments.

Neil Nyren, editor extraordinare at Penguin Putnam Inc., for his sure hand and nimble mind in editing the manuscript.

Liza Darnton for her sensitive note-filled reading.

And, of course, Nina Darnton for providing absolutely everything, from plot and character suggestions to editorial changes to physical and spiritual sustenance.